The JUNIOR CLASSICS

VOLUME THREE • MYTHS AND LEGENDS

Warren Chappell

George took his sword and smote off the dragon's head.

[See page 317]

The JUNIOR CLASSICS

Edited *by* MABEL WILLIAMS *and* MARCIA DALPHIN.

With Introduction *by* WILLIAM ALLAN NEILSON, *Former*
President *of* Smith College; Introduction to First Edition by
CHARLES W. ELIOT, *Former President of Harvard University*

Popular Edition

ILLUSTRATED

VOLUME
THREE

MYTHS AND
LEGENDS

P. F. COLLIER & SON CORPORATION

CONTENTS

STORIES FROM THE MYTHS OF GREECE AND ROME

PAGE

Phaeton . . . . *Thomas Bulfinch* 3

Prometheus the Firebringer . . . . . . *W. M. L. Hutchinson* 10

Perseus . . . . *Charles Kingsley* 20
Illustration After Statue by Cellini

The Argonauts . . . . *Charles Kingsley* 50
Illustrations by H. M. Brock

The Hunting of the Calydonian Boar . . *Elsie Finnimore Buckley* 85
Illustration by Frank C. Pape

The Winning of Atalanta . . . . . . *Elsie Finnimore Buckley* 103

The Divine Musician . . . . *Elsie Finnimore Buckley* 128

The Golden Touch . . . . *Nathaniel Hawthorne* 142

The Chimaera . . . . *Nathaniel Hawthorne* 157
Illustration by Walter Crane

The Miraculous Pitcher . . . . *Nathaniel Hawthorne* 177

STORIES FROM THE NORSE MYTHS
E. M. Wilmot-Buxton

How All Things Began 197
Illustration by Louis Moe

How All-Father Odin Became Wise 203

The Apples of Youth 207

How the Fenris Wolf Was Chained 214
Illustration by Charles Huard

CONTENTS

PAGE

How the Pride of Thor Was Brought Low 219

How Thor's Hammer Was Lost and Found 230

The Story of Balder the Beautiful 238

How Hermod Made a Journey to the Underworld 246
Illustration by Louis Moe

How Loki Was Punished at Last 251

STORIES FROM THE JATAKA TALES OF INDIA
Marie L. Shedlock

The Spirit That Lived in a Tree 257

The Hare That Ran Away 259

The Monkey That Saved the Herd 261

The Elephant That Was Honored in Old Age 263
Illustration by Warren Chappell

The Faithful Friend 265

The Banyan Deer 267

STORIES OF THE AMERICAN INDIAN

The Coyote and the Fox . . . . *Elizabeth Willis DeHuff* 273

Pah-tay and the Wind Witch . . . . . *Elizabeth Willis DeHuff* 275

The Porcupine's Quills . . . . *Arthur C. Parker* 278

How Rock-Dweller the Chipmunk Gained His
Stripes . . . . *Arthur C. Parker* 283

How the Coyote Danced with the
Blackbirds . . . . *Frank Hamilton Cushing* 287

The Serpent of the Sea . . . . . . *Frank Hamilton Cushing* 291

Scarface . . . . *George Bird Grinnell* 298
Illustration by Warren Chappell

CONTENTS

OLD LEGENDS

PAGE

The Proud King . . . . *Horace E. Scudder* 309
Illustration by A. G. Walker

Saint George and the Dragon . . . . . . *Horace E. Scudder* 315
Illustration by Warren Chappell

The Bell of Justice . . . . *Horace E. Scudder* 318

William Tell . . . . *Horace E. Scudder* 319

The Image and the Treasure . . . . . *Horace E. Scudder* 321

The Flying Dutchman . . . . *Horace E. Scudder* 323

Arthur in the Cave . . . . *W. Jenkyn Thomas* 326

The Emperor's Vision . . . . *Selma Lagerlöf* 330

The Legend of St. Christopher . . . *From The Golden Legend* 336

Legends of Beasts and Saints . . . . *Helen Waddell* 339

   The Abbot Gerasimus and the Lion 339

   St. Werburga of Chester and the Wild Geese 341

   St. Godric and the Hunted Stag 342

   St. Cuthbert's Birds and Bartholomew, the Hermit of
   Farne 343

   St. Moling and the Fox 344

   St. Colman and the Cock, the Mouse, and the Fly . . . 345

   St. Kevin and the Blackbird 346

Saint Martin and the Honest Man . . . . . . *Padriac Colum* 347
Illustration by Boris Artzybasheff

How the Son of the Gobhaun Saor Sold the
   Sheepskin . . . . *Ella Young* 352

How the Son of Gobhaun Saor Shortened the
   Road . . . . *Ella Young* 356

(The sources of the stories in this volume will be found listed on page 363.)

vii

Stories From
The Myths of Greece and Rome

A Table of the Principal Gods and Goddesses of
Mythology, Giving Their Latin and
Greek Names

THE GREAT GODS OF OLYMPUS

Latin		Greek
Jupiter	*King of the Gods*	Zeus
Juno	*Queen of the Gods*	Hera
Mars	*God of War*	Ares
Minerva	*Goddess of Wisdom*	Athena, Athene, Pallas Athene
Vulcan	*God of Fire*	Hephæstus
Venus	*Goddess of Love and Beauty*	Aphrodite
Apollo	*God of the Sun; Patron of Music and Poetry*	Apollo
Diana	*Goddess of the Moon; the Maiden Huntress*	Artemis
Mercury	*Messenger of the Gods*	Hermes
Vesta	*Goddess of the Hearth and Home*	Hestia

GODS OF THE EARTH, THE SEA AND THE LOWER WORLD

Latin		Greek
Ceres	*Goddess of the Earth, of Sowing, Reaping and the Harvest*	Demeter
Bacchus	*God of Wine and Feasts*	Dionysus
Neptune	*God of the Sea*	Poseidon
Pluto	*King of the Lower World*	Aidoneus
Proserpina	*Queen of the Lower World*	Persephone

PHAETON

By *THOMAS BULFINCH*

PHAETON was the son of Apollo and the nymph Clymene. One day a schoolfellow laughed at the idea of his being the son of the god, and Phaeton went in rage and shame and reported it to his mother. "If," said he, "I am indeed of heavenly birth, give me, mother, some proof of it, and establish my claim to the honor." Clymene stretched forth her hands toward the skies, and said, "I call to witness the Sun which looks down upon us, that I have told you the truth. If I speak falsely, let this be the last time I behold his light. But it needs not much labor to go and inquire for yourself; the land whence the Sun rises lies next to ours. Go and demand of him whether he will own you as a son." Phaeton heard with delight. He traveled to India, which lies directly in the regions of sunrise; and, full of hope and pride, approached the goal whence his parent begins his course.

The palace of the Sun stood reared aloft on columns, glittering with gold and precious stones, while polished ivory formed the ceilings, and silver the doors. The workmanship surpassed the material, for upon the walls Vulcan had represented earth, sea, and skies, with their inhabitants. In the sea were the nymphs, some sporting in the waves, some riding on the backs of fishes, while others sat upon the rocks and dried their sea-green hair. Their faces were not all alike—but such as sisters' ought to be. The earth had its towns and forests and rivers and rustic divinities. Over all was carved the likeness of the glorious heaven; and on the silver doors the twelve signs of the zodiac, six on each side.

> "The sun's bright palace, on high columns rais'd,
> With burnish'd gold, and flaming jewels blaz'd,
> The folding gates diffus'd a silver light,
> And with a milder gleam refresh'd the sight."
>
> —ADDISON.

3

Clymene's son advanced up the steep ascent, and entered the halls of his disputed father. He approached the paternal presence, but stopped at a distance, for the light was more than he could bear. Phœbus, arrayed in a purple vesture, sat on a throne which glittered as with diamonds. On his right hand and his left stood the Day, the Month, and the Year, and, at regular intervals, the Hours. Spring stood with her head crowned with flowers, and Summer, with garment cast aside, and a garland formed of spears of ripened grain, and Autumn, with his feet stained with grape juice, and icy Winter, with his hair stiffened with hoarfrost.

Surrounded by these attendants, the Sun, with the eye that sees everything, beheld the youth dazzled with the novelty and splendor of the scene, and inquired the purpose of his errand. The youth replied, "O light of the boundless world, Phœbus, my father—if you permit me to use that name—give me some proof, I beseech you, by which I may be known as yours." He ceased; and his father, laying aside the beams that shone all around his head, bade him approach, and embracing him, said, "My son, you deserve not to be disowned, and I confirm what your mother has told you. To put an end to your doubts, ask what you will, the gift shall be yours. I call to witness that dreadful lake, which I never saw, but which we gods swear by in our most solemn engagements." Phaeton immediately asked to be permitted for one day to drive the chariot of the Sun. The father repented of his promise; thrice and four times he shook his radiant head in warning. "I have spoken rashly," said he; "this request only I would fain deny. I beg you to withdraw it. It is not a safe boon, nor one, my Phaeton, suited to your youth and strength. Your lot is mortal, and you ask what is beyond a mortal's power. In your ignorance you aspire to do that which not even the gods themselves may do. None but myself may drive the flaming car of day. Not even Jupiter, whose terrible right arm hurls the thunderbolts. The first part of the way is steep, and such as the horses when fresh in the morning can hardly climb; the middle is high up in the heavens, whence I myself can scarcely, without alarm, look down and behold the earth and sea stretched beneath me. The last part of the road descends rapidly, and requires most careful driving. Tethys, who is waiting to receive me, often trembles for me lest I should fall headlong. Add to all this, the heaven is all the time turning round and carrying the stars with it. I have to be perpetually on my guard lest that movement, which sweeps everything else along, should hurry me also away. Suppose I should lend you the chariot, what would you do? Could you keep your course while the earth was revolving under you? Perhaps you think that there are forests and cities, the abodes of gods, and palaces and temples on the way. On the contrary, the road is through the midst of frightful monsters. You pass by the horns of the Bull, in front of the Archer, and near the Lion's jaws, and where the Scorpion stretches its arms in one direction and the Crab in another. Nor will you find it easy to guide those horses, with their breasts full of fire that they breathe forth from their mouths and nostrils. I can scarcely govern them myself, when they are unruly and resist the reins. Beware, my son, lest I be the donor of a fatal gift, recall your request while yet you may. Do you ask me for a proof that you are sprung from my blood? I give you a proof in my fears for you. Look at my face—I would that you could look into my breast, you would there see all a Father's anxiety. Finally," he continued, "look round the world and choose whatever you will of what earth or sea contains most precious—ask it and fear no refusal. This only I pray you not to urge. It is not honor, but destruction you seek. Why do you hang round my neck and still entreat me? You shall have it if you persist—the oath is sworn and must be kept—but I beg you to choose more wisely."

> "Choose out a gift from seas, or earth, or skies,
> For open to your wish all nature lies;
> Only decline this one unequal task,
> For 'tis a mischief, not a gift, you ask."
>
> —ADDISON.

He ended; but the youth rejected all admonition and held to his demand. So, having resisted as long as he could, Phœbus at last led the way to where stood the lofty chariot.

It was of gold, the gift of Vulcan; the axle was of gold, the pole and wheels of gold, the spokes of silver. Along the seat were rows of chrysolites and diamonds which reflected the brightness of the sun. While the daring youth gazed in admiration, the early Dawn threw open the purple doors of the east, and showed the pathway strewn with roses. The stars withdrew, marshaled by the Day star, which last of all retired also. The father, when he saw the earth beginning to glow, and the Moon preparing to retire, ordered the Hours to harness up the horses. They obeyed, and led forth from the lofty stalls the steeds full fed with ambrosia, and attached the reins. Then the father bathed the face of his son with a powerful ointment, and made him capable of enduring the brightness of the flame. He set the rays on his head, and, with a foreboding sigh, said, "If, my son, you will in this at least heed my advice, spare the whip and hold tight the reins. They go fast enough of their own accord; the labor is to hold them in. You are not to take the straight road directly between the five circles, but turn off to the left. Keep within the limit of the middle zone, and avoid the northern and the southern alike. You will see the marks of the wheels, and they will serve to guide you. And, that the skies and the earth may each receive their due share of heat, go not too high, or you will burn the heavenly dwellings, nor too low, or you will set the earth on fire; the middle course is safest and best. And now I leave you to your chance, which I hope will plan better for you than you have done for yourself. Night is passing out of the western gates and we can delay no longer. Take the reins; but if at last your heart fails you, and you will benefit by my advice, stay where you are in safety, and suffer me to light and warm the earth." The agile youth sprang into the chariot, stood erect, and grasped the reins with delight, pouring out thanks to his reluctant parent.

Meanwhile the horses fill the air with their snortings and fiery breath, and stamp the ground impatiently. Now the bars are let down, and the boundless plain of the universe lies open before them. They dart forward and cleave the opposing clouds, and outrun the morning breezes which started from the same eastern goal. The steeds soon perceived that the load they drew was lighter than usual; and as a ship without ballast is tossed hither and thither on the sea, so the chariot, without its accustomed weight, was dashed about as if empty. They rush headlong and leave the traveled road. Phaeton is alarmed, and knows not how to guide them; nor, if he knew, has he the power. Then, for the first time, the Great and Little Bear were scorched with heat, and would fain, if it were possible, have plunged into the water; and the Serpent which lies coiled up round the north pole, torpid and harmless, grew warm, and with warmth felt its rage revive. Boötes, they say, fled away, though encumbered with his plow, and all unused to rapid motion.

When hapless Phaeton looked down upon the earth, now spreading in vast extent beneath him, he grew pale and his knees shook with terror. In spite of the glare all around him, the sight of his eyes grew dim. He wished he had never touched his father's horses, never learned his parentage, never prevailed in his request. He is borne along like a vessel that flies before a tempest, when the pilot can do no more and betakes himself to his prayers. What shall he do? Much of the heavenly road is left behind, but more remains before. He turns his eyes from one direction to the other; now to the goal whence he began his course, now to the realms of sunset which he is not destined to reach. He loses his self-command, and knows not what to do—whether to draw tight the reins or throw them loose; he forgets the names of the horses. He sees with terror the monstrous forms scattered over the surface of heaven. Here the Scorpion extended his two great arms, with his tail and crooked claws stretching over two signs of the zodiac. When the boy beheld him, reeking with poison and menacing with his fangs, his courage failed, and the reins fell from his hands. The horses, when they felt them loose on their backs, dashed headlong, and unrestrained went off into unknown regions of the sky, in among the stars, hurling the chariot over pathless places, now up in high heaven, now down almost to the earth. The Moon saw with astonishment her brother's chariot running beneath her own. The clouds begin to smoke, and the mountain tops take fire; the fields are parched with heat, the plants wither, the trees with their leafy branches burn, the harvest is ablaze! But these are small things. Great cities perished, with their walls and towers; whole nations with their people were consumed to ashes! The forest-clad mountains burned, Athos and Taurus and Tmolus and Œte; Ida, once celebrated for fountains, but now all are dry; the Muses' mountain Helicon, and Haemus; Ætna, with fires within and without, and Parnassus, with his two peaks, and Rhodope, forced, at last, to part with his snowy crown. Her cold climate was no protection to Scythia, Caucasus burned, and Ossa and Pindus, and, greater than both, Olympus; the Alps high in air, and the Apennines crowned with clouds.

Then Phaeton beheld the world on fire, and felt the heat intolerable. The air he breathed was like the air of a furnace and full of burning ashes, and the smoke was of a pitchy darkness. He dashed forward he knew not whither. Then, it is believed, the people of Æthiopia became black by the blood being forced so suddenly to the surface, and the Libyan desert was dried up to the condition in which it remains to this day. The Nymphs of the fountains, with disheveled hair, mourned their waters, nor were the rivers safe beneath their banks. Tanais smoked, and Caicus, Xanthus and Meander, Babylonian Euphrates and Ganges, Tagus with golden sands, and Cayster where the swans resort. Nile fled away and hid his head in the desert, and there it still remains concealed. Where he used to discharge his waters through seven mouths into the sea, there seven dry channels alone remained. The earth cracked open, and through the chinks light broke into Tartarus, and frightened the King of Shadows and his queen. The sea shrank up. Where before was water, it became a dry plain; and the mountains that lie beneath the waves lifted up their heads and became islands. The fishes sought the lowest depths, and the dolphins no longer ventured as usual to sport on the surface. Even Nereus, and his wife Doris, with the Nereids, their daughters, sought the deepest caves for refuge. Thrice Neptune essayed to raise his head above the surface, and thrice was driven back by the heat. Earth, surrounded as she was by waters, yet with head and shoulders bare, screening her face with her hand, looked up to heaven, and with a husky voice called on Jupiter:

"O ruler of the gods, if I have deserved this treatment, and it is your will that I perish with fire, why withhold your thunderbolts?

Let me at least fall by your hand. Is this the reward of my fertility, of my obedient service? Is it for this that I have supplied herbage for cattle, and fruits for men, and frankincense for your altars? But if I am unworthy of regard, what has my brother Ocean done to deserve such a fate? If neither of us can excite your pity, think, I pray you, of your own heaven, and behold how both the poles are smoking which sustain your palace, which must fall if they be destroyed. Atlas faints, and scarce holds up his burden. If sea, earth, and heaven perish, we fall into ancient Chaos. Save what yet remains to us from the devouring flame. Oh, take thought for our deliverance in this awful moment!"

Thus spoke Earth, and overcome with heat and thirst, could say no more. Then Jupiter omnipotent, calling to witness all the gods, including him who had lent the chariot, and showing them that all was lost unless some speedy remedy were applied, mounted the lofty tower from whence he diffuses clouds over the earth, and hurls the forked lightnings. But at that time not a cloud was to be found to interpose for a screen to earth, nor was a shower remaining unexhausted. He thundered, and brandishing a lightning in his right hand launched it against the charioteer, and struck him at the same moment from his seat and from existence! Phaeton, with his hair on fire, fell headlong, like a shooting star which marks the heavens with its brightness as it falls, and Eridanus, the great river, received him and cooled his burning frame.

The Italian Naiades reared a tomb for him, and inscribed these words upon the stone:

> "Driver of Phoebus' chariot, Phaeton,
>   Struck by Jove's thunder, rest beneath this stone,
>   He could not rule his father's car of fire,
>   Yet was it much so nobly to aspire."
>   —Ovid.

His three sisters, the Heliades, as they were called, lamented his fate, and were turned into poplar trees on the banks of the river, while their tears, which continued to flow, became amber as they dropped into the stream.

PROMETHEUS THE FIREBRINGER

By W. M. L. HUTCHINSON

IN the beginning of the reign of Zeus, his bosom friend and coun-
selor was Prometheus, by whose wisdom he had balked the
Titans of their revenge. But ere long the young King of the Sky
became jealous of that very wisdom to which he owed so much, and
fell to doubting the loyalty of his chief helper.

He began to say to himself that as Prometheus had forsaken
Cronos in his hour of need, so he would forsake Zeus, should he
foresee the coming of some yet mightier god. Had he not, moreover, interceded for Cronos, and given him a sure refuge in those
Happy Isles that lay beyond the range of lightning flash or thunder-
storm—and was he not perhaps already conspiring with the exiled
Titan brethren to restore their ancient king?

Now, what mainly bred suspicion in the mind of Zeus was this:
Prometheus, though he came duly to council and to feast in the
heavenly halls, seemed ever impatient to be gone upon some business
of his own in the world below. It fell on a day that Zeus sat ban-
queting, throned in splendor such as mortal eye hath not seen, and
surrounded by the glorious company of the Olympians, his brothers
and sisters; and Prometheus rose up from his place and made to
depart, after his wont.

And Zeus asked him:

"What is it you will find on earth, Prometheus, fairer than this
house of mine, that you are in such haste to leave?"

"Nothing fairer, nor so fair," answered Prometheus, with a smile,
"but something sweeter to me. For bethink you, King of us all, that
you were born where now you reign, but I am no native of the Sky;
to me, a son of Earth, the green glens of Arcadia are dearer than all
your starry pomp."

So he went his way, but Zeus sat frowning in his place, for the
answer misliked him. Presently he called to him the blithe-faced
Hermes, his herald and messenger, and bade him follow Prometheus

and watch what he did in those glens that he loved better than the golden houses of heaven.

"It is for no good end," he said wrathfully, "that the Titan hides his doings from my view under the dense covert of his oakwoods."

Straightway Hermes put on his shining, winged sandals that bear him over sea and land more swiftly than bird can fly, and sped upon his errand. When he came again, Zeus asked him what he had seen.

"King of Gods," said Hermes, smiling, "have no fear that Prometheus will plot anything against us Olympians. He recks not of us; all his delight is in the race of puny mortals whom he made out of the clay to pleasure old Cronos; and as for his business in Arcadia, it is neither more nor less than devising their welfare.

"He has taught them, it seems, to fashion rude tools and weapons of horn and bone and flint, to build themselves huts, to till and sow the ground, and many other arts that the men of the Gold and Silver Ages knew nothing of. I heard some among them speak of him—they call him the Great Brother whose wisdom helps to lighten their hard lot, and there was word also of a wondrous gift he has promised to bestow on them ere long."

"What gift is that?" asked Zeus uneasily.

"They do not know," answered Hermes; "but Prometheus has told them that it will be to them *a good servant and a bad master.*"

Now Zeus was troubled at these tidings, for he did not believe that the great Titan would thus befriend mere mortals, creatures of a day, without some deep design. In time, perhaps, he would teach them so much that they would become wiser than gods—nay, this unknown gift he had promised them might be some potent charm that would make them strong enough to defy the Lord of the thunder!

Zeus pondered long what this gift might be, but he could make no guess at it. So, when the Immortals were again gathered to the banquet, he put forth a riddle to them all, saying "What is it that is *a good servant and a bad master?*"

Some said one thing, some another; but Prometheus knew that Hermes had spied upon him in Arcadia, and whispered in his ear, "Minion of Zeus, if you would win favor with your master, say *'It is fire.'*" And Hermes said it laughing, after his wont; for he himself never bore ill will to anyone, and dreamed not that a quarrel was toward between his lord and the Titan.

Zeus no sooner heard the answer of Hermes than he perceived that fire was indeed the gift Prometheus was minded to bestow upon men, which, as yet, was unknown to mortals and burned only beneath the earth and on the sacred Hearth of the gods on high. He resolved to defeat the purpose of Prometheus, whatever it might be, and, rising up, he said:

"You have heard, Olympians, my riddle and its answer. Now hear and obey my command. Let none dare to profane the thrice-holy element of fire by bestowing it on mortals, but be it forever consecrate to the use of the gods alone. Swift vengeance will I take on him who shall transgress this my law."

The rest of the Immortals hastily promised obedience, but Prometheus began to plead earnestly with Zeus for the race of mortals, bidding him remember the want and hardship they must endure now that Earth no longer gave her increase freely as in the Age of Gold. Without fire, he said, mankind could not warm their shivering frames in the winter season, nor forge weapons of metal to defend themselves from beasts of prey, nor bring to perfection any of those helpful crafts that he had begun to teach them.

"Forbid them fire," he cried, "and you forbid them all hope of rising above the life of animals; their doom is sure, they must be savages to the end."

But Zeus would not hearken to his pleading, for he could not see that the heart of Prometheus was filled with compassion and loving-kindness for helpless man, being indeed blinded by his jealous mistrust.

"What are this folk of clay to me?" he said disdainfully. "They were not made for my pleasure, that I should show them favor—nay, they belong to Cronos, who bade you provide him new worshipers when he had destroyed the face of Silver. For his sake they are hateful to me, and I have a mind to cut them off as he did those others, and people Earth with a race that has known no other gods but me."

Prometheus made him no answer, but gave him a look at once proud and mournful, and in a little while he departed without word of farewell. And after that he came no more to the board of Zeus. But when some days had passed, Zeus looked forth upon the earth and saw pillars of blue smoke rising among the trees in all the valleys of Arcadia.

For Prometheus had taken fire from the Hearth of the gods by stealth, and brought it to men in a hollow wand of fennel that served him instead of a staff. He had shown them how to make open hearths of sun-baked clay in their poor dwellings and how to kindle dry wood thereon with the new gift, and they cried aloud for joy and wonder as they saw the scarlet flowers of flame blossom from the dead boughs.

Then was Zeus wroth indeed; in the first moment of his fury he stretched forth his hand to his thunderbolts with intent to hurl them upon the land of Arcadia and utterly consume every living thing therein. But he bethought him suddenly of a better way to wreak vengeance upon the rebel Prometheus, and he stayed his hand. Thunderbolts could not slay the Titan, since he was immortal, and to destroy the land and the men he loved would be but small satisfaction, for he could soon make himself another folk in some country fairer than Arcadia.

"These men shall not die," said the angry god, "but I will devise such evils for them that they shall desire death rather than life, and Prometheus shall see their misery and be powerless to succor them. That shall be his keenest pang among the torments I will heap upon him."

Now there are giant Twins whose lot it is to serve him that sits upon the throne of heaven, be he who he may, and the gods call them Kratos and Bia, that is to say, Might and Force. These Zeus called before him, and having laid certain commands on them he sent them to the Forge of the Cyclops in Mount Etna, which he had given to the lame smith god, Hephæstus, the cunning craftsman of the Olympians, to be his workshop.

Meanwhile Prometheus, not ignorant of his doom, betook himself to the house of his brother, Epimetheus, and said to him:

"Brother, I am bound on a far journey, and must bid farewell to to you and to Arcadia, our pleasant home, for the Fates will have it so. Grieve not, nor be amazed at the things you will shortly hear concerning me, since all that must befall me I have foreseen with unshaken mind, but take good heed to yourself and beware above all else of receiving any gift from Zeus."

With that he took leave of his brother, and returned to his own house, to await those whom he knew would come speedily, and that night he went unresisting with Kratos, Bia, and Hephæstus to his place of punishment.

There is a ravine of ice-clad rocks upon the peak of huge Mount Caucasus, so walled about with gaunt black precipices, so ghastly in its frozen desolation, that it might seem a very temple of Death where nothing living had ever come since the making of the world. Not the tiniest, lowliest plant that grows peeps from the crannies of its jagged cliffs; no voice of beast or bird ever echoes there save the scream of a famished eagle far aloft.

Yet it is a solitude without peace, for night and day fierce gusts sweep through the gorge, now wailing like spirits in torment, now with uproar so hideous that to hear it would drive a man from his wits. The bright snow that lies deep on the mountain head is whirled away by those pitiless blasts before it can mantle the unsightly masses of rock that bestrew the floor of the ravine or the lightning-scarred crags whence they have fallen.

Hither now came the captive Titan, led by the ministers of Zeus. They had bound him with fetters of brass and with chains of iron, which Hephæstus had wrought, being so commanded, but sorely against his will. For he and all the Olympians loved Prometheus because of his great and gracious ways and, had they dared, would have interceded for him with their King. But Kratos and Bia, who were by nature without pity, exulted over their mighty prisoner, and when they were now come to the place Zeus had appointed and saw that Hephæstus stood gazing sorrowfully upon him, they were enraged.

"Hephæstus!" cried Kratos fiercely. "Why loiter you now? Have you a mind to take sides with this Fire stealer, or have you so soon forgot the charge Zeus gave you by my mouth?"

"I would he had given it to some other," muttered the lame god. "Have a care, Haltfoot, that he overhear you not," answered Kratos tauntingly. "It is well seen you are loath to do his bidding, and if you make not better speed your pity may shortly be needed for your own plight."

"Savage that you are," retorted Hephæstus, "what needs your rude urging? I know and will perform the sentence of Zeus, but none that has not, like you, a heart of stone could joy in such a task. Come, let us about it, and hold your peace the while."

Forthwith Kratos and Bia caused Prometheus to stand upright against a huge pillar of rock, and they held up his arms above his head while Hephæstus bound him to the pillar by the neck and wrists and ankles, riveting his fetters to the rock with nails of adamant. Slowly he plied his hammer, slowly he limped to and fro, and as he worked he heavily sighed. Meanwhile Kratos feasted his eyes on the sight and exclaimed impatiently against his slackness.

"Bind him faster, Hephæstus!" he cried. "Drive home this spike through the iron collar, that he may not turn his head to right or left! Look you, how loose sits this manacle! Another rivet, I pray you, lest the cunning rebel shake himself free. So—have you done at last? Ah, ha! Prometheus, could not all your foresight save you from this pass? Now learn too late what it is to be the Friend of Man and the Foe of Zeus!"

Never a word answered Prometheus, but Hephæstus angrily bade Kratos and Bia begone, for they had done their office. As they sullenly withdrew, he turned to the motionless figure against the pillar and spoke parting words.

"Son of Earth," he said, "not more unwelcome are those bonds to you who wear them than was the forging of them to me. Alas! that my skill is put to such a proof—that I must bind one of race divine in these shackles which no power can break! Ah! rash Prometheus, why did you flout the majesty of Zeus for the sake of worthless mortals? Know you not that a newcomer makes ever a stern master, jealous of his honor?

"Loath am I to leave you thus, but I can avail you nothing; nor see I whence you are to look for any deliverer. Here then you must bide, shut out from sight and speech of gods or men by these eternal walls; here, unsheltered in the scorching blaze of noon you will pray for the coming of starry-kirtled Night, albeit to you she brings no solace but only exchange of torment—the arrows of frost for the arrows of the sun. Ay, where nought else ever changes, dear to your sleepless eyes shall be the comings of morn and eve."

Having thus spoken, Hephæstus also went his way with halting steps, and all was silence for a space in that prison house. Then a great cry broke from the Titan in his anguish:

"O Earth, Mother of all, O radiant Sky and free Winds of heaven, behold what wrongs are mine! Yea, I call on the Sun's pure splendor, and the multitudinous smile of Ocean waves, and you, O Founts of the rivers, to witness what outrage an Immortal suffers at an Immortal's hand. Behold these shameful bonds, this living tomb where I must wrestle alone with never-ending pain—to this the new Lord of the world has doomed Prometheus for no other crime than giving man fire from heaven."

He paused awhile, communing with his own heart, then said, "Yet why do I lament? All this I foresaw from the beginning, and knew at how great a price I must win for mankind the thrice-blessed gift of fire, whereby alone they shall attain to mastery in every art that ministers to life. Nor will I upbraid the tyrant who has thus repaid my ancient kindness. Not he, but resistless Fate, has decreed my doom, and he also in the hour ordained must learn to submit, as I do."

Now while the captive Titan comforted his heart with the thought of what mankind would be able to accomplish by the means of fire, Zeus sat pondering how he might frustrate that good gift with some countervailing evil. For it is a law to all the Immortals that none may take away what another has bestowed, nor could even he now deprive mortals of their new possession. He purposed therefore to send them some gifts so baneful that they should be never free from misery their lives long, and thus to fill up the measure of his vengeance upon Prometheus.

After long thought, he called Hephæstus to him and said, "Hephæstus, I have devised a new thing that has not its like in earth or heaven; now put forth all your skill, for you must forthwith make it according to the fashion I will tell you."

"Of what shall I make it?" asked Hephæstus.

"Of whatever you can find most fair," said Zeus. "Mingle together all things loveliest, sweetest, and best, but look that you also mingle therewith the opposites of each."

So Hephæstus took gold and dross, wax and flint, pure snow and mud of the highways, honey and gall; he took the bloom of the rose and the toad's venom, the voice of laughing water and the peacock's squall; he took the sea's beauty, and its treachery; the dog's fidelity, the wind's inconstancy; the cruelty of the tiger, and the mother-bird's heart of love. All these, and other contraries past number, he blended cunningly into one substance and this he molded into the shape that Zeus described to him.

When it was finished, Hephæstus looked upon his handiwork and said, "We have made no new thing, but the image of a goddess."

"Nay," said Zeus, "we have made the First Woman," and with that he breathed upon the image, and it lived, and looked upon them wonderingly as one suddenly awakened.

Then he called all the Olympians to behold the First Woman and they marveled at the beauty of her, for in truth she was fair as any goddess. They cried they would each offer her some gift on this her birthday, and so they did; the goddesses arrayed her in glorious apparel, Hephæstus decked her with jewels of cunning workman-ship, and every god gave her some precious thing. Last of all, Zeus himself placed in her hands a casket of lustrous amber, richly over-wrought with flowers and fruit of the pomegranate and having two golden snakes for handles.

"Behold, Immortals," he said, "this new fair creature of my shap-ing thought, endowed with every earthly loveliness, laden with heaven's choicest treasures! Shall she not be named Pandora, All-gifted? Seems she not even as a bride adorned for her husband? But she is no mate for an Olympian, for she is mortal; come, let us send her to wed with Epimetheus, in token that we bear him no ill will for his rebel brother's sake."

The Olympians were well pleased, for they knew not the guileful intent of Zeus, and straightway he bade Hermes lead Pandora to the house of Epimetheus and say to him, "The King of Gods, in sign of his good will toward you, sends you this peerless bride, who brings with her in this casket such a dowry as he only can bestow."

So Hermes brought the First Woman to Arcadia. Now when Epimetheus saw her beauty and heard why she was come, he could scarce contain himself for joy at his good fortune, and he received the bride with her casket into his house and wedded her that day, without once remembering the warning Prometheus gave him not to take any gift from Zeus. But on the morrow it came back to his mind and he repented of what he had done; for this was his nature, that he was never wise until too late. From this he had his name of Epimetheus, which means *Afterthought,* even as his brother was called Prometheus, or *Forethought,* because he was wise about things to come.

Epimetheus now reflected that the dowry Zeus had given his bride was doubtless meant to work him some deadly harm, and he asked Pandora if she knew what lay in her amber box.

"No, my husband," said she, "but I will fetch the box from our chamber and we will open it and see. I long to know what the great King of the Immortals has bestowed on us."

"Bide here, Pandora," said the Titan, "and listen well to what I shall say. My mind misgives me that yonder casket holds some evil secret, and he who sent it is not a friend but a subtle enemy. I was warned erewhile to take no gift at his hand, but in my folly I paid little heed. Now since what is done cannot be undone, and the gift is under my roof, here let it stay; but I charge you on your love and obedience never open the casket. For whatever it holds can do us no mischief while we keep it fast shut, and it is itself so royal-rich and beautiful a thing that I have no heart to cast it away."

Pandora was glad that she might keep the wondrous box, and every day she viewed it with delight as it shone like translucent gold in the sunlight. But after a while she wearied of that pleasure and began to wonder more and more what might be hidden within it. Many a time, alone in her chamber, she sat gazing at the casket until longing to learn its secret so nearly overcame her that she arose and went hastily forth, vowing to look on it no more.

At last, in an accursed hour, she could resist her desire no longer; she laid her hand upon the lid and raised it gently—very gently, half fearful of what she might see. Quick as thought out flew a swarm of tiny winged sprites, soaring and drifting upward like breeze-blown tufts of thistledown, and they vanished like a wreath of smoke through the open doorway.

With a startled cry Pandora closed the box—but, alas! too late; one glance had shown her it was empty and she sat down and wept tears of disappointment. Now, had she known what she had done, she must have grieved a thousand times more bitterly, for the sprites she had let loose were all the cares and woes and fell diseases that afflict mankind, and from that hour to this they fly abroad upon earth, pursuing hapless mortals from the cradle to the grave. Such was the dower that the First Woman brought with her into the world.

Epimetheus found his wife weeping, and she told him what had befallen, and he forgave her and said, "Half the fault is mine, because I left the casket in your keeping. It seems that it is as much a woman's nature to be overcurious as it is mine to be wise too late."

And he forebore to reproach her, although he now knew well enough, by his power of afterthought, what those sprites were. He asked Pandora if she was sure they had all escaped and she said "Yes." But by and by she thought she would look again, and when she opened the casket she saw there was still one left, clinging beneath the gold rim that held up the lid, with its rainbow wings drooping as if broken. And something told Pandora that its name was Hope.

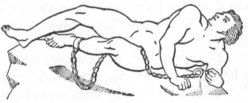

PERSEUS

By CHARLES KINGSLEY

I. HOW PERSEUS AND HIS MOTHER CAME TO SERIPHOS

ONCE upon a time there were two princes who were twins. Their names were Acrisius and Prœtus, and they lived in the pleasant vale of Argos, far away in Hellas. They had fruitful meadows and vineyards, sheep and oxen, great herds of horses feeding down in Lerna Fen, and all that men could need to make them blest; and yet they were wretched, because they were jealous of each other. From the moment they were born they began to quarrel, and when they grew up, each tried to take away the other's share of the kingdom, and keep all for himself. So, first Acrisius drove out Prœtus; and he went across the seas, and brought home a foreign princess for his wife, and foreign warriors to help him, who were called Cyclopes; and drove out Acrisius in his turn; and then they fought a long while up and down the land, till the quarrel was settled; and Acrisius took Argos and one half the land, and Prœtus took Tiryns and the other half. And Prœtus and his Cyclopes built around Tiryns great walls of unhewn stone, which are standing to this day.

But there came a prophet to that hardhearted Acrisius, and prophesied against him, and said "Because you have risen up against your own blood, your own blood shall rise up against you; because you have sinned against your kindred, by your kindred you shall be punished. Your daughter Danae shall bear a son, and by that son's hand you shall die. So the gods have ordained, and it will surely come to pass."

And at that, Acrisius was very much afraid; but he did not mend his ways. He had been cruel to his own family; and, instead of repenting and being kind to them, he went on to be more cruel than ever; for he shut up his fair daughter Danae in a cavern underground, lined with brass, that no one might come near her. So he fancied himself more cunning than the gods; but you will see presently whether he was able to escape them.

Now it came to pass that in time Danae bore a son; so beautiful a babe that any but King Acrisius would have had pity on it. But he had no pity. For he took Danae and her babe down to the seashore, and put them into a great chest, and thrust them out to sea, for the winds and the waves to carry them whithersoever they would.

The northwest wind blew freshly out of the blue mountains, and down the pleasant vale of Argos, and away and out to sea. And away and out to sea before it, floated the mother and her babe, while all who watched them wept, save that cruel father, King Acrisius.

So they floated on and on, and the chest danced up and down upon the billows, and the baby slept upon its mother's breast; but the poor mother could not sleep, but watched and wept, and she sang to her baby as they floated; and the song which she sang you shall learn yourselves some day.

And now they are past the last blue headland, and in the open sea; and there is nothing round them but the waves, and the sky, and the wind. But the waves are gentle, and the sky is clear, and the breeze is tender and low; for these are the days when Halcyone and Ceyx build their nests, and no storms ever ruffle the pleasant summer sea.

And who were Halcyone and Ceyx? You shall hear while the chest floats on. Halcyone was a fairy maiden, the daughter of the beach and of the wind. And she loved a sailor boy, and married him; and none on earth were so happy as they. But at last Ceyx was wrecked; and before he could swim to the shore, the billows swallowed him up. And Halcyone saw him drowning, and leapt into the sea to him; but in vain. Then the Immortals took pity on them both, and changed them into two fair sea birds; and now they build a floating nest every year, and sail up and down happily forever, upon the pleasant seas of Greece.

So a night passed and a day; and a long day it was for Danae; and another night and day beside, till Danae was faint with hunger and weeping, and yet no land appeared. And all the while the babe slept quietly; and at last poor Danae dropped her head and fell asleep likewise, with her cheek against her babe's.

After a while she awakened suddenly; for the chest was jarring and grinding, and the air was full of sound. She looked up, and over her head were mighty cliffs, all red in the setting sun, and around her rocks and breakers, and flying flakes of foam. She clasped her hands together, and shrieked aloud for help. And when she cried, help met her; for now there came over the rocks a tall and stately man, and looked down wondering upon poor Danae tossing about in the chest among the waves.

He wore a rough cloak of frieze, and on his head a broad hat to shade his face; in his hand he carried a trident for spearing fish, and over his shoulder was a casting net; but Danae could see he was no common man by his stature, and his walk, and his flowing golden hair and beard; and by the two servants who came behind him, carrying baskets for his fish. But she had hardly time to look at him, before he had laid aside his trident, and leapt down the rocks, and thrown his casting net so surely over Danae and the chest, that he drew it, and her, and the baby, safe upon a ledge of rock.

Then the fisherman took Danae by the hand, and lifted her out of the chest, and said:

"O beautiful damsel, what strange chance has brought you to this island in so frail a ship? Who are you, and whence? Surely you are some king's daughter; and this boy has somewhat more than mortal."

And as he spoke, he pointed to the babe; for its face shone like the morning star.

But Danae only held down her head, and sobbed out:

"Tell me to what land I have come, unhappy that I am; and among what men I have fallen?"

And he said: "This isle is called Seriphos, and I am a Hellen, and dwell in it. I am the brother of Polydectes the king; and men call me Dictys the netter, because I catch the fish of the shore."

Then Danae fell down at his feet, and embraced his knees, and cried:

"Oh, Sir, have pity upon a stranger, whom a cruel doom has

driven to your land; and let me live in your house as a servant; but treat me honorably, for I was once a king's daughter, and this my boy (as you have truly said) is of no common race. I will not be a charge to you, or eat the bread of idleness; for I am more skillful in weaving and embroidery, than all the maidens of my land."

And she was going on; but Dictys stopped her, and raised her up, and said:

"My daughter, I am old, and my hairs are growing gray; while I have no children to make my home cheerful. Come with me, then, and you shall be a daughter to me and to my wife, and this babe shall be our grandchild. For I fear the gods, and show hospitality to all strangers; knowing that good deeds, like evil ones, always return to those who do them."

So Danae was comforted, and went home with Dictys the good fisherman, and was a daughter to him and to his wife, till fifteen years were past.

II. HOW PERSEUS VOWED A RASH VOW

Fifteen years were past and gone, and the baby was now grown to be a tall lad and a sailor, and went many voyages after merchandise to the islands round. His mother called him Perseus: but all the people in Seriphos said that he was not the son of mortal man, and called him the son of Zeus, the king of the Immortals. For though he was but fifteen, he was taller by a head than any man in the island; and he was the most skillful of all in running and wrestling and boxing, and in throwing the quoit and the javelin, and in rowing with the oar, and in playing on the harp, and in all which befits a man. And he was brave and truthful, gentle and courteous, for good old Dictys had trained him well; and well it was for Perseus that he had done so. For now Danae and her son fell into great danger, and Perseus had need of all his wit to defend his mother and himself.

I said that Dictys's brother was Polydectes, king of the island. He was not a righteous man, like Dictys: but greedy, and cunning, and cruel. And when he saw fair Danae, he wanted to marry her.

But she would not; for she did not love him, and cared for no one but her boy, and her boy's father, whom she never hoped to see again. At last Polydectes became furious; and while Perseus was away at sea, he took poor Danae away from Dictys, saying, "If you will not be my wife, you shall be my slave." So Danae was made a slave, and had to fetch water from the well, and grind in the mill, and perhaps was beaten, and wore a heavy chain, because she would not marry that cruel king. But Perseus was far away over the seas in the isle of Samos, little thinking how his mother was languishing in grief.

Now one day at Samos, while the ship was lading, Perseus wandered into a pleasant wood to get out of the sun, and sat down on the turf, and fell asleep. And as he slept, a strange dream came to him; the strangest dream which he had ever had in his life.

There came a lady to him through the wood, taller than he, or any mortal man: but beautiful exceedingly, with great gray eyes, clear and piercing, but strangely soft and mild. On her head was a helmet, and in her hand a spear. And over her shoulder, above her long blue robes, hung a goatskin, which bore up a mighty shield of brass, polished like a mirror. She stood and looked at him with her clear gray eyes; and Perseus saw that her eyelids never moved, nor her eyeballs, but looked straight through and through him, and into his very heart, as if she could see all the secrets of his soul, and knew all that he had ever thought or longed for since the day that he was born. And Perseus dropped his eyes, trembling and blushing, as the wonderful lady spoke:

"Perseus, you must do an errand for me."

"Who are you, lady? And how do you know my name?"

"I am Pallas Athene; and I know the thoughts of all men's hearts, and discern their manhood or their baseness. And from the souls of clay I turn away; and they are blest, but not by me. They fatten at ease, like sheep in the pasture, and eat what they did not sow, like oxen in the stall. They grow and spread, like the gourd along the ground: but like the gourd, they give no shade to the traveler; and when they are ripe death gathers them, and they go down unloved into hell, and their name vanishes out of the land.

"But to the souls of fire I give more fire, and to those who are manful I give a might more than man's. These are the heroes, the sons of the Immortals, who are blest, but not like the souls of clay. For I drive them forth by strange paths, Perseus, that they may fight the Titans and the monsters, the enemies of Gods and men. Through doubt and need, danger and battle, I drive them; and some of them are slain in the flower of youth, no man knows when or where; and some of them win noble names, and a fair and green old age; but what will be their latter end I know not, and none, save Zeus, the father of Gods and men. Tell me now, Perseus, which of these two sorts of men seem to you more blest?"

Then Perseus answered boldly: "Better to die in the flower of youth, on the chance of winning a noble name, than to live at ease like the sheep, and die unloved and unrenowned."

Then that strange lady laughed, and held up her brazen shield, and cried: "See here, Perseus; dare you face such a monster as this, and slay it, that I may place its head upon this shield?"

And in the mirror of the shield there appeared a face, and as Perseus looked on it his blood ran cold. It was the face of a beautiful woman; but her cheeks were pale as death, and her brows were knit with everlasting pain, and her lips were thin and bitter like a snake's; and instead of hair, vipers wreathed about her temples, and shot out their forked tongues; while round her head were folded wings like an eagle's and upon her bosom claws of brass.

And Perseus looked awhile, and then said: "If there is anything so fierce and foul on earth, it were a noble deed to kill it. Where can I find the monster?"

Then the strange lady smiled again, and said: "Not yet; you are too young, and too unskilled; for this is Medusa the Gorgon, the mother of a monstrous brood. Return to your home, and do the work which waits there for you. You must play the man in that before I can think you worthy to go in search of the Gorgon."

Then Perseus would have spoken, but the strange lady vanished, and he awoke; and behold, it was a dream. But day and night Perseus saw before him the face of that dreadful woman, with the vipers writhing round her head.

So he returned home; and when he came to Seriphos, the first thing he heard was that his mother was a slave of Polydectes.

Grinding his teeth with rage, he went out, and away to the king's palace, and through the men's rooms, and the women's rooms, and so through all the house (for no one dared to stop him, so terrible and fair was he), till he found his mother sitting on the floor, turning the stone hand mill, and weeping as she turned it. And he lifted her up, and kissed her, and bade her follow him forth. But before they could pass out of the room, Polydectes came in, raging. And when Perseus saw him, he flew upon him as the mastiff flies on the boar. "Villain and tyrant!" he cried. "Is this your respect for the Gods, and thy mercy to strangers and widows? You shall die!" And because he had no sword, he caught up the stone hand mill, and he lifted it to dash out Polydectes' brains.

But his mother clung to him, shrieking: "Oh, my son, we are strangers, and helpless in the land; and if you kill the king, all the people will fall on us, and we shall both die."

Good Dictys, too, who had come in, entreated him. "Remember that he is my brother. Remember how I have brought you up, and trained you as my own son, and spare him for my sake."

Then Perseus lowered his hand; and Polydectes, who had been trembling all this while like a coward, because he knew that he was in the wrong, let Perseus and his mother pass.

Perseus took his mother to the temple of Athene, and there the priestess made her one of the temple sweepers; for there they knew she would be safe, and not even Polydectes would dare to drag her away from the altar. And there Perseus, and the good Dictys, and his wife, came to visit her every day; while Polydectes, not being able to get what he wanted by force, cast about in his wicked heart how he might get it by cunning.

Now he was sure that he could never get back Danae as long as Perseus was in the island; so he made a plot to rid himself of him. And first he pretended to have forgiven Perseus, and to have forgotten Danae; so that, for a while, all went as smoothly as ever.

Next he proclaimed a great feast, and invited to it all the chiefs, and landowners, and the young men of the island, and among them

Perseus, that they might all do him homage as their king, and eat of his banquet in his hall.

On the appointed day they all came; and, as the custom was then, each guest brought his present with him to the king: one a horse, another a shawl, or a ring, or a sword; and those who had nothing better brought a basket of grapes, or of game; but Perseus brought nothing, for he had nothing to bring, being but a poor sailor-lad.

He was ashamed, however, to go into the king's presence without his gift, and he was too proud to ask Dictys to lend him one. So he stood at the door sorrowfully, watching the rich men go in; and his face grew very red as they pointed at him, and smiled, and whispered, "What has that foundling to give?"

Now, this was what Polydectes wanted; and as soon as he heard that Perseus stood without, he bade them bring him in, and asked him scornfully before them all, "Am I not your king, Perseus, and have I not invited you to my feast? Where is your present, then?"

Perseus blushed and stammered, while all the proud men round laughed, and some of them began jeering him openly. "This fellow was thrown ashore here like a piece of weed or driftwood, and yet he is too proud to bring a gift to the king."

"And though he does not know who his father is, he is vain enough to let the old women call him the son of Zeus."

And so forth, till poor Perseus grew mad with shame, and hardly knowing what he said, cried out, "A present! Who are you who talk of presents? See if I do not bring a nobler one than all of yours together!"

So he said, boasting; and yet he felt in his heart that he was braver than all those scoffers, and more able to do some glorious deed.

"Hear him! Hear the boaster! What is it to be?" cried they all, laughing louder than ever.

Then his dream at Samos came into his mind, and he cried aloud, "The head of the Gorgon."

He was half afraid after he had said the words; for all laughed louder than ever, and Polydectes loudest of all.

"You have promised to bring me the Gorgon's head? Then never appear again in this island without it. Go!"

Perseus ground his teeth with rage, for he saw that he had fallen into a trap; but his promise lay upon him, and he went out without a word.

Down to the cliffs he went, and looked across the broad blue sea; and he wondered if his dream were true, and prayed in the bitterness of his soul.

"Pallas Athene, was my dream true? And shall I slay the Gorgon? If thou didst really show me her face, let me not come to shame a liar and boastful. Rashly and angrily I promised: but cunningly and patiently will I perform."

But there was no answer, nor sign; neither thunder or any appearance; not even a cloud in the sky.

And three times Perseus called weeping. "Rashly and angrily I promised: but cunningly and patiently will I perform."

Then he saw afar off a small white cloud, as bright as silver. And it came on, nearer and nearer, till its brightness dazzled his eyes.

Perseus wondered at that strange cloud, for there was no other cloud all round the sky; and he trembled as it touched the cliff below. And as it touched, it broke, and parted, and within it appeared Pallas Athene, as he had seen her at Samos in his dream, and beside her a young man more light-limbed than the stag, whose eyes were like sparks of fire. By his side was a scimitar of diamond, all of one clear precious stone, and on his feet were golden sandals, from the heels of which grew living wings.

They looked upon Perseus keenly, and yet they never moved their eyes; and they came up the cliffs toward him more swiftly than the sea gull, and yet they never moved their feet, nor did the breeze stir the robes about their limbs; only the wings of the youth's sandals quivered, like a hawk's when he hangs above the cliff. And Perseus fell down and worshiped, for he knew that they were more than man.

But Athene stood before him and spoke gently, and bid him have no fear. Then—

"Perseus," she said, "he who overcomes in one trial merits thereby a sharper trial still. You have braved Polydectes, and done manfully. Dare you brave Medusa the Gorgon?"

And Perseus said, "Try me; for since you spoke to me in Samos, a new soul has come into my breast, and I should be ashamed not to dare anything which I can do. Show me, then, how I can do this."

"Perseus," said Athene, "think well before you attempt; for this deed requires a seven years' journey, in which you cannot repent or turn back, nor escape; but if your heart fails you, you must die in the unshapen land, where no man will ever find your bones."

"Better so than live here, useless and despised," said Perseus. "Tell me, then, oh tell me, fair and wise Goddess, of your great kindness and condescension, how I can do but this one thing, and then, if need be, die!"

Then Athene smiled and said—

"Be patient, and listen; for if you forget my words, you will indeed die. You must go northward to the country of the Hyperboreans, who live beyond the pole, at the sources of the cold north wind; till you find the three Gray Sisters, who have but one eye and one tooth between them. You must ask them the way to the Nymphs, the daughters of the Evening Star, who dance about the golden tree, in the Atlantic island of the west. They will tell you the way to the Gorgon, that you may slay her, my enemy, the mother of monstrous beasts. Once she was a maiden as beautiful as morn, till in her pride she sinned a sin at which the sun hid his face; and from that day her hair was turned to vipers, and her hands to eagle's claws; and her heart was filled with shame and rage, and her lips with bitter venom; and her eyes became so terrible that whosoever looks on them is turned to stone; and her children are the winged horse, and the giant of the golden sword; and her grandchildren are Echidna the witch adder, and Geryon the three-headed tyrant, who feeds his herds beside the herds of hell. So she became the sister of the Gorgons, Stheino and Euryte the abhorred, the daughters of the Queen of the Sea. Touch them not, for they are immortal: but bring me only Medusa's head."

"And I will bring it!" said Perseus. "But how am I to escape her eyes? Will she not freeze me too into stone?"

"You shall take this polished shield," said Athene; "and when you come near her look not at her herself, but at her image in the brass;

so you may strike her safely. And when you have struck off her head, wrap it, with your face turned away, in the folds of the goatskin on which the shield hangs, the hide of Amaltheie, the nurse of the Ægis-holder. So you will bring it safely back to me, and win to yourself renown and a place among the heroes who feast with the Immortals upon the peak where no winds blow."

Then Perseus said, "I will go, though I die in going. But how shall I cross the seas without a ship? And who will show me my way? And when I find her, how shall I slay her, if her scales be iron and brass?"

Then the young man spoke: "These sandals of mine will bear you across the seas, and over hill and dale like a bird, as they bear me all day long; for I am Hermes, the far-famed Argus-slayer, the messenger of the Immortals who dwell on Olympus."

Then Perseus fell down and worshiped, while the young man spoke again.

"The sandals themselves will guide you on the road, for they are divine and cannot stray; and this sword itself, the Argus-slayer, will kill her, for it is divine, and needs no second stroke. Arise, and gird them on, and go forth."

So Perseus arose, and girded on the sandals and the sword.

And Athene cried, "Now leap from the cliff, and be gone."

But Perseus lingered.

"May I not bid farewell to my mother and to Dictys? And may I not offer burnt offerings to you, and to Hermes, the far-famed Argus-slayer, and to Father Zeus above?"

"You shall not bid farewell to your mother, lest your heart relent at her weeping. I will comfort her and Dictys until you return in peace. Nor shall you offer burnt offerings to the Olympians; for your offering shall be Medusa's head. Leap, and trust in the armor of the Immortals."

Then Perseus looked down the cliff and shuddered; but he was ashamed to show his dread. Then he thought of Medusa and the renown before him, and he leapt into the empty air.

And behold, instead of falling he floated, and stood, and ran along the sky. He looked back, but Athene had vanished, and Hermes;

and the sandals led him on northward ever, like a crane who follows the spring toward the Ister fens.

III. HOW PERSEUS SLEW THE GORGON

So Perseus started on his journey, going dry-shod over land and sea; and his heart was high and joyful, for the winged sandals bore him each day a seven days' journey.

And he went by Cythnus, and by Ceos, and the pleasant Cyclades to Attica; and past Athens, and Thebes, and the Copaic lake, and up the vale of Cephissus, and past the peaks of Œta and Pindus, and over the rich Thessalian plains, till the sunny hills of Greece were behind him, and before him were the wilds of the north. Then he passed the Thracian mountains, and many a barbarous tribe, Paeons and Dardans and Triballi, till he came to the Ister stream, and the dreary Scythian plains. And he walked across the Ister dry-shod, and away through the moors and fens, day and night toward the bleak northwest, turning neither to the right hand nor the left till he came to the Unshapen Land, and the place which has no name.

And seven days he walked through it, on a path which few can tell; for those who have trodden it like least to speak of it, and those who go there again in dreams are glad enough when they awake; till he came to the edge of the everlasting night, where the air was full of feathers, and the soil was hard with ice; and there at last he found the three Gray Sisters, by the shore of the freezing sea, nodding upon a white log of driftwood, beneath the cold white winter moon; and they chanted a low song together, "Why the old times were better than the new."

There was no living thing around them, not a fly, not a moss upon the rocks. Neither seal nor sea gull dare come near, lest the ice should clutch them in its claws. The surge broke up in foam, but it fell again in flakes of snow; and it frosted the hair of the three Gray Sisters, and the bones in the ice cliff above their heads. They passed the eye from one to the other, but for all that they could not see; and they passed the tooth from one to the other, but for all that they could not eat; and they sat in the full glare of the moon, but they were none the warmer for her beams. And Perseus pitied the Gray Sisters; but they did not pity themselves.

So he said, "O venerable mothers, wisdom is the daughter of old age. You therefore should know many things. Tell me, if you can, the path of the Gorgon."

Then one cried, "Who is this who reproaches us with old age?" And another, "This is the voice of one of the children of men."

And he, "I do not reproach, but honor your old age, and I am one of the sons of men and of the heroes. The rulers of Olympus have sent me to you to ask the way to the Gorgon."

Then one—"There are new rulers in Olympus, and all new things are bad." And another—"We hate your rulers, and the heroes, and all the children of men. We are the kindred of the Titans, and the Giants, and the Gorgons, and the ancient monsters of the deep." And another—"Who is this rash and insolent man, who pushes unbidden into our world?" And the first—"There never was such a world as ours, nor will be; if we let him see it, he will spoil it all."

Then one cried, "Give me the eye, that I may see him"; and another, "Give me the tooth, that I may bite him." But Perseus, when he saw that they were foolish and proud, and did not love the children of men, left off pitying them, and said to himself, "Hungry men must needs be hasty; if I stay making many words here, I shall be starved." Then he stepped close to them, and watched till they passed the eye from hand to hand. And as they groped about between themselves, he held out his own hand gently, till one of them put the eye into it, fancying that it was the hand of her sister. Then he sprang back, and laughed, and cried:

"Cruel and proud old women, I have your eye; and I will throw it into the sea, unless you tell me the path to the Gorgon, and swear to me that you tell me right."

Then they wept, chattered, and scolded; but in vain. They were forced to tell the truth, though Perseus could hardly make out the road.

"You must go," they said, "foolish boy, to the southward, into the ugly glare of the sun, till you come to Atlas the Giant, who holds the heaven and the earth apart. And you must ask his daughters, the

Hesperides, who are young and foolish like yourself. And now give us back our eye; for we have forgotten all the rest."

So Perseus gave them back their eye; but instead of using it, they nodded and fell fast asleep, and were turned into blocks of ice, till the tide came up and washed them all away. And now they float up and down like icebergs forever, weeping whenever they meet the sunshine, and the fruitful summer, and the warm south wind, which fill young hearts with joy.

But Perseus leaped away to the southward, leaving the snow and the ice behind; past the isle of the Hyperboreans, and the tin isles, and the long Iberian shore; while the sun rose higher day by day upon a bright blue summer sea. And the terns and the sea gulls swept laughing round his head, and called to him to stop and play, and the dolphins gamboled up as he passed, and offered to carry him on their backs. And all night long the sea nymphs sang sweetly, and the Tritons blew upon their conchs, as they played round Galatæa their queen, in her car of pearled shells. Day by day the sun rose higher, and leaped more swiftly into the sea at night, and more swiftly out of the sea at dawn; while Perseus skimmed over the billows like a sea gull, and his feet were never wetted; and leapt on from wave to wave, and his limbs were never weary, till he saw far away a mighty mountain, all rose-red in the setting sun. Its feet were wrapped in forests, and its head in wreaths of cloud; and Perseus knew that it was Atlas, who holds the heavens and the earth apart.

He came to the mountain, and leapt on shore, and wandered upward among pleasant valleys and waterfalls, and tall trees and strange ferns and flowers; but there was no smoke rising from any glen, nor house, nor sign of man.

At last he heard sweet voices singing; and he guessed that he was come to the garden of the Nymphs, the daughters of the Evening Star.

They sang like nightingales among the thickets, and Perseus stopped to hear their song; but the words which they spoke he could not understand; no, nor no man after him for many a hundred years. So he stepped forward and saw them dancing, hand in hand around the charmed tree, which bent under its golden fruit; and round the tree foot was coiled the dragon, old Ladon the sleepless snake, who lies there forever, listening to the song of the maidens, blinking and watching with dry bright eyes.

Then Perseus stopped, not because he feared the dragon, but because he was bashful before those fair maids; but when they saw him, they too stopped, and called to him with trembling voices,

"Who are you? Are you Heracles the mighty, who will come to rob our garden, and carry off our golden fruit?" And he answered,

"I am not Heracles the mighty, and I want none of your golden fruit. Tell me, fair nymphs, the way which leads to the Gorgon, that I may go on my way and slay her."

"Not yet, not yet, fair boy; come dance with us around the tree, in the garden which knows no winter, the home of the south wind and the sun. Come hither and play with us awhile; we have danced alone here for a thousand years, and our hearts are weary with longing for a play-fellow. So come, come, come!"

"I cannot dance with you, fair maidens, for I must do the errand of the Immortals. So tell me the way to the Gorgon, lest I wander and perish in the waves."

Then they sighed and wept; and answered:

"The Gorgon! She will freeze you into stone."

"It is better to die like a hero than to live like an ox in a stall. The Immortals have lent me weapons, and they will give me wit to use them."

Then they sighed again and answered: "Fair boy, if you are bent on your own ruin, be it so. We know not the way to the Gorgon; but we will ask the giant Atlas, above upon the mountain peak, the brother of our father, the silver Evening Star. He sits aloft, and sees across the ocean, and far away into the Unshapen Land."

So they went up the mountain to Atlas, their uncle, and Perseus went up with them. And they found the giant kneeling, as he held the heavens and the earth apart.

They asked him, and he answered mildly, pointing to the seaboard with his mighty hand: "I can see the Gorgons lying on an island far away, but this youth can never come near them, unless he has the hat of darkness, which whosoever wears cannot be seen."

Then cried Perseus, "Where is that hat, that I may find it?"

But the giant smiled. "No living mortal can find that hat, for it lies in the depths of Hades, in the regions of the dead. But my nieces are immortal, and they shall fetch it for you, if you will promise me one thing and keep your faith."

Then Perseus promised; and the giant said: "When you come back with the head of Medusa, you shall show me the beautiful horror; that I may lose my feeling and my breathing, and become a stone forever; for it is weary labor for me to hold the heavens and the earth apart."

Then Perseus promised; and the eldest of the nymphs went down, and into a dark cavern among the cliffs, out of which came smoke and thunder, for it was one of the mouths of Hell.

And Perseus and the nymphs sat down seven days, and waited trembling, till the nymph came up again; and her face was pale, and her eyes dazzled with the light, for she had been long in the dreary darkness; but in her hand was the magic hat.

Then all the nymphs kissed Perseus, and wept over him a long while; but he was only impatient to be gone. And at last they put the hat upon his head, and he vanished out of their sight.

But Perseus went on boldly, past many an ugly sight, far away into the heart of the Unshapen Land, beyond the streams of Ocean, to the isles where no ship cruises, where is neither night nor day, where nothing is in its right place, and nothing has a name; till he heard the rustle of the Gorgons' wings, and saw the glitter of their brazen talons; and then he knew that it was time to halt, lest Medusa should freeze him into stone.

He thought awhile with himself, and remembered Athene's words. He rose aloft into the air, and held the mirror of the shield above his head, and looked up into it that he might see all that was below him.

And he saw the three Gorgons sleeping, as huge as elephants. He knew that they could not see him, because the hat of darkness hid him; and yet he trembled as he sank down near them, so terrible were those brazen claws.

Two of the Gorgons were foul as swine, and lay sleeping heavily, as swine sleep, with their mighty wings outspread; but Medusa tossed to and fro restlessly, and as she tossed, Perseus pitied her, she looked so fair and sad. Her plumage was like the rainbow, and her face was like the face of a nymph, only her eyebrows were knit, and her lips clenched, with everlasting care and pain; and her long neck gleamed so white in the mirror, that Perseus had not the heart to strike, and said: "Ah, that it had been either of her sisters!"

From Statue by Cellini

He did not need to strike again.

But as he looked, from among her tresses the vipers' heads awoke, and peeped up with their bright dry eyes, and showed their fangs, and hissed; and Medusa, as she tossed, threw back her wings, and showed her brazen claws; and Perseus saw that, for all her beauty, she was as foul and venomous as the rest.

Then he came down and stepped to her boldly, and looked steadfastly on his mirror, and struck with Herpe stoutly once; and he did not need to strike again.

Then he wrapped the head in the goatskin, turning away his eyes, and sprang into the air aloft, faster than he ever sprang before.

For Medusa's wings and talons rattled as she sank dead upon the rocks; and her two foul sisters woke, and saw her lying dead.

Into the air they sprang yelling, and looked for him who had done the deed. Thrice they swung round and round, like hawks who beat for a partridge; and thrice they snuffed round and round, like hounds who draw upon a deer. At last they struck upon the scent of the blood, and they checked for a moment to make sure; and then on they rushed with a fearful howl, while the wind rattled hoarse in their wings.

On they rushed, sweeping and flapping, like eagles after a hare;

and Perseus' blood ran cold, for all his courage, as he saw them come howling on his track; and he cried: "Bear me well, now brave sandals, for the hounds of death are at my heels!"

And well the brave sandals bore him, aloft through cloud and sunshine, across the shoreless sea; and fast followed the hounds of death, as the roar of their wings came down the wind. But the roar came down fainter and fainter, and the howl of their voices died away; for the sandals were too swift, even for Gorgons, and by nightfall they were far behind, two black specks in the southern sky, till the sun sank and he saw them no more.

Then he came again to Atlas, and the garden of the Nymphs; and when the giant heard him coming, he groaned, and said: "Fulfill thy promise to me." Then Perseus held up to him the Gorgon's head, and he had rest from all his toil; for he became a crag of stone, which sleeps forever far above the clouds.

Then he thanked the Nymphs, and asked them: "By what road shall I go homeward again? For I wandered far in coming hither!"

And they wept and cried: "Go home no more, but stay and play with us, the lonely maidens, who dwell forever far away from gods and men."

But he refused, and they told him his road and said: "Take with you this magic fruit, which, if you eat once, you will not hunger for seven days. For you must go eastward and eastward ever, over the doleful Lybian shore, which Poseidon gave to Father Zeus, when he burst open the Bosphorus and the Hellespont, and drowned the fair Lectonian land.

And Zeus took that land in exchange, a fair bargain, much bad ground for a little good, and to this day it lies waste and desert, with shingle, and rock, and sand."

Then they kissed Perseus, and wept over him, and he leapt down the mountain, and went on, lessening and lessening like a sea gull, away and out to sea.

IV. HOW PERSEUS CAME TO THE ÆTHIOPS

So Perseus flitted onward to the northeast over many a league of sea, till he came to the rolling sandhills, and the dreary Lybian shore.

And he flitted on across the desert, over rock-ledges, and banks of shingle, and level wastes of sand, and shell drifts bleaching in the sunshine, and the skeletons of great sea monsters, and dead bones of ancient giants, strewn up and down upon the old sea floor. And as he went, the blood drops fell to the earth from the Gorgon's head, and became poisonous asps and adders, which breed in the desert to this day.

Over the sands he went, he never knew how far or how long, feeding on the fruit which the Nymphs had given him, till he saw the hills of the Psylli, and the Dwarfs who fought with cranes. Their spears were of reeds and rushes, and their houses of the egg-shells of the cranes; and Perseus laughed, and went his way to the northeast, hoping all day long to see the blue Mediterranean sparkling, that he might fly across it to his home.

But now came down a mighty wind, and swept him back southward toward the desert. All day long he strove against it; but even the winged sandals could not prevail. So he was forced to float down the wind all night; and when the morning dawned there was nothing to be seen, save the same old hateful waste of sand.

And out of the north the sandstorms rushed upon him, blood-red pillars and wreaths, blotting out the noonday sun; and Perseus fled before them, lest he should be choked by the burning dust. At last the gale fell calm, and he tried to go northward again; but again came down the sandstorms, and swept him back into the waste, and then all was calm and cloudless as before. Seven days he strove against the storms, and seven days he was driven back, till he was spent with thirst and hunger, and his tongue clove to the roof of his mouth. Here and there he fancied that he saw a fair lake, and the sunbeams shining on the water; but when he came to it it vanished at his feet, and there was nought but burning sand. And if he had not been of the race of the Immortals, he would have perished in the waste; but his life was strong within him, because it was more than man's.

Then he cried to Athene, and said:

"O fair and pure, if thou hearest me, wilt thou leave me here to die of drought? I have brought thee the Gorgon's head at thy bidding, and hitherto thou hast prospered my journey; dost thou desert me at the last? Else why will not these immortal sandals prevail, even against the desert storms? Shall I never see my mother more, and the blue ripple round Seriphos, and the sunny hills of Hellas?"

So he prayed; and after he had prayed there was a great silence.

The heaven was still above his head, and the sand was still beneath his feet; and Perseus looked up, but there was nothing but the blinding sun in the blinding blue; and round him, but there was nothing but the blinding sand.

And Perseus stood still awhile, and waited, and said, "Surely I am not here without the will of the Immortals, for Athene will not lie. Were not these sandals to lead me in the right road? Then the road in which I have tried to go must be a wrong road."

Then suddenly his ears were opened, and he heard the sound of running water.

And at that his heart was lifted up, though he scarcely dare believe his ears; and weary as he was, he hurried forward, though he could scarcely stand upright; and within a bowshot of him was a glen in the sand, and marble rocks, and date trees, and a lawn of gay green grass. And through the lawn a streamlet sparkled and wandered out beyond the trees, and vanished in the sand.

The water trickled among the rocks, and a pleasant breeze rustled in the dry date-branches; and Perseus laughed for joy, and leapt down the cliff, and drank of the cool water, and ate of the dates, and slept upon the turf, and leapt up and went forward again; but not toward the north this time: for he said—"Surely Athene has sent me hither, and will not have me go homeward yet. What if there be another noble deed to be done, before I see the sunny hills of Hellas?"

So he went east, and east forever, by fresh oases and fountains, date-palms, and lawns of grass, till he saw before him a mighty mountain-wall, all rose-red in the setting sun.

Then he towered in the air like an eagle, for his limbs were strong again; and he flew all night across the mountain till the day began to dawn, and rosy-fingered Eos came blushing up the sky. And then, behold, beneath him was the long green garden of Egypt, and the shining stream of Nile.

And he saw cities walled up to heaven, and temples, and obelisks, and pyramids, and giant Gods of stone. And he came down amid fields of barley, and flax, and millet, and clambering gourds; and saw the people coming out of the gates of a great city, and setting to work, each in his place, among the watercourses, parting the streams among the plants cunningly with their feet, according to the wisdom of the Egyptians. But when they saw him they all stopped their work, and gathered round him, and cried:

"Who art thou, fair youth? and what bearest thou beneath thy goatskin there? Surely thou art one of the Immortals; for thy skin is white like ivory, and ours is red like clay. Thy hair is like threads of gold, and ours is black and curled. Surely thou art one of the Immortals;"—and they would have worshiped him then and there, but Perseus said:

"I am not one of the Immortals; but I am a hero of the Hellens. And I have slain the Gorgon in the wilderness, and bear her head with me. Give me food, therefore, that I may go forward and finish my work."

Then they gave him food, and fruit, and wine; but they would not let him go. And when the news came into the city that the Gorgon was slain, the priests came out to meet him, and the maidens, with songs and dances, and timbrels and harps; and they would have brought him to their temple and to their king; but Perseus put on the hat of darkness, and vanished away out of their sight.

Therefore the Egyptians looked long for his return, but in vain, and worshiped him as a hero, and made a statue of him in Chemmis, which stood for many a hundred years; and they said that he appeared to them at times, with sandals a cubit long; and that whenever he appeared the season was fruitful, and the Nile rose high that year.

Then Perseus went to the eastward, along the Red Sea shore; and then, because he was afraid to go into the Arabian deserts, he turned northward once more, and this time no storm hindered him.

He went past the Isthmus, and Mount Casius, and the vast Serbonian bog, and up the shore of Palestine, where the dark-faced Æthiops dwelt.

He flew on past pleasant hills and valleys, like Argos itself, or Lacedæmon, or the fair Vale of Tempe. But the lowlands were all drowned by floods, and the highlands blasted by fire, and the hills heaved like a bubbling cauldron, before the wrath of King Poseidon, the shaker of the earth.

And Perseus feared to go inland, but flew along the shore above the sea; and he went on all the day, and the sky was black with smoke; and he went on all the night, and the sky was red with flame.

And at the dawn of day he looked toward the cliffs; and at the water's edge, under a black rock, he saw a white image stand.

"This," thought he, "must surely be the statue of some sea God; I will go near and see what kind of Gods these barbarians worship."

So he came near; but when he came, it was no statue, but a maiden of flesh and blood; for he could see her tresses streaming in the breeze; and as he came closer still, he could see how she shrank and shivered, when the waves sprinkled her with cold salt spray. Her arms were spread above her head, and fastened to the rock with chains of brass; and her head drooped on her bosom, either with sleep, or weariness, or grief. But now and then she looked up and wailed, and called her mother; yet she did not see Perseus, for the cap of darkness was on his head.

Full of pity and indignation, Perseus drew near and looked upon the maid. Her cheeks were darker than his were, and her hair was blue-black like a hyacinth; but Perseus thought, "I have never seen so beautiful a maiden; no, not in all our Isles. Surely, she is a king's daughter. Do barbarians treat their kings' daughters thus? She is too fair, at least, to have done any wrong. I will speak to her."

And lifting the hat from his head, he flashed into her sight. She shrieked with terror, and tried to hide her face with her hair, for she could not with her hands; but Perseus cried,

"Do not fear me, fair one; I am a Hellen, and no barbarian. What cruel men have bound you? But first I will set you free."

And he tore at the fetters; but they were too strong for him; while the maiden cried, "Touch me not; I am accursed, devoted as a victim to the sea Gods. They will slay you, if you dare to set me free."

"Let them try," said Perseus; and drawing Herpe from his thigh, he cut through the brass as if it had been flax.

"Now," he said, "you belong to me, and not to these sea Gods, whosoever they may be!" But she only called the more on her mother.

"Why call on your mother? She can be no mother to have left you here. If a bird is dropped out of the nest, it belongs to the man who picks it up. If a jewel is cast by the wayside, it is his who dare win it and wear it, as I will win you and will wear you. I know now why Pallas Athene sent me hither. She sent me to gain a prize worth all my toil, and more."

And he clasped her in his arms, and cried, "Where are these sea Gods, cruel and unjust, who doom fair maids to death? I carry the weapons of Immortals. Let them measure their strength against mine! But tell me, maiden, who you are, and what dark fate brought you here."

And she answered, weeping,

"I am the daughter of Cepheus, King of Iopa, and my mother is Cassiopœia of the beautiful tresses, and they called me Andromeda, as long as life was mine. And I stand bound here, hapless that I am, for the sea monster's food, to atone for my mother's sin. For she boasted of me once that I was fairer than Atergatis, Queen of the Fishes; so she in her wrath sent the sea floods, and her brother the Fire King sent the earthquakes, and wasted all the land; and after the floods a monster bred of the slime, who devours all living things. And now he must devour me, guiltless though I am—me who never harmed a living thing, nor saw a fish upon the shore but I gave it life, and threw it back into the sea; for in our land we eat no fish, for fear of Atergatis their Queen. Yet the priests say that nothing but my blood can atone for a sin which I never committed."

But Perseus laughed, and said, "A sea monster? I have fought with worse than him; I would have faced Immortals for your sake; how much more a beast of the sea!"

Then Andromeda looked up at him, and new hope was kindled in her breast, so proud and fair did he stand, with one hand round her, and in the other the glittering sword. But she only sighed, and wept the more, and cried,

"Why will you die, young as you are? Is there not death and sorrow enough in the world already? It is noble for me to die, that I may save the lives of a whole people; but you, better than them all, why should I slay you too? Go you your way; I must go mine."

But Perseus cried, "Not so; for the Lords of Olympus, whom I serve, are the friends of the heroes, and help them on to noble deeds. Led by them, I slew the Gorgon, the beautiful horror; and not without them do I come hither, to slay this monster with that same Gorgon's head. Yet hide your eyes when I leave you, lest the sight of it freeze you, too, to stone."

But the maiden answered nothing, for she could not believe his words. And then, suddenly looking up, she pointed to the sea, and shrieked:

"There he comes, with the sunrise, as they promised. I must die now. How shall I endure it? Oh, go! Is it not dreadful enough to be torn piecemeal without having you to look on?" And she tried to thrust him away.

But he said, "I go; yet promise me one thing ere I go; that if I slay this beast you will be my wife, and come back with me to my kingdom in fruitful Argos, for I am a king's heir. Promise me, and seal it with a kiss." Then she lifted up her face, and kissed him; and Perseus laughed for joy, and flew upward, while Andromeda crouched trembling on the rock, waiting for what might befall.

On came the great sea monster, coasting along like a huge black galley, lazily breasting the ripple, and stopping at times by creek or headland, to watch for the laughter of girls at their bleaching, or cattle pawing on the sandhills, or boys bathing on the beach. His great sides were fringed with clustering shells and seaweeds, and the water gurgled in and out of his wide jaws, as he rolled along, dripping and glistening, in the beams of the morning sun.

At last he saw Andromeda, and shot forward to take his prey, while the waves foamed white behind him, and before him the fish fled leaping.

Then down from the height of the air fell Perseus, like a shooting star; down to the crests of the waves, while Andromeda hid her face as he shouted; and then there was silence for a while.

At last she looked up trembling, and saw Perseus springing toward her; and instead of the monster, a long black rock, with the sea rippling quietly round it.

Who then so proud as Perseus, as he leapt back to the rock, and lifted his fair Andromeda in his arms, and flew with her to the cliff-top, as a falcon carries a dove?

Who so proud as Perseus, and who so joyful as all the Æthiop people? For they had stood watching the monster from the cliffs, wailing for the maiden's fate. And already a messenger had gone to Cepheus and Cassiopœia, where they sat in sackcloth and ashes on the ground, in the innermost palace chambers, awaiting their daughter's end. And they came, and all the city with them, to see the wonder, with songs and with dances, with cymbals and harps, and received their daughter back again, as one alive from the dead.

Then Cepheus said, "Hero of the Hellens, stay here with me and be my son-in-law, and I will give you the half of my kingdom."

"I will be your son-in-law," said Perseus, "but of your kingdom I will have none; for I long after the pleasant land of Greece, and my mother who waits for me at home."

Then Cepheus said, "You must not take my daughter away at once, for she is to us like one alive from the dead. Stay with us here a year, and after that you shall return with honor." And Perseus consented; but before he went to the palace, he bade the people bring stones and wood, and built three altars, one to Athene, and one to Hermes, and one to Father Zeus, and offered bullocks and rams.

And some said, "This is a pious man"; yet the priests said, "The Sea Queen will be yet more fierce against us, because her monster is slain." But they were afraid to speak aloud, for they feared the Gorgon's head. So they went up to the palace; and when they came in, there stood in the hall Phineus, the brother of Cepheus, chafing like a bear robbed of her whelps, and with him his sons, and his servants, and many an armed man; and he cried to Cepheus:

"You shall not marry your daughter to this stranger, of whom no one knows even the name. Was not Andromeda betrothed to my son? And now she is safe again, has he not a right to claim her?"

But Perseus laughed and answered, "If your son is in want of a bride, let him save a maiden for himself. As yet he seems but a helpless bridegroom. He left this one to die, and dead she is to him. I saved her alive, and alive she is to me, but to no one else. Ungrateful man! Have I not saved your land, and the lives of your sons and daughters, and you will requite me thus? Go, or it will be worse for you." But all the men-at-arms drew their swords, and rushed on him like wild beasts.

Then he unveiled the Gorgon's head, and said, "This has delivered my bride from one wild beast; it shall deliver her from many." And as he spoke, Phineus and all his men-at-arms stopped short, and stiffened each man as he stood; and before Perseus had drawn the goatskin over the face again, they were all turned into stone.

Then Perseus bade the people bring levers and roll them out; and what was done with them after that, I cannot tell.

So they made a great wedding feast, which lasted seven whole days, and who so happy as Perseus and Andromeda?

But on the eighth night, Perseus dreamed a dream; and he saw standing beside him Pallas Athene, as he had seen her in Seriphos, seven long years before; she stood and called him by name, and said:

"Perseus, you have played the man, and see, you have your reward. Know now that the Gods are just, and help him who helps himself. Now give me here Herpe the sword, and the sandals, and the hat of darkness, that I may give them back to their owners; but the Gorgon's head you shall keep awhile, for you will need it in your land of Greece. Then you shall lay it up in my temple at Seriphos, that I may wear it on my shield forever, a terror to the Titans and the monsters, and the foes of Gods and men. And as for this land, I have appeased the sea and the fire, and there shall be no more floods nor earthquakes. But let the people build altars to Father Zeus and to me, and worship the Immortals, the Lords of heaven and earth."

And Perseus rose to give her the sword, and the cap, and the sandals: but he woke, and his dream vanished away. And yet it was not altogether a dream; for the goatskin with the head was in its place; but the sword, and the cap, and the sandals were gone, and Perseus never saw them more.

Then a great awe fell on Perseus; and he went out in the morning to the people, and told his dream, and bade them build altars to Zeus, the Father of Gods and men, and to Athene who gives wisdom to heroes; and fear no more the earthquakes and the floods, but sow and build in peace. And they did so for awhile, and prospered: but after Perseus was gone, they forgot Zeus and Athene, and worshiped again Atergatis the queen, and the undying fish of the sacred lake where Deucalion's deluge was swallowed up, and they burnt their children before the Fire King, till Zeus was angry with that foolish people, and brought a strange nation against them out of Egypt, who fought against them and wasted them utterly, and dwelt in their cities for many a hundred years.

V. HOW PERSEUS CAME HOME AGAIN

And when a year was ended, Perseus hired Phœnicians from Tyre, and cut down cedars, and built himself a noble galley; and painted its cheeks with vermilion, and pitched its sides with pitch; and in it he put Andromeda, and all her dowry of jewels, and rich shawls, and spices from the East; and great was the weeping when they rowed away. But the remembrance of his brave deed was left behind; and Andromeda's rock was shown at Jopa in Palestine, till more than a thousand years were past.

So Perseus and the Phœnicians rowed to the westward, across the sea of Crete, till they came to the blue Ægean and the pleasant Isles of Hellas, and Seriphos, his ancient home.

Then he left his galley on the beach, and went up as of old; and he embraced his mother, and Dictys his good foster father, and they wept over each other a long while, for it was seven years and more since they had met.

Then Perseus went out, and up to the hall of Polydectes; and underneath the goatskin he bore the Gorgon's head.

And when he came into the hall, Polydectes sat at the table head, and all his nobles and landowners on either side, each according to his rank, feasting on the fish and the goatflesh, and drinking the blood-red wine. The harpers harped, and the revelers shouted, and the winecups rang merrily as they passed from hand to hand, and great was the noise in the hall of Polydectes.

Then Perseus stood upon the threshold, and called to the king by name. But none of the guests knew Perseus, for he was changed by his long journey. He had gone out a boy, and he was come home a hero; his eye shone like an eagle's, and his beard was like a lion's beard, and he stood up like a wild bull in his pride.

But Polydectes the wicked knew him, and hardened his heart still more; and scornfully he called, "Ah, foundling! Have you found it more easy to promise than to fulfill?"

"Those whom the Gods help, fulfill their promises; and those who despise them, reap as they have sown. Behold the Gorgon's head!"

Then Perseus drew back the goatskin, and held aloft the Gorgon's head.

Pale grew Polydectes and his guests, as they looked upon that dreadful face. They tried to rise up from their seats; but from their seats they never rose, but stiffened, each man where he sat, into a ring of cold gray stones.

Then Perseus turned and left them, and went down to his galley in the bay; and he gave the kingdom to good Dictys, and sailed away with his mother and his bride.

And Polydectes and his guests sat still, with the winecups before them on the board; till the rafters crumbled down above their heads, and the walls behind their backs, and the table crumbled down between them, and the grass sprung up about their feet; but Polydectes and his guests sit on the hillside, a ring of gray stones until this day.

But Perseus rowed westward toward Argos, and landed, and went up to the town. And when he came, he found that Acrisius his grandfather had fled. For Prœtus, his wicked brother, had made war against him afresh; and had come across the river from Tiryns, and conquered Argos, and Acrisius had fled to Larissa, in the country of the wild Pelasgi.

Then Perseus called the Argives together, and told them who he was, and all the noble deeds which he had done. And all the nobles and the yeomen made him king, for they saw that he had a royal heart; and they fought with him against Argos, and took it, and killed Prœtus, and made the Cyclopes serve them, and build them walls round Argos, like the walls which they had built at Tiryns: and there were great rejoicings in the vale of Argos, because they had got a king from Father Zeus.

But Perseus' heart yearned after his grandfather, and he said, "Surely he is my flesh and blood; and he will love me now that I am come home with honor: I will go and find him, and bring him home, and we will reign together in peace."

So Perseus sailed away with his Phœnicians, round Hydrea and Sunium, past Marathon and the Attic shore, and through Euripus, and up the long Eubœan sea, till he came to the town of Larissa, where the wild Pelasgi dwelt.

And when he came there, all the people were in the fields, and there was feasting, and all kinds of games; for Teutamenes their king wished to honor Acrisius, because he was the king of a mighty land.

So Perseus did not tell his name, but went to the games unknown; for he said: "If I carry away the prize in the games, my grandfather's heart will be softened toward me."

So he threw off his helmet, and his cuirass, and all his clothes, and stood among the youths of Larissa, while all wondered and said, "Who is this stranger, who stands like a wild bull in his pride? Surely he is one of the heroes, sons of the Immortals, from Olympus."

And when the games began, they wondered yet more; for Perseus was the best man of all, at running, and leaping, and wrestling, and throwing the javelin; and he won four crowns, and took them, and then he said to himself, "There is a fifth crown yet to be won; I will win that, and lay them all upon the knees of my grandfather."

And as he spoke, he saw where Acrisius sat, by the side of Teutamenes the king, with his white beard flowing down upon his knees, and his royal staff in his hand; and Perseus wept when he looked at him, for his heart yearned after his kin; and he said: "Surely he is a kingly old man, yet he need not be ashamed of his grandson."

Then he took the quoits, and hurled them, five fathoms beyond all the rest; and the people shouted, "Farther yet, brave stranger! There has never been such a hurler in this land."

Then Perseus put out all his strength, and hurled. But a gust of wind came from the sea, and carried the quoit aside, and far beyond all the rest; and it fell on the foot of Acrisius, and he swooned away with the pain.

Perseus shrieked, and ran up to him; but when they lifted the old man up, he was dead; for his life was slow and feeble.

Then Perseus rent his clothes, and cast dust upon his head, and wept a long while for his grandfather. At last he rose, and called to all the people aloud, and said,

"The Gods are true, and what they have ordained must be. I am Perseus, the grandson of this dead man, the far-famed slayer of the Gorgon."

Then he told them how the prophecy had declared that he should kill his grandfather, and all the story of his life.

So they made a great mourning for Acrisius, and burnt him on a right rich pile; and Perseus went to the temple, and was purified from the guilt of the death, because he had done it unknowingly.

Then he went home to Argos, and reigned there well with fair Andromeda; and they had four sons and three daughters.

And when they died, the ancients say, Athene took them up into the sky, with Cepheus and Cassiopœia. And there on starlight nights you may see them shining still: Cepheus with his kingly crown, and Cassiopœia in her ivory chair, plaiting her star-spangled tresses, and Perseus with the Gorgon's head, and fair Andromeda beside him spreading her long white arms across the heaven, as she stood when chained to the stone for the monster. All night long they shine, for a beacon to wandering sailors; but all day they feast with the Gods, on the still blue peaks of Olympus.

THE ARGONAUTS

By CHARLES KINGSLEY

With Illustrations by H. M. Brock

I. HOW THE CENTAUR TRAINED THE HEROES ON PELION

I HAVE told you of a hero who fought with wild beasts and with wild men; but now I have a tale of heroes who sailed away into a distant land to win themselves renown forever, in the adventure of the Golden Fleece.

Whither they sailed, my children, I cannot clearly tell. It all happened long ago; so long that it has all grown dim, like a dream which you dreamt last year. And why they went, I cannot tell; some say that it was to win gold. It may be so; but the noblest deeds which have been done on earth, have not been done for gold. It was not for the sake of gold that the Lord came down and died, and the Apostles went out to preach the good news in all lands. The Spartans looked for no reward in money when they fought and died at Thermopylæ; and Socrates the wise asked no pay from his countrymen, but lived poor and barefoot all his days, only caring to make men good. And there are heroes in our days also, who do noble deeds, but not for gold. Our discoverers did not go to make themselves rich, when they sailed out one after another into the dreary frozen seas; nor did the ladies, who went out last year [1854: the Crimean War], to drudge in the hospitals of the East, making themselves poor, that they might be rich in noble works. And young men, too, whom you know, children, and some of them of your own kin, did they say to themselves, "How much money shall I earn?" when they went out to the war, leaving wealth, and comfort, and a pleasant home, and all that money can give, to face hunger and thirst, and wounds and death, that they might fight for their country and their Queen? No, children, there is a better thing on earth than wealth, a better thing than life itself; and that is, to have done something before you die, for which good men may honor you, and God your Father smile upon your work.

Therefore we will believe—why should we not?—of these same Argonauts of old, that they too were noble men, who planned and did a noble deed; and that therefore their fame has lived, and been told in story and in song, mixed up, no doubt, with dreams and fables, and yet true and right at heart. So we will honor these old Argonauts, and listen to their story as it stands; and we will try to be like them, each of us in our place; for each of us has a Golden Fleece to seek, and a wild sea to sail over, ere we reach it, and dragons to fight ere it be ours.

And what was that first Golden Fleece? I do not know, nor care. The old Hellens said that it hung in Colchis, which we call the Circassian coast, nailed to a beech tree in the war-god's wood; and that it was the fleece of the wondrous ram, who bore Phrixus and Helle across the Euxine sea. For Phrixus and Helle were the children of the cloud nymph, and of Athamas the Minuan king. And when a famine came upon the land, their cruel stepmother, Ino, wished to kill them, that her own children might reign, and said that they must be sacrificed on an altar, to turn away the anger of the gods. So the poor children were brought to the altar, and the priest stood ready with his knife, when out of the clouds came the Golden Ram, and took them on his back, and vanished. Then madness came upon that foolish king Athamas, and ruin upon Ino and her children. For Athamas killed one of them in his fury, and Ino fled from him with the other in her arms, and leaped from a cliff into the sea, and was changed into a dolphin, such as you have seen, which wanders over the waves forever sighing, with its little one clasped to its breast.

But the people drove out King Athamas, because he had killed his child; and he roamed about in his misery, till he came to the Oracle in Delphi. And the Oracle told him that he must wander for his sin, till the wild beasts should feast him as their guest. So he went on in hunger and sorrow for many a weary day, till he saw a pack of wolves. The wolves were tearing a sheep; but when they saw Athamas they fled, and left the sheep for him, and he ate of it; and

The ram carried the children away.

then he knew that the oracle was fulfilled. So he wandered no more; but settled, built a town, and became a king again.

But the ram carried the two children far away over land and sea, till he came to the Thracian Chersonese, and there Helle fell into the sea. So those narrow straits are called "Hellespont," after her; and they bear that name until this day.

Then the ram flew on with Phrixus to the northeast across the sea which we call the Black Sea now; but the Hellens called it Euxine. And at last, they say, he stopped at Colchis, on the steep Circassian coast; and there Phrixus married Chalchiope, the daughter of Aietes the king; and offered the ram in sacrifice; and Aietes nailed the ram's fleece to a beech, in the grove of Ares the war god.

And after awhile Phrixus died, and was buried, but his spirit had no rest; for he was buried far from his native land, and the pleasant hills of Hellas. So he came in dreams to the heroes of the Minuai, and called sadly by their beds, "Come and set my spirit free, that I may go home to my fathers and to my kinsfolk, and the pleasant Minuan land."

And they asked, "How shall we set your spirit free?"

"You must sail over the sea to Colchis, and bring home the golden fleece; and then my spirit will come back with it, and I shall sleep with my fathers and have rest."

He came thus, and called to them often: but when they woke they looked at each other, and said, "Who dare sail to Colchis, or bring home the golden fleece?" And in all the country none was brave enough to try it; for the man and the time were not come.

Phrixus had a cousin called Æson, who was king in Iolcos by the sea. There he ruled over the rich Minuan heroes, as Athamas his uncle ruled in Bœotia; and like Athamas, he was an unhappy man. For he had a stepbrother named Pelias, of whom some said that he was a nymph's son, and there were dark and sad tales about his birth. When he was a babe he was cast out on the mountains, and a wild mare came by and kicked him. But a shepherd passing found the baby, with its face all blackened by the blow; and took him home, and called him Pelias, because his face was bruised and black. And he grew up fierce and lawless, and did many a fearful deed; and at last he drove out Æson his stepbrother, and then his own brother Neleus, and took the kingdom to himself, and ruled over the rich Minuan heroes, in Iolcos by the sea.

And Æson, when he was driven out, went sadly away out of the town, leading his little son by the hand; and he said to himself, "I must hide the child in the mountains; or Pelias will surely kill him, because he is the heir."

So he went up from the sea across the valley, through the vineyards and the olive groves, and across the torrent of Anauros, toward Pelion the ancient mountain, whose brows are white with snow.

He went up and up into the mountain over marsh, and crag, and down, till the boy was tired and footsore, and Æson had to bear him in his arms, till he came to the mouth of a lonely cave, at the foot of a mighty cliff.

Above the cliff the snow wreaths hung, dripping and cracking in the sun; but at its foot around the cave's mouth grew all fair flowers and herbs, as if in a garden, ranged in order, each sort by itself. There they grew gayly in the sunshine, and the spray of the torrent from above; while from the cave came the sound of music, and a man's voice singing to the harp.

Then Æson put down the lad, and whispered,

"Fear not, but go in, and whomsoever you shall find, lay your hands upon his knees, and say, 'In the name of Zeus the father of gods and men. I am your guest from this day forth.'"

Then the lad went in without trembling, for he too was a hero's son: but when he was within, he stopped in wonder, to listen to that magic song.

And there he saw the singer lying, upon bearskins and fragrant boughs; Cheiron, the ancient centaur, the wisest of all things beneath the sky. Down to the waist he was a man; but below he was a noble horse; his white hair rolled down over his broad shoulders, and his white beard over his broad brown chest; and his eyes were wise and mild, and his forehead like a mountain wall.

And in his hands he held a harp of gold, and struck it with a golden key; and as he struck, he sang till his eyes glittered, and filled all the cave with light.

And he sang of the birth of Time, and of the heavens and the dancing stars; and of the ocean, and the ether, and the fire, and the shaping of the wondrous earth. And he sang of the treasures of the hills, and the hidden jewels of the mine, and the veins of fire and metal, and the virtues of all healing herbs, and of the speech of birds, and of prophecy, and of hidden things to come.

Then he sang of health, and strength, and manhood, and a valiant heart; and of music, and hunting, and wrestling, and all the games which heroes love; and of travel, and wars, and sieges, and a noble death in fight; and then he sang of peace and plenty, and of equal justice in the land: and as he sang, the boy listened wide-eyed, and forgot his errand in the song. And at last Old Cheiron was silent, and called the lad with a soft voice.

And the lad ran trembling to him, and would have laid his hands upon his knees: but Cheiron smiled, and said, "Call hither your father Æson, for I know you, and all that has befallen, and saw you both afar in the valley, even before you left the town."

Then Æson came in sadly, and Cheiron asked him, "Why camest you not yourself to me, Æson the Æolid?"

And Æson said: "I thought, Cheiron will pity the lad if he sees him come alone; and I wished to try whether he was fearless, and dare venture like a hero's son. But now I entreat you by Father Zeus, let the boy be your guest till better times, and train him among the sons of the heroes, that he may avenge his father's house."

Then Cheiron smiled, and drew the lad to him, and laid his hand upon his golden locks, and said, "Are you afraid of my horse's hoofs, fair boy, or will you be my pupil from this day?"

"I would gladly have horse's hoofs like you, if I could sing such songs as yours."

And Cheiron laughed, and said, "Sit here by me till sundown, when your playfellows will come home, and you shall learn like them to be a king, worthy to rule over gallant men."

Then he turned to Æson, and said, "Go back in peace, and bend before the storm like a prudent man. This boy shall not cross the Anauros again, till he has become a glory to you and the house of Æolus."

And Æson wept over his son and went away; but the boy did not weep, so full was his fancy of that strange cave, and the Centaur, and his song, and the playfellows whom he was to see.

Then Cheiron put the lyre into his hands, and taught him how to play it, till the sun sank low behind the cliff, and a shout was heard outside. And then in came the sons of the heroes, Æneas, and Heracles, and Peleus, and many another mighty name.

And great Cheiron leapt up joyfully, and his hoofs made the cave resound, as they shouted, "Come out, Father Cheiron; come out and see our game." And one cried, "I have killed two deer," and another "I took a wild cat among the crags"; and Heracles dragged a wild goat after him by its horns, for he was as huge as a mountain crag; and Cæneus carried a bear cub under each arm, and laughed when they scratched and bit; for neither tooth nor steel could wound him.

And Cheiron praised them all, each according to his deserts.

Only one walked apart and silent, Asclepius, the too-wise child, with his bosom full of herbs and flowers, and round his wrist a spotted snake; he came with downcast eyes to Cheiron, and whispered how he had watched the snake cast his old skin, and grow young again before his eyes, and how he had gone down into a village in the vale, and cured a dying man with an herb which he had seen a sick goat eat.

And Cheiron smiled, and said, "To each Athene and Apollo give some gift, and each is worthy in his place; but to this child they have given an honor beyond all honors, to cure while others kill."

Then the lads brought in wood, and split it, and lighted a blazing fire; and others skinned the deer and quartered them, and set them to roast before the fire; and while the venison was cooking they bathed in the snow torrent, and washed away the dust and sweat.

And then all ate till they could eat no more (for they had tasted nothing since the dawn), and drank of the clear spring water, for wine is not fit for growing lads. And when the remnants were put away, they lay down on the skins and leaves about the fire, and each took the lyre in turn, and sang and played with all his heart.

And after a while they all went out to a plot of grass at the cave's mouth, and there they boxed, and ran, and wrestled, and laughed till the stones fell from the cliffs.

Then Cheiron took his lyre, and all the lads joined hands; and as he played, they danced to his measure, in and out, and round and round. There they danced hand in hand, till the night fell over land and sea, while the black glen shone with their broad white limbs, and the gleam of their golden hair.

And the lad danced with them, delighted, and then slept a wholesome sleep, upon fragrant leaves of bay, and myrtle, and marjoram, and flowers of thyme; and rose at the dawn, and bathed in the torrent, and became a schoolfellow to the heroes' sons, and forgot Iolcos, and his father, and all his former life. But he grew strong, and brave and cunning, upon the pleasant downs of Pelion, in the keen hungry mountain air. And he learnt to wrestle, and to box, and to hunt, and to play upon the harp; and next he learnt to ride, for old Cheiron used to mount him on his back; and he learnt the virtues of all herbs, and how to cure all wounds; and Cheiron called him Jason the healer, and that is his name until this day.

II. HOW JASON LOST HIS SANDAL IN ANAUROS

And ten years came and went, and Jason was grown to be a mighty man. Some of his fellows were gone, and some were growing up by his side. Asclepius was gone into Peloponnese, to work his wondrous cures on men; and some say he used to raise the dead to life. And Heracles was gone to Thebes, to fulfill those famous labors which have become a proverb among men. And Peleus had married a sea nymph, and his wedding is famous to this day. And Æneas was gone home to Troy, and many a noble tale you will read of him, and of all the other gallant heroes, the scholars of Cheiron the just. And it happened on a day that Jason stood on the mountain, and looked north and south and east and west; and Cheiron stood by him and watched him, for he knew that the time was come.

And Jason looked and saw the plains of Thessaly, where the Lapithai breed their horses; and the lake of Boibe, and the stream which runs northward to Peneus and Tempe; and he looked north, and saw the mountain wall which guards the Magnesian shore; Olympus, the seat of the Immortals, and Ossa, and Pelion, where he stood. Then he looked east and saw the bright blue sea, which stretched away forever toward the dawn. Then he looked south, and saw a pleasant land, with white-walled towns and farms, nestling along the shore of a landlocked bay, while the smoke rose blue among the trees; and he knew it for the bay of Pagasai, and the rich lowlands of Hæmonia, and Iolcos by the sea.

Then he sighed, and asked: "Is it true what the heroes tell me, that I am heir of that fair land?"

"And what good would it be to you, Jason, if you were heir of that fair land?"

"I would take it and keep it."

"A strong man has taken it and kept it long. Are you stronger than Pelias the terrible?"

"I can try my strength with his," said Jason.

But Cheiron sighed, and said:

"You have many a danger to go through before you rule in Iolcos by the sea; many a danger, and many a woe; and strange troubles in strange lands, such as man never saw before."

"The happier I," said Jason, "to see what man never saw before."

And Cheiron sighed again, and said: "The eaglet must leave the nest when it is fledged. Will you go to Iolcos by the sea? Then promise me two things before you go."

Jason promised, and Cheiron answered: "Speak harshly to no soul whom you may meet, and stand by the word which you shall speak."

Jason wondered why Cheiron asked this of him; but he knew that the Centaur was a prophet, and saw things long before they came. So he promised, and leapt down the mountain, to take his fortune like a man.

He went down through the arbutus thickets, and across the downs of thyme, till he came to the vineyard walls, and the pomegranates and the olives in the glen; and among the olives roared Anauros, all foaming with a summer flood.

And on the bank of Anauros sat a woman, all wrinkled, gray, and old; her head shook palsied on her breast, and her hands shook palsied on her knees; and when she saw Jason, she spoke whining: "Who will carry me across the flood?"

Jason was bold and hasty, and was just going to leap into the flood; and yet he thought twice before he leapt, so loud roared the torrent down, all brown from the mountain rains, and silver-veined with melting snow; while underneath he could hear the boulders rumbling like the tramp of horsemen or the roll of wheels, as they ground along the narrow channel, and shook the rocks on which he stood.

But the old woman whined all the more: "I am weak and old, fair youth. For Hera's sake, carry me over the torrent."

And Jason was going to answer her scornfully, when Cheiron's words came to his mind.

So he said: "For Hera's sake, the Queen of the Immortals on Olympus, I will carry you over the torrent, unless we both are drowned midway."

Then the old dame leapt upon his back, as nimbly as a goat; and Jason staggered in, wondering.

The first step was up to his knees, and the second step was up to his waist; and the stones rolled about his feet, and his feet slipped about the stones; so he went on staggering and panting, while the old woman cried from off his back:

"Fool, you have wet my mantle! Do you make game of poor old souls like me?"

Jason had half a mind to drop her, and let her get through the torrent by herself; but Cheiron's words were in his mind, and he said only: "Patience, mother; the best horse may stumble some day."

At last he staggered to the shore, and set her down upon the bank; and a strong man he needed to have been, or that wild water he never would have crossed.

He lay panting awhile upon the bank, and then leapt up to go upon his journey; but he cast one look at the old woman, for he thought, "She should thank me once at least."

And as he looked, she grew fairer than all women, and taller than all men on earth; and her garments shone like the summer sea, and her jewels like the stars of heaven; and over her forehead was a veil, woven of the golden clouds of sunset; and through the veil she looked down on him, with great soft heifer's eyes; with great eyes, mild and awful, which filled all the glen with light.

And Jason fell upon his knees, and hid his face between his hands.

And she spoke—"I am the Queen of Olympus, Hera the wife of Zeus. As thou hast done to me, so will I do to thee. Call on me in the hour of need, and try if the Immortals can forget."

And when Jason looked up, she rose from off the earth, like a pillar of tall white cloud, and floated away across the mountain peaks, toward Olympus the holy hill.

Then a great fear fell on Jason; but after a while he grew light of heart; and he blessed old Cheiron, and said, "Surely the Centaur is a prophet, and guessed what would come to pass, when he bade me speak harshly to no soul whom I might meet."

Then he went down toward Iolcos, and as he walked, he found that he had lost one of his sandals in the flood.

And as he went through the streets, the people came out to look at him, so tall and fair was he; but some of the elders whispered together; and at last one of them stopped Jason, and called to him, "Fair lad, who are you, and whence come you; and what is your errand in the town?"

"My name, good father, is Jason, and I come from Pelion up above; and my errand is to Pelias your king; tell me then where his palace is."

But the old man started, and grew pale, and said, "Do you not know the oracle, my son, that you go so boldly through the town, with but one sandal on?"

"I am a stranger here, and know of no oracle; but what of my one sandal? I lost the other in Anauros, while I was struggling with the flood."

Then the old man looked back to his companions; and one sighed and another smiled; at last he said: "I will tell you, lest you rush upon your ruin unawares. The oracle in Delphi has said, that a man wearing one sandal should take the kingdom from Pelias, and keep it for himself. Therefore beware how you go up to his palace, for he is the fiercest and most cunning of all kings."

Then Jason laughed a great laugh, like a war horse in his pride, "Good news, good father, both for you and me. For that very end I came into the town." Then he strode on toward the palace of Pelias, while all the people wondered at his bearing.

And he stood in the doorway and cried, "Come out, come out, Pelias the valiant, and fight for your kingdom like a man."

Pelias came out wondering, and "Who are you, bold youth?" he cried.

"I am Jason, the son of Æson, the heir of all this land."

Then Pelias lifted up his hands and eyes, and wept, or seemed to weep; and blessed the heavens which had brought his nephew to him, never to leave him more. "For," said he, "I have but three daughters, and no son to be my heir. You shall be my heir then, and rule the kingdom after me, and marry whichsoever of my daughters you shall choose; though a sad kingdom you will find it, and whosoever rules it a miserable man. But come in, come in, and feast."

So he drew Jason in, whether he would or not, and spoke to him so lovingly and feasted him so well, that Jason's anger passed; and after supper his three cousins came into the hall, and Jason thought that he should like well enough to have one of them for his wife.

But at last he said to Pelias, "Why do you look so sad, my uncle? And what did you mean just now, when you said that this was a doleful kingdom, and its ruler a miserable man?"

Then Pelias sighed heavily again and again and again, like a man who had to tell some dreadful story and was afraid to begin; but at last— "For seven long years and more have I never known a quiet night; and no more will he who comes after me, till the golden fleece be brought home."

Then he told Jason the story of Phrixus, and of the golden fleece; and told him, too, which was a lie, that Phrixus' spirit tormented him, calling to him day and night. And his daughters came, and told the same tale (for their father had taught them their parts), and wept, and said, "Oh, who will bring home the golden fleece, that our uncle's spirit may have rest; and that we may have rest also, whom he never lets sleep in peace?"

Jason sat awhile, sad and silent; for he had often heard of that golden fleece; but he looked on it as a thing hopeless and impossible for any mortal man to win it.

But when Pelias saw him silent, he began to talk of other things, and courted Jason more and more, speaking to him as if he was certain to be his heir, and asking his advice about the kingdom; till Jason, who was young and simple, could not help saying to himself, "Surely he is not the dark man whom people call him. Yet why did he drive my father out?" And he asked Pelias boldly, "Men say that you are terrible, and a man of blood; but I find you a kind and hospitable man; and as you are to me, so will I be to you. Yet why did you drive my father out?"

Pelias smiled and sighed: "Men have slandered me in that, as in all things. Your father was growing old and weary, and he gave the kingdom up to me of his own will. You shall see him tomorrow, and ask him; and he will tell you the same."

Jason's heart leapt in him, when he heard that he was to see his father; and he believed all that Pelias said, forgetting that his father might not dare to tell the truth.

"One thing more there is," said Pelias, "on which I need your advice; for though you are young, I see in you a wisdom beyond your years. There is one neighbor of mine, whom I dread more than all men on earth. I am stronger than he now, and can command him: but I know that if he stay among us, he will work my ruin in the end. Can you give me a plan, Jason, by which I can rid myself of that man?"

After awhile, Jason answered, half laughing, "Were I you, I would send him to fetch that same golden fleece; for if he once set forth after it you would never be troubled with him more."

And at that a bitter smile came across Pelias' lips, and a flash of wicked joy into his eyes; and Jason saw it, and started; and over his mind came the warning of the old man, and his own one sandal, and the oracle, and he saw that he was taken in a trap.

But Pelias only answered gently, "My son, he shall be sent forthwith."

"You mean me?" cried Jason, starting up, "because I came here with one sandal?" And he lifted his fist angrily, while Pelias stood up to him like a wolf at bay; and whether of the two was the stronger and the fiercer, it would be hard to tell.

But after a moment Pelias spoke gently, "Why then so rash, my son? You, and not I, have said what is said; why blame me for what I have not done? Had you bid me love the man of whom I spoke, and make him my son-in-law and heir, I would have obeyed you; and what if I obey you now, and send the man to win himself immortal fame? I have not harmed you, or him. One thing at least I know, that he will go, and that gladly: for he has a hero's heart within him; loving glory, and scorning to break the word which he has given."

Jason saw that he was entrapped: but his second promise to Cheiron came into his mind, and he thought, "What if the Centaur were a prophet in that also, and meant that I should win the fleece!" Then he cried aloud,

"You have well spoken, cunning uncle of mine! I love glory, and I dare keep to my word. I will go and fetch this golden fleece. Promise me but this in return, and keep your word as I keep mine. Treat my father lovingly while I am gone, for the sake of the all-seeing Zeus; and give me up the kingdom for my own, on the day that I bring back the golden fleece."

Then Pelias looked at him and almost loved him, in the midst of all his hate; and said, "I promise, and I will perform. It will be no shame to give up my kingdom to the man who wins that fleece."

Then they swore a great oath between them; and afterwards both went in, and lay down to sleep.

But Jason could not sleep, for thinking of his mighty oath, and how he was to fulfill it, all alone, and without wealth or friends. So he tossed a long time upon his bed, and thought of this plan and of that; and sometimes Phrixus seemed to call him, in a thin voice, faint and low, as if it came from far across the sea, "Let me come home to my fathers and have rest." And sometimes he seemed to see the eyes of Hera, and to hear her words again, "Call on me in the hour of need, and see if the Immortals can forget."

And on the morrow he went to Pelias, and said, "Give me a victim, that I may sacrifice to Hera." So he went up, and offered his sacrifice; and as he stood by the altar, Hera sent a thought into his mind; and he went back to Pelias, and said, "If you are indeed in earnest, give me two heralds, that they may go round to all the princes of the Minuai, who were pupils of the Centaur with me, that we may fit out a ship together, and take what shall befall."

At that Pelias praised his wisdom, and hastened to send the heralds out; for he said in his heart. "Let all the princes go with him, and like him, never return; for so I shall be lord of all the Minuai, and the greatest king in Hellas."

III. HOW THEY BUILT THE SHIP ARGO IN IOLCOS

So the heralds went out, and cried to all the heroes of the Minuai, "Who dare come to the adventure of the golden fleece?"

And Hera stirred the hearts of all the princes, and they came from all their valleys to the yellow sands of Pagasai. And first came Heracles the mighty, with his lion's skin and club, and behind him Hylas his young squire, who bore his arrows and his bow; and Tiphys, the skillful steersman; and Butes, the fairest of all men; and Castor and Pollux the twins, the sons of the magic swan; and Caineus, the strongest of mortals, whom the Centaurs tried in vain to kill, and overwhelmed him with trunks of pine trees, but even so he would not die; and thither came Zetes and Calais, the winged sons of the north wind; and Peleus, the father of Achilles, whose bride was silver-footed Thetis the goddess of the sea. And thither came Telamon and Oileus, the fathers of the two Aiantes, who fought upon the plains of Troy; and Mopsus, the wise soothsayer, who knew the speech of birds; and Idmon, to whom Phœbus gave a tongue to prophesy of things to come; and Ancaios, who could read the stars, and knew all the circles of the heavens; and Argus, the famed shipbuilder, and many a hero more, in helmets of brass and gold with tall dyed horsehair crests, and embroidered shirts of linen beneath their coats of mail, and greaves of polished tin to guard their knees in fight; with each man his shield upon his shoulder, of many a fold of tough bull's hide, and his sword of tempered bronze in his silver-studded belt, and in his right hand a pair of lances, of the heavy white ash staves.

So they came down to Iolcos, and all the city came out to meet them, and were never tired with looking at their height, and their beauty, and their gallant bearing, and the glitter of their inlaid arms. And some said, "Never was such a gathering of the heroes since the Hellens conquered the land." But the women sighed over them, and whispered, "Alas! they are all going to their death."

Then they felled the pines on Pelion, and shaped them with the ax, and Argus taught them to build a galley, the first long ship which ever sailed the seas. They pierced her for fifty oars, an oar for each hero of the crew, and pitched her with coal-black pitch, and painted her bows with vermilion; and they named her *Argo* after Argus, and worked at her all day long. And at night Pelias feasted them like a king, and they slept in his palace porch.

But Jason went away to the northward, and into the land of Thrace, till he found Orpheus, the prince of minstrels, where he dwelt in his cave under Rhodope, among the savage Cicon tribes. And he asked him, "Will you leave your mountains, Orpheus, my fellow scholar in old times, and cross Strymon once more with me, to sail with the heroes of the Minuai, and bring home the golden fleece, and charm for us all men and all monsters with your magic harp and song?"

Then Orpheus sighed, "Have I not had enough of toil and of weary wandering far and wide, since I lived in Cheiron's cave, above Iolcos by the sea? In vain is the skill and the voice which my goddess mother gave me; in vain have I sung and labored; in vain I went down to the dead, and charmed all the kings of Hades, to win back Eurydice my bride. For I won her, my beloved, and lost her again the same day, and wandered away in my madness, even to Egypt and the Libyan sands, and the isles of all the seas, driven on by the terrible gadfly, while I charmed in vain the hearts of men, and the savage forest beasts, and the trees, and the lifeless stones, with my magic harp and song, giving rest, but finding none. But at last Calliope, my mother, delivered me, and brought me home in peace; and I dwell here in the cave alone, among the savage Cicon tribes, softening their wild hearts with music and the gentle laws of Zeus. And now I must go out again, to the ends of all the earth, far away into the misty darkness, to the last wave of the Eastern Sea. But what is doomed must be, and a friend's demand obeyed; for prayers are the daughters of Zeus, and who honors them honors him."

Then Orpheus rose up sighing, and took his harp, and went over Strymon. And he led Jason to the southwest, up the banks of Haliacmon and over the spurs of Pindus, to Dodona the town of Zeus, where it stood by the side of the sacred lake, and the fountain which breathed out fire, in the darkness of the ancient oak wood, beneath the mountain of the hundred springs. And he led him to the holy oak, where the black dove settled in old times, and was changed into the priestess of Zeus, and gave oracles to all nations round. And he bade him cut down a bough, and sacrifice to Hera

They nailed the bough to the beakhead of the ship.

and to Zeus; and they took the bough and came to Iolcos, and nailed it to the beakhead of the ship.

And at last the ship was finished, and they tried to launch her down the beach; but she was too heavy for them to move her, and her keel sank deep in the sand. Then all the heroes looked at each other blushing; but Jason spoke, and said, "Let us ask the magic bough; perhaps it can help us in our need."

Then a voice came from the bough, and Jason heard the words it said, and bade Orpheus play upon the harp, while the heroes waited round, holding the pine-trunk rollers, to help her toward the sea.

Then Orpheus took his harp, and began his magic song: "How sweet it is to ride upon the surges, and to leap from wave to wave, while the wind sings cheerful in the cordage, and the oars flash fast among the foam! How sweet it is to roam across the ocean, and see new towns and wondrous lands, and to come home laden with treasure, and to win undying fame!"

And the good ship *Argo* heard him, and longed to be away and out at sea; till she stirred in every timber, and heaved from stem to stern, and leapt up from the sand upon the rollers, and plunged onward like a gallant horse; and the heroes fed her path with pine trunks, till she rushed into the whispering sea.

Then they stored her well with food and water, and pulled the ladder up on board, and settled themselves each man to his oar, and kept time to Orpheus' harp; and away across the bay they rowed southward, while the people lined the cliffs; and the women wept while the men shouted, at the starting of that gallant crew.

IV. HOW THE ARGONAUTS SAILED TO COLCHIS

And what happened next, my children, whether it be true or not, stands written in ancient songs, which you shall read for yourselves some day. And grand old songs they are, written in grand old rolling verse; and they call them the Songs of Orpheus, or the Orphics, to this day. And they tell how the heroes came to Aphetai, across the bay, and waited for the southwest wind, and chose themselves a captain from their crew: and how all called for Heracles, because he was the strongest and most huge; but Heracles refused, and called for Jason, because he was the wisest of them all. So Jason was chosen captain: and Orpheus heaped a pile of wood, and slew a bull, and offered it to Hera, and called all the heroes to stand round, each man's head crowned with olive, and to strike their swords into the bull. Then he filled a golden goblet with the bull's blood, and with wheaten flour, and honey, and wine, and the bitter salt sea water, and bade the heroes taste. So each tasted the goblet, and passed it round, and vowed an awful vow: and they vowed before the sun, and the night, and the blue-haired sea who shakes the land, to stand by Jason faithfully, in the adventure of the golden fleece; and whosoever shrank back, or disobeyed, or turned traitor to his vow, then justice should witness against him, and the Furies who track guilty men.

Then Jason lighted the pile, and burnt the carcass of the bull; and they went to their ship *Argo* and sailed eastward, like men who have a work to do; and the place from which they went was called Aphetai, the sailing place, from that day forth. Three thousand years and more they sailed away, into the unknown Eastern seas; and great nations have come and gone since then, and many a storm has swept the earth; and many a mighty armament, to which *Argo* would be but one small boat, English and French, Turkish and Russian, have sailed those waters since; yet the fame of that small *Argo* lives forever, and her name is become a proverb among men.

So they sailed past the Isle of Sciathos, with the Cape of Sepius on their left, and turned to the northward toward Pelion, up the long Magnesian shore. On their right hand was the open sea, and on their left old Pelion rose, while the clouds crawled round his dark pine forests, and his caps of summer snow. And their hearts yearned for the dear old mountain, as they thought of pleasant days gone by, and of the sports of their boyhood, and their hunting, and their schooling in the cave beneath the cliff. And at last Peleus spoke:

"Let us land here, friends, and climb the dear old hill once more. We are going on a fearful journey: who knows if we shall see Pelion again? Let us go up to Cheiron our master, and ask his blessing ere we start. And I have a boy, too, with him, whom he trains as he trained me once, the son whom Thetis brought me, the silver-footed lady of the sea, whom I caught in the cave, and tamed her, though she changed her shape seven times. For she changed, as I held her, into water, and to vapor, and to burning flame, and to a rock, and to a black-maned lion, and to a tall and stately tree. But I held her and held her ever, till she took her own shape again, and led her to my father's house, and won her for my bride. And all the rulers of Olympus came to our wedding, and the heavens and the earth rejoiced together, when an Immortal wedded mortal man. And now let me see my son, for it is not often I shall see him upon earth; famous he will be, but short-lived, and die in the flower of youth."

So Tiphys, the helmsman, steered them to the shore under the crags of Pelion; and they went up through the dark pine forests toward the Centaur's cave.

And they came into the misty hall, beneath the snow-crowned crag; and saw the great Centaur lying with his huge limbs spread upon the rock; and beside him stood Achilles, the child whom no steel could wound, and played upon his harp right sweetly, while Cheiron watched and smiled.

Then Cheiron leapt up and welcomed them, and kissed them every one, and set a feast before them, of swine's flesh, and venison, and good wine; and young Achilles served them, and carried the golden goblet round. And after supper all the heroes clapped their hands, and called on Orpheus to sing; but he refused, and said, "How can I, who am the younger, sing before our ancient host?" So they called on Cheiron to sing, and Achilles brought him his harp; and he began a wondrous song; a famous story of old time, of the fight between Centaurs and the Lapithai, which you may still see carved in stone.[1] He sang how his brothers came to ruin by their folly, when they were mad with wine; and how they and the heroes fought, with fists, and teeth, and the goblets from which they drank; and how they tore up the pine trees in their fury, and hurled great crags of stone, while the mountains thundered with the battle, and the land was wasted far and wide; till the Lapithai drove them from their home in the rich Thessalian plains to the lonely glens of Pindus, leaving Cheiron all alone. And the heroes praised his song right heartily; for some of them had helped in that great fight.

Then Orpheus took the lyre, and sang of Chaos, and the making of the wondrous World, and how all things sprang from Love, who could not live alone in the Abyss. And as he sang, his voice rose from the cave, above the crags, and through the tree-tops, and the glens of oak and pine. And the trees bowed their heads when they heard it, and the gray rocks cracked and rang, and the forest beasts crept near to listen, and the birds forsook their nests and hovered round. And old Cheiron clapped his hands together, and beat his hoofs upon the ground, for wonder at that magic song.

Then Peleus kissed his boy, and wept over him, and they went down to the ship; and Cheiron came down with them, weeping, and kissed them one by one, and blessed them, and promised to them great renown. And the heroes wept when they left him, till their great hearts could weep no more; for he was kind and just and pious, and wiser than all beasts and men. Then he went up to a cliff, and prayed for them, that they might come home safe and well; while the heroes rowed away, and watched him standing on his cliff above

[1] In the Elgin Marbles.

the sea, with his great hands raised toward heaven, and his white locks waving in the wind; and they strained their eyes to watch him to the last, for they felt that they should look on him no more.

So they rowed on over the long swell of the sea, past Olympus, the seat of the Immortals, and past the wooded bays of Athos, and Samothrace, the sacred isle; and they came past Lemnos to the Hellespont, and through the narrow strait of Abydos, and so on into the Propontis, which we call Marmora now. And there they met with Cyzicus, ruling in Asia over the Dolions, who, the songs say, was the son of Æneas, of whom you will hear many a tale some day. For Homer tells us how he fought at Troy; and Virgil how he sailed away and founded Rome. Now Cyzicus, the songs say, welcomed the heroes; for his father had been one of Cheiron's scholars; so he welcomed them, and feasted them, and stored their ship with corn and wine, and cloaks and rugs, the songs say, and shirts, of which no doubt they stood in need.

But at night, while they lay sleeping, came down on them terrible men, who lived with the bears in the mountains, like Titans or giants in shape; for each of them had six arms, and they fought with young firs and pines. But Heracles killed them all before morn with his deadly poisoned arrows; but among them, in the darkness, he slew Cyzicus the kindly prince.

Then they got to their ship and to their oars, and Tiphys bade them cast off the hawsers, and go to sea. But as he spoke, a whirlwind came and spun the *Argo* round, and twisted the hawsers together, so that no man could loose them. Then Tiphys dropped the rudder from his hand, and cried, "This comes from the Gods above." But Jason went forward, and asked counsel of the magic bough.

Then the magic bough spoke and answered, "This is because you have slain Cyzicus your friend. You must appease his soul, or you will never leave this shore."

Jason went back sadly, and told the heroes what he had heard. And they leapt on shore, and searched till dawn; and at dawn they found the body, all rolled in dust and blood, among the corpses of those monstrous beasts. And they wept over their kind host, and laid him on a fair bed, and heaped a huge mound over him, and offered black sheep at his tomb, and Orpheus sang a magic song to him, that his spirit might have rest. And then they held games at the tomb, after the custom of those times, and Jason gave prizes to each winner. To Ancæus he gave a golden cup, for he wrestled best of all; and to Heracles a silver one, for he was the strongest of all; and to Castor, who rode best, a golden crest; and Pollux the boxer had a rich carpet, and to Orpheus for his song, a sandal with golden wings. But Jason himself was the best of all the archers, and the Minuai crowned him with an olive crown; and so, the songs say, the soul of good Cyzicus was appeased, and the heroes went on their way in peace.

But when Cyzicus' wife heard that he was dead, she died likewise of grief; and her tears became a fountain of clear water, which flows the whole year round.

Then they rowed away, the songs say, along the Mysian shore, and past the mouth of Rhindacus, till they found a pleasant bay, sheltered by the long ridges of Arganthus, and by high walls of basalt rock. And there they ran the ship ashore upon the yellow sand, and furled the sail, and took the mast down, and lashed it in its crutch. And next they let down the ladder, and went ashore to sport and rest.

And there Heracles went away into the woods, bow in hand, to hunt wild deer; and Hylas the fair boy slipped away after him, and followed him by stealth, until he lost himself among the glens, and sat down weary to rest himself by the side of a lake; and there the water nymphs came up to look at him, and loved him, and carried him down under the lake to be their playfellow, forever happy and young. And Heracles sought for him in vain, shouting his name till all the mountains rang; but Hylas never heard him, far down under the sparkling lake. So while Heracles wandered searching for him, a fair breeze sprang up, and Heracles was nowhere to be found; and the *Argo* sailed away, and Heracles was left behind, and never saw the noble Phasian stream.

Then the Minuai came to a doleful land, where Amycus the giant ruled, and cared nothing for the laws of Zeus, but challenged all strangers to box with him, and those whom he conquered he slew. But Pollux the boxer struck him a harder blow than he ever felt before, and slew him; and the Minuai went on up the Bosphorus, till they came to the city of Phineus, the fierce Bithynian king; Zetes and Calais bade Jason land there, for they had a work to do.

And they went up from the shore toward the city, through forests white with snow; and Phineus came out to meet them with a lean and woeful face, and said, "Welcome, gallant heroes, to the land of bitter blasts, a land of cold and misery; yet I will feast you as best I can." And he led them in, and set meat before them; but before they could put their hands to their mouths, down came two fearful monsters, the like of whom man never saw; for they had the faces and the hair of fair maidens, but the wings and claws of hawks; and they snatched the meat from off the table, and flew shrieking out above the roofs.

Then Phineus beat his breast and cried, "These are the Harpies, whose names are the Whirlwind and the Swift, the daughters of Wonder and of the Amber-nymph, and they rob us night and day. They carried off the daughters of Pandareus, whom all the Gods had blessed; for Aphrodite fed them on Olympus with honey and milk and wine, and Hera gave them beauty and wisdom, and Athene skill in all the arts; but when they came to their wedding, the Harpies snatched them both away, and gave them to be slaves to the Furies, and live in horror all their days. And now they haunt me, and my people, and the Bosphorus, with fearful storms; and sweep away our food from off our tables, so that we starve in spite of all our wealth."

Then up rose Zetes and Calais, the winged sons of the North Wind, and said, "Do you not know us, Phineus, and these wings which grow upon our backs?" And Phineus hid his face in terror; but he answered not a word.

"Because you have been a traitor, Phineus, the Harpies haunt you night and day. Where is Cleopatra our sister, your wife, whom you keep in prison? And where are her two children, whom you blinded in your rage, at the bidding of an evil woman, and cast them out upon the rocks? Swear to us that you will right our sister, and cast out that wicked woman; and then we will free you from your plague, and drive the whirlwind maidens from the south; but if not, we will put out your eyes, as you put out the eyes of your own sons."

Then Phineus swore an oath to them, and drove out the wicked woman; and Jason took those two poor children, and cured their eyes with magic herbs.

But Zetes and Calais rose up sadly, and said, "Farewell now, heroes all; farewell, our dear companions, with whom we played on Pelion in old times; for a fate is laid upon us, and our day is come at last, in which we may hunt the whirlwinds, over land and sea forever; and if we catch them they die, and if not, we die ourselves."

At that all the heroes wept: but the two young men sprang up, and aloft into the air after the Harpies, and the battle of the winds began.

The heroes trembled in silence as they heard the shrieking of the blasts; while the palace rocked and all the city, and great stones were torn from the crags, and the forest pines were hurled eastward, north and south and east and west, and the Bosphorus boiled white with foam, and the clouds were dashed against the cliffs.

But at last the battle ended, and the Harpies fled screaming toward the south, and the sons of the North Wind rushed after them, and brought clear sunshine where they passed. For many a league they followed them, over all the isles of the Cyclades, and away to the southwest across Hellas, till they came to the Ionian sea, and there they fell upon the Echinades, at the mouth of the Achelous; and those isles were called the Whirlwind Isles for many a hundred years. But what became of Zetes and Calais I know not; for the heroes never saw them again: and some say that Heracles met them, and quarreled with them, and slew them with his arrows; and some say that they fell down from weariness and the heat of the summer sun, and that the Sun-god buried them among the Cyclades, in the pleasant Isle of Tenos; and for many hundred years their grave was shown there, and over it a pillar, which turned to every wind. But dark storms and whirlwinds haunt the Bosphorus until this day.

But the Argonauts went eastward, and out into the open sea, which we now call the Black Sea, but it was called the Euxine then. No Hellen had ever crossed it, and all feared that dreadful sea, and its rocks, and shoals, and fogs, and bitter freezing storms; and they told strange stories of it, some false and some half true, how it stretched northward to the ends of the earth, and the sluggish Putrid Sea, and the everlasting night, and the regions of the dead. So the heroes trembled, for all their courage, as they came into that wild Black Sea, and saw it stretching out before them, without a shore, as far as eye could see.

And first Orpheus spoke, and warned them, "We shall come now to the wandering blue rocks; my mother warned me of them, Calliope, the immortal muse."

And soon they saw the blue rocks shining, like spires and castles of gray glass, while an ice-cold wind blew from them, and chilled all the heroes' hearts. And as they neared, they could see them heaving, as they rolled upon the long sea waves, crashing and grinding together, till the roar went up to heaven. The sea sprang up in spouts between them, and swept round them in white sheets of foam; but their heads swung nodding high in air, while the wind whistled shrill among the crags.

The heroes' hearts sank within them, and they lay upon their oars in fear; but Orpheus called to Tiphys the helmsman—"Between them we must pass; so look ahead for an opening, and be brave, for Hera is with us." But Tiphys the cunning helmsman stood silent, clenching his teeth, till he saw a heron come flying mast high toward the rocks, and hover awhile before them, as if looking for a passage through. Then he cried, "Hera has sent us a pilot; let us follow the cunning bird."

Then the heron flapped to and fro a moment, till he saw a hidden gap, and into it he rushed like an arrow, while the heroes watched what would befall.

And the blue rocks clashed together as the bird fled swiftly through; but they struck but a feather from his tail, and then rebounded apart at the shock.

Then Tiphys cheered the heroes, and they shouted; and the oars bent like withes beneath their strokes, as they rushed between those toppling ice crags, and the cold blue lips of death. And ere the rocks could meet again they had passed them, and were safe out in the open sea.

And after that they sailed on wearily along the Asian coast, by the Black Cape and Thyneis, where the hot stream of Thymbris falls into the sea, and Sangarius, whose waters float on the Euxine, till they came to Wolf the river, and to Wolf the kindly king. And there died two brave heroes, Idmon and Tiphys the wise helmsman; one died of an evil sickness, and one a wild boar slew. So the heroes heaped a mound above them, and set upon it an oar on high, and left them there to sleep together, on the far-off Lycian shore. But Idas killed the boar, and avenged Tiphys; and Ancaios took the rudder and was helmsman, and steered them on toward the east.

And they went on past Sinope, and many a mighty river's mouth, and past many a barbarous tribe, and the cities of the Amazons, the warlike women of the East, till all night they heard the clank of anvils and the roar of furnace blasts, and the forge fires shone like sparks through the darkness, in the mountain glens aloft; for they were come to the shores of the Chalybes, the smiths who never tire, but serve Ares the cruel War god, forging weapons day and night.

And at day-dawn they looked eastward, and midway between the sea and the sky they saw white snowpeaks hanging, glittering sharp and bright above the clouds. And they knew that they were come to Caucasus, at the end of all the earth; Caucasus the highest of all mountains, the father of the rivers of the East. On his peak lies chained the Titan, while a vulture tears his heart; and at his feet are piled dark forests round the magic Colchian land.

And they rowed three days to the eastward, while Caucasus rose higher hour by hour, till they saw the dark stream of Phasis rushing headlong to the sea, and shining above the tree-tops, the golden roofs of kind Aietes, the child of the Sun.

Then out spoke Ancaios the helmsman, "We are come to our goal at last; for there are the roofs of Aietes, and the woods where all poisons grow; but who can tell us where among them is hid the golden fleece? Many a toil must we bear ere we find it, and bring it home to Greece."

But Jason cheered the heroes, for his heart was high and bold; he said, "I will go alone up to Aietes, though he be the child of the Sun, and win him with soft words. Better so than to go all together, and to come to blows at once." But the Minuai would not stay behind, so they rowed boldly up the stream.

And a dream came to Aietes, and filled his heart with fear. He thought he saw a shining star, which fell into his daughter's lap; and that Medea his daughter took it gladly, and carried it to the riverside, and cast it in, and there the whirling river bore it down, and out the Euxine Sea.

Then he leapt up in fear, and bade his servants bring his chariot, that he might go down to the riverside and appease the nymphs, and the heroes whose spirits haunt the bank. So he went down in his golden chariot, and his daughters by his side, Medea the fair witch maiden, and Chalciope, who had been Phrixus' wife, and behind him servants and soldiers, for he was a rich and mighty prince.

And as he drove down by the reedy river, he saw *Argo* sliding up beneath the bank, and many a hero in her, like Immortals for beauty and for strength, as their weapons glittered round them in the level morning sunlight, through the white mist of the stream. But Jason was the noblest of all; for Hera who loved him gave him beauty, and tallness, and terrible manhood.

And when they came near together and looked into each other's eyes, the heroes were awed before Aietes as he shone in his chariot, like his father the glorious Sun; for his robes were of rich gold tissue, and the rays of his diadem flashed fire; and in his hand he bore a jeweled scepter, which glittered like the stars; and sternly he looked at them under his brows, and sternly he spoke and loud:

"Who are you, and what want you here that you come to the shore of Cutaia? Do you take no account of my rule, nor of my people the Colchians who serve me, who never tired yet in the battle, and know well how to face an invader?"

And the heroes sat silent awhile before the face of that ancient king. But Hera the awful goddess put courage into Jason's heart, and he rose and shouted loudly in answer, "We are no pirates nor lawless men. We come not to plunder and to ravage, or carry away slaves from your land; but my uncle, the son of Poseidon, Pelias the Minuan king, he it is who has set me on a quest to bring home the golden fleece. And these too, my bold comrades, they are no nameless men; for some are the sons of Immortals, and some of heroes far renowned. And we too never tire in battle, and know well how to give blows and to take; yet we wish to be guests at your table; it will be better so for both."

Then Aietes' rage rushed up like a whirlwind, and his eyes flashed fire as he heard; but he crushed his anger down in his breast, and spoke mildly a cunning speech:

"If you will fight for the fleece with my Colchians, then many a man must die. But do you indeed expect to win from me the fleece in fight? So few you are, that if you be worsted, I can load your ship with your corpses. But if you will be ruled by me, you will find it better far to choose the best man among you, and let him fulfill the labors which I demand. Then I will give him the golden fleece for a prize and a glory to you all."

So saying, he turned his horses and drove back in silence to the town. And the Minuai sat silent with sorrow, and longed for Heracles and his strength; for there was no facing the thousands of the Colchians, and the fearful chance of war.

But Chalciope, Phrixus' widow, went weeping to the town; for she remembered her Minuan husband, and all the pleasures of her youth, while she watched the fair faces of his kinsmen, and their long locks of golden hair. And she whispered to Medea her sister, "Why should all these brave men die? Why does not my father give them up the fleece, that my husband's spirit may have rest?"

And Medea's heart pitied the heroes, and Jason most of all; and she answered, "Our father is stern and terrible, and who can win the golden fleece?" But Chalciope said, "These men are not like our men; there is nothing which they cannot dare nor do."

And Medea thought of Jason and his brave countenance, and said, "If there was one among them who knew no fear, I could show him how to win the fleece."

So in the dusk of evening they went down to the riverside, Chalciope and Medea the witch maiden, and Argus, Phrixus' son. And Argus the boy crept forward, among the beds of reeds, till he came where the heroes were sleeping, on the thwarts of the ship, beneath the bank, while Jason kept ward on shore, and leaned upon his lance full of thought. And the boy came to Jason, and said,

"I am the son of Phrixus, your cousin; and Chalciope my mother waits for you, to talk about the golden fleece."

Then Jason went boldly with the boy, and found the two princesses standing; and when Chalciope saw him she wept, and took his hands, and cried,

"O cousin of my beloved, go home before you die!"

"It would be base to go home now, fair princess, and to have sailed all these seas in vain." Then both the princesses besought him: but Jason said, "It is too late."

"But you know not," said Medea, "what he must do who would win the fleece. He must tame the two brazen-footed bulls, who breathe devouring flame; and with them he must plow ere nightfall four acres in the field of Ares; and he must sow them with serpents' teeth, of which each tooth springs up into an armed man. Then he must fight with all those warriors; and little will it profit him to conquer them; for the fleece is guarded by a serpent, more huge than any mountain pine; and over his body you must step, if you would reach the golden fleece."

Then Jason laughed bitterly. "Unjustly is that fleece kept here, and by an unjust and lawless king; and unjustly shall I die in my youth, for I will attempt it ere another sun be set."

Then Medea trembled, and said, "No mortal man can reach that fleece, unless I guide him through. For round it, beyond the river, is a wall full nine ells high, with lofty towers and buttresses, and mighty gates of threefold brass; and over the gates the wall is arched, with golden battlements above. And over the gateway sits Brimo, the wild witch huntress of the woods, brandishing a pine torch in her hands, while her mad hounds howl around. No man dare meet her or look on her, but only I her priestess, and she watches far and wide lest any stranger should come near."

"No wall so high but it may be climbed at last, and no wood so thick but it may be crawled through; no serpent so wary but he may be charmed, or witch queen so fierce but spells may soothe her. I may yet win the golden fleece, if a wise maiden help bold men."

And he looked at Medea cunningly, and held her with his glittering eye, till she blushed and trembled, and said,

"Who can face the fire of the bulls' breath, and fight ten thousand armed men?"

"He whom you help," said Jason, flattering her, "for your fame is spread over all the earth. Are you not the queen of all enchantresses, wiser even than your sister, Circe, in her fairy island in the West?"

"Would that I were with my sister Circe in her fairy island in the West, far away from sore temptation, and thoughts which tear the heart! But if it must be so—for why should you die?—I have an ointment here; I made it from the magic ice flower which sprang from Prometheus' wound, above the clouds on Caucasus, in the dreary fields of snow. Anoint yourself with that, and you shall have in you seven men's strength; and anoint your shield with it, and neither fire nor sword can harm you. But what you begin you must end before sunset, for its virtue lasts only one day. And anoint your helmet with it before you sow the serpents' teeth; and when the sons of earth spring up, cast your helmet among their ranks, and the deadly crop of the War-god's field will mow itself, and perish."

Then Jason fell on his knees before her, and thanked her and kissed her hands; and she gave him the vase of ointment, and fled trembling through the reeds. And Jason told his comrades what had happened, and showed them the box of ointment; and all rejoiced but Idas, and he grew mad with envy.

And at sunrise Jason went and bathed, and anointed himself from head to foot, and his shield, and his helmet, and his weapons, and bade his comrades try the spell. So they tried to bend his lance, but it stood like an iron bar; and Idas in spite hewed at it with his sword, but the blade flew to splinters in his face. Then they hurled their lances at his shield, but the spear points turned like lead; and Caineus tried to throw him, but he never stirred a foot; and Pollux struck him with his fist, a blow which would have killed an ox; but Jason only smiled, and the heroes danced about him with delight; and he leapt and ran, and shouted, in the joy of that enormous strength, till the sun rose, and it was time to go and to claim Aietes' promise.

So he sent up Telamon and Aithalides to tell Aietes that he was ready for the fight; and they went up among the marble walls, and beneath the roofs of gold, and stood in Aietes' hall, while he grew pale with rage.

"Fulfill your promise to us, child of the blazing sun. Give us the serpents' teeth, and let loose the fiery bulls; for we have found a champion among us who can win the golden fleece."

And Aietes bit his lips, for he fancied that they had fled away by night; but he could not go back from his promise; so he gave them the serpents' teeth. Then he called for his chariot and his horses, and sent heralds through all the town; and all the people went out with him to the dreadful War-god's field.

And there Aietes sat upon his throne, with his warriors on each hand, thousands and tens of thousands, clothed from head to foot in steel-chain mail. And the people and the women crowded to every window, and bank, and wall; while the Minuai stood together, a mere handful in the midst of that great host.

And Chalciope was there and Argus, trembling, and Medea, wrapped closely in her veil; but Aietes did not know that she was muttering cunning spells between her lips.

Then Jason cried, "Fulfill your promise, and let your fiery bulls come forth."

Then Aietes bade open the gates, and the magic bulls leapt out. Their brazen hoofs rang upon the ground, and their nostrils sent out sheets of flame, as they rushed with lowered heads upon Jason; but he never flinched a step. The flame of their breath swept round him, but it singed not a hair of his head; and the bulls stopped short and trembled, when Medea began her spell.

Then Jason sprang upon the nearest, and seized him by the horn; and up and down they wrestled, till the bull fell groveling on his knees; for the heart of the brute died within him, and his mighty limbs were loosed, beneath the steadfast eye of that dark witch maiden, and the magic whisper of her lips.

So both the bulls were tamed and yoked; and Jason bound them to the plow, and goaded them onward with his lance, till he had plowed the sacred field.

And all the Minuai shouted; but Aietes bit his lips with rage; for the half of Jason's work was over, and the sun was yet high in heaven.

Then he took the serpents' teeth and sowed them, and waited what would befall. But Medea looked at him and at his helmet, lest he should forget the lesson she had taught.

And every furrow heaved and bubbled, and out of every clod rose a man. Out of the earth they rose by thousands, each clad from head to foot in steel, and drew their swords, and rushed on Jason, where he stood in the midst alone.

Then the Minuai grew pale with fear for him; but Aietes laughed a bitter laugh: "See! if I had not warriors enough already round me, I could call them out of the bosom of the earth."

But Jason snatched off his helmet, and hurled it into the thickest of the throng. And blind madness came upon them, suspicion, hate, and fear; and one cried to his fellow, "Thou didst strike me!" and another, "Thou art Jason; thou shalt die!" So fury seized those earthborn phantoms, and each turned his hand against the rest; and they fought and were never weary, till they all lay dead upon the ground. Then the magic furrows opened, and the kind earth took them home into her breast; and the grass grew up all green again above them, and Jason's work was done.

Then the Minuai rose and shouted, till Prometheus heard them from his crag. And Jason cried, "Lead me to the fleece this moment, before the sun goes down."

But Aietes thought, "He has conquered the bulls; and sown and reaped the deadly crop. Who is this who is proof against all magic? He may kill the serpent yet." So he delayed, and sat taking counsel with his princes, till the sun went down and all was dark. Then he bade a herald cry, "Every man to his home for tonight. Tomorrow we will meet these heroes, and speak about the golden fleece."

Then he turned and looked at Medea: "This is your doing, false witch maid! You have helped these yellow-haired strangers, and brought shame upon your father and yourself!" Medea shrank and trembled, and her face grew pale with fear; and Aietes knew that she was guilty, and whispered, "If they win the fleece, you die!"

But the Minuai marched toward their ship, growling like lions cheated of their prey; for they saw that Aietes meant to mock them, and to cheat them out of all their toil. And Oileus said: "Let us go to the grove together, and take the fleece by force."

And Idas the rash cried, "Let us draw lots who shall go in first; for while the dragon is devouring one, the rest can slay him, and carry off the fleece in peace." But Jason held them back, though he praised them; for he hoped for Medea's help.

And after awhile Medea came trembling, and wept a long while before she spoke. And at last,

"My end is come, and I must die; for my father has found out that I have helped you. You he would kill if he dared; but he will not harm you, because you have been his guests. Go then, go, and remember poor Medea when you are far away across the sea." But all the heroes cried—

"If you die, we die with you; for without you we cannot win the fleece, and home we will not go without it, but fall here fighting to the last man."

"You need not die," said Jason. "Flee home with us across the sea. Show us first how to win the fleece; for you can do it. Why else are you the priestess of the grove? Show us but how to win the fleece, and come with us, and you shall be my queen, and rule over the rich princes of the Minuai, in Iolcos by the sea."

And all the heroes pressed round, and vowed to her that she should be their queen.

Medea wept, and shuddered, and hid her face in her hands; for her heart yearned after her sisters and her playfellows, and the home where she was brought up as a child. But at last she looked up at Jason, and spoke between her sobs,

"Must I leave my home and my people, to wander with strangers across the sea? The lot is cast, and I must endure it. I will show you how to win the golden fleece. Bring up your ship to the woodside, and moor her there against the bank; and let Jason come up at midnight, and one brave comrade with him, and meet me beneath the wall."

Then all the heroes cried together—"I will go!" "And I!" "And

I!" And Idas the rash grew mad with envy; for he longed to be foremost in all things. But Medea calmed them, and said, "Orpheus shall go with Jason, and bring his magic harp; for I hear that he is the king of all minstrels, and can charm all things on earth."

And Orpheus laughed for joy, and clapped his hands, because the choice had fallen on him; for in those days poets and singers were as bold warriors as the best.

So at midnight they went up the bank, and found Medea; and beside came Absyrtus her young brother, leading a yearling lamb.

Then Medea brought them to a thicket, beside the War-god's gate; and there she bade Jason dig a ditch, and kill the lamb and leave it there, and strew on it magic herbs and honey from the honeycomb.

Then sprang up through the earth, with the red fire flashing before her, Brimo the wild witch huntress, while her mad hounds howled around. She had one head like a horse's, and another like a ravening hound's, and another like a hissing snake's, and a sword in either hand. And she leapt into the ditch with her hounds, and they ate and drank their fill, while Jason and Orpheus trembled, and Medea hid her eyes. And at last the witch queen vanished, and fled with her hounds into the woods; and the bars of the gates fell down, and the brazen doors flew wide, and Medea and the heroes ran forward and hurried through the poison wood, among the dark stems of the mighty beeches, guided by the gleam of the golden fleece, until they saw it hanging on one vast tree in the midst. And Jason would have sprung to seize it: but Medea held him back, and pointed shuddering to the tree foot, where the mighty serpent lay, coiled in and out among the roots, with a body like a mountain pine. His coils stretched many a fathom, spangled with bronze and gold; and half of him they could see, but no more; for the rest lay in the darkness far beyond.

And when he saw them coming, he lifted up his head, and watched them with his small bright eyes, and flashed his forked tongue, and roared like the fire among the woodlands, till the forest tossed and groaned. For his cry shook the trees from leaf to root, and swept over the long reaches of the river, and over Æetes' hall, and woke the sleepers in the city, till mothers clasped their children in their fear.

But Medea called gently to him; and he stretched out his long spotted neck, and licked her hand, and looked up in her face, as if to ask for food. Then she made a sign to Orpheus, and he began his magic song.

And as he sung, the forest grew calm again, and the leaves on every tree hung still; and the serpent's head sank down, and his brazen coils grew limp, and his glittering eyes closed lazily, till he breathed as gently as a child, while Orpheus called to pleasant Slumber, who gives peace to men, and beasts, and waves.

Then Jason leapt forward warily, and stepped across that mighty snake, and tore the fleece from off the tree trunk; and the four rushed down the garden, to the bank where the *Argo* lay.

There was a silence for a moment, while Jason held the golden fleece on high. Then he cried, "Go now, good *Argo,* swift and steady, if ever you would see Pelion more."

And she went, as the heroes drove her, grim and silent all, with muffled oars, till the pinewood bent like willow in their hands, and stout *Argo* groaned beneath their strokes.

On and on, beneath the dewy darkness, they fled swiftly down the swirling stream; underneath black walls, and temples, and the castles of the princes of the East; past sluice mouths, and fragrant gardens, and groves of all strange fruits; past marshes where fat kine lay sleeping, and long beds of whispering reeds; till they heard the merry music of the surge upon the bar, as it tumbled in the moonlight all alone.

Into the surge they rushed, and *Argo* leapt the breakers like a horse; for she knew the time was come to show her mettle, and win honor for the heroes and herself.

Into the surge they rushed, and *Argo* leapt the breakers like a horse, till the heroes stopped all panting, each man upon his oar, as she slid into the still broad sea.

Then Orpheus took his harp and sang a pæan, till the heroes' hearts rose high again; and they rowed on stoutly and steadfastly, away into the darkness of the West.

THE HUNTING OF THE CALYDONIAN BOAR

By ELSIE FINNIMORE BUCKLEY

Illustrations by Frank C. Papé

IN the city of Calydon long ago there were great rejoicings because the queen Althæa had given birth to a son, her first-born, who, if he grew to years of manhood, would in time sit upon the throne of his father Œneus, and rule the land. Some seven days after the child was born it chanced that the queen was lying alone in her chamber, with the babe upon her breast. It was wintertime, and the shades of evening had fallen early about the room, but a bright fire blazed upon the hearth, and the flickering flames threw dancing shadows on the walls. The queen was very happy as she pressed her baby to her breast, and held its soft little hand in hers, and whispered in its ear words which only a mother knows how to use.

As she lay she watched the shadows playing up and down upon the walls, and to her eyes they took strange forms of men and beasts. Now it was a great fight she saw, with horses and chariots rushing over a plain, and mighty warriors meeting face to face in battle; now it was a hunt, with winding of horns and dogs straining at the leash, and a white-tusked boar breaking through a thicket. But whether it was a hunt or whether it was a battle, everywhere there was one figure of a man she watched—a man tall and fair and brave, who stood out conspicuous among his fellows—such a hero as her son might grow to be if he lived till years of manhood. And she prayed that her vision might come true, and her son grow up to be a hero—a man mighty in sport and mighty in battle. In time the flames died down, and the fire burned clear and still upon the hearth.

The queen's eyes grew heavy, and she was about to turn on her side to sleep when a strange thing happened, which took from her all desire for rest. The wall of the room in front of her, which had glowed bright and cheery in the firelight, grew gray and misty and seemed to vanish before her eyes, and through the opening there came toward her the forms of three strange women, taller and more terrible than any women of earth. The first one carried in her hand a skein of thread, the second a spindle, and the third a pair of great sharp shears. The queen lay still and motionless with terror as they came forward slowly arm in arm and stood beside the couch, looking down upon the child at her breast. At length the first one spoke.

"I give to thy child, Althæa, a thread of life exceeding bright and fair."

"And I," said the second, "will weave that thread into dark places, where it will shine the brighter for the darkness round about, and bring him honor and great renown."

The third one said never a word, but walked slowly round the couch till she stood before the fire on the hearth. A great brand had fallen from the grate, and lay smouldering on the stones. Bending down, she took it in her hand, and thrust it deep into the red-hot heart of the fire, and stood watching it till it was well alight, and the tongues of flame shot crackling upward. Then she turned toward the queen.

"As soon as that brand upon the fire is consumed," she said, "I will cut the shining thread with my shears, and his life shall be as ashes cast forth upon the wind."

As she spoke, she held out the shears, and they gleamed sharp and cruel in the firelight.

With a cry of terror the queen sprang up from her couch, forgetful of her weakness, and thinking only of the life of her child; and she rushed across the room, and, drawing forth the blazing brand from the fire, she smothered it in her gown, and crushed it beneath her bare feet, till not a live spark remained about it. Then she hid it in a secret place where she alone could find it, and cast herself upon her couch and knew no more. When the attendants came in, they found the room empty, save for the queen and her child; and she lay senseless on the couch, with her feet and her gown all scarred and burnt.

For many a long day she lay between life and death, but at last the gods had mercy, and her strength came slowly back to her. But when anyone asked her the cause of her burning, she would shudder and mutter some strange tale of a brand which fell from the fire, and would have burnt out the life of her child. What she meant no one ever knew, but they thought that the gods had stricken her with a sudden fever, and that, not knowing what she did, she had burnt herself in the fire. But of the half-burnt brand and of the word of the Fates they knew nothing, for Althæa had said in her heart:

"The Fates have spoken, and their word shall surely come to pass. A fine and fair thread of life has Lachesis given to my son, and Clotho will weave it into dark places, where it shall shine exceeding bright. The gifts they have given are good. The hand of Atropos alone is against him, and she has measured his life by the life of a frail piece of wood. But so long as the gods shall give me strength, no careless hand shall place that brand upon the flames, and no man shall know the secret of his life, for grief or madness may turn even the heart of a friend. On me, and on me alone, shall my son's life rest; for well do I know that neither prayer nor sacrifice can avail to turn the heart of Atropos, the Unswerving One."

So she kept the brand securely hidden where she alone could find it. Many other fair children did she bear to Œneus the king— Phereus and Agelaus and Periphas, and Gorge and Melanippe, and the hapless Dejaneira, who married Heracles, and unwittingly caused his death. But best of them all she loved Meleager, her first-born; for the word that the Fates had spoken came true. He grew to be a great warrior and a mighty man, and was feared by his foes and loved by his friends through the length and breadth of the land; for there were great wars in those days between the Curetes of Pleuron and the Ætolians of Calydon, and on either side fought men whose names were not despised among their fellows, but among them all there was none so famed as Meleager. In all the country-side there was no man who could hurl the javelin with such force and skill as he, and whenever he went forth to battle the victory lay with the men of Calydon, and he was called the savior and protector of his city.

When he was in the flower of his manhood, the call of Jason came from far Iolchos for all the heroes of Hellas to join him in his search for the golden fleece. Amongst them sailed Meleager in the good ship *Argo,* and came to the land of the dusky Colchians on the shores of the Euxine Sea. One tale goes that he slew Æetes their king, the child of the Sun, and saved his comrades from deadly peril. But whether this be true or no, certain it is that he played his part like a man, and came back to Calydon with a fair name for courage and endurance. Then was he hoisted on the shoulders of his countrymen and carried through the streets of the city, and feasted right royally in his father's house.

Soon after his return it chanced that the harvest was more plentiful than it had ever been within the memory of man. The golden corn stood high upon the plains, and on the sunny mountain-sides the olive trees were thick with berries, and the vine branches drooped low with their weight of purple fruit. Wherefore Œneus the king ordered a great thanksgiving to be held throughout the land in honor of Dionysus and Demeter and gray-eyed Pallas Athene, who had given such good gifts to men. At every shrine and temple the altars smoked with sacrifice, and glad bands of youths and maidens with garlands on their heads danced hand in hand around, singing the song of the harvest.

"All hail to thee, Demeter, great Earth-Mother! From Evenus to the silver eddying waters of wide Achelöus thou hast covered the bosom of the plain with golden ears of corn, and they dance beneath the west wind like the waves on summer seas. All hail to thee, Dionysus, who bringest joy to the heart of man! About thine altars the juice of the vine shall flow like water, and the souls of those who were bowed down beneath labor and toil shall be uplifted to thee in the glad harvest time. And Pallas Athene, gray-eyed maiden, thee too we hail, for thy gift of the fragrant olive. The shade of thy trees lies cool upon the panting hillsides, and thou hast looked with kindness on our land. Oh, come hither, all ye townsfolk and ye dwellers on the plains and hills—come hither in your hundreds, and dance about the altars, and sing thanksgiving to the great gods on high."

Thus did they dance and sing, and there was gladness and rejoicing through all the land, and not one soul among them all knew how soon their laughter would be turned to tears. For when Artemis, the huntress, saw that everywhere the altars smoked in honor of Demeter, and Dionysus, and Pallas Athene, but that never a single stone was raised to her, she was filled with jealousy and wrath. One night, when all the land lay sleeping, she left the mountains, where she loved to hunt, and came down to Calydon. The arrows in her quiver rattled as she strode along in her wrath, and the flash of her eyes was as the flash of summer lightning across the sky. With great swinging strides she came and stood over Œneus as he slept.

"O king," she said, "too long have I been patient and waited for my dues; but I will suffer thine ingratitude no more. When the young corn stands green upon the plain, and the vine leaves are shooting, and the trees cast once more their shade upon the bare hillside, then shalt thou have cause to know my power. Demeter may sow her golden grain, and Dionysus and Pallas Athene may fill their fruits with gladdening juice, but thou hast yet to learn that, if it be my will, though the promise of the harvest be fair, the fruits thereof shall lie spoilt and ungathered where they grew. Broad and dark are the forests which cover wild Arachynthus, and deep the ravines, and many a wild beast lurks therein that is tame at my word alone. One of these will I let loose upon thy land. Many a fair field shall be trodden underfoot, and many a vineyard and olive grove laid waste—yea, and red blood shall flow, ere my wrath be assuaged, and I take away the pest from your midst. I have spoken, and no sacrifice shall turn me from my word."

Thus did she speak, saying the words in his ear, and turned and left the room by the way she had come. With a start he awoke from his sleep and looked around him, but no one could he see. Only a sudden storm of wind lashed the branches of the trees against each other, and a dark cloud hid the face of the moon.

"The sad wintertime is coming," he thought, "with its storms and its darkened days. Yet, lest there be aught in my dream, I will remember Artemis tomorrow, and her altars, too, shall smoke with sacrifice."

So on the morrow a great festival was held in honor of Artemis, the maiden huntress, and Œneus laid aside all thought of his dream. But when the springtime came and the early summer, he had cause to remember it with sorrow, for out of the forests of Arachynthus there came a great boar which laid waste all the country, right and left. In size he was more huge than an ox of Epirus, whose oxen are the largest in the world, and the bristles on his neck stood up like spikes. His breath was as a flame of fire that burned up all that stood in his way, and his cruel little eyes gleamed red with blood. Over the cornfields he raged, and trampled the green blades beneath his hoofs, and with his strong white tusks he tore down the vine branches and broke the overhanging boughs of the olive, so that the young berries and fruit lay spoilt upon the ground. Not only did he lay waste the fields, but the flocks and herds on the pasture land were not safe from his attack, and neither shepherds nor dogs could protect them from his fury. Through all the countryside the people fled in terror for their lives, and hid within the city walls, only now and again a band of the bravest would go forth and lay nets and snares for him; but so great was the strength of the beast that he broke through every trap they could devise, and, killing any man who stood in his path, he would return, with greater fury than before, to his attack upon the fields and cattle. At length things came to such a pass that, unless the monster could be checked, famine would ere long stare the people in the face. When Meleager saw that neither prayer nor sacrifice would turn the heart of Artemis, nor any ordinary hunting put an end to the boar, he determined to gather around him a band of heroes who, for the sake of glory, would come together for the hunt, and either kill the beast or perish themselves in the attempt. So he sent a proclamation far and wide through all the kingdoms of Hellas.

"O men of Hellas," he said, "the fair plains of Calydon lie trodden underfoot by a grievous monster, and her people are fallen upon evil days. Come hither and help us, all ye who love adventure, and fear not risk nor peril, ye seasoned warriors whose spirit is not dead within you, and ye young men who have yet your name to win. Come hither to us, and we will give you fair sport and good cheer withal."

In answer to his call there flocked from far and wide to Calydon
a great host of brave men, and mighty was the muster which gathered beneath the roof of Œneus for the hunting of the boar. Jason
himself came, the leader of the Argonauts, and Castor and Pollux,
the great twin brethren, whose stars are in the sky. There was
Theseus, too, who slew the Minotaur, and Peirithous his friend, who
went down with him to Hades, and tried to carry off Persephone
from the king of the Dead. And swift-footed Idas came, and
Lynceus, his brother, whose eyes were so sharp that they could see
into the center of the earth. Others were there besides, whose names
are too many to tell, and Toxeus and Plexippus, the brothers of
Althæa the queen, whom she loved as she loved her own son
Meleager. For as a little maid she had played with them in the
palace of Thestius, her father, and she remembered how she would
watch for them to come home from the hunt and clap her hands
with joy, when from afar she saw them returning home with their
spoil. And they would fondle her and play with her, and so long as
they were with her she was as happy as a bird; but when they went
away, her heart ached for them to come back. The memory of those
days still shone bright within her heart, and when her brothers came
with the other guests for the hunting of the boar, she welcomed
them right gladly. In the great hall a sumptuous feast was spread,
and loud was the laughter and bright were the faces, as one friend
met another he had not seen for many a long day, and sat down by
his side in good fellowship with the groaning board before them.
The feast was well under way when one of the attendants whispered
in the ear of the king that yet another guest had come for the hunting of the boar.

"Who is he?" asked the king.

"My lord, I know not," the man replied.

"Well, keep him not standing without, at all events," said Œneus,
"but show him in here, and we will make him welcome with
the rest."

In a few moments the man returned, and held back the curtain
of the great doorway for the newcomer to enter. All eyes were
turned eagerly that way to see who it might be, and a murmur of

surprise ran round the hall; for they saw upon the threshold no stalwart warrior, as they had expected, but a maiden young and beautiful. She was clad in a hunter's tunic, which fell to her knee, and her legs were strapped about with leathern thongs. Crosswise about her body she wore a girdle, from which hung a quiver full of arrows, and with her right hand she leaned on a great ashen bow like a staff. Her shining hair fell back in waves from her forehead, and was gathered up in a coil behind, and she held her head up proudly and gazed round on the company unabashed. The glow of her cheek and the spring of her step told of life in the open, and of health-giving sport over hill and dale, so that she might have been Artemis herself come down from her hunting on the mountains. She looked round the hall till her eyes fell on Œneus, the host, in the place of honor, and in no wise troubled by the silence which her coming had caused, she said:

"Sire, for my late-coming I crave thy pardon. Doubtless some of thy guests have come from more distant lands than I, but, as ill luck would have it, I chose to come by way of the sea instead of by the isthmus, and for a whole day I ate out my heart with waiting by the shrine of Poseidon for a favoring breeze; for the east wind blew like fury across the Crisæan Gulf, and any barque that had ventured to try the crossing had been blown to the isles of the Hesperides ere it had reached thy land. So I waited perforce till the wind fell and I could cross over in safety."

Concealing his surprise as best he could, Œneus answered:

"Maiden, we thank thee for thy coming, and make thee right welcome in our halls. Yet we fain would know thy name who, a woman all alone, hast crossed barren tracts of land and stormy seas unflinching, and come to take part in a hunt which is no mere child's sport, but a perilous venture, in which strong men might hesitate to risk their lives and limbs."

As she listened to his words she smiled.

"O king," she said, "thou hidest thy surprise but ill. Yet am I not offended, nor will I make a mystery of who I am. My name is Atalanta, and I come from the mountains of Arcadia, where all day long I hunt with the nymphs over hill and over dale, and through the dark forests, following in the footsteps of her we serve, great Artemis the huntress. At her command I stand before thee now, for she said to me, 'Atalanta, the land of Calydon lies groaning beneath the curse, wherewith I cursed them because they forgot me, and gave me not my dues. But do thou go and help them, and for thy sake I will lay aside my wrath, and let them slay the monster that I sent against them. Yet without thee shall they not accomplish it, but the glory of the hunt shall be thine.' Thus did she speak, and in obedience to her word am I come."

When she had spoken, a murmur ran round the hall, and each man's gorge rose within him as he determined in his mind that no mere woman should surpass him in courage and strength. The sons of Thestius, the queen's brothers, especially looked askance at her, and their hearts were filled with jealousy and wrath; for her eye was bright and steady, and her limbs looked supple and swift, and there seemed no reason why she should not be a match for any man among them, in a trial where swiftness of foot and sureness of eye would avail as much as brute force. When Meleager saw their dark looks he was very angry that they should so far forget their good breeding as to fail in welcoming a guest, and he rose from his seat and went toward her.

"O maiden," he said, "we make thee right welcome to our halls, and we thank thee because thou hast heard our appeal, and art come to help us in the day of our trouble. Come, now, and sit thee down, and make glad thy heart with meat and wine, for thou must need it sorely after thy long journeying."

As he spoke, he took her by the hand and set her in a place of honor between his father and himself, and saw that she had her fill of the good fare on the board. As he sat beside her and talked with her, his heart was kindled with love, for she was exceeding fair to look upon; and the more he thought upon the morrow's hunting, the more loath was he that she should risk her life in it. At length he said: "Atalanta, surely thou knowest not what manner of beast it is that we are gathered to destroy. Thou hast hunted the swift-footed stag, perchance, through the greenwood, but never a monster so fierce as this boar that Artemis has sent against us. I tell thee, it will be no child's play, but a matter of death to some of us. Hast thou no mother or father to mourn thee if any evil chance befall, or any lover who is longing for thy return? Think well ere it be too late."

But she laughed aloud at his words.

"Thou takest me for some drooping damsel that sits at home and spins, and faints if she see but a drop of blood. I tell thee, I know neither father, nor mother, nor husband, nor brother, and I love but little the lot of womenkind such as thou knowest. Never have I lived within four walls, and the first roof that covered me was the forest trees of Mount Parthenius, which stands where three lands meet, on the borders of Sparta, Argolis, and wooded Arcadia, that I have chosen for my home. Whence I came or how I got to Parthenius no one can tell, and I have no wish to find out. As for savage beasts, had I not the eyes of a hawk and the feet of a deer, I had not been safe ten seconds on the uplands of Arcadia. For there, as doubtless thou hast heard, there dwells a fierce tribe of centaurs—monsters half human and half horse—who have the passions of men and the strength of beasts. These, when they set eyes upon me, were fired by my beauty, and pursued me over hill and dale, and I fled like the wind before them; but ever and anon I found time to turn and let fly from my bow a dart which fell but seldom short of the mark. So dire was the havoc I wrought in their herd that after a time they gave up in despair, and molested me no more. So talk not to me of fierce beasts or of danger. All my life long I have breathed in danger from the air about me, and I had as soon die outright, as sit with thy womenkind in safety within, whilst all of you went forth for the hunting of the boar."

And nothing that Meleager could say would turn her from her purpose.

"Dost think I have left the mountains of Arcadia, and the nymphs, and the joys and dangers of the hunt, to come and sit with the old wives round thy palace fire in Calydon?" she said with a laugh; and her white teeth shone like pearls in the torchlight, and the gleam of her hair and the fire of her eyes kindled yet more surely the flame of love in his heart, so that he could have fallen at her feet and begged her for his sake to keep away from danger. But across the board he saw the eyes of Toxeus and Plexippus, his mother's brothers, fixed upon him, and their brows were dark and lowering as they frowned upon him and Atalanta. So he said no more, lest they should discover his secret and taunt him for his passion; but in his heart he knew that on the morrow his thought would be as much for her safety as for the killing of the boar. As for Atalanta, a stone would have returned his love as readily as she. For a companion in the hunt she liked him full well, but to give up her maiden life for his sake was as far from her thoughts as the east is from the west. As yet she knew not the love of man, and had vowed in her heart that she never would. Howbeit, such things are not altogether within the power of mortals to will nor not to will, and Atalanta, like any other woman, was destined one day to bow her proud head to the dust before a man's great love, though the gods had not ordained that Meleager should be the one to win her. But more of that hereafter.

When the morrow dawned, great was the bustle and confusion in the court of the palace, where all were to meet together for the hunting of the boar. Attendants ran this way and that to fetch and carry for their masters, and, as the huntsman blew his horn, the hounds barked impatiently, and strained, whining, at their leashes. At length, when all was ready, Althæa with her maidens came forth into the portico, and bade farewell to her guests, her husband, her brothers, and to Meleager, her son.

"God speed thee, my son," she said, as she looked proudly on him, "and good luck to thy hunting."

Then she stood on the step and waved to them with a smile as they turned to look back at her before the curve of the roadway hid them from sight. But though a smile was on her lips, her eyes were full of tears, and her heart within her was dark with a dim foreshadowing of evil. With a heavy step, she turned and went into the house, and as she passed the altar by the hearth she stopped and bowed her head.

"Great Artemis," she prayed, "have mercy and bring my loved ones safely back to me this day."

Then she went to her chamber and drew forth from its hiding place the half-burnt brand on which her son's life depended.

"His life, at any rate, is safe," she thought, "so long as this brand is in my keeping."

And she hid it away again where she knew no one could find it, and set to work restlessly, to while away the hours as best she could, till the hunters should come home.

They, meanwhile, had gone their way up the steep path which led into the mountains and deep into the heart of the forest, where they knew their prey was lurking. Soon they came upon the track of his hoofs leading to the dry bed of a stream, where the rushes and reeds grew high in the marshland, and the bending willows cast their shadow over the spot he had chosen for his lair. Here they spread the nets cautiously about, and stationed themselves at every point of vantage, and, when all was ready, let loose the hounds, and waited for the boar to come forth from his hiding place. Not long did they have to wait. With a snort of rage he rushed out. The breath from his nostrils came forth like steam, and the white foam flew from his mouth and covered his bristly sides and neck. Quick as lightning, he made for the first man he could see, and the tramp of his hoofs reëchoed through the woods like thunder as he came upon the hard ground. As soon as he rushed out, a shower of missiles fell toward him from every side, but some were aimed awry or fell too far or too short of him, and those that touched him slipped aside on his tough hide, as though they had been feathers instead of bronze; and he broke through the nets that had been spread to catch him, and galloped away unharmed, whilst behind him a hound lay dead among the reeds, pierced through with his tusk, and two of the hunters, who stood in his path, and had not been able to rush aside in time, lay groaning on the ground with the iron mark of his hoof upon them, and a gaping wound in the side of one.

When the rest saw that he had escaped them, they gave chase with all speed, headed by Castor and Pollux, on their white horses, and Atalanta close beside them, running swiftly as the wind. Ahead of them the woodland track gave a sudden turn to the left, and the boar, rushing blindly forward, would have plunged into the under-

Frank C. Papé

Meleager buried the spear deep into the beast's shoulder.

[See page 97]

growth and bushes, and escaped beyond range of their darts. But Atalanta, seeing what must happen, stopped short in the chase. Quick as thought, she put an arrow to the string, and let fly at the great beast ahead; and Artemis, true to her word, guided the arrow so that it pierced him in the vital part behind the ear. With a snort of pain and fury, he turned round upon the hunters and charged down toward them as they came up from behind, and great would have been the havoc he had wrought among them but for Meleager. As the brute bore down, he leaped lightly to one side, and, gathering together all his strength, buried the spear deep into the beast's black shoulder, and felled him to the earth with the force of his blow. Immediately the others gathered round, and helped to finish the work that Meleager had begun, and soon the monster lay dead upon the ground in a pool of his own blood. Then Meleager, with his foot upon the boar's head, spoke to the hunters.

"My friends," he said, "I thank you all for the courage and devotion you have shown this day. My land can once more raise her head in joy, for the monster that wrought such havoc in her fields lies dead here at my feet. Yet the price of his death has not been light, my friends." And they bowed their heads in silence, as they remembered the two whom the boar had struck in his rush, one of whom was now dead. "Yet those who have suffered, have suffered gloriously, giving up themselves, as brave men must, for the sake of others, and their names shall surely not be unremembered by us all. Once more, my trusty comrades, I thank you, every man of you. As for thee, lady," he continued, turning to Atalanta, "while all have played their part, yet the glory of the hunt is thine. But for thy sure hand and eye the beast might yet be lurking in the forest. Wherefore, as a token of our gratitude, I will give to thee the boar's head as a trophy to do with as thou wilt."

At his words a murmur of applause went round the ring of them that listened. Only the voices of Toxeus and Plexippus were not heard, for they were mad with jealousy and wrath, and as soon as there was silence they spoke.

"By what right," asked Toxeus, "shall one bear off the trophy of a hunt in which each one of us has played his part?"

The insolence of his words and looks roused the anger of Meleager to boiling point. All through the hunt the brothers had shown scant courtesy to Atalanta, and now their rudeness was past bearing.

"By the same right as the best man bears off the prize in any contest," he answered quietly, though he was pale with rage.

"Happy is that one who has first won the heart of the judge, then," said Plexippus with a sneer, as he looked at Atalanta.

By the truth and the falsehood of his words Meleager was maddened past all bearing. Scarce knowing what he did, he sprang upon him, and before anyone knew what he was about, he had buried his hunting knife in the heart of Plexippus. When Toxeus saw his brother fall back upon the grass, he sprang upon Meleager, and for a moment they swung backward and forward, held each in the other's deadly grip. But Meleager was the younger and the stronger of the two, and soon Toxeus, too, lay stretched upon the ground beside his brother, and a cry of horror went through the crowd of those who stood by. Pale and trembling, Meleager turned toward them.

"My friends," he said, "farewell. You shall look upon my face no more. Whether I slew them justly or no, the curse of Heaven is upon me, and I know that night and day the Furies will haunt my steps, because my hand is red with the blood of my kinsmen. O fair fields of Calydon, that I have loved and served all my days, farewell forever. Nevermore shall I look upon you, nor my home on the steep hillside, nor the face of the queen, my mother; but I must hide my head in shame far from the haunts of men. As for thee, lady," he said, turning to Atalanta, "their taunt was false, yet true. Right honorably didst thou win thy trophy, as all these here will testify"; and he pointed to the hunters standing round. "Yet my soul leapt with joy when I found that into thine hand and none other's I might give the prize of the hunt. Wherefore, think kindly on my memory, lady, when I am far away, for a brave man's heart is in thy keeping. Farewell."

And he turned and went away by the forest path. So surprised were all the company that no man moved hand or foot to stop him. The first to speak was Atalanta.

"Comrades," she said, "do you bear home the dead and break the news as gently as may be to the queen, and I will follow him, if perchance I can comfort him, for the hand of Heaven is heavy upon him."

So firmly did she speak that no man found it in his heart to withstand her; and when she saw that they would do as she bid, she ran swiftly down the path by which he had gone, and disappeared from sight.

Meanwhile the day had been drawing toward its close, and Althæa had come out into the portico to watch for the return of the hunters. The rumor had reached the city that the boar had been killed, but not without loss among the gallant band that had gone out against him, and with a heavy heart Althæa was waiting to know who it was that had fallen. In time she saw them returning home, and in their midst four litters carried on the shoulders of some. When she saw them, her heart stood still with fear, and as they came up and laid down the litters before the doorway she was as one turned to marble, and moved neither hand nor foot. When Œneus the king saw her, he took her gently by the hand.

"Come within, lady," he said; "the hunting of the boar has cost us dear."

"Ah! tell me the worst at once," she cried. "I can bear it better so. The suspense is maddening me."

"Two of those who lie before thee are strangers who have given themselves for us," he said. "One of them is sore wounded, and the other is gone beyond recovery. The other two, Althæa, are very near and dear to us—Toxeus and Plexippus, thy brothers."

And he pointed to two of the bodies which lay side by side with their faces covered before her. With a wild cry she rushed to them, and drew back the coverings, and gazed upon the faces that she loved so well. As she looked, she saw the wound that had killed them, and she knew now that it was no wild beast that had slain them, but the hand of man. Drawing herself up to her full height, she looked round on those who stood by, and the gleam of her eyes was terrible to see. "Deceive me no more," she said, "but tell me how these two came to fall by the hand of man."

"Lady," said Œneus, "they sought a quarrel with one of our company, and in anger he slew them both."

For a moment she was silent, then in a low voice, yet one that all could hear, she spoke.

"My curse be upon him, whosoe'er he be. O Daughters of Destruction, foul wingless Furies, by the blood of my brothers yet wet upon his hand, I bid you track his footsteps night and day. May no roof cover his head nor any man give him food or drink, but let him be a vagabond on the face of the earth till just vengeance overtake him. On thee, Œneus, do I lay this charge, and on my son Meleager, to avenge the death of these my kinsmen, who have been foully slain."

In vain did Œneus try to stop her. She was as one deaf to his entreaties. When she had finished, she looked round for Meleager, and when she could not see him, the blood froze in her veins.

"My son," she cried—"where is my son?"

"Lady," said Œneus, "even now the wingless bearers of thy curse are hunting him through the forest."

For a moment she swayed to and fro as though she would fall.

"Ye gods, what have I done?" she muttered.

Then with a cry she turned and rushed through the doorway, across the deserted palace to her own chamber, and barring the door behind her, she took from its hiding place the brand she had kept jealously so long. As on the day when the Fates had come to her, a bright fire was burning on the hearth, and deep into the heart of it she pushed the log with both her hands.

"O my son, my son!" she cried; "to think that I should come to this! But though the flame that devours thy life burns out my heart within me, yet must I do it. Thus only can I save thee from my curse. For the word, once spoken, never dies, and the Furies, once aroused, sleep never, night nor day. Wherefore Death alone can give thee peace, O Meleager, my first-born and my dearest."

Œneus meanwhile had followed her, and stood without, asking her to open to him. But she cried out to him:

"All is well. I beg thee leave me. I would be alone."

So he left her; and she stood watching the flames slowly eat the wood away, and at last, when the log fell apart in ashes, she sank down upon the floor, and with her son's life hers, too, went out for grief.

Meleager meanwhile had gone blindly forward along the forest track, and from afar Atalanta followed him. For a time he went onward, straight as an arrow, never stopping, never turning. But when his mother's curse was spoken, faster than the whirlwind the Furies flew from the realms of endless night, and came and crouched before his feet, loathsome shapes of darkness and of horror. With a cry he turned aside, and tried to flee from them, but wherever he looked they were there before him, and he reeled backward and forward like a drunken man. But soon his strength seemed to give way, and he fell forward on the grass, and Atalanta ran forward and took his head upon her knee. To her eyes they two were alone in the heart of the forest, for the foul shapes of the Furies he alone had seen. But now he lay with his eyes closed, faint and weak, and she thought that some time in the hunt he must have strained himself, and lay dying of some inward hurt that no man could heal, for on his body she could see not a scratch. So she sat in the gathering gloom with his head upon her lap. There was naught else she could do. Help lay so far away that he would have died alone had she left him. At last, when his heart beat so faint that she thought it had stopped once for all, he opened his eyes and looked up at her, and when he saw her the fear and the madness died out of his face, and he smiled.

"The gods are kind," he said. Once more he closed his eyes, and Atalanta knew that he would open them never again. Gently she laid him with his head on the moss-covered roots of a tree, and sped away to the city to bear the news of his death. In the darkness of night they bore him through the forest, and all the people gathered together and watched from the walls the torchlit procession as it came slowly up the hill; and the heart of each man of them was heavy within him as he thought that the hero and savior of his country was being carried dead into the walls of his native town.

By the side of his mother they laid him, and burned above them the torches of the dead, and the mourners, with heads bowed in grief, stood around.

Thus did it come to pass that the hunting of the boar ended in grief for the land of Calydon, and Atalanta went back to the Arcadian woodlands with a sore place in her heart for Meleager, who had died happy because his head was resting on her knee.

THE WINNING OF ATALANTA

By ELSIE FINNIMORE BUCKLEY

ONCE upon a time there ruled in Arcadian Tegea a proud-hearted king named Schœnus. A tamer of horses was he, and a man mighty in the hunt and in battle. Above every other thing he loved danger and sport and all kinds of manly exercise. Indeed, these things were the passion of his life, and he despised all womenkind because they could take no part nor lot in them. And he wedded Clymene, a fair princess of a royal house, because he wished to raise up noble sons in his halls, who should ride and hunt with him, and carry on his name when he was dead. On his wedding day he swore a great oath, and called upon all the gods to witness it.

"Never," he swore in his pride, "shall a maid child live in my halls. If a maid is born to me, she shall die ere her eyes see the light, and the honor of my house shall rest upon my sons alone."

When a man swears an oath in his pride, he repents full oft in humility, and so it fell out now. For many a long year no child was born to him, and when at last he had hopes of an heir, the babe that was born was a maid. When he saw the child his heart was cut in two, and the pride of a father and the pride of his oath did battle within him for victory. The pride of his oath conquered, for he was afraid to break his word in the face of all his people. He hardened his heart, though he had held the babe in his arms, and its little hand with a birthmark above the wrist had closed about his finger trustfully, and gave orders that the child should be cast out upon the mountains to die of hunger and cold. So the babe was given to a servant, who bore it forth and left it on the slope of bleak Parthenius.

But Fate made a mock of Schœnus, of his pride and of his oath, for no other child, either man or maid, was born to him in his halls. All too late he repented of his folly, when he saw his hearth desolate and no children round his board, and knew that not only

103

his name, but his race, was like to die with him, because of the rash oath which he had sworn.

Yet there was one who had pity on the babe, and whose heart was kinder than the heart of its own sire. When Artemis, the maiden goddess, saw the child cast forth to die, she was filled with anger against Schœnus, and swore that it should live. For it was a fair child, and a maid after her own heart, and no young life ever called to her in vain for mercy. Wherefore she sent a she-bear to the place where the child lay, and softened the heart of the beast, so that she lifted it gently in her mouth and bore it to the cave where her own cubs lay hid. There she suckled it with her own young ones, and tended it night and day, till it grew strong and could walk, and the cave rang with its laughter as it played and gamboled with the young bears. When Artemis knew that the child was old enough to live without its foster mother, she sent her nymphs to fetch it away, and when they bore it to her she was well pleased to find it fair and strong.

"Her name shall be Atalanta," she said to them. "She shall dwell on the mountains and in the woods of Arcadia, and be one of my band with you. A mighty huntress shall she be, and the swiftest of all mortals upon earth; and in time she shall return to her own folk and bring joy and sorrow to their hearts."

Thus it came to pass that Atalanta lived with the nymphs in the woodlands of Arcadia. They taught her to run and to hunt, and to shoot with bow and arrows, till soon the day came when she could do these things as well as any of their band. For the blood of her father ran hot in her veins; and not more easily does a young bird learn to fly than Atalanta learnt to love all manner of sport. So she came to womanhood in the heart of the hills, and as her form grew in height and strength, it grew too in beauty and grace. The light of the sunbeam lay hid in her hair, and the blue of the sky in her eyes, and all the rivers of Arcadia bathed her limbs and made them fresh and white. But she thought little of her beauty, or the power it might have over the hearts of men, for all her delight was in the hunt, and to follow Artemis, her mistress, over hill and over dale. Artemis loved her, and delighted to do her honor; and when the land of Calydon cried to her for mercy, because of the boar she had sent to ravage it in her wrath, she decreed that none but Atalanta should have the glory of that hunt. The tale of how she came to Calydon, and of how the boar was slain at last through her, I have told you before; and of how death came to Meleager, because he loved her, and would not let any man insult her while he stood idly by. By the fame of that hunt her name was carried far and wide through Hellas, so that when she came to the funeral games of Pelias there was no need to ask who she was. She ran in the foot race against the swiftest in the land, and won the prize so easily that when she reached the goal the first man had scarce passed the turning point, though he was no sluggard to make a mock of. When the games were over, she went back to Arcadia without a tear or a sigh, but her face and her memory lived in the heart of many a man whose very name she had not known; and when presently the news went abroad that she would wed the man who could win her, they flocked from far and wide, because they loved her better than life; for they knew that the unsuccessful went forth to certain death.

The tale of how Atalanta went back to her own folk, and of how she was wooed and won, is as follows:

One day, when King Schœnus held a great hunt in the forest on the edge of his domain, it chanced that Atalanta had come to those parts; and when she heard the blare of the bugles and the barking of the hounds, her heart leapt with joy. As a dog, when he hears the voice of his master, pricks up his ears and runs swiftly to meet him, so did Atalanta run swiftly through the woods when she heard the sound of the bugles. Full often had she joined in a hunt on the uplands of Arcadia, and run with the hounds; and when the hunt was over she had fled back into the forest, away from those who had been fain for her to stay. For she loved the hunt, but not the hunters; but because she was a mortal and born of a mortal race, she did not flee from their eyes, as the wood nymphs fled, but hunted with them for joy of the hunt, and left them when it pleased her. So now she joined in the chase as the stag broke loose from cover, and her white feet flashed in the sunlight as she followed the hounds across the moorland. King Schœnus, when he saw her, was glad.

"It is Atalanta, the maiden huntress," he cried. "See that she be treated with due courtesy, for she is the only woman on earth who is fit to look a man in the face."

And he rode eagerly after her. But the best horse in all that company was no match for Atalanta. Far ahead of them all she shot, like an arrow from the bow, and when at last the stag turned at bay in a pool, she was the first to reach him. When the rest had come up, and the huntsman had slain the stag, the king turned to her.

"Atalanta," he said, "the trophy of this chase is thine, and my huntsman shall bear the head of the stag whithersoever thou shalt bid him. In token of our esteem, I beg thee to accept this ring. When thou lookest upon it, think kindly of an old man whose heart is lonely, and who would fain have a daughter like thee."

As he spoke he drew off a gold ring from his finger and held it toward her; the tears stood in his eyes and his hand shook as he looked on her fair young form, and remembered the babe he had cast out on the mountains to die. If she had lived she would have been of an age with Atalanta, and perchance as fair and as strong as she; and his heart was bitter against himself for the folly of his oath.

When Atalanta heard his words, she had a mind at first to refuse his gift. Many a man before had offered her gifts, and she had refused them every one; for she had no wish to be beholden to any man. But when she saw the eyes of the old king dim with tears, and how his hand shook as he held out the ring, her heart was softened, and yearned with a strange yearning toward him. Coming forward, she knelt at his feet and took the ring, and held his hand and kissed it.

"May the gods grant the prayer of thy heart, sire," she said, "and give thee a daughter like unto me, but fairer and more wise than I!"

As he looked down on the hand that held his own the old king trembled more violently than before, for above the wrist was a birthmark like the birthmark above the wrist of the babe he had cast forth to die. And he knew that he made no mistake, for that mark had lived in his mind as though it had been branded with red-hot steel.

"Atalanta," he said, "the gods have heard thy prayer. This is not the first time thy fingers have closed about mine."

"What meanest thou, sire?" she asked.

"As many years ago as the span of thy young life," he said, "I held in my arms a newborn babe, the child that the gods had given me, and its little hand with a birthmark above the wrist closed about my fingers trustfully. But because of my foolish pride I hardened my heart. I cast away the gift of the gods and sent the child to die upon the mountains. But the birthmark on its wrist was branded on my brain so that I could not forget it. Never till this day have I seen that mark again, and now I see it on thy wrist, my child."

He bowed his head as he spoke, and the tears from his eyes fell upon her hand, which lay in his as she knelt before him.

"Oh, my father!" she cried, and bent forward and kissed his hand.

When he found that she did not turn from him, though she knew what he had done, he was more deeply moved than before.

"Atalanta," he said, "when I cast thee forth to die, I gave back to the gods the life they had given me, and now I have no right to claim it again. Yet would thy presence be as sunshine in my halls if thou wert to come back to me, my child."

Thus did the call come to Atalanta to return to her own folk, and the choice lay before her. On the one side was her free life in the forest, with Artemis and her nymphs, the hunt, the fresh air, and all the things that she loved; on the other was life within the walls of a city, and the need to bow her head to the customs and the ways of men. Her heart misgave her when she thought of it.

"My lord," she said, "will a young lion step into the cage of his own free will, think you?"

The old king bowed his head at her words.

"Alas! what other answer could I look for?" he said. "I thank the gods that they have shown me thy fair face this day. Perchance, when we hunt again in these parts, thou wilt join us for love of the chase. Till then, my child, farewell."

With trembling hands he raised her from her knees, and kissed her on the forehead. Then he signed to his men to lead forward his horse, and mounted and rode sadly home through the forest with his company. And Atalanta shaded her eyes and stood watching them till they disappeared from sight. When they had gone, she sighed, and turned and went upon her way. But her eyes were blind and her ears were deaf to the sights and sounds she loved so well, and that night she tossed restlessly upon her couch of moss. For before her eyes was the figure of an old man bowed with sorrow, and in her ear his voice pleaded, trembling with longing and love:

"Thy presence would be as sunshine in my halls if thou wert to come back to me, my child."

In the early dawn, she rose up from her couch, and bathed in a stream close by, and gathered up her shining hair in a coil about her head. Then she put on her sandals and a fresh white tunic, slung her quiver about her shoulders, and bow in hand went forth through the forest. Looking neither to the right nor to the left, she went on her way till she came to the white road that led to the city. Then she turned and looked back at the forest.

"Dear trees and woods," she said, "farewell! And ye nymphs that dwell in the streams and dance on the green sward of the mountains! When I have trodden the white road and gone up to the city, I can live with you no more. As for thee, great Artemis, who saved me in the beginning, I will be thy servant forever, and dwell a maiden all my days, and a lover of the hunt."

She leant her head against a tree close by, and the tears stood in her eyes. It seemed that the breeze bore her words on its wings, for she heard a sigh from the forest, and the waters cried out to her, "Atalanta, come back, come back!"

But she closed her ears, and stepped out bravely on the white highway, and went up into the city. The people as they saw her pass marveled greatly at her beauty, and whispered one to the other, "Surely it is Atalanta, the king's daughter. What doth she here?"

For the tale of how King Schœnus had found his child, and of how she had refused to come home with him, had spread like wildfire through the city; so that when they saw her, they knew full well who she must be. She took no heed of them at all, but went straight forward on her way till she came to the gate of the palace. The gate stood open, and without knocking or calling she passed in, and went across the echoing court and beneath the portico into the great hall, as one who comes by right. When she had entered the hall, she stopped and looked about her. At first all seemed silent and deserted, for the folk had gone their several ways for the work of the day; but at length she spied an old man sitting on a carved chair in one of the alcoves between the pillars. It was the king, her father. He sat with his head upon his hand and his eyes downcast upon the floor, and his face was sad and full of longing, as of one who dreams sweet dreams which he knows will not come true.

Gently she drew near to him, and thanked the gods who had timed her coming so that she should find him alone. And she went and knelt at his feet. The old man gazed for a moment in her face, as though he did not see her; then he started from his chair and laid his hand upon her shoulder.

"Atalanta!" he cried.

"My father," she said, "I have come back to thee."

Then he gathered her up in his arms.

"Oh, my child, my child!" he said. "The gods are kind beyond my desert."

"Thy voice cried out to me in the night-time," she said, "and I could not shut my heart to thy pleading. The call of the free earth was strong, but the call of my blood was stronger."

Thus did Atalanta come back to her own folk, and bring joy to the heart of her father and the mother who had never held her in her arms. A great feast was held in the palace in her honor, and through all the city the people rejoiced because of her. For she was a fair princess of whom any land might be proud, and her fame had spread through the length and breadth of Hellas. Indeed, as soon as it was known who she was, and how she had left the mountains to come and live with her own kin, suitors flocked from far and wide to seek her hand in marriage. But she treated them one and all with scorn, and vowed that she would never wed. At first her father smiled upon her, and looked on her refusal to wed as the sign of a noble nature, that was not to be won for the asking of the first chance comers. So he gathered about him the noblest princes in the land in the hope that among them all there would be one who could win her heart. But the months passed by, and still she vowed that she would never wed. All her delight was in running and hunting, and to ride by her father's side. As for the young princes, she liked them full well for companions in sport, but as soon as they spoke of love and marriage she would turn her back upon them. At length the king grew anxious.

"Surely, my child," he said, "among all these princes there is one whom thou couldst love?"

"I shall never love any man but thee, my father," she replied.

"Yet all the hope of our race lies upon thee, Atalanta," he said. "If thou wilt not wed, our race will die."

"Our race died on the day on which thou didst cast me forth on the mountains," she answered. "If I have lived, it is no thanks to thee or to any of my people, but my life is hers who saved me on that day."

"What meanest thou?" said the king.

"When I left the forest and came back to thee, I vowed a vow to Artemis who saved me in the beginning. I said, 'I will be thy servant for ever, and dwell a maiden all my days and a lover of the hunt.' My life belongs to her, and not to my race, not to any son of man."

"We vow rash vows in ignorance, Atalanta," said the king, as he remembered the oath he had sworn on his wedding day, "and Fate makes a mock of us, and turns our nay to yea."

But Atalanta laughed at his words.

"When Fate mocks at me," she said, "it will be time enough for me to wed and turn my nay to yea."

Nothing that he could say would persuade her to go back from her resolve. But still he reasoned with her night and day, till at length she grew so wearied of the matter that she bethought her of a plan that would rid her of all her suitors.

"My father," she said, "I will wed any man who shall ask for my hand, if he will fulfill one condition."

"My child," cried her father, "I knew that in the end thou wouldst listen to reason. Tell me thy condition, that I may spread it abroad among those who are suing for thy hand."

"Tell them," she said, "that I will wed the first man among them who will run a race with me. If he win, I will be his bride, but if he lose, he must die."

The king's face fell when he heard her words.

"Surely thou speakest in mockery, Atalanta," he said. "No man in all the world can run as swiftly as thou canst, and they know it. Thou wilt drive thy suitors from thee; or if any be foolhardy enough to run with thee, they will run to a certain death."

"No man will run to a certain death, my father," she answered. "When they know that to sigh for me is to sigh for death, they will go back to their own folk, and I shall be troubled with suitors no more."

Herein she spoke in ignorance, and knew not the fatal power of her beauty upon the hearts of men. And her father sighed at her words. Yet he thought within himself:

"Perchance there is more in her words than meets the ear. The deep sea is easier to fathom than the mind of a woman. Either there is one among her suitors whom she favors above the rest, and she will see to it that he is the first to run with her, and will bridle her speed and let him win; or else, Heaven knows, some god has put this whim in her heart, and will send a champion we know not, who can run faster than the fastest, and he will outspeed her and make her his bride. She will never let men die because of her."

But herein he, too, thought in ignorance, and knew not how his own pride and stubbornness lived again in Atalanta, so that she would abide by her word, though it brought grief to herself and death to others. So he published abroad among the suitors the condition she had made. When they heard it there was great consternation among them, and they consulted together as to what they should do, and some sent a deputation to her to find out the meaning of her words.

"Lady," they asked, "when thou speakest of death thou speakest perchance in parables. Those who run in the race with thee and are outstripped must give up all hope of thee, and look upon thy face no more. And this would be death indeed to them that love thee."

But she laughed in their faces.

"If you would hear parables," she said, "go to the oracle at Delphi. I am no raving priestess to utter words that walk two ways at once. He who courts death may race with me at daybreak, and at sunset he shall drink the poison cup without fail, and look neither on my face again nor the face of any living thing. Have I spoken plainly now?"

The next day there was great confusion in the halls of King Schœnus. There was shouting and bustling, and attendants ran this way and that. Chariots clattered through the gateway and drew up in the court, and baggage was piled high behind the horses. And Atalanta laughed aloud at the success of her scheme; for suitor after suitor came and kissed her hand and bade her farewell. They loved her much, but they loved life better, and were content to go home and find mates who, though less fair, were less ferocious, and were like to look upon their lords with eyes more lowly and obedient than Atalanta.

That night the gathering about the board was scantier than it had been for many a long day. Yet a few of the suitors remained, and seemed in no haste to be gone. Day after day passed by, and each night Atalanta said within herself:

"Tomorrow they will surely go. They dwell in distant towns, and they are waiting for a favorable day for their journey."

But favorable days came and went, and still they stayed in the halls of King Schœnus. At last Atalanta could hide the dread in her heart no longer.

"How long will it be, my father," she asked, "ere we are troubled no more with strangers in our halls?"

"If thou wilt wed one of them, we shall be troubled with the rest no more," he replied.

"They know full well I can wed no man of them, because of the condition I have made," she said.

"They are waiting for thee to fulfill thy condition," said the king.

Then Atalanta herself went and pleaded with them.

"My friends," she said, "I pray you to be guided by me. The gods have not fashioned me after the manner of womenkind, and I cannot give myself nor my love to any man. Look upon me as one of yourselves, I pray you, and think not to win me in marriage."

But they replied, "Lady, thou hast given the condition of thy marrying, and we are waiting to fulfill it."

"But my condition means certain death," she cried.

"Nothing in this life is certain," they said, "save death in the end. If it come soon or late, what matter? For thy sake we are willing to face it now."

Thus was she forced to keep her word, and the lists were made ready for the race, and the lots were cast among the suitors as to which of them should be the first to run against her. In the early morning, before the sun was strong, the race was run, and all the city crowded to the course to watch it. The man ran well and bravely, but his speed was as child's play to Atalanta. She put forth her strength like a greyhound that is content to run for awhile before the horses, but when he scents a hare, can leave them far behind. Even so did Atalanta run, and came in cool and fresh at the goal, whilst her rival ran in hot and panting behind her.

Thus did it come to pass that the first man drank the poison cup because of his love of Atalanta. With a smiling face did he drink it, as a man drinks at a feast.

"Farewell, lady," he said; "grieve not for me. With open eyes I chose my fate. I ran for the sake of love and beauty, and I have won death. Such is ever the lot of the nameless many. They fight for the glory of the man whose name shall live. Good luck to my rival!"

And now a time of darkness and mourning fell upon the land, and many a day in the year the city was hung with black for the sake of some noble suitor who had chosen death rather than life without Atalanta. And Atalanta's heart was sore within her, because of the rash condition she had made in her ignorance. When she would fain have recalled her words it was too late, for the suitors bound her to her promise.

"Either give thyself of thine own free will to one of us, or else let us take our chance of winning thee or death," they said.

And so she was forced to run with them. For in her heart she knew that even death was happier for a man than to win her without her love.

Thus were the words of Artemis fulfilled when she said: "In time she shall return to her own folk, and bring joy and sorrow to their hearts."

One day it chanced that a stranger came to the city on a morning that a race was to be run. The night before he had slept in a village near by, and the people had told him the tale of Atalanta, and how on the morrow another suitor was to run to his death. But he scoffed at their words.

"No man would run to certain death," he said, "were the maid as fair as Aphrodite."

"Go and see for thyself," they replied. "Soon we shall hear that thou too wilt run in the race."

"Never," he said; "no woman can cheat my life from me."

But they shook their heads unconvinced. "Many before thee have spoken likewise," said they, "and yet they have run."

"If I run, I will run to win," he answered.

"Can a snail outstrip a deer?" they asked.

"It might so chance," said he.

"Thou art mad," they cried.

"Better to be mad on earth than sane in Hades," he replied.

But they shook their heads the more, and tapped wisely with their fingers on their foreheads, to show that he was mad and spoke at random.

"Well, well," he said, with a laugh, "we shall see what we shall see."

The next morning he set forth early for the city, and, mingling with the crowd, he made his way to the race course, and found for himself a place where he could watch the whole sight with ease. The race was run, and ended as it always ended; and once again the city was hung with black. But in the mind of the stranger an image remained which had not been there before—the image of a maid whose white feet flashed in the sunlight and her tunic swung to and fro as a flag swings in the breeze.

"Great Heracles!" he thought within himself, "to run shoulder to shoulder with her for a moment, even in a race for death, might be worth the while after all. I will make myself known at the palace, and see what the gods will give me."

For some days he lay hid in the city, till he thought the time was ripe for him to go up to the palace of the king. Then he went for a walk along the highway, and when he was covered with dust and grime, he returned to the city and made his way at once to the palace. At the door of the gateway he knocked, and the old porter came out to ask his will.

"I am come from a distant land," he said, "and tomorrow I would journey yet farther on my way. I pray thee to crave hospitality for one night for me from the steward of this house, whoe'er he be. I am a king's son, and worthy to sit at any man's table."

The porter cast a doubtful eye on the travel-worn clothes of the stranger. It seemed unlikely that a king's son would go on a distant journey with no body servant and no horse or baggage. Then he looked in his clear blue eyes, which gazed back at him as innocent as a child's, and he saw that for all his sorry raiment he was by no means ill-favored, but held himself well and proudly. So he opened the door and led him across the court.

"Well, well," he muttered in his beard, "great folk have strange whims in these days. Our king must needs slay his daughter, because she is a maid, and she must needs slay her suitors, because they are men. After that this fellow may well be, as he says, a king's son, who, because he has a palace and plenty, must needs tramp over the face of the earth and beg his bread. Praise be to the gods who put lowly blood in my veins and sense in my head, else had it been better for the gate to keep itself than to have me for a guardian."

Then he cast another look over his shoulder at the young man behind.

"At any rate, for one night he can do no harm," he muttered.

"What didst thou say, father?" asked the stranger.

"I said that for one night thou couldst do no harm," replied the old man.

"On the contrary," said the stranger with a laugh, "in one night

I hope to do more good to this house than thou hast done in all thy life."

"The young have ever a good conceit of themselves," said the porter. "Thou art not like to keep this gate, winter and summer, day and night, for close on three-score years, as I have done, young man."

"On the other hand," said the stranger, "thou art not like to marry the king's daughter within the year, and have the city hung with red instead of black in thine honor, as I am like to do."

"Sir," said the old man, "I know my place too well——"

"—and love thy life too much to aspire to the hand of the princess. Is that not so?"

"Mayhap," said the old man, and shut his mouth with a snap. To all further remarks which the stranger made he answered with a grunt. He took him into the palace and delivered him into the hands of the steward. As he turned to go back to his post, the young man clapped his hand upon his shoulder.

"Good luck to thee and thy gate," he said. "When I come through with the hand of the princess in mine, perchance thou wilt look upon me with greater favor than now."

"Be warned in time, young man," said the porter, "and tarry not overlong in this palace, but go forth on thy journey in the morning, as thou hadst a mind to do in the beginning. Those who tarry too long are apt to go through the gate with nought but a cake in their hand."

This he said, meaning the cake which was put in the hands of the dead for them to give to Cerberus, the watchdog of Hades.

"Fear not for that," said the stranger; "I had as lief go empty-handed."

Thereupon he turned to the steward, who welcomed him sadly to the halls of King Schœnus. All strangers were looked upon askance in those days, lest they came as suitors for the hand of Atalanta, and wished to add to those who had run in the fatal race. When he heard that the young man would depart on the morrow on his journey he was glad, and gave him water to wash with and a change of raiment, and showed him his place at the board, without so much as asking his name. When Atalanta saw a stranger at the board her heart sank within her, and she kept her eyes turned away, as though she had not seen him, for she made sure that he too had come to run in the race with her. It chanced that night that the company was scanty, and no man talked in private to his neighbor, but the conversation leapt from one end of the board to the other, as each one took his share in it and said his say. The stranger, too, took his part with the rest of them, in nowise abashed; and so shrewd were his words, and so full of wit, that soon he had a smile upon the face of each one at the table. For many a long day the talk had not been so merry nor the laughter so loud at the table of King Schœnus. Atalanta, too, forgot her constraint, and talked and laughed freely with the stranger; and he answered her back, as though it had been man to man, and showed no more deference to her than to the others of the company.

When the meal was over, the king approached the stranger, and Atalanta stood beside him.

"Sir," said the king, "thy name and country are still hid from us, but we are grateful for thy coming, and would be fain for thee to stay as long as it shall please thee."

"I thank thee, sire," said the stranger, "but I am bound by a strange vow. I may not reveal my name, nor accept hospitality for more than one night from any man, till I come to a house where none other than the king's daughter shall promise me her hand in marriage. From the tales I have heard in the neighboring country, I have learnt that I may not hope to end my vow beneath this roof— though indeed," he said, turning to Atalanta, "I would fain press my suit if there were any chance of success."

But Atalanta threw back her head at his words.

"Thou hast doubtless heard the condition," she said, "by the fulfillment of which alone a man may win my hand."

"Alas, sir!" said the king, "I would press no man to try his luck in that venture."

"Since that is so," said the stranger, "I will go forth once more upon my journey at break of day, and see what luck the gods will give me. I thank thee for thy kindly hospitality this night, and beg thee to excuse me. I have traveled far, and would fain rest now, as I must go a long distance ere I can rest again."

Thereupon he took his leave of King Schœnus and his daughter. But she, for all her pride, could not forget the man who seemed to bid her farewell with so light a heart. He was well favored, but it was not because he was well favored, or because he had a ready tongue, that she thought on him. Indeed, when she asked herself why she should remember one who by now had doubtless lost all memory of her, she could find no answer. As she tossed on her couch with a troubled mind, she determined that before he left the palace on the morrow she would have some speech with him.

"He thinks no more of me than of a stone upon the wayside," she said within herself, "wherefore I can do him no wrong by letting him speak with me again before he goes."

It was her custom to rise early in the morning, before the rest of the household was stirring, and go forth alone into the woods; and it was the lot of one of the slaves to rouse himself betimes to give her food ere she went, so that when she appeared, as was her wont, he thought nothing of it. The stranger had risen even earlier than she, and the slave was waiting upon him. When Atalanta saw him, her heart gave a sudden thrill, for she had not looked to see him so soon.

"Good morrow, sir," she said. "It is not often I have a companion when I break my fast."

Then she turned to the slave.

"Thou mayest get thee back to thy bed," she said, "and sleep out thy sleep in peace. I will see to the wants of our guest and speed him on his way."

The slave, nothing loath, departed. He was well used to strange commands from his mistress; and, moreover, there was no need to invite him twice to return to his couch.

Thereupon Atalanta sat down at the board beside the stranger, and they fell to with all the appetite of youth and health; and as they ate they laughed and joked, and talked of strange lands they both had seen and adventures that had befallen them. In the space of one half-hour they were as good friends as though they had known each other all their lives, and suitors who had sat at her father's board day after day were much more strangers to Atalanta than this man, who had craved but one night's hospitality.

When they had finished their meal the stranger rose.

"I must bid thee farewell, lady," he said.

"Nay, not yet," she replied; "I will set thee on thy way, and show thee a road through the forest that will bring thee to the city thou seekest. I know every track and path as well as the wild deer know them."

He tried to dissuade her, but she would not listen, and led him out from the palace by a side gate, which she unbarred with her own hands. Down through the sleeping streets they went, where the shadows of the houses lay long upon the ground, and out across the open downs into the shade of the forest. The dew gleamed like jewels on the leaves, as here and there the slanting rays of the sun shone through the trees, and above their heads the lark sang gaily in the bright summer sky. Yet they walked silently side by side, as though, in spite of the brightness of the day, sorrow and not joy were sitting in their hearts; and all their gay talk and laughter of the early morning was dead. At length they came to a broad track that crossed the path they were in, and Atalanta stopped short and pointed to the right.

"From here," she said, "thou canst not miss thy way. Follow the track till it lead thee to the highroad, and when thou strikest the highroad, turn to the left, and thou wilt come to the city thou seekest."

Then she held out her hand to him.

"I must bid thee farewell," she said, "and good luck to the ending of thy vow."

"Lady," he said, and took her hand in his, "if thou wilt, thou canst release me now from my vow."

But she drew her hand away sharply and tossed back her head.

"Many kings have daughters besides King Schœnus," she said, "and any one of them could release thee from thy vow as well as I."

"Atalanta," he said, "no king's daughter save thee shall ever release me from vow. That which all our laughter and our converse last night and this morning strove to hide, our silence as we walked side by side has revealed far better than I can tell thee. Thou knowest that I love. From the first moment that I saw thee I have loved thee."

His words made her heart thrill with a strange joy. But she showed no sign of it, and answered him coldly. She was proud and wished to test him.

"Doubtless the floodgates of love are easily thrown open where a man would be released from a vow. Thou knowest how thou mayest win me. Art thou willing to run in the race?"

At this all his mirth returned to him, and his eyes shone with merriment as he answered:

"Much good would my love do me if I had to drink the poison cup perforce. Nay, nay," he said; "I love thee too well to put my death at thy door. When I have some chance of winning the race, I will come back and claim thee. In the meantime, lady, farewell."

And, bowing to her, he turned and went his way, without so much as looking back at her, as she stood trembling with astonishment and anger. It was not thus her other lovers had spoken. When he had gone from sight, she turned suddenly and went back by the path they had come. Her hands were clenched, and the tears sprang unbidden to her eyes, as she strode forward with long, angry strides that took no heed of where they went.

"He has made a mock of me!" she cried to herself—"he has made a mock of me! He is a base adventurer who seeks release from his vow. He has no heart and no honor. Fool that I was to treat him as a friend!"

Thus did she stride along in her wrath, till it had cooled somewhat, and she was able to think more calmly of the stranger. Then his form came back to her mind, as he had looked when they stood face to face at the parting of the ways, when the sun had glinted down upon them through the trees, and he had looked her straight in the face with his clear blue eyes, and said: "Thou knowest that I love thee. From the first moment I saw thee I have loved thee."

A great sob rose in her throat as she remembered.

"Ah, he spoke the truth!" she said, "I know that he spoke the truth."

Moreover, her heart told her that long before he had spoken the words she had known that he loved her. Yet strange is the bond of love. Its strands are certainty and doubt interwoven. Wherefore Atalanta, though she had heard the words which were but the echo of the silent speech of their hearts, had put him yet further to the test, and had driven him from her side by asking of him a sacrifice she had no wish for him to make.

"If he would come back and run with me," she sighed, "my feet would be as heavy as lead against him."

But she sighed in vain. Day after day passed by, and he came not.

"He is a man of his word," she thought at last. "Till he has some chance of winning he will not come back. And he is no fool. He knows he can never run as I can run. He will never come back."

Yet for all this she watched for him night and day. When she went forth into the road, or into the forest, she looked for his form at every turn of the way. When she entered the great hall of the palace, she looked to see his face at the board. But always she looked in vain, and sometimes her heart grew bitter against him.

"If he were to come now," she would say to herself, "I would show him no mercy. He who takes so much thought before he will risk his life for my sake is not worthy to win me."

Then again she would grow tender, and stand looking down the path by which he gone, and sigh for him.

"Oh, my love, come back, come back! My pride is melted away like the snow, and without any race I will give myself to thee."

Thus would she long for him, and grow near to hating him, because she knew that she loved him. The weeks and months passed by, and still he returned not; winter came and went, and once again the dewdrops shone in the summer sunlight as Atalanta walked in the forest at break of day. She walked with her eyes upon the ground, thinking of the summer morning a long year ago when he had walked by her side in silence along that very path. When by chance she raised her eyes, there, at the parting of the ways, he stood, as though in answer to her thoughts. With a cry she stopped short and gazed at him, and he came forward and bowed to her.

"I have come back, lady," he said.

"Oh!" she cried from her heart, "I am glad thou hast come back."

Then he bent and kissed her hand. So once more they walked in silence side by side along the path they had walked before; and once again the bond of love was knit strong between them, with its strands of certainty and doubt. As they drew near to the edge of the forest, Atalanta was the first to speak.

"And thy vow," she asked—"hast thou found release from it?"

"Not yet," he answered. "I am come back to run the race, that I may win release."

Once again the spirit of perversity came upon her.

"Where has thou learnt to run like the wind?" she asked.

"I have not learnt to run like the wind," he replied. "I have learnt something better than that."

"Few things are better in a race than swiftness," she said.

"True," he answered; "yet I have found the one thing better."

"What is this strange thing?" she asked.

"When we have run the race, thou wilt know," he said.

"I have grown no sluggard," she said, with a toss of her head, as if to warn him that her speed was not a thing to be despised.

"That I can see," he said, as he cast a glance at her straight white limbs and the easy grace of her bearing as she walked beside him. Then they talked of indifferent matters, and each one knew that what they had nearest their hearts they were hiding from each other.

So they came to the palace, and from the lowest to the highest the inmates greeted the stranger with joy. For he had won the hearts of them all by his wit and his genial smile. But they sighed when they heard that he too had come to run in the fatal race.

"Alas!" said the old king, shaking his head, "I had rather not have looked upon thy face again than see thee back on such an errand."

The young man laughed. "He who runs with a fair hope of winning runs swiftly," he said. "The others were dragged down by the shackles of their own despair."

"Thou dost not know my daughter," said the king.

"Mayhap I know her better than thou thinkest, and better than thou knowest her thyself," said the stranger.

No arguments or entreaties would turn him from his purpose.

"I must win release from my vow," he said. "I cannot live all my life a nameless wanderer. Yet will I not wed any woman I love not, for the sake of my release. Atalanta alone can save me, for I love none other."

So the lists once again were prepared, and the course made smooth for the race. With trembling fingers Atalanta tied her girdle about her, and bound her sandals to her feet. Though her heart was crying out for the stranger to win, and praying that her feet might fail her at the last, yet her pride, too, lifted up its head.

"He makes so sure of winning," she thought, "he despises my swiftness. He shall see that nothing he has learnt can teach him to run as I can run. And yet—oh, cursed be the condition I thought so cunning in mine ignorance! Oh, would that he could win me without first outspeeding me!"

Thus did her pride and her desire pull two ways at once.

And now the folk were gathered together round the course, and Atalanta and the stranger stood ready and waiting for the word to be given. She had made it a condition of the race that her rivals should have a good start of her, and she stood with her eyes upon the stranger's back, as he waited many paces before her. All too soon the word was given, and he sprang forward from his place, as a dog which has been straining at his leash springs forward when the hook is unloosed. And Atalanta, too, sprang forward; but whereas the man ran like a hunted thing that strains every muscle to save its life, she ran with the swinging grace of the wild deer that, far away from the hunters and hounds, crosses the springing turf of the lonely moor, fearless and proud, as he throws back his antlers in the breeze. Thus did Atalanta run, as though she had no thought of the race, or of the man who ran for his life. Yet, though she seemed to make no effort, she gained upon her rival at every step, and now she was running close behind him, and now she was almost shoulder to shoulder, and out of the corner of his eye he could see the gleam of her tunic. Then for a moment he slackened his pace, and it seemed that she would pass him, and on every side the people shouted out to him, "Run, run! Faster, faster! She will pass thee."

But he put his hand into the opening of his tunic, and drew forth something from his breast. Then his hand swung up above his head, and from it there flashed a dazzling fiery apple. Up and down through the air it flashed like a meteor, and rolled along the grass, till it stopped far away in the center of the course, and lay shining like a jewel in the rays of the sun. Every eye was turned from the race to watch its gleaming flight, and Atalanta stopped short and watched it too. When she saw it stop still in the middle of the course, flashing and sparkling in the grass, a great desire sprang up in her heart to have it—a mad, unreasoning desire that she could not resist. And she darted aside out of the path of the race, and went and picked up the shining golden apple and put it in the bosom of her tunic. Meanwhile the stranger had lost no time, and when Atalanta came back to the spot she had left, he was far ahead upon the course, and she had to run with a will if she wished to overtake him. But once again she gained upon him, and the space between them grew less and less, till they were running well-nigh shoulder to shoulder. And once again he saw the gleam of her tunic beside him; and again he slackened his speed for a moment, and sent a second gleaming apple into the air. Once more the mad, unreasoning desire sprang up in Atalanta's heart, and, leaving the course, she picked up the second apple and put it in the bosom of her tunic beside the first. By the time she had returned to the path the stranger had rounded the turning point and was well on his way toward the goal, and she put forth all her strength to overtake him. But the ease of her running was gone. She ran as one who runs bearing a burden, yet she would not cast away the golden apples in her bosom; for though they hampered her, she gained upon her rival, and for the third time they were running almost shoulder to shoulder.

And again, the third time, the same thing happened, and Atalanta left the course to pick up the shining fruit. This time when she returned to her place the stranger was close upon the goal, and all around the people were shouting and waving their hands. Blindly she pulled herself together, and with all the strength that was left in her she made a great spurt to overtake him. If she would cast away the golden apples, she might yet win the race; but the same mad desire which had spurred her to pick them up forbade her now to let them go. As she ran, they seemed to grow heavier and heavier in her bosom; yet she struggled and panted on, and step by step did she gain upon him, though her eyes were darkened to all but his form and the goal ahead. On every side the people shouted louder than before, for they knew not now which of them would win. As they drew near to the goal they were again almost shoulder to shoulder, and the stranger saw once more the flash of Atalanta's tunic beside him, while there were yet some paces to run. Then he gave a great spurt forward, and leapt away from her side. She tried to do likewise, but her strength was gone. She had made her last effort before. Thus did it come to pass that the stranger ran in first to the goal, and, running close upon his heels, Atalanta fell breathless into his arms as he turned to catch her. She had run twice as far as he, but what matter if he had not outsped her? He had won the race, and held the woman he loved in his arms. The tears shone in her eyes, but he knew they were not tears of grief; and in the face of all the people he kissed her.

Thus was Atalanta, the swiftest of all mortals, beaten in the race by the stranger, and learnt from his lips what it was that he had found on his travels that had made speed of no avail in the race.

For after they had come back to the city, surrounded by the joyous folk, and had passed hand in hand beneath the gateway, and the stranger had nodded with a smile at the old porter, who stood bowing before them; after he had revealed to them all that he was Meilanion, the son of Amphidamas, and the old king had fallen on his neck and given him his blessing, because he proved to be the son of his own boyhood's friend, and the man of all others he would have chosen for his son-in-law—after all this, when the speeches and the merrymaking were over, they two walked alone in the moonlit court of the palace. At last Atalanta had decked herself in the long saffron robes of a bride, and in her hands she bore the three shining apples. Meilanion's arm was about her, as they walked for a while in silence, but at length she spoke and held out the fruit in her hands.

"Tell me their secret," she said.

"Their secret lies in thy heart, Atalanta," he answered.

"What meanest thou?" she asked.

"I mean that if thou hadst not loved me, they would never have filled thy soul with longing to have them, and thou wouldst never have turned aside from the race."

"And, knowing this, thou didst stake thy life on my love?" she said.

"Knowing that, I staked my life on thy love," he answered.

"Then that was the one thing better than speed in the race?"

"Yes," he answered, "I learnt to trust in thy love."

There was silence for a moment between them, and then again Atalanta spoke.

"And whence came the apples?" she asked him.

"When I left thee at the parting of the ways," he said, "I traveled many a weary league by land, and on the road I passed many a shrine of Aphrodite. But I never passed them by without lifting up my hands in prayer to the goddess, for I knew that she could help me if she would, and I know that to them that love truly she is ever kind in the end. But I wandered till I was footsore and weary, and yet I had no sign. At length I came to the seashore, and took ship for the pleasant isle of Cyprus, which is her own dear home. There at last she came to me, walking on the waves of the sea. As I lay on the shore in the night-time, I saw her as a great light afar, and she drew near to me with the foam playing white about her feet. In her hand she bore three shining golden apples. And she came and stood beside me, and I hid my eyes at the sight of her beauty. But she spoke to me in a voice that was soft and kind, and the melody of it touched my heart like the melody of music.

" 'Fear not, Meilanion,' she said; 'I have heard the cry of thy heart. Here are three apples from mine own apple tree. If she whom thou lovest loves thee in return, she cannot resist the spell of their golden brightness. When thou runnest against her, cast them one by one into the middle of the course. If she love thee she will turn aside to pick them up. For her they will be heavy as the gold they seem made of. For thee they will be light as the fruit whose form they wear. Farewell, and good luck to thy race.'

"Thereupon darkness came over my eyes, and I could find no words to thank her. When I awoke I thought it had been a dream, but lo! by my side upon the sand lay the apples, shining in the sunlight."

"And thy vow?" asked Atalanta. "How camest thou to make such a vow?"

He laughed at her words.

"When a hare is hunted," he said, "thou knowest how he will double and turn, and take a line he has no mind to pursue to the end. So was it with me. Long ago in my father's house I heard of thee and of thy beauty, and how thou couldst cast such a spell upon the hearts of men that for thy sake they would fling away their lives. And a great desire came upon me to see this thing for myself, for I could scarce believe it. So I set forth alone to find thee, and hid my name from all men as I journeyed, for thus could I be more free to act as seemed best in mine own eyes. And I saw thee run in a race, and that glimpse was enough to tell me that I, too, one day must run with thee. Yet was I more wary than my rivals. I knew that to come as a suitor was the way to turn thy heart to stone. Wherefore I pretended to be bound by a vow, which would bring me as a passing stranger before thee. Canst thou forgive the lie?"

She smiled into his face.

"It was a daring venture," she said.

"I knew I was as one who treads unknown paths on a moonless night," he answered. "Yet deep in my heart I felt that when a man desires one thing on earth above every other—when he loves that thing better than life itself, he is like to win it in the end, if he walk patiently step by step in faith. He will win that thing, or death in his struggle for it; and he is content that so it should be."

Such was the winning of Atalanta. As for the golden apples, she placed them in a precious casket, and guarded them jealously all her days, for a memorial of the race that she had failed to win.

THE DIVINE MUSICIAN

By *ELSIE FINNIMORE BUCKLEY*

NORTHWEST of the Ægean, where the cliffs of Pelion rise sheer out of the sea, dwelt long ago Cheiron, the centaur, the wisest of living things, half man, half horse. Many brothers had he, who in form were like himself, but their hearts within were hard and wild, and because of their untamed passions and their cruelty and lust they were hated alike by gods and men. But Cheiron was gentle and mild. He knew all manner of strange things; he could prophesy, and play upon the lyre, and cure men of their hurts by means of healing herbs. He was brave withal, and had been in many a bloody fight, and knew the arts of war full as well as the arts of peace. Wherefore the old Hellenes called Cheiron, the Better One, and sent up their sons to live with him that they might be taught all the things which man should know. In a hollow cave on the mountain-side he had his home. Far up above him the snow-capped peaks of Pelion kept watch over the nestling townships of the plain, and far, far below the waves of the Ægean washed without ceasing on the rocks of that pitiless coast, now soft and soothing as the song a mother sings to her child, now loud and boisterous beneath the lash of the stormwind, when the sea birds fly screaming to the shelter of the shore. All around were dark forests of chestnut, pine and oak, where many a fierce beast had his lair. In the branches of the trees the wild birds built their nests and filled the dark glades with song. About the mouth of the cave the ground was trampled hard beneath the tread of many feet, and paths led this way and that, some into the heart of the forests, others down the steep cliff to the shore.

Every morning at sunrise a troop of boys and youths would come forth from the cave, and, dividing into groups, would go their several ways to fish or to hunt, or to follow the course of some stream to its unknown source in the mountains. Sometimes Cheiron himself would go with them, if he thought they had need of his help;

but more often he left them to their own devices, to follow each one his own bent as Nature prompted him. In the evening they would come home and tell him of their doings in the day; and he would praise or blame them, according as they had done well or ill, and show them how they might do better another time. Then they would go to their couches of dried moss and leaves, and sleep the deep sleep of youth and health, while the cool night breeze blew in upon their faces from the mouth of the cave, and put fresh life and strength into their tired limbs. In the wintertime, when the night was longer than the day, and the snow lay deep upon the hills, they would light a great fire in front of the cave with logs they had stored in the summer months, and Cheiron would take his lyre and sing to them of all things in heaven and earth, while they lay round about and listened.

The songs which he sang to them then they never forgot, because Cheiron was wise, and spoke to their souls in his singing. So they laid up his songs in their hearts; and many a long year after, when they were grown men far away, and some danger or difficulty stood in their path, the drift of his teaching would come back to them in the words of a song, and their hearts would grow brave and strong once more to act worthily of their boyhood's sunny days on Pelion. Many a hero whose name still lives among men had been trained by Cheiron in his youth—Peleus, who married a goddess, and Achilles his son, the swiftest and bravest of mortal men; and Jason, the leader of the Argonauts; and Asklepios, the mighty healer; and, not least among them, Orpheus, the greatest of Greek musicians and mystics, whose tale I will tell you now.

One day, as the shades of evening were beginning to fall, Cheiron stood before the mouth of the cave waiting for the lads to come home. Sooner than he expected he saw one of them far away coming down a path from the mountains, and he marveled that he should return so soon and alone. As he came nearer Cheiron saw that he walked with his eyes upon the ground, deep in thought. Every now and again he stopped and looked round upon the peaceful hillsides stretching calm and smiling in the golden glow of the evening; and when he had gazed for a moment he sighed, as though he would breathe into his soul the beauty he saw around him, and then went on his way once more with his eyes on the ground. So he walked till he came close to the cave and saw Cheiron standing in the entrance. Then he ran up to him and put his hand upon his shoulder.

"My father," he cried, "look round upon the hills; hast thou ever seen them so fair as they have been this day?"

"Orpheus," he said, "the fair face of the earth changes but little. In the soul of man it lies to look upon her and see her beauty, or to be blind."

"Till this day I have been blind, Cheiron," he said.

"And who has lifted the veil from thine eyes, my son?" asked his master.

"I know not," he said. "But this morning, while yet it was dark, there came to me a strange unrest and a longing to be alone. So I crept forth from the cave whilst you were all sleeping, and climbed up the mountain-side—up, up, in the gray light before dawn, till I came to the place where the white snow lies like a cloak about the shaggy shoulders of Pelion. There I left the track of my footsteps where no feet but mine had trod, and climbed up upon a boulder and looked out across the sea. And I saw the great sun rise out of the east. As I looked it seemed that I beheld the face of God; and as the snow and the sea and the forests awoke to life in the light of His glory, my soul awoke within me. All the day long I wandered about the forests and hills; and I saw the beauty of the trees and the grass, and the grace of the wild deer as he bounded over the rocks, as I had never seen it before. The wonder of this day lies like a burden on my heart that I fain would ease, yet I have no words to tell of it."

Then Cheiron took up the lyre which was lying by his side and pressed his fingers gently over the strings.

"Orpheus," he said, "many a long year ago, when thou wast a little lad, thy mother Calliope brought thee to me. And she put thy hand in my hand, and said: 'Cheiron, make a man of my son. Make him brave and fearless and strong, a worthy companion of the noble lads thou hast around thee. When the right time comes I will breathe my spirit upon him, and he shall be great, as few in this world are great.' This day she has kept her word, Orpheus. She has breathed her spirit upon thee, and has opened the eyes of thy soul and made them see."

"Who is my mother Calliope?" asked the lad.

"She is the Fair-voiced One who speaks through the lips of mortals by music and song, Orpheus. With her sisters, she dwells forever by the sunlit streams of Helicon, where they follow in the footsteps of Apollo, their lord, across the green lawns and the flowery meadows. All knowledge, all music of sound and of words, comes to men by their gift—those nine great sisters, the Muses. Happy art thou to be her son. Take now this lyre from mine hand. Ease the burden of thy soul in song, and learn how great is the gift she has given thee."

So Orpheus took the lyre from his master, and struck the chords, as all the lads who dwelt with Cheiron knew full well how to do. But instead of the old songs that he had learnt from his childhood, a new song came to his lips, and he sang as he had never sung before. Far away upon the hillsides his companions heard his voice, and they stopped upon their homeward way to listen, as the evening breeze bore the sound to their ears. When they knew that the voice came from home, they hastened on and drew silently near, that no sound might disturb the singer, and throwing themselves upon the ground at his feet, forgot their weariness and hunger as they listened. On and on he sang, forgetful of all else but his song, till the red glow of the evening died away in the west and the stars shone pale in the twilight. There was a strange magic about his music which drew all living things to his feet, as a magnet draws the cold heart of steel. From the woods and the forests they came, and from the bare hillsides—the lion, the leopard and the trembling fawn. The snake came forth from his hiding place, the rabbit from his hole, and the wild birds wheeled about his head and settled on the brow of the cave. The very trees seemed to hear him, as they swayed their heads to and fro to the rhythm of his song.

As he looked round upon his comrades whilst he sang, his heart grew strong within him, for he felt that a strange new power had been born in his soul, which could bow the heads of men beneath his will as the wind bows the rushes by the stream. So he sang on as the twilight deepened into night, and all the stars of heaven came forth to listen, till at length his song died upon his lips, like a breeze lulled to rest at sunset. For a moment the creatures lay spellbound around him; then one by one they crept back to their homes, with their fears and their hatreds tamed for a while by the magic of his singing. And his companions crowded round him with words of praise and eager questions.

"Who taught thee thy magic song, Orpheus?" they cried.

"The sunrise and the snow," he answered, "and the teaching of Cheiron, and my happy days with you, and the spirit of my mother Calliope—all these have taught me my song."

But his answer was a dark saying to them, and not one of them understood it, save Cheiron. He knew that it is the commonest things in life that are the material of all that is beautiful and fair, just as a temple may be built of common stone; but that the children of the Muses are few, who can by music and art open the blind hearts of men to see.

Thus did the gift of song fall upon Orpheus, so that he became the greatest of all singers upon earth. All day long he would wander about the woods and the hills, and tame the heart of every living thing with the magic of his voice.

One day it chanced that he came into a wood where he had never been before, and he followed a grass-grown track which led to the mouth of a cave. On one side of the cave stood a tall beech tree, whose moss-covered roots offered a tempting seat, and close by a clear stream gushed forth from the rocks. He drank eagerly of the water, for he had wandered far and was thirsty; and when he had quenched his thirst, he sat down on the roots of the beech tree and began his song. As before, the wild things gathered about him, and crouched at his feet, tame and silent, as he sang; and from the shadow of the cave crept a wood nymph, and lay upon the grass, with her chin between her hands, looking up into his face. For a time he did not see her, so silently had she come; but at last the power of her eyes drew his eyes upon her, and he turned his head and looked at her. When he saw her, his arm fell useless by his side and his voice died away in his throat, for he had never looked upon anyone so fair. Her hair was black as the storm cloud, but her eyes were blue as the summer sky, and she lay like a white flower in the grass at his feet. For a long moment he gazed into her face without speaking, as she gazed back at him, and at last he spoke.

"Who art thou, maiden?" he asked.

"I am Eurydice," she answered.

"Thy hair is black as midnight, Eurydice," he said, "and thine eyes are bright as the noonday."

"Are not midnight and noonday fair to thine eyes?" she asked.

"They are fair indeed, but thou art fairer."

"Then I am well content," she said.

"I know not thy name nor thy face, Eurydice," said he, "but my heart beats with thy heart as though we were not strangers."

"When two hearts beat together, Orpheus, they are strangers no more, whether they have known each other all their days or have met as thou and I have met. Long ago the fame of thee and of thy singing reached mine ears, but I hardened my heart against thee, and said, 'It is an idle rumor, and he is no better than other men, before whose face I flee.' But now the gods have brought thy steps to the hollow cave where I dwell, and thou, by thy magic, hast drawn me to thy feet, so that I, who doubted thy power, must follow thee withersoever thou wilt."

"Shall I sing thee a song, Eurydice—the song thou hast sown in my heart?"

"Yes, sing me that song," she answered.

So he struck the chords of his lyre and sang her the song that was born of her beauty. One by one the wild creatures stole back to the forest, for that song was not for them, and they two were left alone beneath the spreading boughs of the beech tree. As he sang, Eurydice crept closer to him, till her head rested on his knee and her long black hair fell in a cloud about his feet. As she drew nearer his voice grew lower, till it became but a whisper in her ear. Then he laid his lyre on the ground beside him and put his arms about her, and their hearts spoke to each other in the tongue that knows not sound nor words.

So it came to pass that Orpheus returned no more to dwell with Cheiron and his companions in the hollow cave below Pelion, but lived with Eurydice, his wife, in her cave in the heart of the forest. But he never forgot his boyhood's happy days, nor all that Cheiron had done for him. He would come often to see him and take counsel with him, and sing to the lads his magic song. For a few short years he lived a life the gods might envy, till the dark days came, when not even music could bring comfort to his heart. For one day, as he roamed with Eurydice through the dark forest, it chanced that she unwittingly trod upon a snake, and the creature turned upon her and pierced her white foot with its venomous fang. Like liquid fire the poison ran through her veins, and she lay faint and dying in his arms.

"O Eurydice," he cried, "Eurydice, open thine eyes and come back to me!"

For a moment the agony of his voice awoke her to life.

"Orpheus," she said, "beloved, this side of the river of death we can dwell together no more. But love, my dear one, is stronger than death, and some day our love shall prevail, never again to be conquered."

When she had spoken, her head sank down upon his breast, and her spirit fled away to return no more. So he bore the fair image of his wife in his arms, and laid her in the depths of the cave that had been their home. Above her head he placed a great pine torch, and all the long night watches he sat with his arms about her and his cheek against her cheek; and his heart groaned within him with a grief too great for words. Ere the day dawned he kissed for the last time the lips that could speak to him never again, and laid back her head on a pillow of leaves and moss. Then he pulled down the earth and stones about the mouth of the cave, so that no one could find the opening, and left forevermore the home he had loved so well. Onward he walked in the gray light of dawn, little caring where he went, and struck the chords of his lyre to tell all the earth of his grief. The trees and the flowers bowed down their heads as they listened, the clouds of heaven dropped tears upon the ground, and the whole world mourned with him for the death of Eurydice his wife.

"Oh, sleep no more, ye woods and forests!" he sang, "sleep no more, but toss your arms in the sighing wind, and bow your heads beneath the sky that weeps with me. For Eurydice is dead. She is dead. No more shall her white feet glance through the grass, nor the field flowers shine in her hair. But, like last year's snow, she is melted away, and my heart is desolate without her. Oh! why may the dried grass grow green again, but my love must be dead for-ever? Oh! ye woods and forests, sleep no more, but awake and mourn with me. For Eurydice is dead; she is dead, dead, dead!"

So he wandered, making his moan and wringing the hearts of all who heard him, with the sorrow of his singing. And when he could find no comfort upon earth he bethought him of the words of his wife:

"This side of the river of death we can dwell together no more. But love, my dear one, is stronger than death, and some day our love shall prevail, never again to be conquered."

He pondered the words in his heart, and wondered what she might mean.

"If love is stronger than death," he thought, "then my love can win her back. If I can charm the hearts of all living things with the magic of my song, I may charm, too, the souls of the dead and of their pitiless king, so that he shall give me back Eurydice, my wife. I will go down to the dark halls of Hades, and bring her up to the fair earth once more."

When hope was thus born anew in his heart he grew brave for any venture, and pressed forward on his way till he came to the place men call the mouth of Hades. Nothing daunted by the tales of horror they told him, he entered the fearsome cave, which led deep down into the bowels of the earth, where noisome vapors choked the breath in his throat, and dark forms crouched in his path and fled shrieking before him, till at last he stood by the shores of the ninefold Styx, that winds about the realms of the dead. Then he shouted aloud to Charon, the ferryman, to row him across in his boat. When the old man heard his voice, he stopped midway across the stream.

"Who is it that calls me in the voice of the living?" he asked.

"It is Orpheus," he answered. "I am come to fetch back Eurydice, my wife."

But the old man laughed, and his laugh cut the heart of Orpheus like a knife.

"O beardless innocent," he said, "who gave thee power over life and death? I tell thee that many have stood by the shores of this stream and entreated me to take them across, that they might bring their dear ones back with them. But no living soul shall sit in my boat; nor shall the dead, who have sat in it once, ever return to sit in it again. Go back to the earth, young man, and when thy time has come, thou too shalt sit in my boat, never fear."

"That time has come, Charon," he said, "and I shall sit in thy boat this day."

Raising his lyre, he struck the chords, and his love taught him the tune and the words to sing. Steadfastly he gazed at Charon, and the magic of his singing drew the old man toward him as surely as though the rope of the boat were in his hands. Without ceasing his song, he took his place in the stern, and in time to the music Charon dipped his oars in the stream, so that the boat swung over the river as it had never swung before. As it stranded in the shallow water, Orpheus leaped lightly to shore.

"Farewell for the present, Charon," he cried; "we shall meet again ere long."

He hastened on his way, playing and singing his magic song. Resting on his pole, the old man looked after him with wonder in his heart, and shaded his eyes with his hand. For a ray of the sun seemed to shine for a moment in that cold gray land as Orpheus passed by. The pale flowers of hell tossed their heads to and fro, as though the west wind played through their leaves, and their color and their scent came back to them once more. With a sigh, Charon breathed in the perfume from the air, and tossed back the gray locks from his brow and straightened his drooping shoulders.

"It is long since I smelt the fresh smell of the earth," he muttered.

"Who is this young god, who can bring light to the darkness and life to the realms of the dead?"

So, till Orpheus passed out of sight and the sound of his singing grew faint in the distance, Charon stood looking after him, and then with a sigh he sat down in his boat and bent to his oars once more.

And Orpheus went on his way, with hope beating high in his heart, till he came to the portals of the palace of Death. On the threshold lay Cerberus, the three-headed hound of hell, who night and day kept watch beside the gate to see that no one passed in save those who had died upon earth, and that those who had passed him once should pass him never again. When he heard Orpheus coming, he sprang to his feet and snarled and growled and bared his sharp white fangs; but as the strains of music grew clearer he sank silent to the ground, and stretched his three great heads between his paws. Orpheus, as he passed by, bent down and stroked him, and the fierce beast licked his hands. So did he enter into the gates of Death, and passed through the shadowy halls, till he stood before the throne of Pluto, the king. A dim and awful form did he sit, wrapped about in darkness and mist, and on his right hand sat Persephone, his wife, whom he stole from the meadows of Sicily. When he saw Orpheus, his eyes gleamed like the gleam of cold steel, and he stretched forth his gaunt right arm toward him.

"What dost thou here, Orpheus?" he asked.

"I am come to ask thee a boon, O king," he answered.

"There be many that ask me a boon," said Pluto, "but none that receive it."

"Yet none have stood before thee in the flesh, as I do, O king, to ask their boon."

"Because thou hast trespassed unlawfully on my domain, dost thou think I will grant thee thy boon?"

"Nay; but because my grief is so great that I have dared what none have dared before me, I pray thee to hear me."

Without waiting for an answer, he struck his lyre and sang to them the story of his life, and of how he had loved and lost Eurydice. The eyes of the pale queen brightened when she heard him, and the color came back to her cheeks, as the song brought back to her mind the days of her girlhood and the sunlit meadows of Sicily. Then a great pity filled her heart for Eurydice, who had left the green earth forever, and might not return, as she herself did, in the springtime, living only the dark winter months below. As Orpheus ceased his song she laid her hand upon her husband's.

"My lord," she said, "grant his boon, I pray thee. He is brave and true-hearted, and he sings as no man has ever sung before."

But the stern king sat with his head upon his hand and eyes cast down, deep in thought. At length he spoke, and his voice was soft and kind.

"Orpheus," he said, "thou hast touched my heart with thy singing. Yet it lies not with me to grant thee thy boon."

"But if the queen, thy wife, may return to the earth in the spring-time, may not Eurydice, too, come back at thy command?" asked Orpheus.

"The ways of the gods are not the ways of mortals, Orpheus; they walk by paths you may not tread. Yet, though I have no power to give thee back Eurydice, thou mayest win her thyself if thou hast the strength."

"How may that be?" cried Orpheus. "For the sake of Eurydice I have strength for any venture."

"No strength of the flesh can win her, Orpheus, but the strength of a faith unfaltering. I will send for her, and when thou seest her stand within the hall, holding out her hands toward thee, thou must harden thy heart, and turn and flee before her by the way thou camest. For the love of thee she will follow, and she will entreat thee to look at her and give her thy hand over the stony way. But thou must neither look at her nor speak to her. One look, one word, will be thine undoing, and she must vanish from thine eyes forever. The spell of thy song still rests upon the guardians of my kingdom, and they will let thee and thy wife pass by. But think not by word nor deed to help her. Alone she passed from life to death, and alone she must pass back from death to life. Her love and thy faith can be the only bond between you. Hast thou the strength for this?"

"My lord," cried Orpheus, " 'tis but a small thing to ask of a love like mine."

"It will be harder than thou thinkest," the king replied. "Nevertheless, I will call Eurydice."

He signed to a messenger to fetch her. In a few moments he returned, and behind him came Eurydice from the garden of Death. The dank dew hung heavy about her, and she walked with her eyes upon the ground, while her long black hair hid the paleness of her face. Thus did she come into the center of the hall, and, not speaking or moving, Orpheus gazed upon her till she raised her eyes and saw him. With a cry she sprang toward him.

"Orpheus!" she said.

But, remembering the words of the king, he turned and fled before her through the misty halls and out by the great gate, where Cerberus lay tamed with his heads between his paws. And he tried to shut his ears to her pleading as they sped across the plain, but every word that she said cut his heart like a stab, and more than once he almost turned to answer her, so piteous was her cry.

"O Orpheus, what have I done? Why dost thou flee from me? O give me one word, one look, to say thou lov'st me still."

But he remained firm in his resolve, and sat himself in Charon's boat, and steeled his heart, whilst she sat beside him, but could not touch him. For he was a living soul, and she was a shade, and might not touch him if she would. But still she pleaded with him.

"O Orpheus, my heart is starving for one look, one word. I know thou lovest me, but oh! to see thine eyes tell me so and hear thy lips say it!"

He longed to turn and clasp her in his arms, and tell her how he loved her better than life. But still he refrained, and hugged his lyre close to his breast in his agony; and as soon as the boat touched the shore he leapt out and hastened up the steep, dark path, whilst the sweat stood out in drops upon his brow, so hard was the way and so stifling the air. Behind him followed Eurydice, and if the way was hard for him, for her it was ten times harder. She had no strength for words, and only by her sobs did Orpheus know she was following still. So they went on, till at length the air grew pure and fresh, and the daylight shone before them at the mouth of the cave. With eager steps Orpheus pressed forward, longing for the moment when he might clasp his wife in his arms and speak to her once more. But as the way grew easier for him, it grew harder for Eurydice; since no one may pass from death to life without sore travail and pain. So she struggled and stumbled after him, and her heart gave way within her as she felt she could follow no farther.

"Orpheus!" she cried in her despair, "thy hand."

Ere reason could restrain him, his heart had answered her sudden cry, and he turned and held out his arms to help her. All too late he knew his folly. Even as he was about to hold her she slipped away, and as smoke is borne away on the wings of the wind, so was she borne away, helpless and lifeless, to the realms of the dead, and her voice floated back like the echo of a dream.

"Farewell, Orpheus. Alas! Alas! Farewell!"

So for the second time did he lose Eurydice; and if his grief was great before, it was ten times greater now. For as the cup of joy had touched his lips it had slipped from his hand and broken, and he knew that the chance the gods had given him once they would give him never again, but that all his life long he must dwell in loneliness without Eurydice his wife. Blindly he went forward with his lyre beneath his arm. The strings hung broken and lifeless, for the rocks and thorns had torn them as he passed on his way up from Hades. But he heeded not nor made any effort to mend them, for the strings of his heart hung broken too, and the music in his soul was dead. In black despair he wandered on, and the sunshine to his eyes was darkness and the fair forms of earth were sadder than the phantoms of Hades had seemed to him while hope still beat in his breast. As a colt that has wandered far by unknown paths returns at last surely to his homestead, so did his feet carry him back to Pelion and the dear home of his boyhood. Not till he stood in the path which led up to the cave did he know where he had come; but when he saw the mouth of the cave before him his eyes were opened once more, and a faint joy stole into his heart as he went on and sat down on a stone outside. All was silent and deserted, and he sat for a while alone with his own sad thoughts, till he felt a touch upon his shoulder, and looked up into the face of Cheiron standing beside him.

"O my master!" he cried.

"My son, thou hast suffered," said Cheiron.

"I have been down into Hades, Cheiron," he answered.

"My child," said Cheiron, "I know it all."

He gazed upon him, his great mild eyes full of pity, and Orpheus gazed back at him, and knew that he understood, though how he had learnt his tale he could not tell. His heart drew comfort from the sympathy that understood without words, and was softened as the parched earth is softened by rain, so that he took Cheiron's hands between his, and bowed his head upon them, and wept.

Thus it came to pass that he returned to his boyhood's home, and dwelt once more with Cheiron and his lads beneath the shade of snow-capped Pelion. In time the bitterness of his grief was purged away, and he remembered Eurydice as something bright and fair that had been woven into the web of his life while yet it was young, and which could never be taken away. As he listened again to the old songs which Cheiron had sung to him and his comrades when they were lads, the fire and the eagerness of his youth were born once more within him. When he saw the elder ones go forth into the world, and little lads brought up to take their place with Cheiron, he felt how life stands ever beckoning and calling to those in whose veins the blood of gods and heroes runs, and they go forth to rule and to serve, to fight and to labor, in answer to the call which the foolish do not hear. So one morning he took his lyre, which for many a long day had lain silent, and putting fresh strings for the ones that were broken, he passed his fingers lovingly over them as of old. And the spirit of music sprang to life once more in his heart, as the flowers spring to life when the winter is past, so that once again he could charm every living thing by the magic of his song.

THE GOLDEN TOUCH

By NATHANIEL HAWTHORNE

ONCE upon a time, there lived a very rich man, and a king besides, whose name was Midas; and he had a little daughter, whom nobody but myself ever heard of, and whose name I either never knew, or have entirely forgotten. So, because I love odd names for little girls, I choose to call her Marygold.

This King Midas was fonder of gold than of anything else in the world. He valued his royal crown chiefly because it was composed of that precious metal. If he loved anything better, or half so well, it was the one little maiden who played so merrily around her father's footstool. But the more Midas loved his daughter, the more did he desire and seek for wealth. He thought, foolish man! that the best thing he could possibly do for this dear child would be to bequeath her the immensest pile of yellow, glistening coin, that had ever been heaped together since the world was made. Thus, he gave all his thoughts and all his time to this one purpose. If ever he happened to gaze for an instant at the gold-tinted clouds of sunset, he wished that they were real gold, and that they could be squeezed safely into his strong box. When little Marygold ran to meet him, with a bunch of buttercups and dandelions, he used to say, "Poh, poh, child! If these flowers were as golden as they look, they would be worth the plucking!"

And yet, in his earlier days, before he was so entirely possessed of this insane desire for riches, King Midas had shown a great taste for flowers. He had planted a garden, in which grew the biggest and beautifullest and sweetest roses that any mortal ever saw or smelt. These roses were still growing in the garden, as large, as lovely, and as fragrant, as when Midas used to pass whole hours in gazing at them, and inhaling their perfume. But now, if he looked at them at all, it was only to calculate how much the garden would be worth if each of the innumerable rose petals were a thin plate of gold. And though he once was fond of music (in spite of an idle story about his ears, which were said to resemble those of an ass), the only music for poor Midas, now, was the chink of one coin against another.

At length (as people always grow more and more foolish, unless they take care to grow wiser and wiser), Midas had got to be so exceedingly unreasonable, that he could scarcely bear to see or touch any object that was not gold. He made it his custom, therefore, to pass a large portion of every day in a dark and dreary apartment, underground, at the basement of his palace. It was here that he kept his wealth. To this dismal hole—for it was little better than a dungeon—Midas betook himself, whenever he wanted to be particularly happy. Here, after carefully locking the door, he would take a bag of gold coin, or a gold cup as big as a washbowl, or a heavy golden bar, or a peck measure of gold dust, and bring them from the obscure corners of the room into the one bright and narrow sunbeam that fell from the dungeon-like window. He valued the sunbeam for no other reason but that his treasure would not shine without its help. And then would he reckon over the coins in the bag; toss up the bar, and catch it as it came down; sift the gold dust through his fingers; look at the funny image of his own face, as reflected in the burnished circumference of the cup; and whisper to himself, "O Midas, rich King Midas, what a happy man art thou!" But it was laughable to see how the image of his face kept grinning at him, out of the polished surface of the cup. It seemed to be aware of his foolish behavior, and to have a naughty inclination to make fun of him.

Midas called himself a happy man, but felt that he was not yet quite so happy as he might be. The very tiptop of enjoyment would never be reached, unless the whole world were to become his treasure room, and be filled with yellow metal which should be all his own.

Now, I need hardly remind such wise little people as you are, that in the old, old times, when King Midas was alive, a great many things came to pass, which we should consider wonderful if they were to happen in our own day and country. And, on the other hand, a great many things take place nowadays, which seem not only wonderful to us, but at which the people of old times would have stared their eyes out. On the whole, I regard our own times as the stranger of the two; but, however that may be, I must go on with my story.

Midas was enjoying himself in his treasure room, one day, as usual, when he perceived a shadow fall over the heaps of gold; and, looking suddenly up, what should he behold but the figure of a stranger, standing in the bright and narrow sunbeam! It was a young man, with a cheerful and ruddy face. Whether it was that the imagination of King Midas threw a yellow tinge over everything, or whatever the cause might be, he could not help fancying that the smile with which the stranger regarded him had a kind of golden radiance in it. Certainly, although his figure intercepted the sunshine, there was now a brighter gleam upon all the piled-up treasures than before. Even the remotest corners had their share of it, and were lighted up, when the stranger smiled, as with tips of flame and sparkles of fire.

As Midas knew that he had carefully turned the key in the lock, and that no mortal strength could possibly break into his treasure room, he, of course, concluded that his visitor must be something more than mortal. It is no matter about telling you who he was. In those days, when the earth was comparatively a new affair, it was supposed to be often the resort of beings endowed with supernatural power, and who used to interest themselves in the joys and sorrows of men, women, and children, half playfully and half seriously. Midas had met such beings before now, and was not sorry to meet one of them again. The stranger's aspect, indeed, was so good-humored and kindly, if not beneficent, that it would have been unreasonable to suspect him of intending any mischief. It was far more probable that he came to do Midas a favor. And what could that favor be, unless to multiply his heaps of treasure?

The stranger gazed about the room; and when his lustrous smile had glistened upon all the golden objects that were there, he turned again to Midas.

"You are a wealthy man, friend Midas!" he observed. "I doubt whether any other four walls, on earth, contain so much gold as you have contrived to pile up in this room."

"I have done pretty well—pretty well," answered Midas, in a discontented tone. "But, after all, it is but a trifle, when you consider that it has taken me my whole life to get it together. If one could live a thousand years, he might have time to grow rich!"

"What!" exclaimed the stranger. "Then you are not satisfied?"

Midas shook his head.

"And pray what would satisfy you?" asked the stranger. "Merely for the curiosity of the thing, I should be glad to know."

Midas paused and meditated. He felt a presentiment that this stranger, with such a golden luster in his good-humored smile, had come hither with both the power and the purpose of gratifying his utmost wishes. Now, therefore, was the fortunate moment, when he had but to speak, and obtain whatever possible, or seemingly impossible thing, it might come into his head to ask. So he thought, and thought, and thought, and heaped up one golden mountain upon another, in his imagination, without being able to imagine them big enough. At last, a bright idea occurred to King Midas. It seemed really as bright as the glistening metal which he loved so much.

Raising his head, he looked the lustrous stranger in the face.

"Well, Midas," observed his visitor, "I see that you have at length hit upon something that will satisfy you. Tell me your wish."

"It is only this," replied Midas. "I am weary of collecting my treasures with so much trouble, and beholding the heap so diminutive, after I have done my best, I wish everything that I touch to be changed to gold!"

The stranger's smile grew so very broad, that it seemed to fill the room like an outburst of the sun, gleaming into a shadowy dell, where the yellow autumnal leaves—for so looked the lumps and particles of gold—lie strewn in the glow of light.

"The Golden Touch!" exclaimed he. "You certainly deserve credit, friend Midas, for striking out so brilliant a conception. But are you quite sure that this will satisfy you,"

"How could it fail?" said Midas.

"And will you never regret the possession of it?"

"What could induce me?" asked Midas. "I ask nothing else, to render me perfectly happy."

"Be it as you wish, then," replied the stranger, waving his hand in token of farewell. "Tomorrow, at sunrise, you will find yourself gifted with the Golden Touch."

The figure of the stranger then became exceedingly bright, and Midas involuntarily closed his eyes. On opening them again, he beheld only one yellow sunbeam in the room, and, all around him, the glistening of the precious metal which he had spent his life in hoarding up.

Whether Midas slept as usual that night, the story does not say. Asleep or awake, however, his mind was probably in the state of a child's, to whom a beautiful new plaything has been promised in the morning. At any rate, day had hardly peeped over the hills, when King Midas was broad awake, and, stretching his arms out of bed, began to touch the objects that were within reach. He was anxious to prove whether the Golden Touch had really come, according to the stranger's promise. So he laid his finger on a chair by the bedside, and on various other things, but was grievously disappointed to perceive that they remained of exactly the same substance as before. Indeed, he felt very much afraid that he had only dreamed about the lustrous stranger, or else that the latter had been making game of him. And what a miserable affair would it be, if, after all his hopes, Midas must content himself with what little gold he could scrape together by ordinary means, instead of creating it by a touch!

All this while, it was only the gray of the morning, with but a streak of brightness along the edge of the sky, where Midas could not see it. He lay in a very disconsolate mood, regretting the downfall of his hopes, and kept growing sadder and sadder, until the earliest sunbeam shone through the window, and gilded the ceiling over his head. It seemed to Midas that this bright yellow sunbeam was reflected in rather a singular way on the white covering of the bed. Looking more closely, what was his astonishment and delight, when he found that this linen fabric had been transmuted to what seemed a woven texture of the purest and brightest gold! The Golden Touch had come to him with the first sunbeam!

Midas started up, in a kind of joyful frenzy, and ran about the room, grasping at everything that happened to be in his way. He seized one of the bedposts, and it became immediately a fluted golden pillar. He pulled aside a window curtain, in order to admit a clear spectacle of the wonders which he was performing; and the tassel grew heavy in his hand—a mass of gold. He took up a book from the table. At his first touch, it assumed the appearance of such a splendidly bound and gilt-edged volume as one often meets with, nowadays; but, on running his fingers through the leaves, behold! it was a bundle of thin golden plates, in which all the wisdom of the book had grown illegible. He hurriedly put on his clothes, and was enraptured to see himself in a magnificent suit of gold cloth, which retained its flexibility and softness, although it burdened him a little with its weight. He drew out his handkerchief, which little Marygold had hemmed for him. That was likewise gold, with the dear child's neat and pretty stitches running all along the border, in gold thread!

Somehow or other, this last transformation did not quite please King Midas. He would rather that his little daugher's handiwork should have remained just the same as when she climbed his knee and put it into his hand.

But it was not worth while to vex himself about a trifle. Midas now took his spectacles from his pocket, and put them on his nose, in order that he might see more distinctly what he was about. In those days, spectacles for common people had not been invented, but were already worn by kings; else, how could Midas have had any?

To his great perplexity, however, excellent as the glasses were, he discovered that he could not possibly see through them. But this was the most natural thing in the world; for, on taking them off, the transparent crystal turned out to be plates of yellow metal, and, of course, were worthless as spectacles, though valuable as gold. It struck Midas as rather inconvenient that, with all his wealth, he could never again be rich enough to own a pair of serviceable spectacles.

"It is no great matter, nevertheless," said he to himself, very philosophically. "We cannot expect any great good, without its being accompanied with some small inconvenience. The Golden Touch is worth the sacrifice of a pair of spectacles, at least, if not of one's very eyesight. My own eyes will serve for ordinary purposes, and little Marygold will soon be old enough to read to me."

Wise King Midas was so exalted by his good fortune, that the palace seemed not sufficiently spacious to contain him. He therefore went downstairs, and smiled, on observing that the balustrade of the staircase became a bar of burnished gold, as his hand passed over it, in his descent. He lifted the door latch (it was brass only a moment ago, but golden when his fingers quitted it), and emerged into the garden. Here, as it happened, he found a great number of beautiful roses in full bloom, and others in all the stages of lovely bud and blossom. Very delicious was their fragrance in the morning breeze. Their delicate blush was one of the fairest sights in the world; so gentle, so modest, and so full of sweet tranquillity, did these roses seem to be.

But Midas knew a way to make them far more precious, according to his way of thinking, than roses had ever been before. So he took great pains in going from bush to bush, and exercised his magic touch most indefatigably; until every individual flower and bud, and even the worms at the heart of some of them, were changed to gold. By the time this good work was completed, King Midas was summoned to breakfast; and as the morning air had given him an excellent appetite, he made haste back to the palace.

What was usually a king's breakfast in the days of Midas, I really do not know, and cannot stop now to investigate. To the best of my belief, however, on this particular morning, the breakfast consisted of hot cakes, some nice little brook trout, roasted potatoes, fresh boiled eggs, and coffee, for King Midas himself, and a bowl of bread and milk for his daughter Marygold. At all events, this is a breakfast fit to set before a king; and, whether he had it or not, King Midas could not have had a better.

Little Marygold had not yet made her appearance. Her father ordered her to be called, and, seating himself at table, awaited the child's coming, in order to begin his own breakfast. To do Midas justice, he really loved his daughter, and loved her so much the more this morning, on account of the good fortune which had befallen him. It was not a great while before he heard her coming along the passageway crying bitterly. This circumstance surprised him, because Marygold was one of the cheerfullest little people whom you would see in a summer's day, and hardly shed a thimbleful of tears in a twelve-month. When Midas heard her sobs, he determined to put little Marygold into better spirits, by an agreeable surprise; so, leaning across the table, he touched his daughter's bowl (which was a China one, with pretty figures all around it), and transmuted it to gleaming gold.

Meanwhile, Marygold slowly and disconsolately opened the door, and showed herself with her apron at her eyes, still sobbing as if her heart would break.

"How now, my little lady!" cried Midas. "Pray what is the matter with you, this bright morning?"

Marygold, without taking the apron from her eyes, held out her hand, in which was one of the roses which Midas had so recently transmuted.

"Beautiful!" exclaimed her father. "And what is there in this magnificent golden rose to make you cry?"

"Ah, dear father!" answered the child, as well as her sobs would let her; "it is not beautiful, but the ugliest flower that ever grew!

"As soon as I was dressed I ran into the garden to gather some roses for you; because I know you like them, and like them the better when gathered by your little daughter. But, oh dear, dear me! What do you think has happened? Such a misfortune! All the beautiful roses, that smelled so sweetly and had so many lovely blushes, are blighted and spoilt! They are grown quite yellow, as you see this one, and have no longer any fragrance! What can have been the matter with them?"

"Poh, my dear little girl—pray don't cry about it!" said Midas, who was ashamed to confess that he himself had wrought the change which so greatly afflicted her. "Sit down and eat your bread and milk! You will find it easy enough to exchange a golden rose like that (which will last hundreds of years) for an ordinary one which would wither in a day."

"I don't care for such roses as this!" cried Marygold, tossing it contemptuously away. "It has no smell, and the hard petals prick my nose!"

The child now sat down to table, but was so occupied with her grief for the blighted roses that she did not even notice the wonderful transmutation of her China bowl. Perhaps this was all the better; for Marygold was accustomed to take pleasure in looking at the queer figures, and strange trees and houses, that were painted on the circumference of the bowl; and these ornaments were now entirely lost in the yellow hue of the metal.

Midas, meanwhile, had poured out a cup of coffee, and, as a matter of course, the coffeepot, whatever metal it may have been when he took it up, was gold when he set it down. He thought to himself, that it was rather an extravagant style of splendor, in a king of his simple habits, to breakfast off a service of gold, and began to be puzzled with the difficulty of keeping his treasures safe. The cupboard and the kitchen would no longer be a secure place of deposit for articles so valuable as golden bowls and coffeepots.

Amid these thoughts, he lifted a spoonful of coffee to his lips, and, sipping it, was astonished to perceive that, the instant his lips touched the liquid, it became molten gold, and the next moment, hardened into a lump! "Ha!" exclaimed Midas, rather aghast.

"What is the matter, father?" asked little Marygold, gazing at him, with the tears still standing in her eyes.

"Nothing, child, nothing!" said Midas. "Eat your milk, before it gets quite cold."

He took one of the nice little trouts on his plate, and, by way of experiment, touched its tail with his finger. To his horror, it was immediately transmuted from an admirably fried brook trout into a gold fish, though not one of those goldfishes which people often keep in glass globes, as ornaments for the parlor. No; but it was really a metallic fish, and looked as if it had been very cunningly made by the nicest goldsmith in the world. Its little bones were now golden wires; its fins and tail were thin plates of gold; and there were the marks of the fork in it, and all the delicate, frothy appearance of a nicely fried fish, exactly imitated in metal. A very pretty piece of work, as you may suppose; only King Midas, just at that moment, would much rather have had a real trout in his dish than this elaborate and valuable imitation of one.

"I don't quite see," thought he to himself, "how I am to get any breakfast."

He took one of the smoking-hot cakes, and had scarcely broken it, when, to his cruel mortification, though, a moment before, it had been of the whitest wheat, it assumed the yellow hue of Indian meal. To say the truth, if it had really been a hot Indian cake, Midas would have prized it a good deal more than he now did, when its solidity and increased weight made him too bitterly sensible that it was gold. Almost in despair, he helped himself to a boiled egg, which immediately underwent a change similar to those of the trout and the cake. The egg, indeed, might have been mistaken for one of those which the famous goose, in the story book, was in the habit of laying; but King Midas was the only goose that had anything to do with the matter.

"Well, this is a quandary!" thought he, leaning back in his chair, and looking quite enviously at little Marygold, who was now eating her bread and milk with great satisfaction. "Such a costly breakfast before me, and nothing that can be eaten!"

Hoping that, by dint of great dispatch, he might avoid what he now felt to be a considerable inconvenience, King Midas next snatched a hot potato, and attempted to cram it into his mouth, and swallow it in a hurry. But the Golden Touch was too nimble for him. He found his mouth full, not of mealy potato, but of solid metal, which so burnt his tongue that he roared aloud, and, jumping up from the table, began to dance and stamp about the room, both with pain and affright.

"Father, dear father!" cried little Marygold, who was a very affectionate child, "pray what is the matter? Have you burnt your mouth?"

"Ah, dear child," groaned Midas, dolefully, "I don't know what is to become of your poor father!"

And, truly, my dear little folks, did you ever hear of such a pitiable case in all your lives? Here was literally the richest breakfast that could be set before a king, and its very richness made it absolutely good for nothing. The poorest laborer, sitting down to his crust of bread and cup of water, was far better off than King Midas, whose delicate food was really worth its weight in gold. And what was to be done? Already, at breakfast, Midas was excessively hungry. Would he be less so by dinner time? And how ravenous would be his appetite for supper, which must undoubtedly consist of the same sort of indigestible dishes as those now before him! How many days, think you, would he survive a continuance of this rich fare?

These reflections so troubled wise King Midas, that he began to doubt whether, after all, riches are the one desirable thing in the world, or even the most desirable. But this was only a passing thought. So fascinated was Midas with the glitter of the yellow metal, that he would still have refused to give up the Golden Touch for so paltry a consideration as a breakfast. Just imagine what a price for one meal's victuals! It would have been the same as paying millions and millions of money (and as many millions more as would take forever to reckon up), for some fried trout, an egg, a potato, a hot cake, and a cup of coffee!

"It would be quite too dear," thought Midas.

Nevertheless, so great was his hunger, and the perplexity of his situation, that he again groaned aloud, and very grievously too. Our pretty Marygold could endure it no longer. She sat, a moment, gazing at her father, and trying, with all the might of her little wits, to find out what was the matter with him. Then, with a sweet and sorrowful impulse to comfort him, she started from her chair, and, running to Midas, threw her arms affectionately about his knees. He bent down and kissed her. He felt that his little daughter's love was worth a thousand times more than the Golden Touch.

"My precious, precious Marygold!" cried he.

But Marygold made no answer.

Alas, what had he done? How fatal was the gift which the stranger bestowed! The moment the lips of Midas touched Marygold's forehead, a change had taken place. Her sweet, rosy face, so full of affection as it had been, assumed a glittering yellow color, with yellow teardrops congealing on her cheeks. Her beautiful brown ringlets took the same tint. Her soft and tender little form grew hard and inflexible within her father's encircling arms. Oh, terrible misfortune! The victim of his insatiable desire for wealth, little Marygold was a human child no longer, but a golden statue!

Yes, there she was, with the questioning look of love, grief, and pity, hardened into her face. It was the prettiest and most woeful sight that ever mortal saw. All the features and tokens of Marygold were there; even the beloved little dimple remained in her golden chin. But the more perfect was the resemblance, the greater was the father's agony at beholding this golden image, which was all that was left him of a daughter. It had been a favorite phrase of Midas, whenever he felt particularly fond of the child, to say that she was worth her weight in gold. And now the phrase had become literally true. And now, at last, when it was too late, he felt how infinitely a warm and tender heart, that loved him, exceeded in value all the wealth that could be piled up betwixt the earth and sky!

It would be too sad a story, if I were to tell you how Midas, in the fullness of all his gratified desires, began to wring his hands and bemoan himself; and how he could neither bear to look at Marygold, nor yet to look away from her. Except when his eyes were fixed on the image, he could not possibly believe that she had been changed to gold.

But, stealing another glance, there was the precious little figure, with a yellow teardrop on its yellow cheek, and a look so piteous and tender, that it seemed as if that very expression must needs soften the gold, and make it flesh again. This, however, could not be. So Midas had only to wring his hands, and to wish that he were the poorest man in the wide world, if the loss of all his wealth might bring back the faintest rose color to his dear child's face.

While he was in this tumult of despair, he suddenly beheld a stranger standing near the door. Midas bent down his head, without speaking; for he recognized the same figure which had appeared to him, the day before, in the treasure room, and had bestowed on him this disastrous faculty of the Golden Touch. The stranger's countenance still wore a smile, which seemed to shed a yellow luster all about the room, and gleamed on little Marygold's image, and on the other objects that had been transmuted by the touch of Midas.

"Well, friend Midas," said the stranger, "pray how do you succeed with the Golden Touch?"

Midas shook his head.

"I am very miserable," said he.

"Very miserable, indeed!" exclaimed the stranger. "And how happens that? Have I not faithfully kept my promise with you? Have you not everything that your heart desired?"

"Gold is not everything," answered Midas. "And I have lost all that my heart really cared for."

"Ah! So you have made a discovery, since yesterday?" observed the stranger. "Let us see, then. Which of these two things do you think is really worth the most—the gift of the Golden Touch, or one cup of clear cold water?"

"O blessed water!" exclaimed Midas. "It will never moisten my parched throat again!"

"The Golden Touch," continued the stranger, "or a crust of bread?"

"A piece of bread," answered Midas, "is worth all the gold on earth!"

"The Golden Touch," asked the stranger, "or your own little Marygold, warm, soft, and loving as she was an hour ago?"

"Oh, my child, my dear child!" cried poor Midas, wringing his hands. "I would not have given that one small dimple in her chin for the power of changing this whole big earth into a solid lump of gold!"

"You are wiser than you were, King Midas!" said the stranger, looking seriously at him. "Your own heart, I perceive, has not been entirely changed from flesh to gold. Were it so, your case would indeed be desperate. But you appear to be still capable of understanding that the commonest things, such as lie within everybody's grasp, are more valuable than the riches which so many mortals sigh and struggle after. Tell me, now, do you sincerely desire to rid yourself of this Golden Touch?"

"It is hateful to me!" replied Midas.

A fly settled on his nose, but immediately fell to the floor; for it, too, had become gold. Midas shuddered.

"Go, then," said the stranger, "and plunge into the river that glides past the bottom of your garden. Take likewise a vase of the same water, and sprinkle it over any object that you may desire to change back again from gold into its former substance. If you do this in earnestness and sincerity, it may possibly repair the mischief which your avarice has occasioned."

King Midas bowed low; and when he lifted his head the lustrous stranger had vanished.

You will easily believe that Midas lost no time in snatching up a great earthen pitcher (but, alas me! it was no longer earthen after he touched it), and hastening to the riverside. As he scampered along, and forced his way through the shrubbery, it was positively marvelous to see how the foliage turned yellow behind him, as if the autumn had been there, and nowhere else. On reaching the river's brink, he plunged headlong in, without waiting so much as to pull off his shoes.

"Poof! poof! poof!" snorted King Midas, as his head emerged out of the water. "Well; this is really a refreshing bath, and I think it must have quite washed away the Golden Touch. And now for filling my pitcher!"

As he dipped the pitcher into the water, it gladdened his very heart to see it change from gold into the same good, honest earthen vessel which it had been before he touched it. He was conscious, also, of a change within himself. A cold, hard, and heavy weight seemed to have gone out of his bosom. No doubt, his heart had been gradually losing its human substance, and transmuting itself into insensible metal, but had now softened back again into flesh. Perceiving a violet, that grew on the bank of the river, Midas touched it with his finger, and was overjoyed to find that the delicate flower retained its purple hue, instead of undergoing a yellow blight. The curse of the Golden Touch had, therefore, really been removed from him.

King Midas hastened back to the palace; and, I suppose, the servants knew not what to make of it when they saw their royal master so carefully bringing home an earthen pitcher of water. But that water, which was to undo all the mischief that his folly had wrought, was more precious to Midas than an ocean of molten gold could have been. The first thing he did, as you need hardly be told, was to sprinkle handfuls over the golden figure of little Marygold.

No sooner did it fall on her than you would have laughed to see how the rosy color came back to the dear child's cheek! and how she began to sneeze and sputter!—and how astonished she was to find herself dripping wet, and her father still throwing more water over her!

"Pray do not, dear father!" cried she. "See how you have wet my nice frock, which I put on only this morning!"

For Marygold did not know that she had been a little golden statue; nor could she remember anything that had happened since the moment when she ran with outstretched arms to comfort poor King Midas.

Her father did not think it necessary to tell his beloved child how very foolish he had been, but contented himself with showing how much wiser he had now grown. For this purpose, he led little Marygold into the garden, where he sprinkled all the remainder of the water over the rose bushes, and with such good effect that above five thousand roses recovered their beautiful bloom. There were two circumstances, however, which, as long as he lived, used to put King Midas in mind of the Golden Touch. One was, that the sands of the river sparkled like gold; the other, that little Marygold's hair had now a golden tinge, which he had never observed in it before she had been transmuted by the effect of his kiss. This change of hue was really an improvement, and made Marygold's hair richer than in her babyhood.

When King Midas had grown quite an old man, and used to trot Marygold's children on his knee, he was fond of telling them this marvelous story, pretty much as I have now told it to you. And then would he stroke their glossy ringlets, and tell them that their hair, likewise, had a rich shade of gold, which they had inherited from their mother.

"And to tell you the truth, my precious little folks," quoth King Midas, diligently trotting the children all the while, "ever since that morning, I have hated the very sight of all other gold, save this!"

THE CHIMAERA

By NATHANIEL HAWTHORNE

Illustration by Walter Crane

ONCE, in the old, old times (for all the strange things which I tell you about happened long before anybody can remember), a fountain gushed out of a hillside, in the marvelous land of Greece. And, for aught I know, after so many thousand years, it is still gushing out of the very selfsame spot. At any rate, there was the pleasant fountain, welling freshly forth and sparkling a-down the hillside, in the golden sunset, when a handsome young man named Bellerophon drew near its margin. In his hand he held a bridle, studded with brilliant gems, and adorned with a golden bit. Seeing an old man, and another of middle age, and a little boy, near the fountain, and likewise a maiden, who was dipping up some of the water in a pitcher, he paused, and begged that he might refresh himself with a draught.

"This is very delicious water," he said to the maiden as he rinsed and filled her pitcher, after drinking out of it. "Will you be kind enough to tell me whether the fountain has any name?"

"Yes; it is called the Fountain of Pirene," answered the maiden; and then she added, "My grandmother has told me that this clear fountain was once a beautiful woman; and when her son was killed by the arrows of the huntress Diana, she melted all away into tears. And so the water, which you find so cool and sweet, is the sorrow of that poor mother's heart!"

"I should not have dreamed," observed the young stranger, "that so clear a well spring, with its gush and gurgle, and its cheery dance out of the shade into the sunlight, had so much as one teardrop in its bosom! And this, then, is Pirene? I thank you, pretty maiden, for telling me its name. I have come from a far-away country to find this very spot." A middle-aged country fellow (he had driven his cow to drink out of the spring) stared hard at young Bellerophon, and at the handsome bridle he carried in his hand.

"The watercourses must be getting low, friend, in your part of the world," remarked he, "if you come so far only to find the Fountain of Pirene. But pray, have you lost a horse? I see you carry the bridle in your hand; and a very pretty one it is with that double row of bright stones upon it. If the horse was as fine as the bridle, you are much to be pitied for losing him."

"I have lost no horse," said Bellerophon, with a smile. "But I happen to be seeking a very famous one, which, as wise people have informed me, must be found hereabouts, if anywhere. Do you know whether the winged horse Pegasus still haunts the Fountain of Pirene, as he used to do in your forefathers' days?"

But then the country fellow laughed.

Some of you, my little friends, have probably heard that this Pegasus was a snow-white steed, with beautiful silvery wings, who spent most of his time on the summit of Mount Helicon. He was as wild, and as swift, and as buoyant, in his flight through the air, as any eagle that ever soared into the clouds. There was nothing else like him in the world. He had no mate; he never had been backed or bridled by a master; and, for many a long year, he led a solitary and a happy life.

Oh, how fine a thing it is to be a winged horse! Sleeping at night, as he did, on a lofty mountain-top, and passing the greater part of the day in the air, Pegasus seemed hardly to be a creature of the earth. Whenever he was seen, up very high above people's heads, with the sunshine on his silvery wings, you would have thought that he belonged to the sky, and that, skimming a little too low, he had got astray among our mists and vapors, and was seeking his way back again. It was very pretty to behold him plunge into the fleecy bosom of a bright cloud, and be lost in it, for a moment or two, and then break forth from the other side. Or, in a sullen rainstorm, when there was a gray pavement of clouds over the whole sky, it would sometimes happen that the winged horse descended right through it, and the glad light of the upper region would gleam after him. In another instant, it is true, both Pegasus and the pleasant light would be gone away together. But anyone that was fortunate enough to see this wondrous spectacle felt cheerful the whole day after, and as much longer as the storm lasted,

In the summertime, and in the beautifullest of weather, Pegasus often alighted on the solid earth, and, closing his silvery wings, would gallop over hill and dale for pastime, as fleetly as the wind. Oftener than in any other place, he had been seen near the Fountain of Pirene, drinking the delicious water, or rolling himself upon the soft grass of the margin. Sometimes, too (but Pegasus was very dainty in his food), he would crop a few of the clover blossoms that happened to be sweetest.

To the Fountain of Pirene, therefore, people's great-grandfathers had been in the habit of going (as long as they were youthful, and retained their faith in winged horses), in hopes of getting a glimpse at the beautiful Pegasus. But, of late years, he had been very seldom seen. Indeed, there were many of the country folk, dwelling within half an hour's walk of the fountain, who had never beheld Pegasus, and did not believe that there was any such creature in existence. The country fellow to whom Bellerophon was speaking chanced to be one of those incredulous persons.

And that was the reason why he laughed.

"Pegasus, indeed!" cried he, turning up his nose as high as such a flat nose could be turned up—"Pegasus, indeed! A winged horse, truly! Why, friend, are you in your senses? Of what use would wings be to a horse? Could he drag a plow so well, think you? To be sure, there might be a little saving in the expense of shoes; but then, how would a man like to see his horse flying out of the stable window?—yes, or whisking him up above the clouds, when he only wanted to ride to mill? No, no! I don't believe in Pegasus. There never was such a ridiculous kind of a horse-fowl made!"

"I have some reason to think otherwise," said Bellerophon, quietly.

And then he turned to an old, gray man, who was leaning on a staff, and listening very attentively, with his head stretched forward, and one hand at his ear, because, for the last twenty years, he had been getting rather deaf.

"And what say you, venerable sir?" inquired he. "In your younger days, I should imagine, you must frequently have seen the winged steed!"

"Ah, young stranger, my memory is very poor!" said the aged man. "When I was a lad, if I remember rightly, I used to believe there was such a horse, and so did everybody else. But, nowadays, I hardly know what to think, and very seldom think about the winged horse at all. If I ever saw the creature, it was a long, long while ago; and, to tell you the truth, I doubt whether I ever did see him. One day, to be sure, when I was quite a youth, I remember seeing some hoof-tramps round about the brink of the fountain. Pegasus might have made those hoof-marks; and so might some other horse."

"And have you never seen him, my fair maiden?" asked Bellerophon of the girl, who stood with the pitcher on her head, while this talk went on. "You certainly could see Pegasus, if anybody can, for your eyes are very bright."

"Once I thought I saw him," replied the maiden, with a smile and a blush. "It was either Pegasus, or a large white bird, a very great way up in the air. And one other time, as I was coming to the fountain with my pitcher, I heard a neigh. Oh, such a brisk and melodious neigh as that was! My very heart leaped with delight at the sound. But it startled me, nevertheless; so that I ran home without filling my pitcher."

"That was truly a pity!" said Bellerophon.

And he turned to the child, whom I mentioned at the beginning of the story, and who was gazing at him, as children are apt to gaze at strangers, with his rosy mouth wide open.

"Well, my little fellow," cried Bellerophon, playfully pulling one of his curls, "I suppose you have often seen the winged horse."

"That I have," answered the child, very readily. "I saw him yesterday, and many times before."

"You are a fine little man!" said Bellerophon, drawing the child closer to him. "Come, tell me all about it."

"Why," replied the child. "I often come here to sail little boats in the fountain, and gather pretty pebbles out of its basin. And sometimes, when I look down into the water, I see the image of the winged horse, in the picture of the sky that is there. I wish he would come down, and take me on his back, and let me ride him up to the moon! But, if I so much as stir to look at him, he flies far away out of sight."

And Bellerophon put his faith in the child, who had seen the image of Pegasus in the water, and in the maiden, who had heard him neigh so melodiously, rather than in the middle-aged clown, who believed only in cart horses, or in the old man who had forgotten the beautiful things of his youth.

Therefore, he haunted about the Fountain of Pirene for a great many days afterwards. He kept continually on the watch, looking upward at the sky, or else down into the water, hoping forever that he should see either the reflected image of the winged horse, or the marvelous reality. He held the bridle, with its bright gems and golden bit, always ready in his hand. The rustic people, who dwelt in the neighborhood, and drove their cattle to the fountain to drink, would often laugh at poor Bellerophon, and sometimes take him pretty severely to task. They told him that an able-bodied young man, like himself, ought to have better business than to be wasting his time in such an idle pursuit. They offered to sell him a horse, if he wanted one; and when Bellerophon declined the purchase, they tried to drive a bargain with him for his fine bridle.

Even the country boys thought him so very foolish, that they used to have a great deal of sport about him, and were rude enough not to care a fig, although Bellerophon saw and heard it. One little urchin, for example, would play Pegasus, and cut the oddest imaginable capers, by way of flying; while one of his schoolfellows would scamper after him, holding forth a twist of bulrushes, which was intended to represent Bellerophon's ornamental bridle. But the gentle child, who had seen the picture of Pegasus in the water, comforted the young stranger more than all the naughty boys could torment him. The dear little fellow, in his play-hours, often sat down beside him, and, without speaking a word, would look down into the fountain and up toward the sky, with so innocent a faith, that Bellerophon could not help feeling encouraged.

Now you will, perhaps, wish to be told why it was that Bellerophon had undertaken to catch the winged horse. And we shall find no better opportunity to speak about this matter than while he is waiting for Pegasus to appear.

If I were to relate the whole of Bellerophon's previous adventures, they might easily grow into a very long story. It will be quite enough to say, that, in a certain country of Asia, a terrible monster, called a Chimæra, had made its appearance, and was doing more mischief than could be talked about between now and sunset. According to the best accounts which I have been able to obtain, this Chimæra was nearly, if not quite, the ugliest and most poisonous creature, and the strangest and unaccountablest, and the hardest to fight with, and the most difficult to run away from, that ever came out of the earth's inside. It had a tail like a boa constructor; its body was like I do not care what; and it had three separate heads, one of which was a lion's, the second a goat's, and the third an abominably great snake's. And a hot blast of fire came flaming out of each of its three mouths! Being an earthly monster, I doubt whether it had any wings; but, wings or no, it ran like a goat and a lion, and wriggled along like a serpent, and thus contrived to make about as much speed as all three together.

Oh, the mischief, and mischief, and mischief that this naughty creature did! With its flaming breath, it could set a forest on fire, or burn up a field of grain, or, for that matter, a village, with all its fences and houses. It laid waste the whole country round about, and used to eat up people and animals alive, and cook them afterwards in the burning oven of its stomach. Mercy on us, little children, I hope neither you nor I will ever happen to meet a Chimæra!

While the hateful beast (if a beast we can anywise call it) was doing all these horrible things, it so chanced that Bellerophon came to that part of the world, on a visit to the king. The king's name was Iobates, and Lycia was the country which he ruled over. Bellerophon was one of the bravest youths in the world, and desired nothing so much as to do some valiant and beneficent deed, such as would make all mankind admire and love him. In those days, the only way for a young man to distinguish himself was by fighting battles, either with the enemies of his country, or with wicked giants, or with troublesome dragons, or with wild beasts, when he could find nothing more dangerous to encounter. King Iobates, perceiving the courage of his youthful visitor, proposed to him to go and fight the Chimæra, which everybody else was afraid of, and which, unless it should be soon killed, was likely to convert Lycia into a desert. Bellerophon hesitated not a moment, but assured the king that he would either slay this dreaded Chimæra, or perish in the attempt.

But, in the first place, as the monster was so prodigiously swift, he bethought himself that he should never win the victory by fighting on foot. The wisest thing he could do, therefore, was to get the very best and fleetest horse that could anywhere be found. And what other horse, in all the world, was half so fleet as the marvelous horse Pegasus, who had wings as well as legs, and was even more active in the air than on the earth? To be sure, a great many people denied that there was any such horse with wings, and said that the stories about him were all poetry and nonsense. But, wonderful as it appeared, Bellerophon believed that Pegasus was a real steed, and hoped that he himself might be fortunate enough to find him; and, once fairly mounted on his back, he would be able to fight the Chimæra at better advantage.

And this was the purpose with which he had traveled from Lycia to Greece, and had brought the beautifully ornamented bridle in his hand. It was an enchanted bridle. If he could only succeed in putting the golden bit into the mouth of Pegasus, the winged horse would be submissive, and would own Bellerophon for his master, and fly whithersoever he might choose to turn the rein.

But, indeed, it was a weary and anxious time, while Bellerophon waited and waited for Pegasus, in hopes that he would come and drink at the Fountain of Pirene. He was afraid lest King Iobates should imagine that he had fled from the Chimæra. It pained him, too, to think how much mischief the monster was doing, while he himself, instead of fighting with it, was compelled to sit idly poring over the bright waters of Pirene, as they gushed out of the sparkling sand. And as Pegasus came thither so seldom in these latter years, and scarcely alighted there more than once in a lifetime, Bellerophon feared that he might grow an old man, and have no strength left in his arms nor courage in his heart, before the winged horse would appear. Oh, how heavily passes the time, while an adventurous youth is yearning to do his part in life, and to gather in the harvest of his renown! How hard a lesson it is to wait! Our life is brief, and how much of it is spent in teaching us only this!

Well was it for Bellerophon that the gentle child had grown so fond of him, and was never weary of keeping him company. Every morning the child gave him a new hope to put in his bosom, instead of yesterday's withered one.

"Dear Bellerophon," he would cry, looking up hopefully into his face, "I think we shall see Pegasus today!"

And, at length, if it had not been for the little boy's unwavering faith, Bellerophon would have given up all hope, and would have gone back to Lycia, and have done his best to slay the Chimæra without the help of the winged horse. And in that case poor Bellerophon would at least have been terribly scorched by the creature's breath, and would most probably have been killed and devoured. Nobody should ever try to fight an earthborn Chimæra, unless he can first get upon the back of an aerial steed.

One morning the child spoke to Bellerophon even more hopefully than usual.

"Dear, dear Bellerophon," cried he, "I know not why it is, but I feel as if we should certainly see Pegasus today!"

And all that day he would not stir a step from Bellerophon's side; so they ate a crust of bread together, and drank some of the water of the fountain. In the afternoon, there they sat, and Bellerophon had thrown his arm around the child, who likewise had put one of his little hands in Bellerophon's. The latter was lost in his own thoughts, and was fixing his eyes vacantly on the trunks of the trees that overshadowed the fountain, and the grapevines that clambered up among their branches. But the gentle child was gazing down into the water; he was grieved, for Bellerophon's sake, that the hope of another day should be deceived, like so many before it; and two or three quiet teardrops fell from his eyes, and mingled with what were said to be the many tears of Pirene, when she wept for her slain children.

But, when he least thought of it, Bellerophon felt the pressure of the child's little hand, and heard a soft, almost breathless, whisper.

"See there, dear Bellerophon! There is an image in the water!"

The young man looked down into the dimpling mirror of the fountain, and saw what he took to be the reflection of a bird which seemed to be flying at a great height in the air, with a gleam of sunshine on its snowy or silvery wings.

"What a splendid bird it must be!" said he. "And how very large it looks, though it must really be flying higher than the clouds!"

"It makes me tremble!" whispered the child. "I am afraid to look up into the air! It is very beautiful, and yet I dare only look at its image in the water. Dear Bellerophon, do you not see that it is no bird? It is the winged horse Pegasus!"

Bellerophon's heart began to throb! He gazed keenly upward, but could not see the winged creature, whether bird or horse; because, just then, it had plunged into the fleecy depths of a summer cloud. It was but a moment, however, before the object reappeared, sinking lightly down out of the cloud, although still at a vast distance from the earth. Bellerophon caught the child in his arms, and shrank back with him, so that they were both hidden among the thick shrubbery which grew all around the fountain. Not that he was afraid of any harm, but he dreaded lest, if Pegasus caught a glimpse of them, he would fly far away, and alight in some inaccessible mountain-top. For it was really the winged horse. After they had expected him so long, he was coming to quench his thirst with the water of Pirene.

Nearer and nearer came the aerial wonder, flying in great circles, as you may have seen a dove when about to alight. Downward came Pegasus, in those wide, sweeping circles, which grew narrower, and narrower still, as he gradually approached the earth. The nigher the view of him, the more beautiful he was, and the more marvelous the sweep of his silvery wings. At last, with so light a pressure as hardly to bend the grass about the fountain, or imprint a hoof-tramp in the sand of its margin, he alighted, and, stooping his wild head, began to drink. He drew in the water, with long and pleasant sighs, and tranquil pauses of enjoyment; and then another draught, and another, and another. For, nowhere in the world, or up among the clouds, did Pegasus love any water as he loved this of Pirene. And when his thirst was slaked, he cropped a few of the honey blossoms of the clover, delicately tasting them, but not caring to make a hearty meal, because the herbage, just beneath the clouds, on the lofty sides of Mount Helicon, suited his palate better than this ordinary grass.

After thus drinking to his heart's content, and, in his dainty fashion, condescending to take a little food, the winged horse began to caper to and fro, and dance as it were, out of mere idleness and sport. There never was a more playful creature made than this very Pegasus. So there he frisked, in a way that it delights me to think about, fluttering his great wings as lightly as ever did a linnet, and running little races, half on earth and half in air, and which I know not whether to call a flight or a gallop. When a creature is perfectly able to fly, he sometimes chooses to run, just for the pastime of the thing; and so did Pegasus, although it cost him some little trouble to keep his hoofs so near the ground. Bellerophon, meanwhile, holding the child's hand, peeped forth from the shrubbery, and thought that never was any sight so beautiful as this, nor ever a horse's eyes so wild and spirited as those of Pegasus. It seemed a sin to think of bridling him and riding on his back.

Once or twice, Pegasus stopped, and snuffed the air, pricking up his ears, tossing his head, and turning it on all sides, as if he partly suspected some mischief or other. Seeing nothing, however, and hearing no sound, he soon began his antics again.

At length—not that he was weary, but only idle and luxurious— Pegasus folded his wings, and lay down on the soft green turf. But, being too full of aerial life to remain quiet for many moments together, he soon rolled over on his back, with his four slender legs in the air. It was beautiful to see him, this one solitary creature, whose mate had never been created, but who needed no companion, and, living a great many hundred years, was as happy as the centuries were long. The more he did such things as mortal horses are accustomed to do, the less earthly and the more wonderful he seemed. Bellerophon and the child almost held their breath, partly from a delightful awe, but still more because they dreaded lest the slightest stir or murmur should send him up, and with the speed of an arrow flight, into the farthest blue of the sky.

Walter Crane

Bellerophon leaped astride his back.

Finally, when he had had enough of rolling over and over, Pegasus turned himself about, and, indolently, like any other horse, put out his forelegs, in order to rise from the ground; and Bellerophon, who had guessed that he would do so, darted suddenly from the thicket, and leaped astride of his back.

Yes, there he sat, on the back of the winged horse!

But what a bound did Pegasus make, when, for the first time, he felt the weight of a mortal man upon his loins! A bound, indeed! Before he had time to draw a breath, Bellerophon found himself five hundred feet aloft, and still shooting upward, while the winged horse snorted and trembled with terror and anger. Upward he went, up, up, up, until he plunged into the cold misty bosom of a cloud, at which, only a little while before, Bellerophon had been gazing, and fancying it a very pleasant spot. Then again, out of the heart of the cloud, Pegasus shot down like a thunderbolt, as if he meant to dash both himself and his rider headlong against a rock. Then he went through about a thousand of the wildest caprioles that had ever been performed either by a bird or a horse.

I cannot tell you half that he did. He skimmed straight forward, and sideways, and backward. He reared himself erect, with his forelegs on a wreath of mist, and his hind legs on nothing at all. He flung out his heels behind, and put down his head between his legs, with his wings pointing right upward. At about two miles' height above the earth, he turned a somerset, so that Bellerophon's heels were where his head should have been, and he seemed to look down into the sky, instead of up. He twisted his head about, and, looking Bellerophon in the face, with fire flashing from his eyes, made a terrible attempt to bite him. He fluttered his pinions so wildly that one of the silver feathers was shaken out, and floating earthward, was picked up by the child, who kept it as long as he lived, in memory of Pegasus and Bellerophon.

But the latter (who, as you may judge, was as good a horseman as ever galloped) had been watching his opportunity, and at last clapped the golden bit of the enchanted bridle between the winged steed's jaws. No sooner was this done, than Pegasus became as manageable as if he had taken food, all his life, out of Bellerophon's hand. To speak what I really feel, it was almost a sadness to see so wild a creature grow suddenly so tame. And Pegasus seemed to feel it so, likewise. He looked round to Bellerophon with the tears in his beautiful eyes, instead of the fire that so recently flashed from them. But when Bellerophon patted his head, and spoke a few authoritative, yet kind and soothing words, another look came into the eyes of Pegasus; for he was glad at heart, after so many lonely centuries, to have found a companion and a master.

Thus it always is with winged horses, and with all such wild and solitary creatures. If you can catch and overcome them, it is the surest way to win their love.

While Pegasus had been doing his utmost to shake Bellerophon off his back, he had flown a very long distance; and they had come within sight of a lofty mountain by the time the bit was in his mouth. Bellerophon had seen this mountain before, and knew it to be Helicon, on the summit of which was the winged horse's abode. Thither (after looking gently into his rider's face, as if to ask leave) Pegasus now flew, and, alighting, waited patiently until Bellerophon should please to dismount. The young man, accordingly, leaped from his steed's back, but still held him fast by the bridle. Meeting his eyes, however, he was so affected by the gentleness of his aspect, and by the thought of the free life which Pegasus had heretofore lived, that he could not bear to keep him a prisoner, if he really desired his liberty.

Obeying this generous impulse he slipped the enchanted bridle off the head of Pegasus, and took the bit from his mouth.

"Leave me, Pegasus!" said he. "Either leave me, or love me."

In an instant, the winged horse shot almost out of sight, soaring straight upward from the summit of Mount Helicon. Being long after sunset, it was now twilight on the mountain-top, and dusky evening over all the country round about. But Pegasus flew so high that he overtook the departed day, and was bathed in the upper radiance of the sun. Ascending higher and higher, he looked like a bright speck, and, at last, could no longer be seen in the hollow waste of the sky. And Bellerophon was afraid that he should never behold him more. But, while he was lamenting his own folly, the bright speck reappeared, and drew nearer and nearer, until it descended lower than the sunshine; and behold, Pegasus had come back! After this trial there was no more fear of the winged horse's making his escape. He and Bellerophon were friends, and put loving faith in one another.

That night they lay down and slept together, with Bellerophon's arm about the neck of Pegasus, not as a caution, but for kindness. And they awoke at peep of day, and bade one another good morning, each in his own language.

In this manner, Bellerophon and the wondrous steed spent several days, and grew better acquainted and fonder of each other all the time. They went on long aerial journeys, and sometimes ascended so high that the earth looked hardly bigger than—the moon. They visited distant countries, and amazed the inhabitants, who thought that the beautiful young man, on the back of the winged horse, must have come down out of the sky. A thousand miles a day was no more than an easy space for the fleet Pegasus to pass over. Bellerophon was delighted with this kind of life, and would have liked nothing better than to live always in the same way, aloft in the clear atmosphere; for it was always sunny weather up there, however cheerless and rainy it might be in the lower region. But he could not forget the horrible Chimæra, which he had promised King

Iobates to slay. So, at last, when he had become well accustomed to feats of horsemanship in the air, and could manage Pegasus with the least motion of his hand, and had taught him to obey his voice, he determined to attempt the performance of this perilous adventure.

At daybreak, therefore, as soon as he unclosed his eyes, he gently pinched the winged horse's ear, in order to arouse him. Pegasus immediately started from the ground and pranced about a quarter of a mile aloft, and made a grand sweep around the mountain-top, by way of showing that he was wide awake, and ready for any kind of an excursion. During the whole of this little flight, he uttered a loud, brisk, and melodious neigh, and finally came down at Bellerophon's side, as lightly as ever you saw a sparrow hop upon a twig.

"Well done, dear Pegasus! well done, my sky-skimmer!" cried Bellerophon, stroking the horse's neck. "Now, my fleet, beautiful friend, we must break our fast. Today we fight the terrible Chimæra."

As soon as they had eaten their morning meal, and drank some sparkling water from a spring called Hippocrene, Pegasus held out his head, of his own accord, so that his master might put on the bridle. Then, with a great many playful leaps and airy caperings, he showed his impatience to be gone; while Bellerophon was girding on his sword, and hanging his shield about his neck, and preparing himself for battle. When everything was ready, the rider mounted, and (as was his custom, when going a long distance) ascended five miles perpendicularly, so as the better to see whither he was directing his course. He then turned the head of Pegasus toward the east, and set out for Lycia. In their flight they overtook an eagle, and came so nigh him, before he could get out of their way, that Bellerophon might easily have caught him by the leg. Hastening onward at this rate, it was still early in the forenoon when they beheld the lofty mountains of Lycia, with their deep and shaggy valleys. If Bellerophon had been told truly, it was in one of those dismal valleys that the hideous Chimæra had taken up its abode.

Being now so near their journey's end, the winged horse gradually descended with his rider; and they took advantage of some clouds that were floating over the mountain-tops, in order to conceal themselves. Hovering on the upper surface of a cloud, and peeping over its edge, Bellerophon had a pretty distinct view of the mountainous part of Lycia, and could look into all its shadowy vales at once. At first there appeared to be nothing remarkable. It was a wild, savage, and rocky tract of high and precipitous hills. In the more level part of the country, there were the ruins of houses that had been burnt, and, here and there, the carcasses of dead cattle, strewn about the pastures where they had been feeding.

"The Chimæra must have done this mischief," thought Bellerophon. "But where can the monster be?"

As I have already said, there was nothing remarkable to be detected, at first sight, in any of the valleys and dells that lay among the precipitous heights of the mountains. Nothing at all; unless, indeed, it were three spires of black smoke, which issued from what seemed to be the mouth of a cavern, and clambered sullenly into the atmosphere. Before reaching the mountain-top, these three black smoke wreaths mingled themselves into one. The cavern was almost directly beneath the winged horse and his rider, at the distance of about a thousand feet. The smoke, as it crept heavily upward, had an ugly, sulphurous, stifling scent, which caused Pegasus to snort and Bellerophon to sneeze. So disagreeable was it to the marvelous steed, accustomed to breathe only the purest air, that he waved his wings, and shot half a mile out of range of this offensive vapor.

But, on looking behind him, Bellerophon saw something that induced him first to draw the bridle, and then to turn Pegasus about. He made a sign, which the winged horse understood, and sunk slowly through the air, until his hoofs were scarcely more than a man's height above the rocky bottom of the valley. In front, as far off as you could throw a stone, was the cavern's mouth, with the three smoke wreaths oozing out. And what else did he behold?

There seemed to be a heap of strange and terrible creatures curled up within the cavern. Their bodies lay so close together, that Bellerophon could not distinguish them apart; but, judging by their heads, one of these creatures was a huge snake, the second a fierce

lion, and the third an ugly goat. The lion and the goat were asleep;
the snake was broad awake, and kept staring around him with a
great pair of fiery eyes. But—and this was the most wonderful part
of the matter—the three spires of smoke evidently issued from the
nostrils of these three heads! So strange was the spectacle, that,
though Bellerophon had been all along expecting it, the truth did
not immediately occur to him, that here was the terrible three-
headed Chimæra. He had found out the Chimæra cavern. The
snake, the lion, and the goat, as he supposed them to be, were not
three separate creatures, but one monster!

The wicked, hateful thing! Slumbering as two thirds of it were,
it still held, in its abominable claws, the remnant of an unfortunate
lamb—or possibly (but I hate to think so) it was a dear little boy—
which its mouths had been gnawing, before two of them fell asleep!

All at once, Bellerophon started as from a dream, and knew it
to be the Chimæra. Pegasus seemed to know it, at the same instant,
and sent forth a neigh, that sounded like the call of a trumpet to
battle. At this sound the three heads reared themselves erect, and
belched out great flashes of flame. Before Bellerophon had time to
consider what to do next, the monster flung itself out of the cavern
and sprung straight toward him, with its immense claws extended,
and its snaky tail twisting itself venomously behind. If Pegasus had
not been as nimble as a bird, both he and his rider would have
been overthrown by the Chimæra's headlong rush, and thus the battle have been ended before it was well begun. But the winged horse
was not to be caught so. In the twinkling of an eye he was up
aloft, halfway to the clouds, snorting with anger. He shuddered,
too, not with affright, but with utter disgust at the loathsomeness of
this poisonous thing with three heads.

The Chimæra, on the other hand, raised itself up so as to stand
absolutely on the tip-end of its tail, with its talons pawing fiercely
in the air, and its three heads spluttering fire at Pegasus and his
rider. How it roared, and hissed, and bellowed! Bellerophon, meanwhile, was fitting his shield on his arm, and drawing his sword.

"Now, my beloved Pegasus," he whispered in the winged horse's
ear, "thou must help me to slay this insufferable monster; or else

thou shalt fly back to thy solitary mountain-peak without thy friend Bellerophon. For either the Chimæra dies, or its three mouths shall gnaw this head of mine, which has slumbered upon thy neck!"

Pegasus whinnied, and, turning back his head, rubbed his nose tenderly against his rider's cheek. It was his way of telling him that, though he had wings and was an immortal horse, yet he would perish, if it were possible for immortality to perish, rather than leave Bellerophon behind.

"I thank thee, Pegasus," answered Bellerophon. "Now, then, let us make a dash at the monster!"

Uttering these words, he shook the bridle; and Pegasus darted down aslant, as swift as the flight of an arrow, right toward the Chimæra's three-fold head, which, all this time, was poking itself as high as it could into the air. As he came within arm's length, Bellerophon made a cut at the monster, but was carried onward by his steed, before he could see whether the blow had been successful. Pegasus continued his course, but soon wheeled round, at about the same distance from the Chimæra as before. Bellerophon then perceived that he had cut the goat's head of the monster almost off, so that it dangled downward by the skin, and seemed quite dead.

But, to make amends, the snake's head and the lion's head had taken all the fierceness of the dead one into themselves, and spit flame, and hissed, and roared, with more fury than before.

"Never mind, my brave Pegasus!" cried Bellerophon. With another stroke like that, we will stop either its hissing or its roaring."

And again he shook the bridle. Dashing aslantwise, as before, the winged horse made another arrow flight toward the Chimæra, and Bellerophon aimed another downright stroke at one of the two remaining heads, as he shot by. But this time, neither he nor Pegasus escaped so well as at first. With one of its claws, the Chimæra had given the young man a deep scratch in his shoulder, and had slightly damaged the left wing of the flying steed with the other. On his part, Bellerophon had mortally wounded the lion's head of the monster, insomuch that it now hung downward, with its fire almost extinguished, and sending out gasps of thick black smoke. The snake's head, however (which was the only one now left), was twice as fierce and venomous as ever before. It belched forth shoots of fire five hundred yards long, and emitted hisses so loud, so harsh, and so ear-piercing, that King Iobates heard them, fifty miles off, and trembled till the throne shook under him.

"Well-a-day!" thought the poor king; "the Chimæra is certainly coming to devour me!"

Meanwhile Pegasus had again paused in the air, and neighed angrily, while sparkles of a pure crystal flame darted out of his eyes. How unlike the lurid fire of the Chimæra! The aerial steed's spirit was all aroused, and so was that of Bellerophon.

"Dost thou bleed, my immortal horse?" cried the young man, caring less for his own hurt than for the anguish of this glorious creature, that ought never to have tasted pain. "The execrable Chimæra shall pay for this mischief with his last head!"

Then he shook the bridle, shouted loudly, and guided Pegasus, not aslantwise as before, but straight at the monster's hideous front. So rapid was the onset, that it seemed but a dazzle and a flash before Bellerophon was at close grips with his enemy.

The Chimæra, by this time, after losing its second head, had got into a red-hot passion of pain and rampant rage. It so flounced about, half on earth and partly in the air, that it was impossible to say which element it rested upon. It opened its snake jaws to such an abominable width, that Pegasus might almost, I was going to say, have flown right down its throat, wings outspread, rider and all! At their approach it shot out a tremendous blast of its fiery breath, and enveloped Bellerophon and his steed in a perfect atmosphere of flame, singeing the wings of Pegasus, scorching off one whole side of the young man's golden ringlets, and making them both far far hotter than was comfortable, from head to foot.

But this was nothing to what followed.

When the airy rush of the winged horse had brought him within the distance of a hundred yards, the Chimæra gave a spring, and flung its huge, awkward, venomous, and utterly detestable carcass right up on poor Pegasus, clung round him with might and main, and tied up its snaky tail into a knot! Up flew the aerial steed, higher, higher, higher, above the mountain-peaks, above the clouds, and almost out of sight of the solid earth. But still the earthborn monster kept its hold, and was borne upward, along with the creature of light and air. Bellerophon, meanwhile, turning about, found himself face to face with the ugly grimness of the Chimæra's visage, and could only avoid being scorched to death, or bitten right in twain, by holding up his shield. Over the upper edge of the shield, he looked sternly into the savage eyes of the monster.

But the Chimæra was so mad and wild with pain, that it did not guard itself so well as might else have been the case. Perhaps, after all, the best way to fight a Chimæra is by getting as close to it as you can. In its efforts to stick its horrible iron claws into its enemy, the creature left its own breast quite exposed; and perceiving this, Bellerophon thrust his sword up to the hilt into its cruel heart. Immediately the snaky tail untied its knot. The monster let go its hold of Pegasus, and fell from the vast height, downward; while the fire within its bosom, instead of being put out burned fiercer than ever, and quickly began to consume the dead carcass. Thus it fell out of the sky, all a-flame, and (it being nightfall before it reached the earth) was mistaken for a shooting star or a comet. But, at early sunrise, some cottagers were going to their day's labor, and saw, to their astonishment, that several acres of ground were strewn with black ashes. In the middle of a field, there was a heap of whitened bones, a great deal higher than a haystack. Nothing else was ever seen of the dreadful Chimæra!

And when Bellerophon had won the victory, he bent forward and kissed Pegasus, while the tears stood in his eyes. "Back now, my beloved steed!" said he. "Back to the Fountain of Pirene!"

Pegasus skimmed through the air, quicker than ever he did before, and reached the fountain in a very short time. And there he found the old man leaning on his staff, and the country fellow watering his cow, and the pretty maiden filling her pitcher.

"I remember now," quoth the old man, "I saw this winged horse once before, when I was quite a lad. But he was ten times handsomer in those days."

"I own a cart horse, worth three of him!" said the country

fellow. "If this pony were mine, the first thing I should do would be to clip his wings!"

But the poor maiden said nothing, for she had always the luck to be afraid at the wrong time. So she ran away, and let her pitcher tumble down, and broke it.

"Where is the gentle child," asked Bellerophon, "who used to keep me company, and never lost his faith, and never was weary of gazing into the fountain?"

"Here am I, dear Bellerophon!" said the child, softly.

For the little boy had spent day after day, on the margin of Pirene, waiting for his friend to come back; but when he perceived Bellerophon descending through the clouds, mounted on a winged horse, he had shrunk back into the shrubbery. He was a delicate and tender child, and dreaded lest the old man and the country fellow should see the tears that were gushing from his eyes.

"Thou hast won the victory," said he, running to the knee of Bellerophon, who still sat on Pegasus. "I knew thou wouldst."

"Yes, dear child!" replied Bellerophon, alighting from the winged horse. "But if thy faith had not helped me, I should never have waited for Pegasus, and never have gone up above the clouds, and never have conquered the terrible Chimæra. Thou, my beloved little friend, hast done it all. And now let us give Pegasus his liberty."

So he slipped off the enchanted bridle from the head of the marvelous steed.

"Be free, forevermore, my Pegasus!" cried he, with a shade of sadness in his tone. "Be as free as thou art fleet."

But Pegasus rested his head on Bellerophon's shoulder, and would not be persuaded to take flight.

"Well, then," said Bellerophon, caressing the airy horse, "thou shalt be with me, as long as thou wilt; and we will go together. forthwith, and tell King Iobates that the Chimæra is destroyed."

Then Bellerophon embraced the gentle child, and promised to come to him again, and departed. But, in after years, that child took higher flights upon the aerial steed than ever did Bellerophon, and achieved more honorable deeds than his friend's victory over the Chimæra. For, gentle and tender, he grew to be a mighty poet!

THE MIRACULOUS PITCHER

By NATHANIEL HAWTHORNE

ONE evening, in times long ago, old Philemon and his old wife Baucis sat at their cottage door, enjoying the calm and beautiful sunset. They had already eaten their frugal supper, and intended now to spend a quiet hour or two before bedtime. So they talked together about their garden, and their cow, and their bees, and their grapevine, which clambered over the cottage wall, and on which the grapes were beginning to turn purple. But the rude shouts of children and the fierce barking of dogs, in the village near at hand, grew louder and louder, until, at last, it was hardly possible for Baucis and Philemon to hear each other speak.

"Ah, wife," cried Philemon, "I fear some poor traveler is seeking hospitality among our neighbors yonder, and, instead of giving him food and lodging, they have set their dogs at him, as their custom is!"

"Well-a-day!" answered old Baucis, "I do wish our neighbors felt a little more kindness for their fellow creatures. And only think of bringing up their children in this naughty way, and patting them on the head when they fling stones at strangers!"

"Those children will never come to any good," said Philemon, shaking his white head. "To tell you the truth, wife, I should not wonder if some terrible thing were to happen to all the people in the village unless they mend their manners. But, as for you and me, so long as Providence affords us a crust of bread, let us be ready to give half to any poor, homeless stranger that may come along and need it."

"That's right, husband," said Baucis. "So we will!"

These old folk, you must know, were quite poor, and had to work pretty hard for a living. Old Philemon toiled diligently in his garden, while Baucis was always busy with her distaff, or making a little butter and cheese with their cow's milk, or doing one thing and another about the cottage. Their food was seldom anything but bread, milk, and vegetables, with sometimes a portion of honey from their beehive, and now and then a bunch of grapes, that had ripened against the cottage wall. But they were two of the kindest old people in the world, and would cheerfully have gone without their dinners any day rather than refuse a slice of their brown loaf, a cup of new milk, and a spoonful of honey, to the weary traveler who might pause before their door. They felt as if such guests had a sort of holiness, and that they ought, therefore, to treat them better and more bountifully than their own selves.

Their cottage stood on a rising ground, at some short distance from a village, which lay in a hollow valley, that was about half a mile in breadth. This valley, in past ages, when the world was new, had probably been the bed of a lake. There, fishes had glided to and fro in the depths, and waterweeds had grown along the margin, and trees and hills had seen their reflected images in the broad and peaceful mirror. But, as the waters subsided, men had cultivated the soil, and built houses on it, so that it was now a fertile spot, and bore no traces of the ancient lake, except a very small brook which meandered through the midst of the village and supplied the inhabitants with water. The valley had been dry land so long, that oaks had sprung up and grown great and high, and perished with old age and been succeeded by others, as tall and stately as the first. Never was there a prettier or more fruitful valley. The very sight of the plenty around them should have made the inhabitants kind and gentle, and ready to show their gratitude to Providence by doing good to their fellow creatures.

But, we are sorry to say, the people of this lovely village were not worthy to dwell in a spot on which Heaven had smiled so beneficently. They were a very selfish and hardhearted people, and had no pity for the poor, nor sympathy with the homeless. They would only have laughed had anybody told them that human beings owe a debt of love to one another, because there is no other method of paying the debt of love and care which all of us owe to Providence. You will hardly believe what I am going to tell you. These naughty people taught their children to be no better than themselves, and used to clap their hands, by way of encouragement, when they saw the little boys and girls run after some poor stranger, shouting at his heels and pelting him with stones. They kept large and fierce dogs, and whenever a traveler ventured to show himself in the village street, this pack of disagreeable curs scampered to meet him, barking, snarling, and showing their teeth. Then they would seize him by his leg, or by his clothes, just as it happened; and if he were ragged when he came, he was generally a pitiable object before he had time to run away. This was a very terrible thing to poor travelers, as you may suppose, especially when they chanced to be sick, or feeble, or lame, or old. Such persons (if they once knew how badly these unkind people, and their unkind children and curs, were in the habit of behaving) would go miles and miles out of their way, rather than try to pass through the village again.

What made the matter seem worse, if possible, was that when rich persons came in their chariots, or riding on beautiful horses, with their servants in rich liveries attending on them, nobody could be more civil and obsequious than the inhabitants of the village. They would take off their hats and make the humblest bows you ever saw. If the children were rude, they were pretty certain to get their ears boxed; and as for the dogs, if a single cur in the pack presumed to yelp, his master instantly beat him with a club, and tied him up without any supper. This would have been all very well, only it proved that the villagers cared much about the money that a stranger had in his pocket, and nothing whatever for the human soul which lives equally in the beggar and the prince.

So now you can understand why old Philemon spoke so sorrowfully, when he heard the shouts of the children and the barking of the dogs, at the farther extremity of the village street. There was a confused din, which lasted a good while, and seemed to pass quite through the breadth of the valley.

"I never heard the dogs so loud!" observed the good old man.

"Nor the children so rude!" answered his good old wife.

They sat shaking their heads, one to another, while the noise came nearer and nearer; until, at the foot of the little eminence on which their cottage stood, they saw two travelers approaching on foot. Close behind them came the fierce dogs, snarling at their very heels.

A little farther off, ran a crowd of children, who sent up shrill cries, and flung stones at the two strangers, with all their might. Once or twice, the younger of the two men (he was a slender and very active figure) turned about and drove back the dogs with a staff which he carried in his hand. His companion, who was a very tall person, walked calmly along, as if disdaining to notice either the naughty children or the pack of curs whose manners the children seemed to imitate.

Both of the travelers were very humbly clad, and looked as if they might not have money enough in their pockets to pay for a night's lodging. And this, I am afraid, was the reason why the villagers had allowed their children and dogs to treat them so rudely.

"Come, wife," said Philemon to Baucis, "let us go and meet these poor people. No doubt, they feel almost too heavy-hearted to climb the hill."

"Go you and meet them," answered Baucis, "while I make haste within doors, and see whether we can get them anything for supper. A comfortable bowl of bread and milk would do wonders toward raising their spirits."

Accordingly, she hastened into the cottage. Philemon, on his part, went forward, and extended his hand with so hospitable an aspect that there was no need of saying what nevertheless he did say, in the heartiest tone imaginable, "Welcome, strangers! Welcome!"

"Thank you!" replied the younger of the two, in a lively kind of way, notwithstanding his weariness and trouble. "This is quite another greeting than we have met with yonder in the village. Pray, why do you live in such a bad neighborhood?"

"Ah!" observed old Philemon, with a quiet and benign smile, "Providence put me here, I hope, among other reasons, in order that I may make you what amends I can for the inhospitality of my neighbors."

"Well said, old father!" cried the traveler, laughing; "and if the truth must be told, my companion and myself need some amends. Those children (the little rascals!) have bespattered us finely with their mud balls; and one of the curs has torn my cloak, which was ragged enough already. But I took him across the muzzle with my staff; and I think you may have heard him yelp, even thus far off."

Philemon was glad to see him in such good spirits; nor, indeed, would you have fancied, by the traveler's look and manner, that he was weary with a long day's journey, besides being disheartened by rough treatment at the end of it. He was dressed in rather an odd way, with a sort of cap on his head, the brim of which stuck out over both ears. Though it was a summer evening, he wore a cloak which he kept wrapt closely about him, perhaps because his under garments were shabby. Philemon perceived, too, that he had on a singular pair of shoes; but, as it was now growing dusk, and as the old man's eyesight was none the sharpest, he could not precisely tell in what the strangeness consisted. One thing, certainly, seemed queer. The traveler was so wonderfully light and active, that it appeared as if his feet sometimes rose from the ground of their own accord, or could only be kept down by an effort.

"I used to be light-footed, in my youth," said Philemon to the traveler. "But I always found my feet grow heavier toward nightfall."

"There is nothing like a good staff to help one along," answered the stranger; "and I happen to have an excellent one, as you see."

This staff, in fact, was the oddest-looking staff that Philemon had ever beheld. It was made of olive wood, and had something like a little pair of wings near the top. Two snakes, carved in the wood, were represented as twining themselves about the staff, and were so very skillfully executed that old Philemon (whose eyes, you know, were getting rather dim) almost thought them alive, and that he could see them wriggling and twisting.

"A curious piece of work, sure enough!" said he. "A staff with wings! It would be an excellent kind of stick for a little boy to ride astride of!" By this time, Philemon and his two guests had reached the cottage door.

"Friends," said the old man, "sit down and rest yourselves here on this bench. My good wife Baucis has gone to see what you can have for supper. We are poor folks; but you shall be welcome to whatever we have in the cupboard."

The younger stranger threw himself carelessly on the bench, letting his staff fall, as he did so. And here happened something rather marvelous, though trifling enough, too. The staff seemed to get up from the ground of its own accord, and, spreading its little pair of wings, it half hopped, half flew, and leaned itself against the wall of the cottage. There it stood quite still, except that the snakes continued to wriggle. But, in my private opinion, old Philemon's eyesight had been playing him tricks again.

Before he could ask any questions, the elder stranger drew his attention from the wonderful staff, by speaking to him.

"Was there not," asked the stranger, in a remarkably deep tone of voice, "a lake, in very ancient times, covering the spot where now stands yonder village?"

"Not in my day, friend," answered Philemon; "and yet I am an old man, as you see. There were always the fields and meadows, just as they are now, and the old trees, and the little stream murmuring through the midst of the valley. My father, nor his father before him, ever saw it otherwise, so far as I know; and doubtless it will still be the same, when old Philemon shall be gone and forgotten!"

"That is more than can be safely foretold," observed the stranger; and there was something very stern in his deep voice. He shook his head, too, so that his dark and heavy curls were shaken with the movement. "Since the inhabitants of yonder village have forgotten the affections and sympathies of their nature, it were better that the lake should be rippling over their dwellings again!"

The traveler looked so stern that Philemon was really almost frightened; the more so, that, at his frown, the twilight seemed suddenly to grow darker, and that, when he shook his head, there was a roll of thunder in the air.

But, in a moment afterwards, the stranger's face became so kindly and mild that the old man quite forgot his terror. Nevertheless, he could not help feeling that this elder traveler must be no ordinary personage, although he happened now to be attired so humbly and to be journeying on foot. Not that Philemon fancied him a prince in disguise, or any character of that sort; but rather some exceedingly wise man, who went about the world in this poor garb, despising wealth and all worldly objects, and seeking everywhere to add a nite to his wisdom. This idea appeared the more probable, because, when Philemon raised his eyes to the stranger's face, he seemed to see more thought there in one look than he could have studied out in a lifetime.

While Baucis was getting the supper, the travelers both began to talk very sociably with Philemon. The younger, indeed, was extreme loquacious, and made such shrewd and witty remarks that the good old man continually burst out a-laughing, and pronounced him the merriest fellow whom he had seen for many a day.

"Pray, my young friend," said he, as they grew familiar together, "what may I call your name?"

"Why, I am very nimble, as you see," answered the traveler. "So, if you call me Quicksilver, the name will fit tolerably well."

"Quicksilver? Quicksilver?" repeated Philemon, looking in the traveler's face, to see if he were making fun of him. "It is a very odd name! And your companion there? Has he as strange a one?"

"You must ask the thunder to tell it you!" replied Quicksilver, putting on a mysterious look. "No other voice is loud enough."

This remark, whether it were serious or in jest, might have caused Philemon to conceive a very great awe of the elder stranger, if, on venturing to gaze at him, he had not beheld so much beneficence in his visage. But, undoubtedly, here was the grandest figure that ever sat so humbly beside a cottage door. When the stranger conversed, it was with gravity, and in such a way that Philemon felt irresistibly moved to tell him everything which he had most at heart. This is always the feeling that people have when they meet with anyone wise enough to comprehend all their good and evil, and to despise not a tittle of it.

But Philemon, simple and kind-hearted old man that he was, had not many secrets to disclose. He talked, however, quite garrulously, about the events of his past life, in the whole course of which he had never been a score of miles from this very spot. His wife Baucis and himself had dwelt in the cottage from their youth upward, earning their bread by honest labor, always poor, but still contented. He told what excellent butter and cheese Baucis made, and how nice were the vegetables which he raised in his garden. He said, too, that, because they loved one another so very much, it was the wish of both that death might not separate them, but that they should die, as they had lived, together.

As the stranger listened, a smile beamed over his countenance, and made its expression as sweet as it was grand.

"You are a good old man," said he to Philemon, "and you have a good old wife to be your helpmeet. It is fit that your wish be granted."

And it seemed to Philemon just then as if the sunset clouds threw up a bright flash from the west, and kindled a sudden light in the sky.

Baucis had now got supper ready, and, coming to the door, began to make apologies for the poor fare which she was forced to set before her guests.

"Had we known you were coming," said she, "my good man and myself would have gone without a morsel, rather than you should lack a better supper. But I took the most part of today's milk to make cheese; and our last loaf is already half eaten. Ah me! I never feel the sorrow of being poor, save when a poor traveler knocks at our door."

"All will be very well; do not trouble yourself, my good dame," replied the elder stranger, kindly. "An honest, hearty welcome to a guest works miracles with the fare, and is capable of turning the coarsest food to nectar and ambrosia."

"A welcome you shall have," cried Baucis, "and likewise a little honey that we happen to have left, and a bunch of purple grapes besides."

"Why, Mother Baucis, it is a feast!" exclaimed Quicksilver, laughing, "an absolute feast! and you shall see how bravely I will play my part at it! I think I never felt hungrier in my life."

"Mercy on us!" whispered Baucis to her husband. "If the young man has such a terrible appetite, I am afraid there will not be half enough supper!" They all went into the cottage.

And now, my little auditors, shall I tell you something that will make you open your eyes very wide? It is really one of the oddest circumstances in the whole story. Quicksilver's staff, you recollect, had set itself up against the wall of the cottage. Well; when its master entered the door, leaving this wonderful staff behind, what should it do but immediately spread its little wings, and go hopping and fluttering up the doorsteps! Tap, tap, went the staff, on the kitchen floor; nor did it rest until it had stood itself on end, with the greatest gravity and decorum, beside Quicksilver's chair. Old Philemon, however, as well as his wife, was so taken up in attending to their guests, that no notice was given to what the staff had been about.

As Baucis had said, there was but a scanty supper for two hungry travelers. In the middle of the table was the remnant of a brown loaf, with a piece of cheese on one side of it, and a dish of honeycomb on the other. There was a pretty good bunch of grapes for each of the guests. A moderately sized earthern pitcher, nearly full of milk, stood at a corner of the board; and when Baucis had filled two bowls, and set them before the strangers, only a little milk remained in the bottom of the pitcher. Alas! it is a very sad business when a bountiful heart finds itself pinched and squeezed among narrow circumstances. Poor Baucis kept wishing that she might starve for a week to come, if it were possible by so doing to provide these hungry folk a more plentiful supper.

And, since the supper was so exceedingly small, she could not help wishing that their appetites had not been quite so large. Why, at their very first sitting down, the travelers both drank off all the milk in their two bowls, at a draught.

"A little more milk, kind Mother Baucis, if you please," said Quicksilver. "The day has been hot, and I am very much a-thirst."

"Now, my dear people," answered Baucis, in great confusion, "I am so sorry and ashamed! But the truth is, there is hardly a drop more milk in the pitcher. O husband! husband! why didn't we go without our supper?"

"Why, it appears to me," cried Quicksilver, starting up from the table and taking the pitcher by the handle, "it really appears to me that matters are not quite so bad as you represent them. Here is certainly more milk in the pitcher."

So saying, and to the vast astonishment of Baucis, he proceeded to fill not only his own bowl but his companion's likewise, from the pitcher that was supposed to be almost empty. The good woman could scarcely believe her eyes. She had certainly poured out nearly all the milk, and had peeped in afterwards and seen the bottom of the pitcher as she set it down upon the table.

"But I am old," thought Baucis to herself, "and apt to be forgetful. I suppose I must have made a mistake. At all events, the pitcher cannot help being empty now, after filling the bowls twice over."

"What excellent milk!" observed Quicksilver, after quaffing the contents of the second bowl. "Excuse me, my kind hostess, but I must really ask you for a little more."

Now Baucis had seen, as plainly as she could see anything, that Quicksilver had turned the pitcher upside down, and consequently had poured out every drop of milk in filling the last bowl. Of course, there could not possibly be any left. However, in order to let him know precisely how the case was, she lifted pitcher and made a gesture as if pouring milk into Quicksilver's bowl, but without the remotest idea that any milk would stream forth. What was her surprise, therefore, when such an abundant cascade fell bubbling into the bowl, that it was immediately filled to the brim and overflowed upon the table! The two snakes that were twisted about Quicksilver's staff (but neither Baucis nor Philemon happened to observe this circumstance) stretched out their heads, and began to lap the spilt milk.

And then what a delicious fragrance the milk had! It seemed as if Philemon's only cow must have pastured, that day, on the richest herbage that could be found anywhere in the world. I only wish that each of you, my beloved little souls, could have a bowl of such nice milk at supper time!

"And now a slice of your brown loaf, Mother Baucis," said Quicksilver, "and a little of that honey!"

Baucis cut him a slice, accordingly; and though the loaf, when she and her husband ate of it, had been rather too dry and crusty to be palatable, it was now as light and moist as if but a few hours out of the oven. Tasting a crumb, which had fallen on the table, she found it more delicious than bread ever was before, and could hardly believe that it was a loaf of her own kneading and baking. Yet, what other loaf could it possibly be?

But, oh, the honey! I may just as well let it alone, without trying to describe how exquisitely it smelt and looked. Its color was that of the purest and most transparent gold; and it had the odor of a thousand flowers; but of such flowers as never grew in an earthly garden, and to seek which the bees must have flown high above the clouds. The wonder is, that, after alighting on a flower bed of so delicious fragrance and immortal bloom, they should have been content to fly down again to their hive in Philemon's garden. Never was such honey tasted, seen, or smelt. The perfume floated around the kitchen, and made it so delightful, that, had you closed your eyes you would instantly have forgotten the low ceiling and smoky walls, and have fancied yourself in an arbor, with celestial honeysuckles creeping over it.

Although good Mother Baucis was a simple old dame, she could not but think that there was something rather out of the common way in all that had been going on. So, after helping the guests to bread and honey, and laying a bunch of grapes by each of their plates, she sat down by Philemon, and told him what she had seen, in a whisper. "Did you ever hear the like?" asked she.

"No, I never did," answered Philemon, with a smile. "And I rather think, my dear old wife, you have been walking about in a sort of a dream. If I had poured out the milk, I should have seen through the business at once. There happened to be a little more in the pitcher than you thought—that is all."

"Ah, husband," said Baucis, "say what you will, these are very uncommon people."

"Well, well," replied Philemon, still smiling, "perhaps they are. They certainly do look as if they had seen better days; and I am heartily glad to see them making so comfortable a supper."

Each of the guests had now taken his bunch of grapes upon his plate. Baucis (who rubbed her eyes in order to see the more clearly) was of opinion that the clusters had grown larger and richer and that each separate grape seemed to be on the point of bursting with ripe juice. It was entirely a mystery to her how such grapes could ever have been produced from the old stunted vine that climbed against the cottage wall.

"Very admirable grapes these!" observed Quicksilver, as he swallowed one after another, without apparently diminishing his cluster. "Pray, my good host, whence did you gather them?"

"From my own vine," answered Philemon. "You may see one of its branches twisting across the window, yonder. But wife and I never thought the grapes very fine ones."

"I never tasted better," said the guest. "Another cup of this delicious milk, if you please, and I shall then have supped better than a prince."

This time, old Philemon bestirred himself and took up the pitcher; for he was curious to discover whether there was any reality in the marvels which Baucis had whispered to him. He knew that his good old wife was incapable of falsehood, and that she was seldom mistaken in what she supposed to be true; but this was so very singular a case that he wanted to see into it with his own eyes. On taking up the pitcher, therefore, he slyly peeped into it, and was fully satisfied that it contained not so much as a single drop. All at once, however, he beheld a little white fountain which gushed up from the bottom of the pitcher, and speedily filled it to the brim with foaming and deliciously fragrant milk. It was lucky that Philemon, in his surprise, did not drop the miraculous pitcher from his hand.

"Who are ye, wonder-working strangers?" cried he, even more bewildered than his wife had been.

"Your guests, my good Philemon, and your friends," replied the elder traveler, in his mild, deep voice, that had something at once sweet and awe-inspiring in it. "Give me likewise a cup of the milk; and may your pitcher never be empty for kind Baucis and yourself, any more than for the needy wayfarer!"

The supper being now over, the strangers requested to be shown to their place of repose. The old people would gladly have talked with them a little longer, and have expressed the wonder which they felt, and their delight at finding the poor and meager supper prove so much better and more abundant than they hoped. But the elder

traveler had inspired them with such reverence that they dared not
ask him any questions. And when Philemon drew Quicksilver aside,
and inquired how under the sun a fountain of milk could have got
into an old earthen pitcher, this latter personage pointed to his staff.

"There is the whole mystery of the affair," quoth Quicksilver;
"and if you can make it out, I'll thank you to let me know. I can't
tell what to make of my staff. It is always playing such odd tricks as
this; sometimes getting me a supper, and, quite as often, stealing
it away. If I had any faith in such nonsense, I should say the stick
was bewitched!"

He said no more, but looked so slyly in their faces that they rather
fancied he was laughing at them. The magic staff went hopping at
his heels as Quicksilver quitted the room. When left alone, the good
old couple spent some little time in conversation about the events of
the evening, and then lay down on the floor and fell fast sleep.
They had given up their sleeping room to the guests, and had no
other bed for themselves save these planks, which I wish had been
as soft as their own hearts.

The old man and his wife were stirring betimes in the morning,
and the strangers likewise arose with the sun, and made their preparations to depart. Philemon hospitably entreated them to remain a
little longer, until Baucis could milk the cow, and bake a cake upon
the hearth, and, perhaps, find them a few fresh eggs for breakfast.
The guests, however, seemed to think it better to accomplish a good
part of their journey before the heat of the day should come on.
They therefore persisted in setting out immediately, but asked
Philemon and Baucis to walk forth with them a short distance, and
show them the road which they were to take.

So they all four issued from the cottage, chatting together like old
friends. It was very remarkable, indeed, how familiar the old couple
insensibly grew with the elder traveler, and how their good and
simple spirits melted into his, even as two drops of water would melt
into the illimitable ocean. And as for Quicksilver, with his keen,
quick, laughing wits, he appeared to discover every little thought
that but peeped into their minds, before they suspected it themselves. They sometimes wished, it is true, that he had not been quite

so quick-witted, and also that he would fling away his staff, which
looked so mysteriously mischievous with the snakes always writhing
about it. But then, again, Quicksilver showed himself so very good-
humored, that they would have been rejoiced to keep him in their
cottage, staff, snakes, and all, every day, and the whole day long.

"Ah me! Well-a-day!" exclaimed Philemon, when they had
walked a little way from their door. "If our neighbors only knew
what a blessed thing it is to show hospitality to strangers, they would
tie up all their dogs and never allow their children to fling another
stone."

"It is a sin and shame for them to behave so—that it is!" cried
good old Baucis, vehemently. "And I mean to go this very day, and
tell some of them what naughty people they are!"

"I fear," remarked Quicksilver, slyly smiling, "that you will find
none of them at home."

The elder traveler's brow just then assumed such a grave, stern,
and awful grandeur, yet serene withal, that neither Baucis nor Philemon dared to speak a word. They gazed reverently into his face,
as if they had been gazing at the sky.

"When men do not feel toward the humblest stranger as if he
were a brother," said the traveler in tones so deep that they sounded
like those of an organ," they are unworthy to exist on earth, which
was created as the abode of a great human brotherhood!"

"And, by the by, my dear old people," cried Quicksilver, with the
liveliest look of fun and mischief in his eyes, "where is this same
village that you talk about? On which side of us does it lie?
Methinks I do not see it hereabouts."

Philemon and his wife turned toward the valley, where, at sunset,
only the day before, they had seen the meadows, the houses, the
gardens, the clumps of trees, the wide, green-margined street, with
children playing in it, and all the tokens of business, enjoyment, and
prosperity. But what was their astonishment! There was no longer
any appearance of a village! Even the fertile vale in the hollow of
which it lay had ceased to have existence. In its stead, they beheld
the broad, blue surface of a lake, which filled the great basin of the
valley from brim to brim, and reflected the surrounding hills in its

bosom with as tranquil an image as if it had been there ever since the creation of the world. For an instant, the lake remained perfectly smooth. Then a little breeze sprang up, and caused the water to dance, glitter, and sparkle in the early sunbeams, and to dash with a pleasant rippling murmur against the hither shore.

The lake seemed so strangely familiar that the old couple were greatly perplexed, and felt as if they could only have been dreaming about a village having lain there. But, the next moment, they remembered the vanished dwellings and the faces and characters of the inhabitants far too distinctly for a dream. The village had been there yesterday, and now was gone!

"Alas!" cried these kindhearted old people, "what has become of our poor neighbors?"

"They exist no longer as men and women," said the elder traveler, in his grand and deep voice, while a roll of thunder seemed to echo it at a distance. "There was neither use nor beauty in such a life as theirs; for they never softened or sweetened the hard lot of mortality by the exercise of kindly affections between man and man. They retained no image of the better life in their bosoms; therefore, the lake that was of old has spread itself forth again, to reflect the sky!"

"And as for those foolish people," said Quicksilver, with his mischievous smile, "they are all transformed to fishes. There needed but little change, for they were already a scaly set of rascals and the coldest-blooded beings in existence. So, kind Mother Baucis, whenever you or your husband have an appetite for a dish of broiled trout, he can throw in a line, and pull out half a dozen of your old neighbors!"

"Ah," cried Baucis, shuddering, "I would not, for the world, put one of them on the gridiron!"

"No," added Philemon, making a wry face, "we could never relish them!"

"As for you, good Philemon," continued the elder traveler—"and you, kind Baucis—you, with your scanty means, have mingled so much heartfelt hospitality with your entertainment of the homeless stranger, that the milk became an inexhaustible fount of nectar and the brown loaf and the honey were ambrosia. Thus, the divinities have feasted, at your board, off the same viands that supply their banquets on Olympus. You have done well, my dear old friends. Wherefore, request whatever favor you have most at heart and it is granted."

Philemon and Baucis looked at one another, and then—I know not which of the two it was who spoke, but that one uttered the desire of both their hearts.

"Let us live together while we live, and leave the world at the same instant when we die! For we have always loved one another!"

"Be it so!" replied the stranger, with majestic kindness. "Now, look toward your cottage!"

They did so. But what was their surprise on beholding a tall edifice of white marble, with a wide-open portal, occupying the spot where their humble residence had so lately stood!

"There is your home," said the stranger, beneficently smiling on them both. "Exercise your hospitality in yonder palace as freely as in the poor hovel to which you welcomed us last evening."

The old folk fell on their knees to thank him; but, behold! neither he nor Quicksilver was there.

So Philemon and Baucis took up their residence in the marble palace and spent their time, with vast satisfaction to themselves, in making everybody jolly and comfortable who happened to pass that way. The milk pitcher, I must not forget to say, retained its marvelous quality of being never empty when it was desirable to have it full. Whenever an honest, good-humored, and freehearted guest took a draught from this pitcher, he invariably found it the sweetest and most invigorating fluid that ever ran down his throat. But, if a cross and disagreeable curmudgeon happened to sip, he was pretty certain to twist his visage into a hard knot and pronounce it a pitcher of sour milk!

Thus the old couple lived in their palace a great, great while, and grew older and older, and very old indeed. At length, however, there came a summer morning when Philemon and Baucis failed to make their appearance as on other mornings, with one hospitable smile overspreading both their pleasant faces, to invite the guests of overnight to breakfast. The guests searched everywhere from top to bottom of the spacious palace, and all to no purpose. But, after a great deal of perplexity, they espied, in front of the portal, two venerable trees, which nobody could remember to have seen there the day before. Yet there they stood, with their roots fastened deep into the soil, and a huge breadth of foliage overshadowing the whole front of the edifice. One was an oak, and the other a linden tree. Their boughs—it was strange and beautiful to see—were intertwined together, and embraced one another, so that each tree seemed to live in the other tree's bosom much more than in its own.

While the guests were marveling how these trees that must have required at least a century to grow could have come to be so tall and venerable in a single night, a breeze sprang up, and set their intermingled boughs astir. And then there was a deep, broad murmur in the air, as if the two mysterious trees were speaking.

"I am old Philemon!" murmured the oak.

"I am old Baucis!" murmured the linden tree.

But, as the breeze grew stronger, the trees both spoke at once—"Philemon! Baucis! Baucis! Philemon!"—as if one were both and both were one, and talking together in the depth of their mutual heart. It was plain enough to perceive that the good old couple had renewed their age and were now to spend a quiet and delightful hundred years or so, Philemon as an oak, and Baucis as a linden tree. And oh, what a hospitable shade did they fling around them! Whenever a wayfarer paused beneath it, he heard a pleasant whisper of the leaves above his head, and wondered how the sound should so much resemble words like these:

"Welcome, welcome, dear traveler, welcome!"

And some kind soul, that knew what would have pleased old Baucis and old Philemon best, built a circular seat around both their trunks, where, for a great while afterwards, the weary, and the hungry, and the thirsty used to repose themselves, and quaff milk abundantly out of the miraculous pitcher.

And I wish, for all our sakes, that we had the pitcher here now!

Stories From
The Norse Myths

HOW ALL THINGS BEGAN

By E. M. WILMOT-BUXTON

Illustration by Louis Moe

ONCE upon a time, before ever this world was made, there was neither earth nor sea, nor air, nor light, but only a great yawning gulf, full of twilight, where these things should be.

To the north of this gulf lay the Home of Mist, a dark and dreary land, out of which flowed a river of water from a spring that never ran dry. As the water in its onward course met the bitter blasts of wind from the yawning gulf, it hardened into great blocks of ice, which rolled far down into the abyss with a thunderous roar and piled one on another until they formed mountains of glistening ice.

South of this gulf lay the Home of Fire, a land of burning heat, guarded by a giant with a flaming sword, which, as he flashed it to and fro before the entrance, sent forth showers of sparks. And these sparks fell upon the ice blocks and partly melted them, so that they sent up clouds of steam; and these again were frozen into hoarfrost, which filled all the space left in the midst of the mountains of ice.

Then one day, when the gulf was full to the very top, this great mass of frosty rime, warmed by the flames from the Home of Fire and frozen by the cold airs from the Home of Mist, came to life and became the Giant Ymir, with a living, moving body and cruel heart.

Now there was as yet no tree, nor grass, nor anything that would serve for food, in this gloomy abyss. But when the Giant Ymir began to grope around for something to satisfy his hunger, he heard a sound as of some animal chewing the cud; and there among the ice hills he saw a gigantic cow, from whose udder flowed four great streams of milk, and with this his craving was easily stilled.

But the cow was hungry also, and began to lick the salt off the block of ice by which she was surrounded. And presently, as she went on licking with her strong, rough tongue, a head of hair pushed itself through the melting ice. Still the cow went on licking, until she had at last melted all the icy covering and there stood fully revealed the frame of a mighty man.

Ymir looked with eyes of hatred at this being, born of snow and ice, for somehow he knew that his heart was warm and kind, and that he and his sons would always be the enemies of the evil race of the Frost Giants.

So, indeed, it came to pass. For from the sons of Ymir came a race of giants whose pleasure was to work evil on the earth; and from the Sons of the Iceman sprang the race of the gods, chief of whom was Odin, Father of All Things that ever were made; and Odin and his brothers began at once to war against the wicked Frost Giants, and most of all against the cold-hearted Ymir, whom in the end they slew.

Now when, after a hard fight, the Giant Ymir was slain, such a river of blood flowed forth from his wounds that it drowned all the rest of the Frost Giants save one, who escaped in a boat with only his wife on board and sailed away to the edge of the world. And from him sprang all the new race of Frost Giants, who at every opportunity issued from their land of twilight and desolation to harm the gods in their abode of bliss.

Now when the giants had been thus driven out, All-Father Odin set to work with his brothers to make the earth, the sea, and the sky; these they fashioned from the great body of the Giant Ymir.

Out of his flesh they formed Midgard, the earth, which lay in the center of the gulf; and all round it they planted his eyebrows to make a high fence which should defend it from the race of giants.

With his bones they made the lofty hills, with his teeth the cliffs, and his thick curly hair took root and became trees, bushes, and the green grass.

With his blood they made the ocean, and his great skull, poised aloft, became the arching sky. Just below this they scattered his brains, and made of them the heavy gray clouds that lie between earth and heaven.

The sky itself was held in place by four strong dwarfs, who support it on their broad shoulders as they stand east and west and south and north.

The next thing was to give light to the new-made world. So the gods caught sparks from the Home of Fire and set them in the sky for stars; and they took the living flame and made of it the sun and moon, which they placed in chariots of gold and harnessed to them beautiful horses with flowing manes of gold and silver. Before the horses of the sun, they placed a mighty shield to protect them from its hot rays; but the swift moon-steeds needed no such protection from its gentle heat.

And now all was ready save that there was no one to drive the horses of the sun and moon. This task was given to Mani and Sol, the beautiful son and daughter of a giant; and these fair charioteers drive their fleet steeds along the paths marked out by the gods, and not only give light to the earth but mark out months and days for the sons of men.

Then All-Father Odin called forth Night, the gloomy daughter of the cold-hearted giant folk, and set her to drive the dark chariot drawn by the black horse, Frosty-mane, from whose long wavy hair the drops of dew and hoarfrost fall upon the earth below. After her drove her radiant son, Day, with his white steed Shining-Mane, from whom the bright beams of daylight shine forth to gladden the hearts of men.

But the wicked giants were very angry when they saw all these good things; and they set in the sky two hungry wolves, that the fierce, gray creatures might forever pursue the sun and moon and devour them and so bring all things to an end. Sometimes, indeed, or so say the men of the North, the gray wolves almost succeed in swallowing sun or moon; and then the earth children make such an uproar that the fierce beasts drop their prey in fear. And the sun and moon flee faster than before, still pursued by the hungry monsters.

One day, so runs the tale, as Mani, the Man in the Moon, was hastening on his course, he gazed upon the earth and saw two beautiful little children, a boy and a girl, carrying between them a pail of water. They looked very tired and sleepy, and indeed they were, for a cruel giant made them fetch and carry water all night long when they should have been in bed. So Mani put out a long, long arm and snatched up the children and set them in the moon, pail and all; there you can see them on any moonlight night for yourself.

But that happened a long time after the beginning of things; for as yet there was no man or woman or child upon the earth.

And now that this pleasant Midgard was made, the gods determined to satisfy their desire for an abode where they might rest and enjoy themselves in their hours of ease.

Louis Moe

The gray wolves almost succeed in swallowing sun or moon.

They chose a suitable place far above the earth, on the other side of the great river which flowed from the Home of Mist where the giants dwelt, and here they made for their abode Asgard, wherein they dwelt in peace and happiness and from whence they could look down upon the sons of men.

From Asgard to Midgard they built a beautiful bridge of many colors, to which men gave the name of Rainbow Bridge, and up and down which the gods could pass on their journeys to the earth.

Here in Asgard stood the mighty forge where the gods fashioned their weapons wherewith they fought the giants, and the tools wherewith they built their palaces of gold and silver.

Meantime, no human creature lived upon the earth, and the giants dared not cross its borders for fear of the gods. But one of them, clad in eagles' plumes, always sat at the north side of Midgard, and whenever he raised his arms and let them fall again an icy blast rushed forth from the Mist Home and nipped all the pleasant things of earth with its cruel breath. In due time the earth was no longer without life, for the ground brought forth thousands of tiny creatures, which crawled about and showed signs of great intelligence. And when the gods examined these little people closely, they found that they were of two kinds.

Some were ugly, misshapen, and cunning-faced, with great heads, small bodies, long arms and feet. These they called Trolls or Dwarfs or Gnomes, and sent them to live underground, threatening to turn them into stone should they appear in the daytime. And this is why the Trolls spend all their time in the hidden parts of the earth, digging for gold and silver and precious stones, and hiding their spoil away in secret holes and corners. Sometimes they blow their tiny fires and set to work to make all kinds of wonderful things from this buried treasure; and that is what they are doing when, if one listens very hard on the mountains and hills of the Northland, a sound of tap-tap-tapping is heard far underneath the ground.

The other small earth creatures were very fair and light and slender, kindly of heart, and full of good will. These the gods called Fairies or Elves, and gave to them a charming place called Elfland in which to dwell. Elfland lies between Asgard and Midgard, and since all fairies have wings they can easily flit down to the earth to play with the butterflies, teach the young birds to sing, water the flowers, or dance in the moonlight round a fairy ring.

Last of all, the gods made a man and woman to dwell in fair Midgard; and this is the manner of their creation.

All-Father Odin was walking with his brothers in Midgard where, by the seashore, they found growing two trees, an ash and an elm. Odin took these trees and breathed on them, whereupon a wonderful transformation took place. Where the trees had stood, there were a living man and woman, but they were stupid, pale, and speechless, until Hœnir, the god of Light, touched their foreheads and gave them sense and wisdom; and Loki, the Fire god, smoothed their faces, giving them bright color and warm blood, and the power to speak and see and hear. It only remained that they should be named, and they were called Ask and Embla, the names of the trees from which they had been formed. From these two people sprang all the race of men which lives upon this earth.

And now All-Father Odin completed his work by planting the Tree of Life.

This immense tree had its roots in Asgard and Midgard and the Mist Land; and it grew to such a marvelous height that the highest bough, the Bough of Peace, hung over the Hall of Odin on the heights of Asgard; and the other branches overshadowed both Midgard and the Mist Land. On the top of the Peace Bough was perched a mighty eagle, and ever a falcon sat between his eyes and kept watch on all that happened in the world below, that he might tell to Odin what he saw.

Heidrun, the goat of Odin, who supplied the heavenly mead, browsed on the leaves of this wonderful tree, and from them fed also the four mighty stags from whose horns honeydew dropped on to the earth beneath and supplied water for all the rivers of Midgard.

The leaves of the Tree of Life were ever green and fair, despite the dragon which, aided by countless serpents, gnawed perpetually at its roots, in order that they might kill the Tree of Life and thus bring about the destruction of the gods.

Up and down the branches of the tree scampered the squirrel, Ratatosk, a malicious little creature whose one amusement it was to make mischief by repeating to the eagle the rude remarks of the dragon, and to the dragon those of the eagle, in the hope that one day he might see them in actual conflict.

Near the roots of the Tree of Life is a sacred well of sweet water from which the three Weird Sisters, who know all that shall come to pass, sprinkle the tree and keep it fresh and green. And the water, as it trickles down from the leaves, falls as drops of honey on the earth and the bees take it for their food.

Close to this sacred well is the Council Hall of the gods, to which every morning they rode over the Rainbow Bridge to hold converse together.

And this is the end of the tale of How All Things Began.

HOW ALL-FATHER ODIN
BECAME WISE

By E. M. WILMOT-BUXTON

ON the highest hill of Asgard, upon a great chair, sat All-Father Odin watching from thence all that was happening on and above and under the earth.

The Father of Asas and of men had long gray locks and thick curling beard, and he wore a great blue coat flecked with gray like unto the sky when the fleecy clouds scud across it.

In his hand he carried a spear so sacred that, if anyone swore an oath upon its point, that oath could never be broken.

On his head he wore, when sitting upon his watchtower throne, a helmet shaped like an eagle; but when he wandered as he loved to do about the earth, he wore a large broad-brimmed hat drawn low over his forehead.

Perched on his broad shoulders sat two inky-black ravens, Hugin and Munin, whom every morning he sent to wing their flight about the world to see what was going on. Every evening when they returned, they whispered all that they had seen and heard in his ears.

At Odin's feet crouched two great wolves whom he fed from the meat set before him; for he himself cared not to eat flesh food, and preferred rather to drink the sacred mead provided by the goat who fed upon the leaves of the Tree of Life.

Sometimes Odin left his watchtower throne for the great Council Hall where the twelve Asas sat and took counsel together; but his favorite seat of all was in his own palace of Valhalla, or the Hall of the Chosen Slain.

This palace stood in the midst of a wonderful grove of trees, whose leaves were all of red gold, rustling and shimmering in the breeze. Five and forty doors opened into it, each wide enough to allow eight hundred warriors to enter abreast, and over the chief entrance was a boar's head and a great eagle, whose keen gaze looked forth over all the world. The walls of the palace were built of spears of polished steel so bright that they lighted the whole building; and the roof was made of golden shields.

> "And wondrous gleamed Valhalla on the heights—
> Her walls shone bright as rows of glittering spears;
> The roof resplendent like great golden shields;
> Hundreds of open gates and welcoming doors
> For myriad warriors from the fields of earth—
> The chosen heroes of the future years,
> To be great Odin's mighty bodyguard
> Against the awful prophecies of doom."

From end to end of the great hall stood long tables and benches loaded with armor, ready prepared for the fortunate guests. And this was the manner of their selection. Whenever a great battle was about to be fought on the earth, Odin sent forth the nine Valkyrs, or Battle Maidens, his especial attendants, to watch the progress of the fight and to choose from the fallen warriors half of their number. These the Battle Maidens carried on their swift steeds over the Rainbow Bridge into the great hall of Valhalla, where they were welcomed by the sons of Odin and taken to the All-Father's throne to receive his greeting. But if one had shown himself especially heroic in the fight, Odin would descend from his throne and advance to the door to bid him welcome.

And now, seated at the long tables loaded with great beakers of mead and dishes of boar flesh, the warriors feasted merrily, tended by the fair Battle Maidens,

> "The blazing roof resounds
> The genial uproar of those shades who fall
> In desperate fight, or by some brave attempt."

When they had eaten all they could, the warriors would call for their weapons, ride out into the great courtyard, and there wage desperate fights in the course of which many a man would be sorely wounded. But this mattered little, for at the sound of the dinner horn all wounds were healed.

"And all day long they there are hacked and hewn
'Mid dust, and groans, and limbs lopped off, and blood,
But all at night return to Odin's hall
Woundless and fresh; such lot is theirs in heaven."

These warriors were Odin's special joy and delight, and he was never weary of watching them at feast or in the combat. Sometimes, indeed, when some battle on earth was impending, he would appear riding upon his eight-footed gray horse and with white shield on arm would fling his glittering spear into the ranks of the warriors as signal for the fight to begin, and would rush into the fray with his war cry, "Odin has you all!"

Now, though all this shows very clearly that All-Father Odin was a warlike Asa and delighted in battles, there was another side to his character, for beyond all the other Asas he cared for wisdom.

Very early in the morn of time All-Father Odin discovered that beneath the roots of the Tree of Life, just where sky and ocean met, there was a marvelous spring of water, "the fountain of all wit and wisdom." Looking into its crystal depths, all that was going to happen in the future was revealed, and anyone drinking of it received the gifts of wisdom, knowledge, and right judgment about all things. Now this spring was guarded by the Giant Mimir, who prided himself upon being wiser than any other giants or Asas could be, for he alone had the right to draw water from the well; and every morning, dipping his glittering horn therein, he drank a long draught, and with every draught he grew wiser, till he knew everything that was past and present and is to come.

When Odin became aware of the marvelous properties of the spring, he was eager to drink of it, "for," said he, "it is not fitting that a giant should know more than the Father of Asas and men."

So early one morn he entered a dark grove of trees, where amidst great arching roots fantastically intertwined bubbled the spring; and keeping watch beside it sat Giant Mimir, his long gray beard sweeping over his knees and his great piercing eyes shining with fierce light as the newcomer approached.

"What do you want here?" he demanded, in a voice that sounded like the muttering of thunder before a storm.

"I want a drink of yon water from your glittering horn, good Mimir," said Odin.

But Giant Mimir sunk his great head upon his chest, and looking from under his shaggy eyebrows, growled again:

"Begone, I tell you. I give no man drink from my well."

Then Odin drew himself up to his full height, and in a voice that was more thunderous than that of the giant himself, cried:

"No man am I, O Mimir, but Odin, Father of Asas and men. Refuse not to me the gift of wisdom; for though I can see all things that happen in heaven and earth, I cannot see what lies beneath the deep nor can I see what shall happen in the future. Give, me, therefore, the draught of wisdom and I will pay you whatsoever you demand."

But Mimir still refused. "We giants are of elder race than ye Asas be," he said, "and all the wisdom in the world is in our hands. If I give you to drink of this water you will become wise even as we are, and an enemy more dangerous than ever."

"Nevertheless," replied Odin firmly, "you must give me the water, and I will pay you whatsoever you may ask."

Then Mimir, feeling sure that such a payment would be refused, said, "I will give you the magic draught in return for one of your eyes."

But to his amazement, for the god was very proud of his keen vision, Odin at once plucked forth an eye and handed it to him, saying: "No price is too high to pay for wisdom."

So Mimir was obliged to hand him the horn filled with precious water, and Odin drank a full draught, caring not at all that henceforth he was to have but one eye, for he knew that he had gained the precious gift of wisdom beyond any in the world save Mimir himself.

Meantime, Mimir dropped the eye of the Asa into the well, where it shines bright as the moon reflected in still waters; and he bade Odin depart, saying heavily, "This day is the beginning of trouble betwixt your race and mine."

THE APPLES OF YOUTH

By E. M. WILMOT-BUXTON

SWEETEST of all the Asa folk was Idun, the fair young goddess of Springtime and Youth, and dearly loved was she by the other Asas, both for herself and for her magic apples.

Fast locked in a golden casket were her apples, ripe and sweet and rosy. And each day, at dawn, Idun came to the table where the gods sat and feasted together, and gave those who wished a taste of the fruit.

And it came to pass that everyone who ate the magic fruit grew fresh and young again, however old and weary he had been before. For even the gods of Asgard grew old and weary sometimes; and then nothing would make them young again but the Apples of Youth. So Idun treasured the fruit with the greatest care, and never let it out of her charge for a moment. And however many she took out of her casket wherewith to feed the gods, there always remained just the same number as before.

> "Bright Iduna, maid immortal!
> Standing at Valhalla's portal,
> In her casket has rich store
> Of rare apples, gilded o'er;
> Those rare apples, not of earth,
> To ageing Asas gave new birth."

It was only to be expected, of course, that the fame of this magic fruit should spread, and as nobody liked to grow old, many of the giants, as well as the little dwarf people, used to come to the gates of Asgard and beg that Idun would give them a taste of her apples. But this, though they offered her the richest gifts they could think of, she never would do.

Now one day it so fell out that Odin grew weary of watching his heroes feast and fight in Valhalla, and determined to go forth and seek an adventure elsewhere.

So he called for his brother Hœnir, the clear-eyed Asa who first gave hope to the heart of man, and Loki, the mischievous fellow who yet by reason of his fun and gayety was no bad traveling companion, and bade them accompany him on a journey.

Speeding over the Rainbow Bridge, they came down to the world below and presently found themselves in a desolate region of mountain and moorland, through which they wandered for a long, long time, without coming across any kind of human habitation.

At length, grown weary and very hungry, they began to look about for food, and presently saw to their great joy a herd of oxen feeding upon the mountain-side. It took no long time to kill a fine bull and to kindle an immense fire; after which the Asas hung up the animal to roast and sat down to wait till it was done.

But though the fire flamed bravely over the logs, it made no difference whatever to the meat, which remained raw and cold.

Heaping on fresh fuel, the three Asas put the carcass still nearer the flame and waited hungrily. All in vain; the meat remained uneatable.

Looking at each other in dismay, the Asas exclaimed:

"There is some magic spell at work here."

And at that very moment they heard the loud croak of a bird in the tree above them.

Hastily searching the branches, the Asas soon found an immense eagle perched there and looking down upon them with an evil expression.

"Ho!" cried Odin, "is it you who has bewitched our food?"

The eagle nodded and croaked maliciously again.

"Then come at once and remove the spell," cried the famished Hœnir.

"If I do so, will you give me as much as I want to eat?" asked the eagle.

At this Odin hesitated, for he feared a trick, but Loki's mouth was watering and he called out: "Yes, yes, anything you like if you will only let the meat be cooked."

Then the great bird swooped down and began to fan the flame with his huge wings, and behold! in a very few minutes the gravy began to run, a delicious smell of roast beef filled the air, and there was the meat done to a turn.

Just as the three Asas were putting out hungry hands to seize their portions, however, the eagle, which had been hovering overhead, swooped down and seized more than three-quarters of the animal, leaving barely enough for one of the famished gods.

This was too much for Loki. With a roar of rage like that of an angry lion, he seized a great stake that stood near and struck with all his might at the greedy bird.

The eagle shook himself after the blow, but instead of dropping his booty he rose slowly into the air. And then, to Loki's dismay, he found that one end of the pole had stuck fast to the body of the bird, the other to his own hands.

Try as he would he could not let go, and so found himself being dragged along over stones and bushes and briers, while his arms were almost torn out of their sockets.

In vain he begged and implored the eagle to let him go; it took no notice of him whatever, but flew on and on just a little way above the earth, until at length Loki, feeling he could endure no longer, promised him anything he asked if he would only release him.

Then at last the eagle spoke, telling him that he would set him free on one condition only, and that was that he should manage by some trick to tempt Idun out of Asgard, in order that he could obtain possession of her and of the magic fruit. He told Loki, moreover, that he was the Storm Giant Thiassi in disguise, and bade him beware of the consequences if he broke his solemn promise to one of giant race.

By this time Loki was ready to promise anything to save his life, and so at length he found himself free.

Bruised and torn he made his way back to Odin and Hœnir, by whom he was closely questioned concerning his adventures.

But Loki never hesitated to depart from the truth, and, knowing that it would not do to tell what he had promised, he answered glibly that the eagle had captured him in mistake for someone else, and that when he found out it was Red Loki himself, he had set him free, with many expressions of sorrow for his error.

So the three Asas returned to Asgard, and from that moment Loki did not cease to plot and plan the means by which he could entice Idun outside the gates.

And indeed this was no easy matter, for the Apples of Youth were so precious to the gods that Idun was well guarded by night and day. Sometimes, however, even the Asas were off their guard, and that was the opportunity for Loki.

Strolling one day through the groves of Asgard, Loki found the beautiful maiden all alone in a sunny corner playing at ball with her golden fruit.

"Aha!" cried he, approaching gently so as not to startle her, "what a fair game thou playest here, maiden!" But Idun only smiled at him happily and went on tossing her apples.

Then Loki pulled a long face and came nearer, and said:

"Till this day, fair Idun, I had said that nowhere in the wide world grew apples like thine. But now have I found a tree whereon the fruit is of finer gold, and of greater size than these, and a taste of it needs not to be renewed again, but makes one young forevermore."

Then Idun stopped playing and her blue eyes grew dark and stormy, for she could not bear to think that her apples would no longer be the joy and delight of the Asas.

But then she remembered Loki's deceitful ways and said: "I believe thee not. This is one of thy tricks, Red Loki."

"Ho, you think so, do you?" said the crafty one. "Then come and see them for yourself, and bring your own to compare with them."

"Are they near by?" said Idun, rising doubtfully to her feet and still holding fast to the casket of fruit.

"Only just a little way off," replied Loki, and taking hold of her hand he drew her outside the thicket.

On and on they went, and when she asked where they were going he always replied that the grove where the apples grew was just a little farther than he had thought.

At length, without noticing that she had passed the boundaries, Idun stood outside the walls of Asgard on a dreary region of barren heath and then she at last began to suspect mischief.

"Where am I?" she cried, "and where, O Loki, are the golden apples?"

But she only heard the jeering "Ha! Ha! Ha!" of the Asa as he returned to Asgard, and that was soon lost in the *whirr-r-r* of wings as a mighty eagle, swooping down upon her, fixed his talons in her girdle and rose with her into the air.

And this of course was Thiassi, the Storm Giant, who had been on the watch for her all the time, and who now carried her off, casket and all, to the bleak and desolate abode over which he ruled. Well had it been said that Loki was at the bottom of all the misfortunes that ever befell in Asgard. And never until the End of All Things would he work so dire a mischief again.

Poor Idun grew pale and thin and sad in her captivity, but she would not purchase freedom with a taste of the Apples of Youth, although the Storm Giant coaxed and begged and threatened by turns.

For a time the Asas took little notice of her absence, for they thought she was amusing herself somewhere in the sunny groves of Asgard and had forgotten her daily visit. Then they began to feel old and weary, and at first scarcely knew what was wrong.

Glancing at each other they saw, with startled eyes, wrinkles and lines and gray hairs where these things were not wont to be. Their youth and beauty were disappearing, and then they suddenly awoke to the need of a thorough search for the missing Idun.

And when she could nowhere be found, All-Father Odin, mindful of former tricks, sent for Red Loki and began very closely to question him. Others had seen Idun in his company on that eventful day when she had been carried away, and so, finding it impossible to keep the matter hidden, Loki confessed with a mocking laugh that he had betrayed her into the power of the Storm Giant.

Then all the Asas arose in hot wrath and threatened Loki with death or torture if he did not at once restore the beautiful Goddess of Youth with her magic fruit. And at length, being fairly frightened, he undertook to bring her back if Freya would lend him her falcon plumes that he might disguise himself as a bird.

Thus equipped, Loki flew off to Giantland, and arrived, for-tunately for him, just as Thiassi had gone out a-fishing.

High up at the window of a great stone castle fair Idun looked with tearful eyes upon the stormy sea, and, as she thought of the sunny groves of Asgard, suddenly the plumage of a great falcon almost brushed against her face. Drawing back in alarm, she saw the cunning red eyes of Loki looking at her from the bird's head.

"See how kind am I!" he jeered. "I am come to take thee back to Asgard."

Then Idun almost wept for joy, till she remembered that she was a prisoner, and so cried pitifully.

"I cannot win forth from this cold stone tower, O Loki, and even if I could, thou canst never carry me and my casket back to Asgard. And lo! I cannot outrun the wicked Storm Giant, and though the fruit be heavy I will not leave it behind."

Then Loki soothed her and by his magic arts he changed her into a nut, which he took up in one talon, while the casket he carried with the other, and so set off to fly back to Asgard.

Now Thiassi, the Storm Giant, was ill at ease that day, for he felt the pangs and pains of old age upon him as he went a-fishing. So he determined to return earlier than usual in order to try once more to get the magic fruit from Idun.

Judge then of his dismay when he found his prisoner flown!

Hastily transforming himself into an eagle, Thiassi began to scour the regions of the air, looking everywhere for the maiden, and before long he noted the steady flight of a falcon toward the walls of Asgard.

Sweeping toward him through the air, the keen eyes of the eagle saw the gleam of a golden casket in his talons, and he knew that it was an Asa who had come to the rescue of Idun.

And now it seemed that Loki would be hard put to it to reach Asgard before he was overtaken; for the eagle swept through the air with his great wings much faster than the falcon could fly, and the Asas, who had assembled on the battlements of the city to watch the race, trembled for its issue.

Then some of them remembered how once before they had played a trick upon the pursuer in a similar conflict, and they collected pine shavings in great abundance and piled them on the walls, and stood ready to fire them when the moment came.

On, on flew Loki, hard beset; and close behind him came, with steady rush, the mighty eagle Thiassi. He was almost upon his prey as they neared the walls, but Loki made a last violent effort which was successful, and he fell exhausted into the midst of the Asas.

At the same moment the pile of fuel was lighted, and Thiassi, blinded with smoke and singed with flame, dropped over the battlements and thus fell an easy prey to his waiting enemies. In admiration of his good race, however, the Asas placed his eyes as stars in the heavens, and there they shine to this day.

So the Apples of Youth returned to Asgard, and all the Asas hastened to eat of them and became young and beautiful again. And fair Idun once more resumed her shape, and never again was tricked by wicked Loki but played with her magic fruit in the golden groves of Asgard till the End of All Things.

And this is how the Apples of Youth were once very nearly lost to Asgard.

HOW THE FENRIS WOLF
WAS CHAINED

By E. M. WILMOT-BUXTON

Illustration by Charles Huard

FAIR as were the meads of Asgard, we have seen that the Asa folk were fond of wandering far afield in other regions. Most restless of all was Red Loki, that cunning fellow who was always bringing trouble upon himself or upon his kindred. And because he loved evil, he would often betake himself to the gloomy halls of Giantland and mingle with the wicked folk of that region.

Now one day he met a hideous giantess named Angur-Boda. This creature had a heart of ice, and because he loved ugliness and evil she had a great attraction for him, and in the end he married her and they lived together in a horrible cave in Giantland.

Three children were born to Loki and Angur-Boda in this dread abode, and they were even more terrible in appearance than their mother. The first was an immense wolf called Fenris, with a huge mouth filled with long white teeth which he was constantly gnashing together. The second was a wicked-looking serpent with a fiery-red tongue lolling from its mouth. The third was a hideous giantess, partly blue and partly flesh-color, whose name was Hela.

No sooner were these three terrible children born than all the wise men of the earth began to foretell the misery they would bring upon the Asa folk. In vain did Loki try to keep them hidden within the cave wherein their mother dwelt. They soon grew so immense in size that no dwelling would contain them, and all the world began to talk of their frightful appearance.

It was not long before All-Father Odin, from his high seat in Asgard, heard of the children of Loki. He said to the Asas:

"Much evil will come upon us, O my children, from this giant brood if we defend not ourselves against them. For their mother will teach them wickedness and still more quickly will they learn the cunning wiles of their father. Fetch me them here, therefore, that I may deal with them forthwith."

So, after somewhat of a struggle, the Asas captured the three giant children and brought them before Odin's judgment seat.

Then Odin looked first at Hela, and when he saw her gloomy eyes full of misery and despair he was sorry, and dealt kindly with her, saying: "Thou art the bringer of Pain to man and Asgard is no place for such as thou. But I will make thee ruler of the Mist Home, and there shalt thou rule over that unlighted world, the Region of the Dead."

Forthwith he sent her away over rough roads to the cold, dark region of the North called the Mist Home. And there did Hela rule over a grim crew, for all those who had done wickedness in the world above were imprisoned by her in those gloomy regions. To her came also all those who had died not on the battlefield but of old age or disease. And though these were treated kindly enough, theirs was a joyless life in comparison with that of the dead warriors who were feasting and fighting in the halls of Valhalla, under the kindly rule of All-Father Odin.

Having thus disposed of Hela, Odin next turned his attention to the serpent. And when he saw his evil tongue and cunning, wicked eyes, he said: "Thou art he who bringest Sin into the world of men; therefore the ocean shall be thy home forever."

Then he threw that horrid serpent into the deep sea which surrounds all lands, and there the creature grew so fast that when he stretched himself one day he encircled all the earth and held his own tail fast in his mouth. And sometimes he grew angry to think that he, the son of a god, had thus been cast out; and at those times he would writhe with his huge body and lash his tail till the sea spouted up to the sky. And when that happened the men of the North said that a great tempest was raging. But it was only the Serpent-son of Loki writhing in his wrath.

Then Odin turned to the third child. And behold! the Fenris Wolf was so appalling to look upon that Odin feared to cast him forth, and he decided to endeavor to tame him by kindness so that he should not wish them ill.

But when he bade them carry food to the Fenris Wolf, not one of the Asas would do so for they feared a snap from his great jaws. Only the brave Tyr had courage enough to feed him, and the wolf ate so much and so fast that the business took him all his time. Meantime, too, the Fenris grew so rapidly and became so fierce that the gods were compelled to take counsel and consider how they should get rid of him. They remembered that it would make their peaceful halls unholy if they were to slay him, and so they resolved instead to bind him fast that he should be unable to do them harm.

So those of the Asa folk who were clever smiths set to work and made a very strong, thick chain; and when it was finished they carried it out to the yard where the wolf dwelt, and said to him as though in jest: "Here is a fine proof of thy boasted strength, O Fenris. Let us bind this chain about thee, that we may see if thou canst break it asunder."

Then the wolf gave a great grin with his wide jaws, and came and stood still that they might bind the chain about him; for he knew what he could do. And it came to pass that directly they had fastened the chain, and had slipped aside from him, the great beast gave himself a shake and the chain fell about him in little bits.

At this the Asas were much annoyed, but they tried not to show it and praised him for his strength.

Then they set to work again upon a chain much stronger than the last, and brought it to the Fenris Wolf, saying:

"Great will be thy renown, O Fenris, if thou canst break this chain as thou didst the last."

But the wolf looked at them askance, for the chain they brought was very much thicker than the one he had already broken. He reflected, however, that he himself had grown stronger and bigger, and moreover that one must risk something in order to win renown.

So he let them put the chain upon him, and when the Asas said that all was ready he gave a good shake and stretched himself a few times, and again the fetters lay in fragments on the ground.

Then the gods began to fear that they would never hold the wolf in bonds; and it was All-Father Odin who persuaded them to make one more attempt.

Charles Huard

Only the brave Tyr had courage to feed him.

[See page 216]

So they sent a messenger to Dwarfland bidding him ask the Little Men to make a chain which nothing could possibly destroy.

Setting at once to work, the clever little smiths soon fashioned a slender silken rope, and gave it to the messenger, saying that no strength could break it and that the more it was strained the stronger it would become.

It was made of the most mysterious things—the sound of a cat's footsteps, the roots of a mountain, the sinews of a bear, the breath of fishes, and other such strange materials which only the dwarfs knew how to use.

With this chain the messenger hastened back over the Rainbow Bridge to Asgard.

By this time the Fenris Wolf had grown too big for his yard, so he lived on a rocky island in the middle of the lake that lies in the midst of Asgard. And here the Asas now betook themselves with their chain, and began to play their part with wily words.

"See," they cried, "O Fenris! Here is a cord so soft and thin that none would think of it binding such strength as thine."

And they laughed great laughs, and handed it to one another, and tried its strength by pulling at it with all their might, but it did not break. Then they came nearer and used more wiles, saying:

"*We* cannot break the cord, for 'tis stronger than it looks, but thou, O mighty one, wilt be able to snap it in a moment."

But the wolf tossed his head in scorn, and said: "Small renown would there be to me, O Asa folk, if I were to break yon slender string. Save therefore your breath, and leave me now alone."

"Aha!" cried the Asas. "Thou fearest the might of the silken cord, thou false one, and that is why thou wilt not let us bind thee!"

"Not I," said the Fenris Wolf, growing rather suspicious, "but if it is made with craft and guile it shall never come near my feet."

"But," said the Asas, "thou wilt surely be able to break this silken cord with ease, since that hast already broken the great iron fetters."

To this the wolf made no answer, pretending not to hear.

"Come!" said the Asas again, "why shouldst thou fear? For even if thou couldst not break the cord we would immediately let thee free again. To refuse is a coward's piece of work."

Then the wolf gnashed his teeth at them in anger and said:

"Well I know you, Asas! For if you bind me so fast that I cannot get loose you will skulk away, and it will be long before I get any help from you; and therefore am I loath to let this band be laid upon me."

But still the Asas continued to persuade him and to twit him with cowardice, until at length the Fenris Wolf said with a sullen growl:

"Have it your own way then. But, as a pledge that this is done without deceit, let one of you lay his hand in my mouth while you are binding me and afterwards while I try to break the bonds."

Then the Asa folk looked at one another in dismay, for they knew very well what this would mean. And while they consulted together the wolf stood gnashing his teeth at them with a horrid grin.

At length Tyr the Brave hesitated no longer. Boldly he stalked up to the wolf and thrust his arm into his enormous mouth, bidding the Asas bind fast the beast. Scarce had they done so when the wolf began to strain and pull, but the more he did so the tighter and stiffer the rope became.

The gods shouted and laughed with glee when they saw how all his efforts were in vain. But Tyr did not join them in their mirth, for the wolf in his rage snapped his great teeth together and bit off his hand at the wrist.

Now when the Asas discovered that the animal was fast bound they took the chain which was fixed to the rope and drew it through a huge rock, and fastened this rope deep down in the earth so that it could never be moved. And this they fastened to another great rock which was driven still deeper into the ground.

When the Fenris Wolf found that he had been thus secured he opened his mouth terribly wide, and twisted himself right and left and tried his best to bite the Asa folk. He uttered, moreover, such terrible howls that at length the gods could bear it no longer. So they took a sword and thrust it into his mouth so that the hilt rested on his lower, and the point against his upper jaw. And there he was doomed to remain until the end of All Things shall come, when he

"Freed from the Chain
Shall range the Earth."

HOW THE PRIDE OF THOR
WAS BROUGHT LOW

By E. M. WILMOT-BUXTON

FROM the sunny heights of Asgard, the Asa folk were wont to look upon the earth and to take pleasure in its welfare and in the happiness of its people. But all too often they saw with dismay that the Frost Giants from their cold Northern home of ice and snow sent forth cruel blasts which nipped the buds, withered the flowers of spring, and saddened the hearts of men. So one day that mighty Asa who is called Thor determined to go forth and teach these Giant folk how to behave themselves better. Calling for his chariot of brass, which was drawn by two mighty goats from whose teeth and hoofs sparks continually flew, he was about to drive away when Red Loki came running up and begged to be taken, too.

To this Thor agreed, for he had rather a liking for Loki in spite of his mischievous tricks, and in a few minutes they were hurtling through the air at a great rate.

All day long they drove, and at evening time reached the borders of Giantland where stood the hut of a poor peasant. Seeing this, the two Asas determined to try to obtain shelter for the night.

The peasant was a goodhearted fellow and gladly welcomed them under his roof; but he had only a bit of black bread to offer them for supper, and this was by no means a satisfactory meal for two hungry gods. But Thor was quite equal to the occasion.

"Fear not," said he kindly, "I will provide meat in plenty for you and your family as well as for ourselves."

Then he went out, killed his two goats, cut them up, and threw them into a great cauldron which the peasant's wife at his request had set to boil upon the fire. The skins meantime he spread with care upon the floor.

The stew was soon cooked to perfection, whereupon Thor invited the man and his wife and children to eat as much as they would.

"Be careful, however," said he, "not to break a single bone, but to throw them all into the skins spread out on the floor."

This they promised to do, but during the meal Red Loki, wishing to see what would happen if they disobeyed, persuaded the boy, Thialfi, the peasant's son, to break one of the bones in order to suck out the marrow, saying that no one could possibly know that he had done so. Then they lay down to sleep, the bones of the animals wrapped in the goatskins being upon the floor.

Next morning, just before daybreak Thor arose, and having stretched himself took up his mighty hammer and gave the goat-skins a tap. Immediately the goats sprang up as much alive as ever they were, and perfectly well save that one of them limped.

Then Thor knew at once that his commands had been disobeyed and the whole household soon knew it too. His brows sank over his eyes and he grasped his hammer so hard that his knuckles grew white. The terrified peasant fell down on his face before him; and when Thor lifted the hammer to destroy him the whole household wept aloud and begged for mercy, promising to give him all they had in the world as an atonement.

When Thor saw their terror, his anger left him and he agreed to take as a ransom the children of the peasant, a boy and girl, called Thialfi and Roskva. And they became his servants and have been always in his company since that time.

Leaving his goats in charge of the peasant, Thor went forward toward Giantland accompanied by Loki and the two children; and the boy Thialfi, who was the fleetest of foot of all living creatures, carried Thor's bag.

After walking all day through a bleak and barren country wrapped in a thick mist, they came at nightfall to a great wood which seemed to offer neither provisions, nor roof to shelter under for the night. At length, after searching about for a very long time they came to what seemed to be a large hall of misty and uncertain shape, the door of which was as wide as the whole building.

So they entered, and finding everything within empty and dark they determined to go no farther, and stretched themselves, hungry and weary as they were, upon the ground.

In the middle of the night they were awakened by what seemed to be a great earthquake. The earth trembled beneath them and the house shook.

Calling upon his companions, Thor arose, and fearing lest the roof should fall upon them he drew them into an inner room, and, seating himself in the doorway, took up his hammer and prepared to defend himself and them if anything should befall. But nothing further happened save a renewed trembling of the ground and a curious, regularly recurring sound, like a loud groan or roar.

When it began to grow light Thor went out and saw, not far off, a huge giant lying on the ground fast asleep; and he understood that it was his snores which had caused the ground to shake and which had sounded like a roar or groan.

Suddenly the giant awoke, and sprang up so quickly that Loki and the children, who had followed Thor, jumped behind a tree. But Thor, who was afraid of nothing, only grasped his hammer tightly and asked his name.

"I am called Skrymir," said the giant, looking down at him, and, catching sight of his hammer of which all in heaven and earth had heard, he went on: "I don't need to ask *your* name, for I see you are Thor. But what have you done with my glove?"

As he said these last words, he stretched out a huge hand and picked up his glove, which Thor to his great astonishment found to be the house in which he had spent the night; and the inner room was the place for the thumb.

Hearing that they were on their way toward Giantland, Skrymir asked if he might accompany them; and as he seemed a good-natured fellow they agreed. But first they sat down to eat their breakfast. Skrymir ate his huge meal out of a great provision sack, and eyed with much merriment the wallet which held the food of Thor and his companions.

" 'Tis like a little toy," said he; but Thialfi answered crossly:

"Toy it may be to you, but it has made my shoulders ache very finely, I can tell you. I could hardly sleep all night for the pain."

Then Skrymir laughed, and took the bag and put it into his sack, slinging the whole over his shoulder as if it had been a feather.

After this they all set off together, and that day they covered an immense distance, for the giant took such huge strides that they had to run the whole time in order to keep up with him.

When it grew dark, Skrymir led them into a vast wood where no habitation was to be found, and bade them take up their quarters under a huge oak. The others were weary and hungry beyond words, for they had not stopped all day either to eat or rest; but Skrymir seemed only sleepy, and was preparing to begin his snores when Loki, whom fasting had put decidedly out of temper, sharply reminded him that they had had no supper. Pushing the great sack over to them, the giant sleepily replied that they were welcome to all that it contained and immediately fell into a deep slumber.

But when Loki tried to undo the mouth of the sack he could not get one knot loosened, nor could he even get one of the strings to stir. Then Thor tried with all his strength, but could do nothing. This was a serious matter, for they were all starving with hunger by this time; so Thor in a great rage snatched up his hammer in both hands, stepped up to where Skrymir was lying and dashed the hammer with all his force at his head.

At this blow, which would have smashed the skull of most men, the giant drowsily opened one eye, saying: "Did a leaf fall on my head just now? Good night to all of you. I suppose you have now had your supper and are going to bed."

At this the Asas were so astonished that they meekly replied that they were just going to do that very thing. And they went and lay down under another oak. But there was no sleep for them, for, besides their fear and hunger, the whole wood resounded with the giant's snores so that it seemed as though it thundered all the time.

At last Thor could stand it no longer, so he went over to him, and swinging his hammer with all his skill brought it down with such a crash that he knew by the feel of it that it had sunk deep into the head.

But the giant only turned over, saying sleepily: "What was that? Did an acorn fall upon my head? How is it with you, friend Thor?"

Then Thor answered hastily that he had only just waked up, and that it was midnight and still time to sleep.

The god was now alarmed, and he decided that if it were possible he would get in a third blow which should put an end altogether to the most extraordinary companion he had ever had.

So he lay watching for Skrymir to go fast asleep again, and shortly before daybreak his chance came.

Creeping up, he clutched the hammer with all his might and dashed it at the giant's temples with such force that it sank up to the handle.

Scarcely had he time to pull it out again than Skrymir sat up and began to yawn, rubbing his eyes and stroking his temples and saying:

"Are there any birds sitting in the tree above me? I thought, as I woke up, that some moss from the branches fell upon my head. Ho, there! Thor, are you awake? You seem to be moving early this morning. Let us all get up and continue our journey, for we are now not far from Giant Town."

Filled with astonished dismay at the failure of his attempts, Thor roused his companions, and all set off hungry and dispirited at the giant's heels. Presently they began to whisper together as to the events of the night, and of the enormous strength and size of their companion, but after awhile Skrymir looked down at them and said:

"We have now come to two ways: mine goes to the north where you see yon mountains; yours, if you still wish to reach Giant Town, lies there to the east. So here we part company, but first let me give you some useful advice.

"I have heard you whispering to one another that I am not small of stature; but when you come to Giant Town you will see greater folk still. So do not brag too much of your own powers, for the Giant folk will not put up with the boasting of such insignificant little fellows as you be.

"But if you want to be quite wise, turn back now to your own place, for that is the best thing you can do."

So saying, Skrymir shouldered his great sack and, turning his back upon them, went off through the forest with such huge strides that he was soon lost to sight.

Now Loki was much disposed to follow the advice of the giant and turn back to Asgard, but of this Thor would not hear. So they continued their journey until noonday, when they saw before them a great town standing in the midst of an immense plain. The walls and gates of the town were so high that they had to bend their necks right back before they could see the top of them, and when they came nearer still they found the gate was fast shut.

But this gate had bars, and was made to keep in the Giant folk, not to keep out smaller people of whose visits they had never thought. So the two Asas and their servants found little difficulty in creeping through the bars and so getting into the town.

The first thing they saw was a great hall, toward which they went, and finding the door open they entered, and saw in the center of it two benches, enormously high and wide upon which sat a number of giants. In their midst, upon a platform high as the roof of an ordinary house, sat the King of the Giants, to whom they advanced and made their bows. At first the King looked about on the floor as though they were too small for him to see, but at length he cast a scornful glance upon them, and with a grin that showed all his teeth said:

"Is this little fellow the great god Thor, of whom we have heard so much? Perhaps, however, you are bigger in strength than in size. Now, for what feats are you and your companions prepared? For you must know this, that no one is allowed to stay here unless he be more skilled in some craft or accomplishment than any other man."

At this Red Loki, who was so dreadfully hungry that he scarcely knew what he was saying, called out: "I know what I can do better than anyone else! I will soon prove that there is no one present who can eat his food faster than I can."

Then said the King of the Giants: "That is a feat to be proud of if you speak the truth, and you shall try it immediately."

So he called from the bench a man named Logi, and bade him come out on the floor and try his strength against Loki.

The others took a huge trough full of meat and set it on the floor, and they put Logi at one end and Loki at the other.

Both of them ate as fast as they possibly could, and met in the middle of the trough. But though Loki had such an immense appetite and had eaten every scrap of meat off the bones, Logi had eaten up the flesh and bones and the trough as well.

So Loki had to confess that he had been beaten.

Then the Giant King looked at the boy Thialfi and asked: "What use is that lad in heaven or earth?"

And Thialfi answered that he would run faster than anyone whom the Giant King liked to name.

"That is a good feat," said the King, "but it is to be hoped you can run *really* fast, for you will have something to do to win this race."

So saying, he took them outside where there was an excellent race course along the flat plain; and he called up a young man whose name was Hugi, and bade him run a race with Thialfi.

In the first heat of that race, although Hugi ran so fast, yet, when he turned to run back, he met Thialfi face to face. Then the King of the Giants encouraged the lad, saying: "Never before has come anyone hither who was swifter of foot than you."

Then they ran the second heat, and when Hugi reached the goal, Thialfi was three-quarters of the way thither.

Then said the giant: "Well run, Thialfi; yet I do not think that you will win this race. However, we shall see what happens in the third heat."

When this was run, Hugi had reached the goal and turned back again ere poor Thialfi was barely half way there.

At this all the giants began to applaud Hugi, saying that he had fairly won the race; and Thialfi was obliged to go sadly away.

The King of the Giants next inquired what feats Thor could show to prove the truth of the tales men told of his great strength; and the Asa, who was now very thirsty, and at all times a mighty man at the bowl, said that he would drink deeper than anyone in the whole world.

So they returned to the hall, where the King called upon his cupbearer to bring the horn out of which his valiant giants drank; and this was filled with ale and handed to Thor.

Then said the King of the Giants: "With us 'tis thought that the man is a good drinker who empties his horn at one drought; he who takes it off in two is but moderately thirsty; but he who cannot empty in three is but a wretched drinker, and not worthy of the name."

Thor looked at the horn, and thinking within himself: "This is not a difficult task, for the horn though it seems deep is not very large," took a drink which he quite thought would have drained the vessel. But when he could drink no longer for lack of breath, he looked in the horn and there was the ale still brimming over the edge.

Then the giant chuckled and said: "Well drunk, good Thor, but you have by no means emptied the horn. It seems to me, indeed, that men have boasted too much of your fine deeds. I would not have believed that you would have taken so long to drink up the ale. However, I don't doubt you will finish it at the second draught."

Thor reddened with wrath at these scoffing words, and took up the horn intending to drink the ale to the last dregs. But, try as he would, he could not get the end of the horn to tip up completely, and when he set it down it seemed to him that he had drunk less than at the first time. Yet some difference had been made, for the horn could now be carried without spilling.

"Ha! ha!" laughed the giant. "Is this your skill, good Thor? Are you not leaving rather much for your third draught? It looks to me as if that will have to be the greatest of them all."

Then Thor got very angry indeed, and, setting the horn to his mouth, drank with all his might and main, so that when he could do no more and had set it down again the ale had certainly grown less.

"Ha! ha!" roared the giant. "They think too highly of you in the world above, my little Thor. Now what other game would you like to try?"

"Whatever you like," answered Thor very grumpily, for none of the Asas liked being laughed at.

So the giant said: "Young lads here think it nothing but play to lift my cat up from the ground, and I should never have suggested such a feat to the strength of Asa Thor had I not discovered that he is much less of a man than I thought."

Then he called: "Puss! Puss!" in a voice that shook the house; upon which an enormous gray cat sprang forth on the floor before them.

Rather annoyed at being asked to do such an easy thing, Thor went over to the animal, put his arm round it and tried to lift it up. But the more he tugged and strained the more the cat arched its back, so that his strength was exerted vainly; and in the end, when he was black in the face with the efforts he had made, he had only succeeded in lifting up one paw.

Then the giant repeated his scornful laugh, saying: "That's just as I expected. The cat is rather large, and Thor is small—tiny, indeed, compared with the great men who are here with us."

"Tiny, indeed!" roared Thor, in great wrath. "Let anyone you like come and wrestle with me and I will show you if my strength is as tiny as you seem to think."

At this the giant pretended to look about him on the benches, saying: "I don't see anyone here who would not think it beneath him to wrestle with such a puny fellow. Let me see! Let me see! Ah! call hither my old nurse, Elli, and let Thor wrestle with her if he wants to. She has thrown to the ground before now men who thought themselves as strong as this little Thor."

At his call there came into the hall an old woman—so old that Thor refused at first to close with her. But the giants mocked him so that at length he seized her round the waist. Yet the tighter he grasped her the firmer she stood. At length she began to grip him in her turn. Thor lost his footing almost at once and, though he wrestled valiantly, she brought him onto his knee.

At this the giant interfered, saying that no more was necessary to show who was the stronger and that it was getting too late for any more contests. Then he bade them seat themselves at supper, and after a royal feast conducted them to their beds with the kindest hospitality. But Thor spent all that night in bitterness, for his pride had been brought very low.

At daybreak next morning the Asas and their companions arose and prepared to depart. Before they set out, however, their host appeared on the scene and insisted upon their eating a hearty breakfast, after which he offered to show them the most direct way out of the city.

As they set out, the Giant King grew strangely silent and thoughtful and did not speak to them until they stood outside the gates. Then, as they were about to bid him farewell, he suddenly asked Thor how he thought his journey had turned out.

To this, Thor, deeply humbled and mortified by all that had occurred, said that he felt much disgraced at the knowledge that henceforth the giants would call him a man of little account. But to his intense surprise the giant shook his head, saying: "Had I my way, you should never enter this city again, and if I had known before how strong you were you should never have come into it, for you have very nearly brought utter ruin upon us all.

"Know then, first of all, that I have deceived you with magical delusions the whole time. For I was that giant Skrymir who met you in the woods, and who tied up the mouth of the provision sack with invisible iron threads so that you could not unloose it.

"That same night you struck with your hammer three great blows upon my head, the least of which would have made an end of me if it had hit me. But in the darkness I managed each time to bring a mountain between me and your hammer without your seeing it; and if you want to see the marks you made in it you have but to look at that mountain above my city, with its top cloven into three great dales.

"Next, when you came to my hall, Loki contested with Logi, my courtier, as to who should eat the fastest. But he whose name was Logi is really *Fire*, and in consequence he could eat up trough and bones and all in no time. When Thialfi ran his race, he ran against Hugi who is no other than *Thought*, and no one, of course, can run as fast as he.

"When you yourself drank from that horn, then indeed was seen a marvel which I should never have thought possible. You did not see that one end of the horn stood in the sea, which you were drinking all the time. And when you reach the shore you will see how much the sea has ebbed by your draughts.

"Nor was it less marvelous to me that you lifted up the paw of the cat. For that cat was none other than the Serpent which lies around the whole earth with its tail in its mouth. When it took the form of a cat you lifted it so that it was obliged to arch itself almost up to the sky; and then we all trembled, for we feared that you would pull it altogether out of the sea.

"Your struggle with Elli was perhaps the most amazing of all. For she is *Old Age,* of whom none has ever got the better.

"And now depart, O Asa folk, and 'twill be better for us both if we never see each other again."

Now when Thor heard how he had been tricked, he grasped his hammer with intent to dash both the giant and his city to pieces. But when he looked for them, both had disappeared, and he found himself standing with his companions in the midst of a large plain on which was no sign of habitation.

Then he knew that the power of the Giant folk would not yield to force, and thinking of their strange adventures Thor and his companions returned to Asgard.

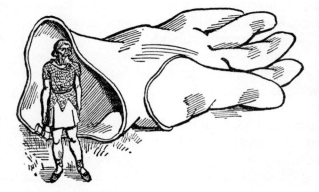

HOW THOR'S HAMMER WAS LOST AND FOUND

By E. M. WILMOT-BUXTON

MOST precious in the eyes of Thor was his magic hammer, Miölnir, of which even the mighty Frost Giants stood in dread.

Always he laid it by his side when he went to rest, and always it was the first thing for which his hand was outstretched when he awoke. Judge then of his horror and dismay when, on opening his eyes one morning, the hammer was nowhere to be seen.

Starting up with a roar of rage, Thor commenced to search everywhere for the missing weapon. Up and down his wonderful palace built of the thunder clouds, he tramped, with a noise that shook the whole city of Asgard. But the hammer was not to be found.

Then he called upon golden-haired Sif, his wife, and bade her help in the search; and still the hammer was nowhere to be seen. It was clear that someone must have stolen it, and when he realized this Thor's wrath broke all bounds. His bristling red hair and beard stood up on end, and from them flew a whole volley of fiery sparks.

Presently, as the angry Asa was shaking the palace with his thunderous voice, Red Loki came along to inquire into the trouble. He was not likely to sympathize with Thor, but, always brimful of curiosity, he loved to have a part in everything that happened.

"What's the matter, Asa Thor?" said he; and Thor replied, lowering his voice as he spoke, for he did not want his loss to be too widely known:

"Now listen to what I tell thee, Loki—'tis a thing which is known neither on earth below nor in heaven above. My hammer's gone."

This news was most interesting to Loki, who had long owed Thor a grudge which he was afraid to pay openly. "Ho! ho!" said he. "Then shall we soon have the giants turning us out of Asgard, brother Thor." "Not if you use your wits as you know how," growled Thor, still in a very bad temper. "Come, you call yourself a clever fellow. Find out for me who has robbed me of my thunderbolt, my hammer, my Miölnir."

Then Loki gave a grin and a wink, and promised to do what he could—not because he cared for Thor but because he loved to be of importance, and was, moreover, really frightened as to what might happen to Asgard if the magic hammer was not at hand.

It was not long before he noticed that an extraordinary kind of tempest was raging in the regions below—not an orderly kind of tempest, with first some thunder and then some rain and then a gust of wind or two, such as Thor was wont to arrange, but a mixture of hail and wind and thunder and lightning and rain and snow, all raging together in a tremendous muddle, so that the earth folk thought the end of the world was come.

This gave Loki a hint, and he began to peer about between the clouds until at length he saw that the trouble was coming from a certain hill which stood in the center of Giantland.

Now on the top of this hill lived a certain Thrym, prince of the Frost Giants, who for a long time past had been very envious of the might of Thor. He had indeed done his best to imitate him as far as he could, and had managed to get up a very good imitation of lightning and hail and rain; but he had not been able to manage the thunderbolts, for they could only be made by means of Thor's hammer, Miölnir. All this was well known to Red Loki, and he was therefore not at all surprised to find that somehow or other Thrym must have got hold of the magic weapon; for here were thunderbolts crashing about the earth and sky at a terrible rate.

When informed of the discovery, Thor flew into a still more tremendous rage, and wanted to rush off at once to try conclusions with the giant. But Loki, who loved rather to get a thing by trickery and deceit, persuaded him that violence would never do.

"Remember," said he, "that Thrym *with* the hammer is much stronger than Thor without it. This is a matter which must be managed by clever wit and craft, not by force and loud talking. Leave therefore the whole matter to me."

To this Thor very reluctantly agreed.

Then Loki bethought him of some disguise wherein he might visit Giantland in safety, for he was not at all anxious to risk his life. He betook himself to the House of Maidens, over which ruled Freya, fairest of all in Asgard, she who was wont to shake the spring flowers from her golden locks as she passed over the frozen uplands, leaving behind her a region of green and smiling beauty. Loki found the goddess, and begged the loan of her magic falcon plumes in which she was wont to flit to and fro over the earth; and when she learnt for what purpose he needed them she gladly assented.

Then Loki took the appearance of a great brown bird, and spreading his wings he flew toward Giantland.

It was a long journey, as he already knew, and, although the tempest had now ceased to rage, he found the country of the giants darker and colder and drearier than ever.

The longest journey comes to an end, and at length Loki reached a mountain where sat the Giant Thrym, his huge legs dangling to the ground, playing with a puppy as large as an elephant.

Perching as near as he dared, Loki gazed at the giant with his bright, round eyes, and was wondering how to begin, when Thrym, who at a glance had seen completely through his disguise, said calmly, in a voice as much as possible like Thor's thunderous roar: "Oh, ho! Loki, what are you doing so far from Asgard? Are you not afraid, little fellow as you are, to venture into our country?"

Then Loki, thinking to win his way by flattery, replied: "Sad indeed is it in Asgard, now that Miölnir has vanished. Clever was that one who spirited it away from the very side of Thor. Methinks none but you could have done it, O mighty Thrym!"

Pleased with the compliment to his cleverness the giant chuckled before admitting: "Ay, Loki, the hammer is mine, 'tis very true; and now men will know who really is the Thunderer."

"Ah, well!" sighed cunning Loki. "Some men are strong by reason of their weapons, and some are just as strong without. Small need have you, O mighty Thrym, for hammers, but Thor is nought without it. Yet, since all the world knows that you are his master, let him have his plaything back that we may cease to be troubled by his peevish outcry."

But though Thrym was as stupid as he was big, he was not to be caught thus.

"No, no, my little Loki," he said. "Mine is the hammer, and deep have I buried it beneath the bottom of the sea. Go tell this to your Asa folk, and say to them that I will give it back on one condition only—and that is that they send me Freya, that fairest of maidens, to be my wife."

At this suggestion Loki could scarcely keep from laughing, for the idea of sending the beautiful Freya, the joy and delight of Asgard to be the wife of this ill-favored Frost Giant was too absurd for words.

It was not much to him, however, what happened to anyone except himself, so he hastened to reply: "Be sure, O Thrym, that everything I can do to further the matter shall be done. And if Freya is of the same mind as I you will soon be welcoming that most sweet maiden to Giantland—Farewell!"

So saying, he spread his brown wings and flew back to Asgard, delighted to think of the mischief he could now set brewing.

First of all he visited Thor and told him of what had passed. And the Thunderer, when he heard of Thrym's boastful words, was filled with wild wrath and wanted to start off, then and there, and wrest the hammer from the depths of the sea. But Loki pointed out the difficulties that stood in the way and, leaving the Asa to ponder over his words, he hurried off to Freya and informed her of Thrym's proposal.

The beautiful Freya was walking in her garden, and round her neck she wore her famous necklet of stars. When she heard Loki's suggestion that she should wed a hideous giant she fell into such a rage that she broke her necklace, and all the stars went falling through the sky, so that men cried: "See how the stars are shooting!"

Meantime the Asa folk had met together to consider all that had happened, and, having calmed the fury of Thor, they pointed out to him that Asgard stood in the gravest danger of an attack which would find them quite unprotected. When they had said this several times over, Thor began to weary of the subject, and he replied with great surliness: "Very well, then. Let Freya go to Thrym as his wife, and then shall we be as before, with Miölnir to defend us."

When Freya heard this, her rage turned to tears and lamentations, and she declared that it would be death to her to send her to the gloomy halls of Giantland, whence she could never hope to revisit the flowery meads and grassy slopes of Asgard. And the Asas, unable to bear the sight of her grief, with one voice declared that they would never spare her from the Home of Bliss.

Then there stepped forward Heimdall, the watchman who sits on guard over the Rainbow Bridge by night and day.

Now Heimdall had the gift of seeing into the future, and the Asas were always ready to hear his words, well knowing them to be wise.

"My plan is this," said he. "Let Thor borrow the clothes of Freya and put a thick veil over his face; and let him go thus to Thrym's castle and pass for his bride. And if he cannot by some means manage to get hold of the hammer when he is there—why, he must give it up altogether."

At this suggestion the Asas clapped their hands with approval— all, indeed, save Thor, who looked most glum and was extremely unwilling to agree to the plan.

"Dress me as a bride!" he grumbled. "A pretty maiden I shall make! Ready enough am I to fight, but I will not make myself a laughing-stock if I know it."

But the Asas besought him to give way, while Loki twitted him with cowardice. Fair Freya, too, appealed with tearful eyes; and so at length, with great reluctance, the Thunderer agreed to do what they wished.

Fortunately the maiden Freya was very tall, but even so it was with some difficulty that they managed to cover the burly form of Thor with her robes.

He insisted, moreover, upon wearing his own shirt of mail and his girdle of strength; and these took much drapery to hide. Great was the laughter in the halls of Asgard that night as the Battle Maidens brushed and curled Thor's long yellow hair, and set a jeweled headdress upon it; and finally, when the maidens proceeded to cover up his thick beard and angry eyes with a silken veil, the mirth of the Asas was unrestrained. To complete the disguise, the maidens hung round his neck the famous necklet which had now been restrung, and finally Frigga, the wife of All-Father Odin, secured at his girdle the great bunch of keys proper to brides at a wedding in the Northland.

While this was being done, Loki more than all had been convulsed with merriment at the success of his mischief-making. The very sight of Thor's disgusted looks, and of his great hands clenched with rage under the delicate veil, nearly killed him with laughter; and when all was ready he declared himself unable to lose an atom of the fun in store.

"Let me go with you," he implored. "See, I will dress myself as your handmaiden. Ah, you had better agree, for without me to prompt you, you will never play your part."

So Loki was dressed as a waiting maid and took his seat very demurely by the side of Thor in the goat car. Loud was the laughter in Asgard as the Asas watched the two drive off together and heard the roar of the Thunderer's voice issuing from the folds of a meek maiden's veil as he urged his goats upon their course. Long and stormy was that ride to Giantland, for Thor was still in the worst of tempers and drove his chariot so furiously that

> "The mountains crashed,
> The earth stood in flames,"

as the hoofs of the goats clattered over mountains and waters, striking sparks wherever they touched a rock.

Thrym was much overjoyed when he heard that a chariot containing the two maidens was approaching his door. Away ran his servants in different directions, some with orders to make ready a grand banquet, some to prepare the chamber of the bride, some to receive her at the door.

The giant himself assisted them to alight and looked with admiration at the stately figure of his bride; but he made no attempt to see her face, since it is the custom in the Northland for the bride to remain veiled until the marriage has been completed.

"A bride worthy of a giant!" murmured his servants, as he led her to a lofty seat beside his own great throne of gold; and they looked with approval also on the buxom form of the waiting maid, who stood, closely veiled, behind her mistress' chair.

Now the journey had been long and cold, and it was with joy that the newcomers noticed that the preparations for the banquet were complete, for they were exceedingly hungry.

The giants are huge eaters, and they gathered round the board, whereon were displayed an enormous ox roasted whole, a vast dish of salmon and various other dainties. But because the bride was a woman, and modest withal, they brought her tiny morsels on a dainty golden plate.

This was too much for Thor, who had always possessed a most healthy appetite and was now more than usually ready for his supper. Gradually drawing nearer to the table, whilst the others were busy with the meal, he managed to get hold of the dish of roasted ox and within a few minutes the whole of the animal had disappeared.

Then he put out his hand to the platter of salmon, and in eight mouthfuls disposed of eight of the great fish. After this he noticed a large plate full of cakes and sweetmeats which was set apart for the ladies of the party. Of these, too, he made short work. Finally, feeling thirsty after his huge meal, he took up two barrels of mead and tossed them off, one after another, down his capacious throat. Then he sat back on his chair with a sigh of deep content.

These proceedings had been watched by Loki with uneasiness, but by Thrym with open-mouthed dismay. Was this the usual appetite of this dainty maiden, who had eaten more than the company of giants? But Loki bent toward him and whispered in his ear that the thought of marrying had so excited Freya that she had eaten nothing for eight days, and had therefore been on the point of starvation.

This reassured the giant, and being now himself filled with mead he drew nearer and, lifting a corner of the veil, tried to kiss the cheek of his future bride.

But Thor, who was longing to be at close grips with him, threw him such a fiery glance that he drew quickly back, saying: "Why does fair Freya's eye burn like a spark from a furnace?" "Pooh!" whispered Loki again, "that is nothing but her love for you, which for eight days has raged like a flaming fire."

This news was still more pleasant to hear, and Thrym in high good humor cried: "Bring in the hammer, my wedding gift, wherewith to plight the maid. For when I have laid it on her lap she will be my own forever, and together we will work dire evil against the Asa folk whom I hate with all my heart."

What was that unmaidenly sound that issued from under the silken veil at these words? But though Loki turned pale to hear it, Thrym, busy sending for the hammer, did not pay any heed.

Back came the giant's servants at length, bending under the weight of Miölnir. And as they bowed before the silent maiden, sitting with meekly bent head upon the throne, Thrym cried with a merry jest: "See, here is little Thor's tiny plaything—a pretty toy truly for his feeble hands. Take it, fair Freya, as my wedding gift."

"And take *that* as mine!" roared Thor in a voice of thunder, as he flung off the veil and rose to his full height. And with the words he swung the hammer once—and ere the eye could follow its movement, it had crashed through Thrym's skull and had knocked over a round dozen of his guests. Yet again did it swing in the Asa's hand, and this time it left not a giant standing in the hall.

A third time it was swung, and on this occasion the roof and walls of the palace came tumbling on every side, and only Thor and Loki were left alive amid the ruins.

"Ha! ha!" laughed Red Loki, "that was neatly done, fair Freya."

Thor, who was now busily tearing off the hated robes and veil, stayed to look threateningly at his companion. "No more of that, Loki," said he, "the thing had to be done, 'tis true, but talk not to me again of this woman's work. We will remember only that I am the Thunderer, and that my hammer that was lost is found."

So they drove back peacefully to Asgard.

And this is the end of the tale of how Thor's hammer was lost and found.

THE STORY OF BALDER
THE BEAUTIFUL

By E. M. WILMOT-BUXTON

FAIR beyond all the sons of Odin was Balder the Beautiful, Balder of the snow-white brow and golden locks, and he was well beloved not only by the Asa folk, but also by the men of the earth below.

> "Of all the twelve round Odin's throne,
> Balder, the Beautiful, alone,
> The Sun god, good and pure and bright,
> Was loved by all, as all love light."

Balder had a twin brother named Hoder, who was born blind. Gloomy and silent was he, but none the less he loved his bright sun-brother best of all in heaven or earth.

The home of Balder was a palace with silver roof and pillars of gold, and nothing unclean or impure was allowed to come inside its doors.

Very wise in all magic charms was this radiant young god; and for all others save himself he could read the future; but "to keep his own life safe and see the sun" was not granted to him.

Now there came a time when Balder's bright face grew sad and downcast; and when his father Odin and his mother Frigga perceived this they implored him to tell them the cause of his grief. Then Balder told them that he had been troubled by strange dreams; and, since in those days men believed that dreams were sent as a warning of what was about to happen, he had gone heavily since these visions had come to him.

First he had dreamt that a dark cloud had arisen which came before the sun and shut out all brightness from the land.

The next night he dreamt that Asgard lay in darkness and that her bright flowers and radiant trees were withered and lifeless, and that the Asa folk, dull and withered also, were sorrowing as though from some great calamity.

The third night he dreamt yet again that Asgard was dark and lifeless and that from out of the gloom one sad voice cried:

"Woe! Woe! Woe! For Balder the Beautiful is dead—is dead!"

Odin listened to the recital of this story with heavy heart, and at its conclusion he mounted his coal-black horse and rode over many a hard and toilsome road till he came to the dark abode of Hela. And there he saw, to his surprise, that a great banquet was being prepared in the gloomy hall. Dishes of gold were set upon the table and all the couches were covered with the richest silken tapestry, as though some honored guest were expected. But a throne that stood at the head of the table was empty.

Very thoughtfully Odin rode on through those dim halls, till he came to one where dwelt an ancient prophetess whose voice no man had heard for many a long year.

Silent he stood before her until she asked in a voice that sounded as though it came from far away: "Who art thou, and from whence dost thou come to trouble my long rest?"

Now Odin was fearful that she would not answer him did he give his real name, so he told her that he was the son of Valtam, and asked anxiously for whom the grim goddess of death was preparing her banquet.

Then, to his great grief, the hollow voice of the prophetess replied that Balder was the expected guest, and he would shortly be sent thither, slain by the hand of Hoder, the blind god of darkness.

"Who then," asked Odin, in sorrowful tones, "shall avenge the death of Balder?"

And she answered that the son of the Earth goddess, Vali by name, should neither

> "Comb his raven hair
> Nor wash his visage in the stream,
> Nor see the sun's departing beam,
> Till He on Hoder's corse shall smile
> Flaming on the funeral pile."

And learning thus of the fate of his two favorite sons, All-Father Odin went sadly back to Asgard.

Meantime Mother Frigga had not been idle. Filled with anxiety for her darling son, she decided to send her servants throughout the earth, bidding them exact a promise from all things—not only living creatures, but plants, stones, and metals, fire, water, trees and diseases of all kinds—that they would do harm in no way to Balder the Beautiful.

Theirs was an easy task, for all things loved the bright Sun-god and readily agreed to give the pledge. Nothing was overlooked, save only the mistletoe growing upon the oak tree that shaded the entrance of Valhalla. It seemed so insignificant that no one thought it worth while to ask this plant to take the oath.

The servants returned to Frigga with all the vows and compacts that had been made; and the Mother of Gods and Men went back with heart at ease to her spinning wheel.

The Asa folk, too, were reassured, and, casting aside the burden of care that had fallen upon them, they resumed their favorite game upon the plains of Idavold, where they were wont to contend with one another in the throwing of golden disks.

And when it became known among them that nothing would hurt Balder the Beautiful they invented a new game.

Placing the young Sun-god in their midst they would throw stones at him, or thrust at him with their knives, or strike with their wooden staves; and the wood or the knife or the stone would glance off from Balder and leave him quite unhurt.

This new game delighted both Balder and the Asa folk, and so loud was their laughter that Loki, who was some distance away pursuing one of his schemes in the disguise of an old woman, shook with rage at the sound. For Loki was jealous of Balder and, as is usual with people who make themselves disliked, nothing gave him such displeasure as to see a group of the Asas on such happy terms with each other.

Presently in his wanderings Loki passed by the house of Fensalir, in the doorway of which sat Frigga, at her spinning wheel. She did not recognize Red Loki but greeted him kindly and asked:

"Old woman, dost thou know why the gods are so merry this evening?"

And Loki answered: "They are casting stones and throwing sharp knives and great clubs at Balder the Beautiful, who stands smiling in their midst daring them to hurt him."

Then Frigga smiled tranquilly and turned again to her wheel, saying: "Let them play on, for no harm will come to him whom all things in heaven and earth have sworn not to hurt."

"Art thou sure, good mother, that *all* things in heaven and earth have taken this vow?"

"Ay, indeed," replied Frigga, "all save a harmless little plant, the mistletoe, which grows on the oak by Valhalla, and this is far too small and weak to be feared."

And to this Loki replied in musing voice, nodding his head as he spoke: "Yea, thou art right, great Mother of Gods and Men."

But the wicked Asa had learnt what he desired to know. The instrument by which he might bring harm to Balder the Beautiful was now awaiting him, and he determined to use it to the dire sorrow of Asgard.

Hastening to the western gate of Valhalla, he pulled a clump of the mistletoe from the oak, and fashioned therefrom a little wand, or stick, and with this in his hand he returned to the plain of Idavold. He was far too cunning, however, to attempt to carry out his wicked design himself. His malicious heart was too well known to the Asa folk. But he soon found an innocent tool. Leaning against a tree and taking no part in the game was Hoder, the blind god, the twin brother of Balder, and to him he began:

"Hark to the Asas—how they laugh! Do you take no share in the game, good Hoder?"

"Not I," said Hoder gloomily, "for I am blind, and know not where to throw."

"I could show you that," said Loki, assuming a pleasant tone; "'tis no hard matter, Hoder, and methinks the Asas will call you proud and haughty if you take no share in the fun."

"But I have nothing to throw," said poor blind Hoder.

Then Loki said: "Here, at least, is a small shaft, 'twill serve your purpose," and leading innocent Hoder into the ring he cunningly guided his aim. Hoder, well pleased to be able to share in a game with his beloved brother, boldly sped the shaft, expecting to hear the usual shouts of joyous laughter which greeted all such attempts. There fell instead dead silence on his ear, and immediately on this followed a wail of bitter agony. For Balder the Beautiful had fallen dead without a groan, his heart transfixed by the little dart of mistletoe.

> "So on the floor lay Balder dead; and round
> Lay thickly strewn swords, axes, darts, and spears,
> Which all the gods in sport had idly thrown
> At Balder, whom no weapon pierced or clove;
> But in his breast stood fixed the fatal bough
> Of mistletoe, which Loki the Accuser gave
> To Hoder, and unwitting Hoder threw—
> 'Gainst that alone had Balder's life no charm."

Dreading he knew not what, Hoder stood in doubt for some moments. But soon the meaning of that bitter wail was borne in upon him, piercing the cloud of darkness in which he always moved. He opened wide his arms as though to clasp the beloved form, and then with: "I have slain thee, my brother," despair seized him and he fell prostrate in utter grief.

Meantime, the Asa folk crowded round the silent form of Balder, weeping and wailing; but, alas! their moans and tears could not bring Balder back. At length, All-Father Odin, whose grief was too deep for lamentations, bade them be silent and prepare to bear the body of the dead Asa to the seashore.

The unhappy Hoder, unable to take part in these last offices, made his way sadly through Asgard, beyond the walls and along the seashore until he came to the house Fensalir.

Frigga was seated upon her seat of honor before the fire against the inner wall, and standing before her with bent head and woeful sightless gaze Hoder told her of the dread mishap that had befallen.

"Tell me, O Mother," he cried in ending, and his voice sounded like the wail of the wind on stormy nights, "tell me, is there aught I can do to bring my brother back? Or can I make agreement with the dread mother of the Underworld, giving my life in exchange for his?"

Woe crowded upon woe in the heart of Frigga as she listened to the story. The doom was wrought that she had tried so vainly to avert, and not even her mother's love had availed to safeguard the son so dearly cherished.

"On Balder Death hath laid her hand, not thee, my son," she said; "yet though we fail in the end, there is much that may be tried before all hope is lost." Then she told Hoder of a road by which the abode of Hela could be reached, one which had been traveled by none living save Odin himself:

> "Who goes that way must take no other horse
> To ride, but Sleipnir, Odin's horse, alone.
> Nor must he choose that common path of gods
> Which every day they come and go in heaven,
> O'er the bridge Bifrost, where is Heimdall's watch.
>
> But he must tread a dark untraveled road
> Which branches from the north of heaven, and ride
> Nine days, nine nights, toward the northern ice,
> Through valleys deep engulfed, with roaring streams.
> And he will reach on the tenth morn a bridge
> Which spans with golden arches Giöll's stream.
> Then he will journey through no lighted land,
> Nor see the sun arise, nor see it set;
>
> And he must fare across the dismal ice
> Northward, until he meets a stretching wall
> Barring his way, and in the wall a grate,
> But then he must dismount and on the ice
> Tighten the girths of Sleipnir, Odin's horse,
> And make him leap the grate, and come within."

There in that cheerless abode dead Balder was enthroned, but, said Frigga, he who braves that dread journey must take no heed of him, nor of the sad ghosts flitting to and fro like eddying leaves. First he must accost their gloomy queen and entreat her with prayers:

> "Telling her all that grief they have in heaven
> For Balder, whom she holds by right below."

A bitter groan of anguish escaped from Hoder when Frigga had finished her recital of the trials which must be undergone:

"Mother, a dreadful way is this thou showest;
No journey for a sightless god to go."

And she replied:

"... Thyself thou shalt not go, my son;
But he whom first thou meetest when thou com'st
To Asgard and declar'st this hidden way,
Shall go; and I will be his guide unseen."

Meantime the Asa folk had felled trees and had carried to the seashore outside the walls of Asgard a great pile of fuel, which they laid upon the deck of Balder's great ship, *Ringhorn,* as it lay stranded high up on the beach.

"Seventy ells and four extended
On the grass the vessel's keel;
High above it, gilt and splendid,
Rose the figurehead ferocious
With its crest of steel."

Then they adorned the funeral pyre with garlands of flowers, with golden vessels and rings, with finely wrought weapons and rich necklets and armlets; and when this was done they carried out the fair body of Balder the Beautiful, and bearing it reverently upon their shields they laid it upon the pyre.

Then they tried to launch the good ship, but so heavily laden was she that they could not stir her an inch.

The Mountain Giants, from their heights afar, had watched the tragedy with eyes that were not unpitying, for even they had no ill will for Balder, and they sent and told of a giantess called Hyrroken, who was so strong that she could launch any vessel whatever its weight might be.

So the Asas sent to fetch her from Giantland, and she soon came, riding a wolf for steed and twisted serpents for reins.

When she alighted, Odin ordered four of his mightiest warriors to hold the wolf, but he was so strong that they could do nothing until the giantess had thrown him down and bound him fast.

Then with a few enormous strides, Hyrroken reached the great vessel, and set her shoulder against the prow, sending the ship rolling into the deep. The earth shook with the force of the movement as though with an earthquake, and the Asa folk collided with one another like pine trees during a storm. The ship, too, with its precious weight, was well-nigh lost. At this Thor was wroth and, seizing his hammer, would have slain the giantess had not the other Asas held him back, bidding him not forget the last duty to the dead god. So Thor hallowed the pyre with a touch of his sacred hammer and kindled it with a thorn twig, which is the emblem of sleep.

Last of all, before the pyre blazed up, All-Father Odin added to the pile of offerings his magic ring, from which fell eight new rings every ninth night, and bending he whispered in Balder's ear.

But none to this day know the words that Odin spake thus in the ear of his dead son.

Then the flames from the pyre rose high and the great ship drifted out to sea, and the wind caught the sails and fanned the flames till it seemed as though sky and sea were wrapped in golden flame.

> "And while they gazed, the sun went lurid down
> Into the smoke-wrapt sea, and night came on.
> But through the dark they watched the burning ship
> Still carried o'er the distant waters. . . .
> But fainter, as the stars rose high, it flared;
> And as, in a decaying winter fire,
> A charr'd log, falling, makes a shower of sparks—
> So, with a shower of sparks, the pile fell in,
> Reddening the sea around; and all was dark."

And thus did Balder the Beautiful pass from the peaceful steads of Asgard, as passes the sun when he paints the evening clouds with the glory of his setting.

HOW HERMOD MADE A JOURNEY TO THE UNDERWORLD

By E. M. WILMOT-BUXTON

Illustration by Louis Moe

OF all the Asa folk most fleet of foot was Hermod, but on that sad eve when Balder was laid upon the funeral pyre his step was lagging and slow as he went to his home by the city wall.

As he approached, there met him in the gloom a vague figure that walked with outstretched hands and faltering steps like one that is blind. And Hermod knew it to be the form of Hoder of the sightless eyes, brother to Balder and to him.

But when he would have spoken Hoder brushed past, murmuring in his ear:

"Take Sleipnir, Hermod, and set forth with dawn
To Hela's kingdom, to ask Balder back;
And they shall be thy guides who have the power."

Hermod bowed his head and passed on; but poor blind Hoder, heartbroken, went his way to his own house and shut the door upon his grief.

When the first rosy fingers of dawn touched the clouds of morning Hermod led out Sleipnir, the steed of Odin, from Valhalla, and rode away. Sleipnir was not wont to permit any to mount him, or even to touch his mane, save the All-Father himself; but he stood meekly as Hermod mounted; for he knew upon what errand they were bound.

Nine long days and nine long nights rode Hermod toward the realms of ice and snow; and on the tenth morn he drew near to the golden bridge which spanned Giöll, the greatest river in the world. A maiden of pale and downcast mien kept this bridge with unsleeping vigilance and she now challenged Hermod as he approached:

246

"Who art thou on thy black and fiery horse,
Under whose hoofs the bridge o'er Giöll's stream
Rumbles and shakes? Tell me thy race and home.
But yestermorn, five troops of dead passed by,
Bound on their way below to Hela's realm,
Nor shook the bridge so much as thou alone.
And thou hast flesh and color on thy cheeks,
Like men who live, and draw the vital air;
Nor look'st thou pale and wan, like men deceased,
Souls bound below, my daily passers here."

Then Hermod told his name and whence he came, and asked eagerly if Balder had already crossed that bridge. And the maiden

Louis Moe

So Hermod galloped through the mist.

told him that Balder had indeed passed that way along the road to Hela's kingdom.

So Hermod galloped over the golden bridge, and resumed his way through a darksome tract of frozen country, and over fields of ice unlighted save by dim stars that shone uncertainly through the mist.

At length farther passage was barred by a high wall in which was a gate. Without hesitation Hermod put Sleipnir to this obstacle; he surmounted it with the ease and grace of a fawn, and they found themselves in Hela's realm.

On passed Hermod, all unheeding the murmuring shades that flocked around, and he did not draw rein until, coming to Hela's hall, he saw there Balder, his brother, and, near by, the awful goddess.

Leaping from Sleipnir, the young Asa knelt before Hela and besought her that Balder might ride home with him, that the heavy hearts of all in Asgard might be comforted.

But dark Hela shook her head, reminding him how Odin had cast her out with her two brothers, the Serpent and the Fenris Wolf; why should she grant the Asa folk this boon?

Then Hermod laid his hands upon her knees. "All things in heaven and earth grieve for Balder, therefore restore him, good mother, and darken not our lives for evermore," he answered.

The appeal in his mournful eyes, as well as in his words, somewhat moved Hela, though her heart was still hardened against Odin, and she said: "Come now, let us see if all things love Balder as you say:

> "Show me through all the world the signs of grief!
> Fails but one thing to grieve, here Balder stops!
> Let all that lives and moves upon the earth
> Weep him, and all that is without life weep:
> Let gods, men, brutes, beweep him; plants and stones.
> So shall I know the lost was dear indeed,
> And bend my heart, and give him back to heaven."

Then Hermod was given permission to greet his brother, and Balder answered him with faint voice. They spoke of Asgard, the beloved land of living gods and heroes, and at parting Balder charged his brother to carry the magic ring, Draupnir, back to Odin, and a kerchief and other gifts to Frigga, as tokens of his love. And Hermod rode sadly back along the weary road to Asgard.

All-Father Odin from his high seat saw his son returning, and he hastened forth to receive him.

> "And Hermod came, and leapt from Sleipnir down,
> And in his father's hand put Sleipnir's rein
> And greeted Odin and the gods."

Then all the Asa folk assembled in the Council Hall, at the root of the Tree of Life, to hear the message that Hermod had brought from the joyous realms; and he told them of Hela's reply to his request, saying:

"... To your prayer she sends you this reply:
Show her through all the world the signs of grief!
Fails but one thing to grieve, there Balder stops!
Let gods, men, brutes, beweep him; plants and stones;
So shall she know your loss was dear indeed,
And bend her heart, and give you Balder back."

When Hermod had ceased speaking, All-Father Odin arose, and leaning on his great staff he looked slowly around and commanded: "Go ye quickly forth through all the world and pray all living and unliving things to weep for Balder dead."

Then the gods arose willingly and went their way through all the world, Thor in his goat chariot, and Freya in her carriage drawn by white cats, but most of the others on swift horses. North, South, East, and West they rode, entreating all things to weep for Balder's death.

"And all that lived, and all without life, wept."

Just as at the end of winter, before the springtime, when a warm southwest wind blows over the land and melts the ice and snow,

"A dripping sound is heard
In all the forests....
And, in fields sloping to the south, dark plots
Of grass peep out amid surrounding snow,
And widen, and the peasant's heart is glad"—

so through the whole world was now heard the sound of falling tears, as all things living and dead wept for Balder's sake.

Hermod rode with the Storm god, Niörd, who knew all the creeks and hidden bays of the coastline of the earth; and when the sea creatures and those that live on the borders of the ocean heard the message, they all added their tribute of tears to the common cause.

Now, as the Asas rode home together they came to a great wood upon the borders of Giantland, where all the trees are of iron. And in the midst of this wood was a cave, at the mouth of which sat an ancient giantess gnashing her teeth at all who passed by.

This seeming giantess was none other but wicked Loki in disguise, but this Hermod did not know.

As the Asas came near, she greeted them with shrill laughter and asked them if it was dull in Asgard that they came thither to her iron wood. But they answered that they came not for gibes but for tears, that Balder might be saved. Then she laughed louder and cried:

> "Is Balder dead? And do ye come for tears?
> Weep him all other things, if weep they will:
> I weep him not! Let Hela keep her prey."

And with these mocking words she fled to the dark recesses of her cave, repeating again and again:

> "Neither in life, nor yet in death,
> Gave he me gladness.
> Let Hela keep her prey."

Heavy were the steps with which Hermod returned to Asgard, and when they had heard the news of how one creature had refused her tears the eager faces of the Asa folk grew dark with woe, for they knew that never more would they see Balder—Balder the Beautiful.

But the future days brought peace to the tormented soul of Hoder, the innocent cause of all their grief.

For there was born to Odin a child who grew to his full size within a few short hours. And on the first day that he arrived in Asgard he fared forth with bow and arrow, and one of his shafts found mark in the heart of Hoder.

And so, from henceforth, the blind god and his twin brother are together in the realms of Hela.

HOW LOKI WAS PUNISHED AT LAST

By E. M. WILMOT-BUXTON

WHEN the Asas knew that it was Loki, disguised as Thok, the giant woman, who had refused to shed the tears that would have won Balder's release, they determined to bear with his presence in Asgard no longer.

So with many a hard word and ugly look they drove him forth, bidding him never enter those gates again.

But the Asa folk were still sad and heavy of heart: for at every moment the gloom that lay over the city reminded them of the loss of their bright young Balder.

Ægir, god of the sea, saw their forlorn condition, and he prepared a great banquet in the caves of coral that lie underneath the sea, and bade all the Asas attend it as his guests.

> "That though for Balder every guest
> Was grieving yet,
> He might forget
> Awhile his woe in friendly feast."

The invitation was pleasing to the gods, and on the day appointed they came attired in their richest cloaks of silk and satin, green and blue and yellow and purple, by a path through the waters whereby they reached the coral caves of the Sea god. Very beautiful were these caves. The walls and ceilings were carved with the most delicate fretwork of pink and cream and white, and a faint green light shone into them from the ocean without.

The floor was covered with the finest silver sand, encrusted with beautiful sea shells, and the flowers with which the tables were adorned with feathery seaweeds and glowing sea anemones. In the midst of the floor was a mass of gold so bright that it lighted up the whole place as though with fire.

The dishes upon the table were filled with the most delicious fish of every kind and variety, and the gods sat down to the feast well pleased, regretting only the absence of the well-loved Balder, and the fact that Thor had been detained by a tempest which kept him busy in the regions of the dwarfs, from whence he hoped to travel to the sea caves directly his work was done.

Merrily went the banquet, for all the Asas were filled with good will toward one another and toward their burly host, who sat at the head of the board with his long gray beard sweeping his broad chest.

Suddenly into the midst of this cheerful scene fell a black shadow from the entrance to the cave; and there, red and gaunt, and evil of countenance, stood Loki, glowering upon them all.

At first the Asas sat in silence, their anger too deep for words. Then Odin arose and sternly bade the intruder begone.

This was the signal for a storm of hatred in words so evil that they poisoned the air. For a time the Asas pretended not to heed, but went on quietly with the meal. One of them even tried to drown his speech by talking loudly to old Ægir in praise of the servant who waited so deftly upon them all. But at the word Loki sprang forward, knife in hand, and killed the unfortunate serving-man before their eyes.

Then the Asa folk arose and cast out Loki with violence, threatening dire punishment should he appear in their presence again.

Resuming their seats at the interrupted feast, they made brave efforts to appear gay and cheerful; but scarcely had they begun to eat when Loki came creeping in again disguised as a sea serpent. Once in, he resumed his proper form and began as before to revile the gods, taunting them one after another with the mistakes which each had made, and telling his malicious stories, so that the gods were filled with dismay and with suspicion each of his neighbor.

Louder and louder grew the voice of Loki, the Asas all the time sitting as if turned to stone, and now he began to heap abuse on the head of Sif, the fair-haired wife of Thor.

Suddenly there was heard outside the noise of goats' feet clattering over the rocks, and in another moment the Thunderer entered, brandishing his hammer about his head and crying:

"Silence, thou wicked wretch, or my mighty hammer shall put a stop to thy prating. At one blow will I strike thy head from thy neck, and then will thy evil tongue be silenced once for all!"

But Loki did not wait for Thor to strike. Quick as light he dashed out of the cave and disappeared. He well knew that now at length he had indeed lost all hope of forgiveness. Wandering in dismal wise about the earth, fear seized him lest Odin or the Thunderer should find and slay him in order to prevent further annoyance.

So he made his way to the mountains of the North, and there he built for himself a hut with four doors, open to every quarter of the earth, that if need arose he might be able to escape quickly.

He built this hut, moreover, close to a mountain side, down which rushed a mighty cataract of water. For he intended, if the Asas found him, to spring into the stream, change himself into a salmon, and so make good his escape.

But when, sitting within his cold and draughty hut, he began to consider the matter afresh, he remembered that even if he carried out this plan he would not yet be quite safe.

For though he could easily avoid any hook that ever was made, he would find it very difficult to evade capture if the gods should think of making a net like that which the Sea goddess, Ran, spreads for unwary men when they are fishing or bathing in the sea, and all the time she is lurking near in some cavern on the shore, or enmeshed in the dark folds of a giant seaweed in the ocean depths.

So much and so long did Loki brood over the thought of Ran's fishing net, that at length he began to wonder if such a thing could really be made, and then to try to weave one out of twine as much like it as possible. He had not quite finished his curious task when upon the mountain, just above the hut, he suddenly perceived the two mighty figures of his dreaded foes. Knowing that their intention must be to enter his hut and make him prisoner, Loki hastily threw the half-made net upon the fire, and rushing forth he flung himself into the waterfall, where he quickly changed himself into a salmon and lurked unseen among the stones in the torrent's bed. Meantime, the two Asas had entered the hut.

"Ho! ho!" said Odin, as he noted the silence of the place, "our bird has flown."

"What fresh mischief doth he plan?" muttered Thor, looking closely about him.

"Let us look farther afield," urged Odin; but Thor kicked over the logs on the hearth and picked out the half-burned net.

Now Odin well knew the net of Ran, and the half-burned strands suggested to him the truth. So he set to work and, with Thor's assistance, quickly mended the net, and they proceeded to drag the mountain stream with it.

At their first attempt sly Loki hid between two stones at the bottom of the river, laughing in scorn as the net passed over his head.

Then the Asas weighted the net with stones and tried again; but Loki gave a great leap over the net and dashed up stream.

A third time they made the attempt, and now Loki, grown reckless, leaped out of the water. But this time Thor caught him by his tail, and held it fast in spite of its slipperiness.

Then the gods forced him to resume his usual shape, and they carried him off to an underground cavern far below the earth, and there they bound him fast to a rock with iron fetters.

Most things in heaven and earth rejoiced at the downfall of wicked Red Loki, but above all rejoiced Skadi the giantess. Her home was in the cold mountain stream which Loki had invaded, and he had done her many an ill turn in bygone days.

This Skadi now took a poisonous serpent and fastened it above his head, so that the venom of the reptile falling, drop by drop, upon his face, would cause the most terrible pain. But Sigyn, Loki's loyal wife, the only person in heaven or earth who cared what became of him, took a cup and held it up to catch the burning drops as they fell, and she only left his side when the cup was full and she had to empty it.

In these brief periods, the fettered god howled with rage and pain, in tones which echoed through the dismal caverns of earth like mighty peals of thunder, and his writhing shook the earth to its foundations, bringing the Northmen from their dwellings in terror of what they thought to be violent earthquakes. But his efforts can avail nothing until the day of Ragnarok. Then shall his bonds be loosed, and he shall fight his last battle and fall, never to rise again.

Stories From
The Jataka Tales of India

THE SPIRIT THAT LIVED IN A TREE

By MARIE L. SHEDLOCK

AND it came to pass that the Buddha was reborn as a Tree Spirit. Now there reigned at Benares at that time a King who said to himself: "All over India, the kings live in palaces supported by many a column. *I* will build me a palace resting on one column only—then shall I in truth be the chiefest of all kings."

Now in the King's Park was a lordly Sal tree, straight and well-grown, worshiped by village and town, and to this tree even the Royal Family also paid tribute, worship, and honor. And then suddenly there came an order from the King that the tree should be cut down.

And the people were sore dismayed, but the woodmen, who dared not disobey the orders of the king, came to the Park with hands full of perfumed garlands, and encircling the tree with a string, fastened to it a nosegay of flowers, and kindling a lamp, they did worship, exclaiming: "O Tree! on the seventh day must we cut thee down, for so hath the King commanded. Now let the Deities who dwell within thee go elsewhither, and since we are only obeying the King's command, let no blame fall upon us and no harm come to our children because of this."

And the Spirit who lived in the tree, hearing these words, reflected within himself and said: "These builders are determined to cut down this tree and to destroy my place of dwelling. Now my life lasts only as long as this tree. And lo! all the young Sal trees that stand around, where dwell the Deities my kinsfolk—and they are many—will be destroyed! My own destruction does not touch me so near as the destruction of my children: therefore must I protect their lives."

Accordingly, at the hour of midnight, adorned in divine splendor, he entered into the magnificent chamber of the King, and filling the whole chamber with a bright radiance, stood weeping beside the King's pillow. At the sight of him, the King, overcome with terror, said: "Who art thou, standing high in the air, and why do thy tears flow?"

And the Tree God made answer: "Within thy realm I am known as the Lucky Tree. For sixty thousand years have I stood, and all have worshiped me, and though they have built many a house and many a town no violence has been done to me. Spare thou me, also, O King."

Then the King made answer and said: "Never have I seen so mighty a trunk, so thick and strong a tree; but I will build me a palace, and thou shalt be the only column on which it shall rest, and thou shalt dwell there forever."

And the Tree said: "Since thou art resolved to tear my body from me, I pray thee cut me down gently, one branch after another—the root last of all."

And the King said: "O Woodland Tree! what is this thou askest of me? It were a painful death to die. One stroke at the root would fell thee to the ground. Why wouldst thou die piecemeal?"

And the Tree made answer: "O King! My children, the young Sal trees, all grow at my feet: they are prosperous and well sheltered. If I should fall with one mighty crash, behold these young children of the forest would perish also!"

And the King was greatly moved by this spirit of sacrifice, and said: "O great and glorious Tree! I set thee free from thy fear, and because thou wouldst willingly die to save thy kindred, thou shalt not be cut down. Return to thy home in the Ancient Forest."

THE HARE THAT RAN AWAY

By MARIE L. SHEDLOCK

AND it came to pass that the Buddha (to be) was born again as a Lion. Just as he had helped his fellow men, he now began to help his fellow animals, and there was a great deal to be done. For instance, there was a little nervous Hare who was always afraid that something dreadful was going to happen to her. She was always saying: "Suppose the Earth were to fall in, what would happen to me?" And she said this so often that at last she thought it really was about to happen. One day, when she had been saying over and over again, "Suppose the Earth were to fall in, what would happen to me?" she heard a slight noise: it really was only a heavy fruit which had fallen upon a rustling leaf, but the little Hare was so nervous she was ready to believe anything, and she said in a frightened tone: "The Earth *is* falling in." She ran away as fast as she could go, and presently she met an old brother Hare, who said: "Where are you running to, Mistress Hare?"

And the little Hare said: "I have no time to stop and tell you anything. The Earth is falling in, and I am running away."

"The Earth is falling in, is it?" said the old brother Hare, in a tone of much astonishment; and he repeated this to *his* brother hare, and *he* to *his* brother hare, and *he* to *his* brother hare, until at last there were a hundred thousand brother hares, all shouting: "The Earth is falling in." Now presently the bigger animals began to take the cry up. First the deer, and then the sheep, and then the wild boar, and then the buffalo, and then the camel, and then the tiger, and then the elephant.

Now the wise Lion heard all this noise and wondered at it. "There are no signs," he said, "of the Earth falling in. They must have heard something." And then he stopped them all short and said: "What is this you are saying?"

And the Elephant said: "I remarked that the Earth was falling in."

259

"How do you know this?" asked the Lion.

"Why, now I come to think of it, it was the Tiger that remarked it to me."

And the Tiger said: "*I* had it from the Camel," and the Camel said: "*I* had it from the Buffalo." And the buffalo from the wild boar, and the wild boar from the sheep, and the sheep from the deer, and the deer from the hares, and the Hares said: "Oh! *we* heard it from *that* little Hare."

And the Lion said: "Little Hare, *what* made you say that the Earth was falling in?"

And the little Hare said: "I *saw* it."

"You saw it?" said the Lion. "Where?"

"Yonder, by the tree."

"Well," said the Lion, "come with me and I will show you how——"

"No, no," said the Hare, "I would not go near that tree for any-thing, I'm *so* nervous."

"But," said the Lion, "I am going to take you on my back." And he took her on his back, and begged the animals to stay where they were until they returned. Then he showed the little Hare how the fruit had fallen upon the leaf, making the noise that had frightened her, and she said: "Yes, I see—the Earth is *not* falling in." And the Lion said: "Shall we go back and tell the other animals?" And they went back. The little Hare stood before the animals and said: "The Earth is *not* falling in." And all the animals began to repeat this to one another, and they dispersed gradually, and you heard the words more and more softly.

"The Earth is *not* falling in," etc., etc., etc., until the sound died away altogether.

THE MONKEY THAT SAVED THE HERD

By MARIE L. SHEDLOCK

IT came to pass that the Buddha was reborn as the King of the monkeys. He lived with his herd of 80,000 monkeys in a thick forest near a lake. In this lake there lived an ogre who used to devour all those who went down to the water.

The Buddha spoke to his subjects and said:

"My friends, in this forest there are trees that are poisoned, and lakes that are haunted by ogres. Eat no fruit and drink no water of which you have not already tasted, without consulting me."

This they agreed to. And one day, having arrived at a spot which they had never visited before, they found a great lake. They did not drink, but awaited the return of their King.

Now when he arrived he went round the lake, and found that all the footsteps led down to the lake but none came up again. And he said:

"Without doubt this is the haunt of an ogre."

When this water ogre saw that they were not invading his domain he appeared in the form of a terrible monster with a blue belly, a white face, and bright red hands and feet. In this shape he came out of the water and said to the King: "Why are you seated here? Go down to the lake to drink." But the King said: "Are you not the ogre of this water?" "Yes, I am," was the answer. "Do you take as your prey all those who go down into this water?" "Yes, I do, from small birds upward. I never let anything go which comes down into this water. I will eat the lot of you, too." "But we shall not let you eat us." "Just drink the water." "Yes, we will drink the water, and yet not fall into your power." "How do you propose to drink the water, then?" "Ah, you think we shall have to go down to the water to drink; whereas we shall not enter the water at all, but the whole eighty thousand of us will take a cane each and drink therewith from your lake as easily as through the hollow stalk of a lotus. And so you will not be able to eat us."

So saying, the King had a cane brought to him, and in true belief that the miracle would take place he blew down the cane, which straightway became hollow throughout without a single knot being left in its length. In this fashion he had another, and another brought, and blew down them. Then he made the tour of the lake and commanded, saying, "Let all canes growing here become hollow throughout." Now, thanks to the saving goodness of their reborn chiefs, their commands are always fulfilled. And henceforth every single cane that grew round that lake became hollow throughout. After giving his commands the King seated himself with a cane in his hand. All the other 80,000 monkeys, too, seated themselves round the lake each with a cane in his hands. At the same moment when the King sucked up the water through his cane, they all drank in the same manner, as they sat on the bank. This was the way they drank, and the ogre could get no power over any of them, so he went off in a rage to his habitation. The King, with his following of 80,000 monkeys, went back into the forest.

THE ELEPHANT THAT WAS HONORED IN OLD AGE

By MARIE L. SHEDLOCK

Illustration by Warren Chappell

AND the Buddha as Prime Minister served the King. Now there was a certain She-Elephant, endowed with great might which enabled her to go a hundred leagues a day. She did the duties of messenger to the King, and in battle she fought and crushed the enemy. The King said: "She is very serviceable to me."

He gave her ornaments and caused all honor to be shown her. Then, when she was weak from age, the King took away all the honor he had bestowed.

From that time she was unprotected, and lived by eating grass and leaves in the forest.

And one day the chief Potter had not enough oxen to yoke to the carts which carried the material for making clay. And the King said: "Where is our She-Elephant?"

"O King! she is wandering at her will in the forest."

And the King said: "Do thou yoke her to the cart."

And the Potter said: "Good, O King!" And he did even as the King commanded.

But when this insult was offered to the Elephant, she came to the Prime Minister and said: "O Wise Being! I pray you listen to my tale. When I was young, great strength was mine; and I did walk a hundred leagues to bear the King's messages, and, with weapons bound upon my body, I did take part in battle, crushing the enemy beneath my feet. And now I am old, and the King hath withdrawn all the honors he bestowed upon me, and not content with allowing me to wander and feed on grass, unprotected in my old age, he has *even caused me to be yoked to* the Potter's cart as are the oxen."

Then the Buddha promised that he would plead her cause, and appearing before the King, he asked: "Great King, did not a She-Elephant covered with weapons do battle for thee; and on such and such a day, with a writing upon her neck, did she not go a hundred leagues on a message? Thou didst bestow upon her great honor. I pray thee tell me, where is she now?"

Warren Chappell

The King restored the Elephant to her place of honor.

And the King, in some confusion, made answer: "Behold, she is yoked to a cart."

Then did the Buddha speak in sorrowful anger to the King, and rebuked him, saying: "Thou hast yoked this Elephant to a cart after all the services she has rendered. Then was the honor only bestowed because of more services expected?"

And all who heard him received his instruction, and the King restored the She-Elephant to her former place of honor.

THE FAITHFUL FRIEND

By MARIE L. SHEDLOCK

LONG ago, when Brahma-datta was reigning in Benares, the
Bodisat became his Minister.

At that time a dog used to go to the state elephant's stable and
feed on the lumps of rice which fell where the elephant fed. Being
attracted there by the food, he soon became great friends with the
elephant and used to eat close by him.

At last neither of them was happy without the other; and the
dog used to amuse himself by catching hold of the elephant's trunk
and swinging to and fro.

But one day there came a peasant who gave the elephant-keeper
money for the dog, and took it back with him to his village. From
that time the elephant, missing the dog, would neither eat nor drink
nor bathe. And they let the King know about it.

He sent the Bodisat, saying: "Do you go, Pandit, and find out
what's the cause of the elephant's behavior."

So he went to the stable, and seeing how sad the elephant looked,
said to himself: "There seems to be nothing bodily the matter with
him. He must be so overwhelmed with grief by missing someone,
I should think, who had become near and dear to him." And he
asked the elephant-keepers: "Is there anyone with whom he is particularly intimate?"

"Certainly, Sir! There was a dog of whom he was very fond
indeed."

"Where is it now?"

"Some man or other took it away."

"Do you know where the man lives?"

"No, Sir!"

Then the Bodisat went and told the King: "There's nothing the
matter with the elephant, Your Majesty; but he was great friends
with a dog, and I fancy it's through missing it that he refuses his
food."

When the King heard what he said, he asked what was now to be done.

"Have a proclamation made, O King, to this effect: 'A man is said to have taken away a dog of whom our state elephant was fond. In whose house soever that dog shall be found, he shall be fined so much.' "

The King did so; and as soon as he heard of it the man turned the dog loose. The dog hastened back, and went close up to the elephant. The elephant took him up in his trunk and placed him on his forehead, and wept and cried, and took him down again, and watched him as he fed. And then he took his own food.

Then the King paid great honor to the Bodisat for knowing the motives even of animals.

THE BANYAN DEER

By MARIE L. SHEDLOCK

LONG ago the Bodisat came to life like a deer. When he was born he was of a golden color; his eyes were like round jewels; his horns were white as silver; his mouth was red as a cluster of kamala flowers; his hoofs were as bright and hard as lacquer work; his tail as fine as the tail of a Thibetan ox; and his body as large in size as a foal's.

He lived in the forest with an attendant herd of five hundred deer, under the name of the King of the Banyan Deer; and not far from him there dwelt another deer, golden as he, under the name of the Monkey Deer, with a like attendant herd.

The King of that country was devoted to hunting, never ate without meat, and used to summon all the townspeople to go hunting every day to the destruction of their ordinary work. The people thought, "This King puts an end to all our work. Suppose we make a park, provide food for the deer. Then we will drive them into the park, close the entrance and deliver them to the King."

This they did, surrounding the very place where the Banyan Deer and the Monkey Deer were living. When the King heard this he went to the park, and seeing there the two golden-colored deer, he granted them their lives. But henceforth he would go himself to shoot the dear and bring it home. Sometimes his cook would go and shoot one. The deer, as soon as they saw the bow, would quake with fear of Death, and run away; but when they had been hit once or twice, they became weary or wounded and were killed. And the herd told their King, who sent for the Monkey Deer and said: "Friend, almost all the Deer are being destroyed. Now, though they certainly must die, yet henceforth let them not be wounded with arrows. Let the deer take it by turns to go to the place of the execution. One day let the lot fall on my herd and the next day on yours." He agreed, and thenceforth the deer whose turn it was used to go down and lie down after placing his neck on the block of execution. And the cook used to come and carry off the one lying there. But one day the lot fell upon a roe in the Monkey Deer who was with young. She went to the Monkey Deer and said: "Lord! I am with young. When I have brought forth my son, we will both take our turn. Order the bows to pass me by."

"I cannot make your lot," said he, "fall upon the others. You know well enough it has fallen upon you. Go away!" Receiving no help from him, she went to the Bodisat and told him the matter. He listened to her quietly and said: "Be it so! Do you go back. I will relieve you of your turn." And he went himself and laid his head on the block of execution.

The cook, seeing him, exclaimed: "The King of the Deer whose life was promised to him is lying in the place of execution. What does it mean?" And he went hastily and told the King.

The King no sooner heard it than he mounted his chariot and proceeded with a great retinue to the place, and beholding the Bodisat, said: "My friend, the King of the Deer! Did I not grant you your life? Why are you lying here?"

"O great King! A roe with young came and told me that the lot had fallen upon her. Now I could not ask another to take her place, so I, giving my life for her, have lain down. Harbor no further suspicion, O great King!"

"My Lord, the golden-colored King of the Deer! I never yet saw, even among men, one so full of forbearance, kindness and compassion. I am pleased with thee in this matter! Rise up. I grant your lives, both to you and to her!"

"But though we be safe, what shall the rest do, O King of men?"

"Then I grant their lives to the rest, my Lord."

"Thus, then, great King, the deer in the park will have gained security, but what will the others do?"

"They also shall not be molested."

"Great King! even though the deer dwell secure, what shall the rest of the four-footed creatures do?"

"They shall also be free from fear."

"Great King, even though the quadrupeds are in safety, what shall the flock of birds do?"

"Well, I grant the same boon to them."

"Great King! the birds then will obtain peace; but what of the fish who dwell in the water?"

"They shall have peace as well."

Then the Great Being having interceded with the King for all creatures, said:

"Walk in righteousness, O great King! Doing justice to fathers and mothers, to townsmen and landsmen, you shall enter, when your body is dissolved, the happy world of Heaven."

. . . . .

The roe gave birth to a son as beautiful as buds of flowers; and he went to playing about with the Monkey Deer's herd. But when its mother saw that, she said, "My son, henceforth go not in his company. You may keep to the Banyan Deer's herd."

Now after that, the deer, secure of their lives, began to eat men's crops. And the men dared not strike them or drive them away, recollecting how it had been granted to them that they should dwell secure. So they met together in front of the King's palace, and told the matter to the King.

"When I was well pleased, I granted to the leader of the Banyan herd a boon," said he. "I may give up my kingdom but not my oaths! Begone with you! Not a man in my kingdom shall be allowed to hurt the deer."

When the Banyan King heard that, he assembled his herd, and said:

"Henceforth you are not allowed to eat other people's crops." And so forbidding them, he sent a message to the men: "Henceforth let the husbandmen put up no fence to guard their crops: but let them tie leaves round the edge of the field as a sign."

From that time, they say, the sign of the tying of the leaves was seen in the fields, and from that time not a single deer trespassed beyond it: for such was the instruction they received from their King, the Bodisat.

And the Bodisat continued thus his life long to instruct the deer, and passed away with his herd, according to his deeds.

Stories of
The American Indian

THE COYOTE AND THE FOX

By ELIZABETH W. DE HUFF

O-WAY-WAY-HAM-BY-YOH, which means long time ago, a fox felt very hungry, so he went down into prairie-dog town and caught a fine fat prairie dog. Then he built a fire of dry rabbit brush. When the brush had all burned up and left a pile of coals, Mr. Fox took his prairie dog and covered him all up with the hot ashes. That was the way he always roasted meat for his dinner. It required some time for the prairie dog to roast, so Mr. Fox lay down and went to sleep.

Very soon Mr. Coyote came along. Sniff! Sniff! He could smell meat roasting and it smelt very delicious. He saw Mr. Fox fast asleep; so he slipped quietly over to the pile of ashes, stuck his paw in and pulled out the prairie dog. He ran behind a bush and ate all of the meat off, but he left the bones. Then he took a bone and greased the fox's mouth all around with a greasy end of it. After that he put the bones back under the hot ashes and ran away.

When Mr. Fox awoke, he could smell prairie-dog grease. He licked his tongue out and tasted grease all around his mouth. "Surely I have not eaten the prairie dog while I was asleep. No, I feel too hungry; but where did this grease come from on my mouth if I did not eat him?" Mr. Fox was very much puzzled. He went over to the ashes and caught hold of a prairie dog foot and pulled. Out came a long leg bone without any meat on it. "This is funny," thought he.

Just then he spied some tracks in the sand. "Oho!" said he, "Now I understand it all. Coyote-man has played a trick on me and eaten my prairie dog. I'll catch him and kill him for this."

So Mr. Fox trotted off, following the coyote tracks. He found the coyote by a high cliff. Mr. Coyote saw Mr. Fox coming and he knew he was angry. He did not have time to run away, so he just leaned against the cliff and called, "Oh, Fox-man, come here quick and help me! Look up there, this cliff is falling! It will kill us both!"

Mr. Fox looked up. The clouds were passing over the cliff and made the cliff look as if it were really falling. Mr. Fox jumped quickly over by Mr. Coyote and leaned against the cliff just as hard as he could to hold it up. As soon as Mr. Fox leaned on the cliff, Mr. Coyote jumped away. He made a big jump, just as if the cliff might really fall on him.

"Hold the cliff up, Fox-man, while I go to get a stick to prop it with."

Then Mr. Coyote ran away and left Mr. Fox leaning hard against the cliff.

Mr. Fox stayed there all day waiting for Mr. Coyote to come with the stick. Late that evening he looked up and there were no clouds passing, so he could see that the cliff was not falling. He knew that the coyote had played another trick on him, so he was angrier than ever.

Again he followed the coyote tracks and found the coyote down by the river.

When Mr. Coyote saw Mr. Fox coming, he called:

"Oh, Fox-man, come quick and see what I have for you. I found a cheese and I saved half of it for you; but it has fallen into the river. Look!"

And Mr. Fox looked down into the water. There was the reflection of the half-moon in the water. It looked just like the half of a round cheese, and Mr. Fox's mouth began to water for a taste of it. He was very hungry. "I wonder how I can get that cheese!" he said.

"I'll tell you how. Let me tie the end of this rope"—for Mr. Coyote had a rope all ready—"around your tail and tie the other end to this big stone. Then you can jump into the river and get the cheese. When you have got hold of it, call me and I will pull you out."

Mr. Fox thought that was a good scheme, so he let Mr. Coyote tie the rope around his tail and around the stone. Then Mr. Fox jumped into the river with a big splash.

As soon as he did, Mr. Coyote threw the stone in after him, and if the rope had not slipped off of Mr. Fox's tail when it got wet, that would have been the end of poor old Mr. Fox.

PAH-TAY AND THE WIND WITCH

By ELIZABETH W. DE HUFF

PAH-TAY was a little Indian boy who lived long, long, long ago. One night when he was going to bed on his pile of pretty red and yellow blankets, he said to his mother:

"Ye-ah, it is going to snow tomorrow. I will go hunting and kill you some rabbits. Please put my quiver of arrows, my new bow that Tay-tay made me, and some lunch by the door before you go to bed; for I shall leave early in the morning."

Just like all other mothers, Pah-tay's mother did as he asked her. She put his new bow and arrows against the doorpost. She wrapped up some hard baked bread in some corn husks for his lunch. She put this lunch beside the bow and arrows; and right on top of it she placed a little bag made of buckskin filled with corn meal. Ye-ah wanted Pah-tay to sprinkle a little sacred meal over all the water he passed, so that the Rain God would give him luck and bring him safely home again.

Next morning when Ye-ah awoke, the little bed on the floor next to her blanket bed was empty. She looked over by the door and the things she had placed there were gone. She got up quickly and looked out of the little peephole window; it was snowing and the big round red sun was hidden. Pah-tay had already gone out over the prairie to hunt rabbits. Quickly Ye-ah went into the little room where outsiders were never allowed to go, and took some sacred corn meal out of a jar. She dropped the meal into the center of a round pile of sacred rocks, so that the good spirits would take care of her little boy out in the snow.

For many hours Pah-tay wandered about in the snow storm killing rabbits. He killed so many that they were hanging thick all around his belt. It had been growing dark and the snow had gotten so deep that it was difficult to walk through it; but little Pah-tay had been so interested in his rabbits that he did not notice either the darkness or the snow until he had used his last arrow.

Then he was ready to go home; but when he turned around, all parts of the country, being covered with snow, looked just alike and he did not know which way to go. He went up on top of a little hill to look for a light. He knew a light would come from a house.

Sure enough he saw a light. He went to the light, and climbed the ladder he found beside the house. Then he called down through the open door: "Does a friend live here?"

"Yes, a friend lives here, come down!"

Pah-tay climbed down the inside ladder to the floor, and an old woman roughly caught his arm.

"I am glad you have come, for I eat little children," she said, "and I am starving for raw meat."

Poor Pah-tay began to tremble. He tried to pull his arm away from the old witch, for that is what she was, but she held him tight.

"Aha, what is this you have here! Rabbits!" and the old witch began to smack her lips.

"I shall eat these rabbits first and then I will eat you."

She pushed Pah-tay down into the corner and began to skin the rabbits. She ate the rabbits one by one with her sharp teeth. Pah-tay tried to slip by her to run away; but she pushed him back with her bloody hands. He watched her eat all of the big pile of rabbits but two, and he shivered to think how soon she would eat him.

"It is warm down here. I would like to go up and sit on the roof," he said.

"No," said the witch, "I will not give you a chance to get away."

"But if I am too warm, I will not taste good."

"That is true; but you will taste better than no boy at all."

There was only one more rabbit!

"You tie all of your pelts together," suggested Pah-tay, "to make a strong rope, and then tie one end to my leg and hold the other end while I go up on the roof."

The old witch agreed, so she made a rope of all of her pelts. She tied one end to Pah-tay's leg and he climbed up the ladder. As soon as he was up, he untied the rope from his leg and tied it to the ladder. Then he whispered: "Little fairy in the ladder, whenever the old witch calls me, please answer 'Here I am.'" And then he climbed quickly and quietly down the outside ladder and ran up on the hill to look for another light. He saw one and ran to it.

In the doorway of the house, Pah-tay found two men singing and beating a drum. "Please let me in. An old witch is trying to eat me up and I want to hide."

The men let him in, and inside some women were grinding corn on big stones. Pah-tay hid behind one of the stones.

All the while the witch was eating the last rabbit, she kept jerking the rope and calling, "Are you there, little boy?" And each time the little fairy in the ladder answered, "Here I am."

But the last time she jerked, the rope came untied. The witch looked up and did not see Pah-tay. "He has run away, but I'll catch him," and she showed her sharp teeth.

She turned around and around and changed herself into the north wind. Then she went whistling after Pah-tay. She followed him to the house where the men were singing. There she changed herself back from the wind to an old woman.

"Where is that little boy who came here a few minutes ago? I want him," she wheezed.

"Go in," replied the men, "and if you find him, he is yours."

The old witch went in and looked in all of the dark corners. When Pah-tay saw her coming toward the stone where he was hiding, he ran outside again. He saw another light and ran to it. This light was in a kiva and the medicine men were dancing inside with their rattles. Down into the kiva climbed Pah-tay. He jumped into a hole in the big rattle of one of the medicine men. He bumped around in the rattle with a funny noise; but the medicine men kept on singing and dancing.

As soon as the old witch found that Pah-tay had left the house where the women were grinding meal, she whirled around and changed herself again into the north wind and followed him. She went down into the kiva to get him; for she had changed into an old woman again. But the sound of the rattles confused her. She tried to climb the ladder to get out again, but before she reached the top the rhythm made her fall back dead.

And Pah-tay went back home to Ye-ah.

THE PORCUPINE'S QUILLS

By *ARTHUR C. PARKER*

G ET out of my way, Gray One," growled the Bear, "hurry up, hurry up!"

"I don't like to hurry," answered Gray One, the soft-skinned Porcupine.

"Then I'll step on you," said Bear. "You can't block this path."

"It's my path; I made it," said Gray One.

"Well, if I want to walk in it, I will," said Bear gruffly.

"Let me take my time then," begged Gray One.

"I'll take my own time," said Bear, stepping right on Gray One, and sticking his claws right in the poor fellow's back.

"Oh, oh," groaned Gray One, "everybody abuses me."

And so Bear went on, laughing at the soft-skinned Gray One who would not hurry, but Gray One did not laugh; he wept, for some other four-foot was coming along.

"Get out of my way, Gray One," snarled Bobcat.

"Oh, I don't like to hurry," pleaded Gray One.

"Oh, don't block the path," said Bobcat.

"It's my own path; I made it," wept Gray One.

"Well, a path's a path, and I'll walk in it if I want to," said Bobcat with a grin, as he stuck out his claws.

"Let me take my time," pleaded Gray One.

"After I pass by," said Bobcat, grabbing Gray One by the neck and flinging him aside, at the same time batting him with one sharp clawed paw.

"Oh, oh," moaned Gray One, weeping. "Everybody abuses me."

One by one the animals stalked down Gray One's path, pushing him aside and doing him some injury.

Now Gray One was not a bothersome fellow at all. He was just soft and good-natured. He disliked to hurry, for what was the use? Anyone who hurried got there sooner and only had to come back, and so life became just hurry-scurry to him.

Gray One had a coat of fine soft wool, like a 'Possum, but he was no 'Possum. He looked his foes right in the eye. I mustn't forget to tell you either that Gray One could climb trees, and when he wanted to do so he could run as fast as a Fox, which is very fast. Most of the time, however, he didn't want to run; he just didn't want to.

Along came Red Fox and saw Gray One licking his scratches. "Hi, there, Gray One," said Fox. "What's the matter?"

"They all scratch and bite me," said the abused one.

"Never mind that," said Fox. "Do me a favor."

"What's that?" inquired Gray One.

"Climb that pine and pick off a cone."

"What for?"

"Just because I say so," said Fox.

"All right," answered Gray One moodily. "I'll go up."

Up he went with great agility and plucked a cone.

"Thank you," said Fox. "You are a pretty fine fellow. Say, would you like to be my friend?"

"And have you eat me?" inquired Gray One.

"No," answered Fox. "You see, I don't like Bobcat and I don't like Bear, while Dog just gets me mad. I do not choose friends very often, but I do like you."

"I wonder," replied Gray One. "Well, what next?"

"Roll over in the clay," said Fox.

"And get my woolly coat all plastered?" inquired Gray One.

"That's it exactly," said Fox. "Go on and do as I say."

"Oh, all right," said Gray One. "Just so long as you don't bite me or stick your claws through my skin."

"You'll soon forget your skin," said Fox, as he watched his friend roll over and over in the mud.

After a while Fox began to laugh. "Ho-hoh!" he roared. "You look like a chunk of mud rolled off a clay bluff. Well, that's just what I want, ho-hoh!"

Fox now began to pick thorns off a haw tree and after he had a big pile of them he peeled off the bark. The ends of the thorns wouldn't peel, but most of the thorn showed up nice and white.

Fox now sorted the thorns and then started to stick them into Gray One's mud coating. After a time he finished the work and stepped back to admire his effort. Gray One now looked like a formidable beast.

"Now, look here," said Fox. "Remember I'm your friend. You just do as I say, and don't you ever crawl in my bed or chase me. Now then, I am going to sit on that hummock of grass and watch the fun when Bear and Bobcat come back from their hunting."

"What will I do then?" asked Gray One, feeling uncomfortable in his prickly coat.

"Just as you have always done. Keep in your own path and take your time," answered Fox.

Gray One dried out, and soon his coat fitted better. He crouched in his path and waited.

Along came the Bear, grouchy as ever that food was so scarce. "Get out of my way, Gray One," he snorted, trotting up to the abused one.

"I don't like to hurry," came the answer.

"Then I'll step on you," said Bear. "I told you once before that you can't block the path."

"Well, it's my path; I made it," said Gray One, crouching in the grass.

"Go ahead and toss him out," shouted Fox. "Don't take orders from the soft-skinned one."

"You are no friend of mine," growled Bear, "but your idea is a good one." So saying, he grasped Gray One and lifted him up.

"Grr-oof, grr-oof," snorted Bear. "What is this that pierces my hands?" And he put Gray One down.

"Let me alone," screamed Gray One.

"I'll let you alone all right," said Bear, trotting off and licking his punctured paws.

"Go on and eat him alive," shouted Fox, laughing until he rolled off his grassy knoll.

"I'll eat you," snorted Bear.

"Come on and catch me," replied Fox, laughing the louder.

Then who should come along but cross old Bobcat.

"Get out of my way, Gray One," he shouted.

"I'll stay right here," came the answer.

"Oh, you will, will you? We'll see about that."

"Go on and give him a good bite," called out Fox.

"You are no friend of mine, but your idea is good," snarled Bobcat, leaping upon Gray One and giving him a savage bite.

"Rao-ow, spputt," spat Bobcat. "What is this that pierces my mouth? Oh, those thorns have torn me terribly. Oh, my tongue!"

Bobcat fell to plucking out the thorns, but they had grown barbs, and such a sputtering was never heard before.

Fox just rolled over and over with laughter, until his sides ached. "Eat him up, the monster!" he shouted, and laughed again.

"I'll eat you," snarled Bobcat. "You fooled me."

"Come on and catch me, I might make a good meal," laughed Fox.

Then who should come along but Dog, the matchless hunter.

"Get out of my way, Gray One," snapped Dog.

"I'll stay right here," came the answer.

"So you want another shaking?" asked Dog.

"Let me alone," replied Gray One.

"Go on and give him the shaking of his life," called out Fox.

"You are no friend of mine," said Dog, "but your idea is a good one."

So saying, he gave a great leap and landed right on Gray One, his jaws snapping right on the abused one's neck.

"Mmmmmmmm-ee, yow yip!" yelled Dog. "What horrible thing has pierced me all over like arrows?" And he leaped away whining, to pluck out the thorns, but the thorns all had cruel barbs.

As Dog wept and whined, Fox rolled over and laughed. "Say, Dog," said he, "why don't you just eat up that soft, flabby Gray One?"

"I'll eat you," snapped Dog, twisting into knots, so painful were the stings of the thorns.

"Come on and catch me," invited Fox, but Dog was in no mood for a chase. He had other troubles and they were thorny ones.

Fox now scampered off seeking more foes to set on Gray One,

but the word had gone forth that Gray One had become Prickly One and was to be respected.

"So now," said Fox, "I have made a man of you. You just do as you please and treat all of my enemies as though they were yours. You gave me the magic pine cone that gives me great speed; I gave you some magic hair that will enable you to take your time and command your own path."

"Thanks," said the Prickly One. "I always did like to take my time."

And so, O nephew, the Porcupine takes his own time and anyone who argues with him will have troubles of his own, and they'll be prickly ones, too. So it is said by the wise ones. Na-hoh.

HOW ROCK-DWELLER THE CHIPMUNK GAINED HIS STRIPES

By ARTHUR C. PARKER

YEH-HEY, yeh-hey, nephew, nephew! Story now!
Long ago there were four of them, what we call nutcrackers
—squirrels. Ho-hoh, squirrels!
Long time ago four squirrels climbed up a chestnut tree, and ho-
hoh! how they did talk and scold. Then the fifth one climbed up
and all four pounced on him, for he was a little rock-dweller—
whom we call chipmunk. Ho-hoh!
"Go away, rock-dweller," scolded Gray Squirrel.
"Guess not," answered Chipmunk.
"Go away, rock-dweller, you can't have any of our chestnuts,"
said Red Squirrel.
"Guess not," said Chipmunk.
"Go away, rock-dweller," said Black Squirrel, "you can't steal any
of our chestnuts."
"Guess not," said Chipmunk.
"Go away, rock-dweller," said Flying Squirrel, "you can't have
any of our chestnuts."
"Guess not," answered Chipmunk.
Then all the squirrels looked at each other and asked, "What does
rock-dweller mean by 'guess not'?"
"What do you mean by 'guess not'?" asked Gray Squirrel.
"I quit," answered Chipmunk.
"What did you say you meant?" inquired Red Squirrel.
"I quit, quit," answered Chipmunk.
"What does 'quit' mean?" asked Black Squirrel.
"I quit, quit, quit," retorted Chipmunk.
"Meaning what?" inquired Flying Squirrel.
"I quit, quit, quit, quit!" chattered Chipmunk.
"Then run away as quick as you can—you, the most ugly of all

our clan, you, the outcast without a totem mark," said Gray Squirrel. *"My* totem mark is a bushy gray tail."

"My totem mark," said Red Squirrel, "is a bushy red tail."

"My totem mark," said Black Squirrel, "is a bushy black tail."

"My totem mark," said Flying Squirrel, "is my blanketed legs that help me fly."

The little Chipmunk was only a dismal clay color, and his tail a poor apology for one. He was greatly ashamed.

"I quit, I quit, I quit, I quit!" he chattered, as he slid away from the feast in the tree. When he was safely down he called back, "Oh, cousins, when may I join you at the feast?"

"When you have a totem mark," called they all together, which made Chipmunk sad, for he had no totem mark and did not know where to get one, for no warrior was he.

Robbed of all chance at chestnuts, Chipmunk scampered away to the deep woods, hungry and sad. So hungry was he that he fell to eating fat grubs that he found in the leaves, and the fat bugs didn't like it one bit. Chipmunk didn't care one chatter whether or not the grubs liked it; he was hungry and the grubs were very filling. But, ho-hoh! suddenly a big bear came into sight. Brother Bear saw Chipmunk, and Brother Bear was hungry too. "Whoof," said he. "If I can't find honey or berries, little rock-dweller will do." Thereupon he gave a pounce and landed on Chipmunk with both paws.

"Quit, quit, quit, quit!" chattered Chipmunk.

"Sing your last song," counseled Brother Bear. "I am hungry and won't wait very long. Sing, sing, for I am going to eat you!"

"Oh, Brother Bear," pleaded Chipmunk, "let me dance too, for that is the custom of my tribe. I must sing and dance my last song and dance."

"Then dance quickly," said the hungry Bear.

Chipmunk now began to dance, singing in his own tongue, one which Brother Bear did not understand, of course, nephew:

> "Oh, for a hole made by a mole,
>   As quick as I see it I'll duck.
> Oh, for a hole made by a mole—
>   Oh, now that I see it—here's luck!"

Chipmunk, standing on his hind legs, espied the hole of the mole at the foot of the tree and with a quick dart he ducked into the burrow, breathless but out of sight of the hungry Bear.

"Whoof," said Brother Bear, "not so quick," and he pounced on the tunnel of the mole, driving his long claws into the ground and right through the underground runway.

As luck would have it one paw struck Chipmunk right on his shoulders and pricked him deep. "I quit," he squealed, as he struggled to run down the burrow, but the claw held him fast. He struggled again and then something ripped; Chipmunk had torn himself loose and raked his back under the sharp claws of Brother Bear, scratching his clay-colored hide from shoulders to hips. The scratches were deep and the blood ran fast, but Chipmunk ran faster and escaped way down in the earth.

"Whoof," said the Bear, ambling away with a grouch.

Long Chipmunk lay in the dark in the hole of the mole. He licked his sores and scratched off the clots of blood. At length he recovered and cautiously emerged from his hiding place. He was very hungry and sneaked back to the chestnut tree to find a stray nut or two.

But there, as before, were the four cousins, chattering and scolding as they ever do when collecting nuts.

Chipmunk was frightened when Gray Squirrel espied him and shouted, "Who are you, who are you, who are you, stripes upon his back?"

"Stripes on his back," chattered Red Squirrel, "who are you with a warrior's totem marks?"

"Stripes, stripes, stripes, stripes," echoed Black Squirrel. "Who are you with the stripes?"

"Stripes on his back, who are you?" mimicked Flying Squirrel. "What right have you won to gain totem marks?"

"I am rock-dweller," answered Chipmunk. "I am hungry for nuts after my big fight with Brother Bear."

"Fight with Brother Bear?" questioned Gray Squirrel. "Why, you couldn't fight me. Come up if you dare, and if you win you can have my store of nuts in a secret place at the foot of this tree."

Chipmunk didn't want to fight, so he said, "I'll sing a war song in my own language; then look out for me!" So he sang:

> "Oh, for a hole made by a mole,
>   As quick as I see it, I'll duck.
>   Oh for a hole made by a mole—
>   And now that I see it—here's luck!"

Chipmunk, standing on his hind legs, espied the hole of the mole at the foot of the tree and with a quick dart he ducked into the burrow, and it was filled with meaty brown chestnuts. So quickly did he disappear that the stingy squirrels in the tree never saw where Chipmunk went. They only said, "That new totem is full of power."

But down under the ground Chipmunk gloated over his store of food. "No," he chattered, "I can't have any of *their* chestnuts. Guess not, guess not, guess not."

Way up in the tree the four nutcrackers heard rock-dweller snipping out, "Guess not, guess not," and Gray Squirrel asked, "Brothers, what did rock-dweller mean when he said, 'guess not'?"

Then they all shouted again, "Chipmunk with the totem mark, come out where we can see you." But Chipmunk only answered, "Guess not." Ho-hoh, nephew. Now you know how the Chipmunk got his stripes. That's all.

HOW THE COYOTE DANCED
WITH THE BLACKBIRDS

By FRANK HAMILTON CUSHING

ONE late autumn day in the times of the ancients, a large
council of Blackbirds were gathered, fluttering and chattering, on the smooth, rocky slopes of Gorge Mountain, northwest of
Zuñi. Like ourselves, these birds, as you are well aware, congregate
together in autumn time when the harvests are ripe, to indulge in
their festivities before going into winter quarters; only we do not
move away, while they, on strong wings and swift, retreat for a
time to the Land of Everlasting Summer.

Well, on this particular morning they were making a great noise
and having a grand dance, and this was the way of it: They would
gather in one vast flock, somewhat orderly in its disposition, on the
sloping face of Gorge Mountain—the older birds in front, the
younger ones behind—and down the slope, chirping and fluttering,
they would hop, hop, hop, singing:

> *"Ketchu, Ketchu, oñtila, oñtila,*
> *Ketchu, Ketchu, oñtila, oñtila!*
> *Âshokta a yá-à-laa Ke-e-tchu,*
> ***Oñtila,***
> ***Oñtila!"***—
> Blackbirds, Blackbirds, dance away, O, dance away, O!
> Blackbirds, Blackbirds, dance away, O, dance away, O!
> Down the Mountain of the Gorges, Blackbirds,
> > Dance away, O!
> > Dance away, O!—

and spreading their wings with many a flutter, flurry, and scurry,
keh keh—keh keh—keh keh—keh keh—they would fly away into
the air, swirling off in a dense, black flock, circling far upward and
onward; then, wheeling about and darting down, they would dip
themselves in the broad spring which flows out at the foot of the
mountain, and return to their dancing place on the rocky slopes.

287

A Coyote was out hunting (as if he could catch anything, the beast!) and saw them, and was enraptured.

"You beautiful creatures!" he exclaimed. "You graceful dancers! Delight of my senses! How do you do that, anyway? Couldn't I join in your dance—the first part of it, at least?"

"Why, certainly; yes," said the Blackbirds. "We are quite willing," the masters of the ceremony said.

"Well," said the Coyote, "I can get on the slope of the rocks and I can sing the song with you; but I suppose that when you leap off into the air I shall have to sit there patting the rock with my paw and my tail and singing while you have the fun of it."

"It may be," said an old Blackbird, "that we can fit you out so that you can fly with us."

"Is it possible!" cried the Coyote. "Then by all means do so. By the Blessed Immortals! Now, if I am only able to circle off into the air like you fellows, I'll be the biggest Coyote in the world!"

"I think it will be easy," resumed the old Blackbird. "My children," said he, "you are many, and many are your wing feathers. Contribute each one of you a feather to our friend." Thereupon the Blackbirds, each one of them, plucked a feather from his wing. Unfortunately they all plucked feathers from the wings on the same side.

"Are you sure, my friend," continued the old Blackbird, "that you are willing to go through the operation of having these feathers planted in your skin? If so, I think we can fit you out."

"Willing?—why, of course I am willing." And the Coyote held up one of his arms, and, sitting down, steadied himself with his tail. Then the Blackbirds thrust in the feathers all along the rear of his forelegs and down the sides of his back, where wings ought to be. It hurt, and the Coyote twitched his mustache considerably; but he said nothing. When it was done, he asked: "Am I ready now?"

"Yes," said the Blackbirds; "we think you'll do."

So they formed themselves again on the upper part of the slope, sang their songs, and hopped along down with many a flutter, flurry, and scurry—*Keh keh, keh keh, keh keh*—and away they flew off into the air.

The Coyote, somewhat startled, got out of time, but followed bravely, making heavy flops; but, as I have said before, the wings he was supplied with were composed of feathers all plucked from one side, and therefore he flew slantingly and spirally and brought up with a whack which nearly knocked the breath out of him, against the side of the mountain. He picked himself up and shook himself, and cried out: "Hold! Hold! Hold on, hold on, there!" to the fast-disappearing Blackbirds. "You've left me behind!"

When the birds returned they explained: "Your wings are not quite thick enough, friend; and, besides, even a young Blackbird, when he is first learning to fly, does just this sort of thing that you have been doing—makes bad work of it."

"Sit down again," said the old Blackbird. And he called out to the rest: "Get feathers from your other sides also, and be careful to select a few strong feathers from the tips of the wings, for by means of these we cleave the air, guide our movements, and sustain our flight."

So the Blackbirds all did as they were bidden, and after the new feathers were planted, each one plucked out a tail feather, and the most skillful of the Blackbirds inserted these feathers into the tip of the Coyote's tail. It made him wince and "yip" occasionally; but he stood it bravely and reared his head proudly, thinking all the while: "What a splendid Coyote I shall be! Did ever anyone hear of a Coyote flying?"

The procession formed again. Down the slope they went, hopity-hop, hopity-hop, singing their song, and away they flew into the air, the Coyote in their midst. Far off and high they circled and circled, the Coyote cutting more eager pranks than any of the rest. Finally they returned, dipped themselves again into the spring, and settled on the slopes of the rocks.

"There, now," cried out the Coyote, with a flutter of his feathery tail, "I can fly as well as the rest of you."

"Indeed, you do well!" exclaimed the Blackbirds. "Shall we try it again?"

"Oh, yes! Oh, yes! I'm a little winded," cried the Coyote, "but this is the best fun I ever had."

The Blackbirds, however, were not satisfied with their companion. They found him less sedate than a dancer ought to be, and, moreover, his irregular cuttings-up in the air were not to their taste. So the old ones whispered to one another: "This fellow is a fool, and we must pluck him when he gets into the air. We'll fly so far this time that he will get a little tired out and cry to us for assistance."

The procession formed, and hopity-hop, hopity-hop, down the mountain slope they went, and with many a flutter and flurry flew off into the air. The Coyote, unable to restrain himself, even took the lead. On and on and on they flew, the Blackbirds and the Coyote, and up and up and up, and they circled round and round, until the Coyote found himself missing a wing stroke occasionally and falling out of line; and he cried out: "Help! help, friends, help!"

"All right!" cried the Blackbirds. "Catch hold of his wings; hold him up!" cried the old ones. And the Blackbirds flew at him; and every time they caught hold of him (the old fool all the time thinking they were helping) they plucked out a feather, until at last the feathers had become so thin that he began to fall, and he fell and fell and fell—flop, flop, flop, he went through the air—the few feathers left in his forelegs and sides and the tip of his tail just saving him from being utterly crushed as he fell with a thud to the ground. He lost his senses completely, and lay there as if dead for a long time. When he awoke he shook his head sadly, and, with a crestfallen countenance, and tail dragging between his legs, betook himself to his home over the mountains.

The agony of that fall had been so great and the heat of his exertions so excessive, that the feathers left in his forelegs and tail tip were all shriveled up into little ugly black fringes of hair.

His descendants were many. Therefore you will often meet coyotes to this day who have little black fringes along the rear of their forelegs, and the tips of their tails are often black. Thus it was in the days of the ancients.

Thus shortens my story.

THE SERPENT OF THE SEA

By *FRANK HAMILTON CUSHING*

IN THE TIMES of our forefathers, under Thunder Mountain was a village called K'iákime ("Home of the Eagles"). It is now in ruins; the roofs are gone, the ladders have decayed, the hearths grown cold. But when it was all still perfect, and, as it were, new, there lived in this village a maiden, the daughter of the priest chief. She was beautiful, but possessed of a certain peculiarity of character. There was a sacred spring of water at the foot of the terrace whereon stood the town. We now call it the Pool of the Apaches; but then it was sacred to Kólowissi (the Serpent of the Sea). Now, at this spring the girl displayed her peculiarity, which was that of a passion for neatness and cleanliness of person and clothing. She could not endure the slightest speck or particle of dust or dirt upon her clothes or person, and so she spent most of her time in washing all the things she used and in bathing herself in the waters of this spring.

Now, these waters, being sacred to the Serpent of the Sea, should not have been defiled in this way. As might have been expected, Kolowissi became troubled and angry at the sacrilege committed in the sacred waters by the maiden, and he said:

"Why does this maiden defile the sacred waters of my spring with the dirt of her apparel and the dun of her person? I must see to this." So he devised a plan by which to prevent the sacrilege and to punish its author.

When the maiden came again to the spring, what should she behold but a beautiful little child seated amidst the waters, splashing them, cooing and smiling. It was the Sea Serpent, wearing the semblance of a child—for a god may assume any form at its pleasure, you know. There sat the child, laughing and playing in the water. The girl looked around in all directions—north, south, east, and west—but could see no one, nor any traces of persons who might have brought hither the beautiful little child. She said to herself:

"I wonder whose child this may be! It would seem to be that of some unkind and cruel mother, who has deserted it and left it here to perish. And the poor little child does not yet know that it is left all alone. Poor little thing! I will take it in my arms and care for it."

The maiden then talked softly to the young child, and took it in her arms, and hastened with it up the hill to her house, and, climbing up the ladder, carried the child in her arms into the room where she slept.

Her peculiarity of character, her dislike of all dirt or dust, led her to dwell apart from the rest of her family, in a room by herself above all of the other apartments.

She was so pleased with the child that when she had got him into her room she sat down on the floor and played with him, laughing at his pranks and smiling into his face; and he answered her in baby fashion with cooings and smiles of his own, so that her heart became very happy and loving. So it happened that thus was she engaged for a long while and utterly unmindful of the lapse of time.

Meanwhile, the younger sisters had prepared the meal, and were awaiting the return of the elder sister.

"Where, I wonder, can she be?" one of them asked.

"She is probably down at the spring," said the old father; "she is bathing and washing her clothes, as usual, of course! Run down and call her."

But the younger sister, on going, could find no trace of her at the spring. So she climbed the ladder to the private room of this elder sister, and there found her, as has been told, playing with the little child. She hastened back to inform her father of what she had seen. But the old man sat silent and thoughtful. He knew that the waters of the spring were sacred. When the rest of the family were excited, and ran to behold the pretty prodigy, he cried out, therefore: "Come back! Come back! Why do you make fools of yourselves? Do you suppose any mother would leave her own child in the waters of this or any other spring? There is something more of meaning than seems in all this."

When they again went and called the maiden to come down to

the meal spread for her, she could not be induced to leave the child.

"See! It is as you might expect," said the father. "A woman will not leave a child on any inducement; how much less her own."

The child at length grew sleepy. The maiden placed it on a bed, and, growing sleepy herself, at length lay by its side and fell asleep. Her sleep was genuine, but the sleep of the child was feigned. The child became elongated by degrees, as it were, fulfilling some horrible dream, and soon appeared as an enormous Serpent that coiled itself round and round the room until it was full of scaly, gleaming circles. Then, placing its head near the head of the maiden, the great Serpent surrounded her with its coils, taking finally its own tail in its mouth.

The night passed, and in the morning when the breakfast was prepared, and yet the maiden did not descend, and the younger sisters became impatient at the delay, the old man said: "Now that she has the child to play with, she will care little for aught else. That is enough to occupy the entire attention of any woman."

But the little sister ran up to the room and called. Receiving no answer, she tried to open the door; she could not move it, because the Serpent's coils filled the room and pressed against it. She pushed the door with all her might, but it could not be moved. She again and again called her sister's name, but no response came. Beginning now to be frightened, she ran to the skyhole over the room in which she had left the others and cried out for help. They hastily joined her—all save the old father—and together were able to press the door sufficiently to get a glimpse of the great scales and folds of the Serpent. Then the women all ran screaming to the old father. The old man, priest and sage as he was, quieted them with these words: "I expected as much as this from the first report which you gave me. It was impossible, as I then said, that a woman should be so foolish as to leave her child playing even near the waters of the spring. But it is not impossible, it seems, that one should be so foolish as to take into her arms a child found as this one was."

Thereupon he walked out of the house, deliberately and thoughtful, angry in his mind against his eldest daughter. Ascending to her room, he pushed against the door and called to the Serpent of the

Sea: "Oh, Kólowissi! It is I, who speak to thee, O Serpent of the Sea; I thy priest. Let, I pray thee, let my child come to me again, and I will make atonement for her errors. Release her, though she has been so foolish, for she is thine, absolutely thine. But let her return once more to us that we may make atonement to thee more amply." So prayed the priest to the Serpent of the Sea.

When he had done this the great Serpent loosened his coils, and as he did so the whole building shook violently, and all the villagers became aware of the event and trembled with fear.

The maiden at once awoke and cried piteously to her father for help.

"Come and release me, O my father! Come and release me!" she cried.

As the coils loosened she found herself able to rise. No sooner had she done this than the great Serpent bent the folds of his large coils nearest the doorway upward so that they formed an arch. Under this, filled with terror, the girl passed. She was almost stunned with the dread din of the monster's scales, rasping past one another with a noise like the sound of flints trodden under the feet of a rapid runner, and once away from the writhing mass of coils, the poor maiden ran like a frightened deer out of the doorway, down the ladder and into the room below, casting herself on the breast of her mother.

But the priest still remained praying to the Serpent; and he ended his prayer as he had begun it, saying: "It shall be even as I have said; she shall be thine!"

He then went away and called the two warrior priest chiefs of the town, and these called together all the other priests in sacred council. Then they performed the solemn ceremonies of the sacred rites—preparing plumes, prayer wands, and offerings of treasure.

After four days of labor, these things they arranged and consecrated to the Serpent of the Sea. On that morning the old priest called his daughter and told her she must make ready to take these sacrifices and yield them up, even with herself—most precious of them all—to the great Serpent of the Sea; that she must yield up also all thoughts of her people and home forever, and go hence to the house of the great Serpent of the Sea, even in the Waters of the

World. "For it seems," said he, "to have been your desire to do thus, as manifested by your actions. You used even the sacred water for profane purposes; now this that I have told you is inevitable. Come; the time when you must prepare yourself to depart is near at hand."

She went forth from the home of her childhood with sad cries, clinging to the neck of her mother and shivering with terror. In the plaza, amidst the lamentations of all the people, they dressed her in her sacred cotton robes of ceremonial, embroidered elaborately, and adorned her with earrings, bracelets, beads—many beautiful, precious things. They painted her cheeks with red spots as if for a dance; they made a road of sacred meal toward the Door of the Serpent of the Sea—a distant spring in our land known to this day as the Doorway to the Serpent of the Sea—four steps toward this spring did they mark in sacred terraces on the ground at the western way of the plaza. And when they had finished the sacred road, the old priest, who never shed one tear, although all the villagers wept sore —for the maiden was very beautiful—instructed his daughter to go forth on the terraced road, and, standing there, call the Serpent to come to her.

Then the door opened, and the Serpent descended from the high room where he was coiled, and, without using ladders, let his head and breast down to the ground in great undulations. He placed his head on the shoulder of the maiden, and the word was given—the word: "It is time"—and the maiden slowly started toward the west, cowering beneath her burden; but whenever she staggered with fear and weariness and was like to wander from the way, the Serpent gently pushed her onward and straightened her course.

Thus they went toward the river trail and in it, on and over the Mountain of the Red Paint; yet still the Serpent was not all uncoiled from the maiden's room in the house, but continued to crawl forth until they were past the mountain—when the last of his length came forth. Here he began to draw himself together again and to assume a new shape. So that ere long his serpent form contracted, until, lifting his head from the maiden's shoulder, he stood up, in form a beautiful youth in sacred gala attire! He placed the scales of his serpent form, now small, under his flowing mantle, and called out to the maiden in a hoarse, hissing voice: "Let us speak one to the other. Are you tired, girl?" Yet she never moved her head, but plodded on with her eyes cast down.

"Are you weary, poor maiden?"—then he said in a gentler voice, as he arose erect and fell a little behind her, and wrapped his scales more closely in his blanket—and he was now such a splendid and brave hero, so magnificently dressed! And he repeated, in a still softer voice: "Are you still weary, poor maiden?"

At first she dared not look around, though the voice, so changed, sounded so far behind her and thrilled her wonderfully with its kindness. Yet she still felt the weight on her shoulder, the weight of that dreaded Serpent's head; for you know after one has carried a heavy burden on his shoulder or back, if it be removed he does not at once know that it is taken away; it seems still to oppress and pain him. So it was with her; but at length she turned around a little and saw a young man—a brave and handsome young man.

"May I walk by your side?" said he, catching her eye. "Why do you not speak with me?"

"I am filled with fear and sadness and shame," said she.

"Why?" asked he. "What do you fear?"

"Because I came with a fearful creature forth from my home, and he rested his head upon my shoulder, and even now I feel his presence there," said she, lifting her hand to the place where his head had rested, even still fearing that it might be there.

"But I came all the way with you," said he, "and I saw no such creature as you describe."

Upon this she stopped and turned back and looked again at him, and said: "You came all the way? I wonder where this fearful being has gone!"

He smiled, and replied: "I know where he has gone."

"Ah, youth and friend, will he now leave me in peace," said she, "and let me return to the home of my people?"

"No," replied he, "because he thinks very much of you."

"Why not? Where is he?"

"He is here," said the youth smiling, and laying his hand on his own heart. "I am he."

"You are he?" cried the maiden. Then she looked at him again, and would not believe him.

"Yea, my maiden, I am he!" said he. And he drew forth from under his flowing mantle the shriveled serpent scales, and showed them as proofs of his word. It was wonderful and beautiful to the maiden to see that he was thus, a gentle being; and she looked at him long.

Then he said: "Yes, I am he. I love you, my maiden! Will you not haply come forth and dwell with me? Yes, you will go with me, and dwell with me, and I will dwell with you, and I will love you. I dwell not now, but ever, in all the Waters of the World, and in each particular water. In all and each you will dwell with me forever, and we will love each other."

Behold! As they journeyed on, the maiden quite forgot that she had been sad; she forgot her old home, and followed and descended with him into the Doorway of the Serpent of the Sea and dwelt with him ever after.

It was thus in the days of the ancients. Therefore the ancients, no less than ourselves, avoided using springs, except for the drinking of their water; for to this day we hold the flowing springs the most precious things on earth, and therefore use them not for any profane purposes whatsoever.

Thus shortens my story.

SCARFACE

Origin of the Medicine Lodge

By GEORGE BIRD GRINNELL

Illustration by Warren Chappell

I

IN THE earliest times there was no war. All the tribes were at peace. In those days there was a man who had a daughter, a very beautiful girl. Many young men wanted to marry her, but every time she was asked, she only shook her head and said she did not want a husband.

"How is this?" asked her father. "Some of these young men are rich, handsome, and brave."

"Why should I marry?" replied the girl. "I have a rich father and mother. Our lodge is good. The parfleches[1] are never empty. There are plenty of tanned robes and soft furs for winter. Why worry me, then?"

The Raven Bearers held a dance; they all dressed carefully and wore their ornaments, and each one tried to dance the best. Afterwards some of them asked for this girl, but still she said no. Then the Bulls, the Kit foxes, and others of the *I-kun-uh'-kah-tsi* held their dances, and all those who were rich, many great warriors, asked this man for his daughter, but to every one of them she said no. Then her father was angry and said: "Why, now, this way? All the best men have asked for you and still you say no. I believe you have a secret lover."

"Father! Mother!" replied the girl, "pity me. I have no secret lover, but now hear the truth. That Above Person, the Sun, told me, 'Do not marry any of those men, for you are mine; thus you shall be happy, and live to great age'; and again he said, 'Take heed. You must not marry. You are mine.'"

---

[1] Rawhide saddlebags.

"Ah!" replied her father. "It must always be as he says."

And they talked no more about it.

There was a poor young man, very poor. His father, mother, all his relations, had gone to the Sand Hills. He had no lodge, no wife to tan his robes or sew his moccasins. He stopped in one lodge to-day, and tomorrow he ate and slept in another; thus he lived. He was a good-looking young man, except that on his cheek he had a scar, and his clothes were always old and poor.

After those dances some of the young men met this poor Scarface, and they laughed at him, and said: "Why don't you ask that girl to marry you? You are so rich and handsome!" Scarface did not laugh; he replied: "Ah! I will do as you say. I will go and ask her." All the young men thought this was funny. They laughed a great deal. But Scarface went down by the river. He waited by the river, where the women came to get water, and by and by the girl came along. "Girl," he said, "wait. I want to speak with you. Not as a designing person do I ask you, but openly where the Sun looks down, and all may see."

"Speak then," said the girl.

"I have seen the days," continued the young man. "You have refused those who are young, and rich, and brave. Now, today, they laughed and said to me, 'Why do you not ask her?' I am poor, very poor. I have no lodge, no food, no clothes, no robes and warm furs. I have no relations; all have gone to the Sand Hills; yet, now, today, I ask you, take pity, be my wife."

The girl hid her face in her robe and brushed the ground with the point of her moccasin, back and forth, back and forth; for she was thinking. After a time she said: "True. I have refused all those rich young men, yet now the poor one asks me and I am glad. I will be your wife and my people will be happy. You are poor, but it does not matter. My father will give you dogs. My mother will make us a lodge. My people will give us robes and furs. You will be poor no longer."

Then the young man was happy and he started to kiss her, but she held him back and said: "Wait! The Sun has spoken to me. He says I may not marry; that I belong to him. He says if I listen to him, I shall live to great age. But now I say: Go to the Sun. Tell him, 'She whom you spoke with heeds your words. She has never done wrong, but now she wants to marry. I want her for my wife.' Ask him to take that scar from your face. That will be his sign. I will know he is pleased. But if he refuses, or if you fail to find his lodge, then do not return to me."

"Oh!" cried the young man, "at first your words were good. I was glad. But now it is dark. My heart is dead. Where is that far-off lodge? Where the trail, which no one yet has traveled?"

"Take courage, take courage!" said the girl and went to her lodge.

II

Scarface was very sad. He sat down and covered his head with his robe and tried to think what to do. After a while he got up, and went to an old woman who had been kind to him. "Pity me," he said. "I am very poor. I am going away now on a long journey. Make me some moccasins."

"Where are you going?" asked the old woman. "There is no war; we are very peaceful here."

"I do not know where I shall go," replied Scarface. "I am in trouble, but I cannot tell you now what it is."

So the old woman made him some moccasins, seven pairs, with parfleche soles, and also she gave him a sack of food—pemmican of berries, pounded meat, and dried back fat; for this old woman had a good heart. She liked the young man.

All alone, and with a sad heart, he climbed the bluffs and stopped to take a last look at the camp. He wondered if he would ever see his sweetheart and the people again. "Hai-yu! Pity me, O Sun," he prayed, and turning, he started to find the trail.

For many days he traveled on, over great prairies, along timbered rivers and among the mountains, and every day his sack of food grew lighter; but he saved it as much as he could, and ate berries and roots, and sometimes he killed an animal of some kind. One night he stopped by the home of a wolf. "Hai-yah!" said that one; "what is my brother doing so far from home?"

"Ah!" replied Scarface, "I seek the place where the Sun lives; I am sent to speak with him."

"I have traveled far," said the wolf. "I know all the prairies, the valleys, and the mountains, but I have never seen the Sun's home. Wait; I know one who is very wise. Ask the bear. He may tell you."

The next day the man traveled on again, stopping now and then to pick a few berries, and when night came he arrived at the bear's lodge.

"Where is your home?" asked the bear. "Why are you traveling alone, my brother?"

"Help me! Pity me!" replied the young man; "Because of her words[1] I seek the Sun. I go to ask him for her."

"I know not where he stops," replied the bear. "I have traveled by many rivers, and I know the mountains, yet I have never seen his lodge. There is someone beyond, that striped-face, who is very smart. Go and ask him."

The badger was in his hole. Stooping over, the young man shouted: "Oh, cunning striped-face! Oh, generous animal! I wish to speak with you."

"What do you want?" said the badger, poking his head out of the hole.

"I want to find the Sun's home," replied Scarface. "I want to speak with him."

"I do not know where he lives," replied the badger. "I never travel very far. Over there in the timber is a wolverine. He is always traveling around, and has much knowledge. Maybe he can tell you."

Then Scarface went to the woods and looked all around for the wolverine, but could not find him. So he sat down to rest. *"Hai-yu! Hai-yu!"* he cried. "Wolverine, take pity on me. My food is gone, my moccasins worn out. Now I must die."

"What is it, my brother?" he heard, and looking around, he saw the animal sitting near.

"She whom I would marry," said Scarface, "belongs to the Sun; I am trying to find where he lives to ask him for her."

"Ah!" said the wolverine. "I know where he lives. Wait; it is

[1] A Blackfoot often talks of what this or that person said, without mentioning names.

nearly night. Tomorrow I will show you the trail to the big water. He lives on the other side of it."

Early in the morning the wolverine showed him the trail, and Scarface followed it until he came to the water's edge. He looked out over it, and his heart almost stopped. Never before had anyone seen such a big water. The other side could not be seen, and there was no end to it. Scarface sat down on the shore. His food was all gone, his moccasins worn out. His heart was sick. "I cannot cross this big water," he said. "I cannot return to the people. Here, by this water, I shall die."

Not so. His Helpers were there. Two swans came swimming up to the shore. "Why have you come here?" they asked him. "What are you doing? It is very far to the place where your people live."

"I am here," replied Scarface, "to die. Far away, in my country, is a beautiful girl. I want to marry her, but she belongs to the Sun. So I started to find him and ask for her. I have traveled many days. My food is gone. I cannot go back. I cannot cross this big water, so I am going to die."

"No," said the swans; "it shall not be so. Across this water is the home of that Above Person. Get on our backs, and we will take you there."

Scarface quickly arose. He felt strong again. He waded out into the water and lay down on the swans' backs, and they started off. Very deep and black is that fearful water. Strange people live there, mighty animals which often seize and drown a person. The swans carried him safely, and took him to the other side. Here was a broad hard trail leading back from the water's edge.

"*Kyi*," said the swans. "You are now close to the Sun's lodge. Follow that trail, and you will soon see it."

III

Scarface started up the trail, and pretty soon he came to some beautiful things lying in it. There was a war shirt, a shield, and a bow and arrows. He had never seen such pretty weapons; but he did

Warren Chappell

They were married and made the first Medicine Lodge.

[See page 306]

not touch them. He walked carefully around them, and traveled on.
A little way farther on, he met a young man, the handsomest person
he had ever seen. His hair was very long, and he wore clothing
made of strange skins. His moccasins were sewn with bright colored
feathers. The young man said to him, "Did you see some weapons
lying on the trail?"

"Yes," replied Scarface; "I saw them."

"But did you not touch them?" asked the young man.

"No; I thought someone had left them, so I did not take them."

"You are not a thief," said the young man. "What is your name?"

"Scarface."

"Where are you going?"

"To the Sun."

"My name," said the young man, "is A-pi-sú-ahts.[1] The Sun is
my father; come, I will take you to our lodge. My father is not now
at home, but he will come in at night."

Soon they came to the lodge. It was very large and handsome;
strange medicine animals were painted on it. Behind, on a tripod,
were strange weapons and beautiful clothes—the Sun's. Scarface was
ashamed to go in, but Morning Star said, "Do not be afraid, my
friend; we are glad you have come."

They entered. One person was sitting there, Ko-ko-mik'-e-is,[2] the
Sun's wife, Morning Star's mother. She spoke to Scarface kindly and
gave him something to eat. "Why have you come so far from your
people?" she asked.

Then Scarface told her about the beautiful girl he wanted to
marry. "She belongs to the Sun," he said. "I have come to ask him
for her."

When it was time for the Sun to come home, the Moon hid Scarface under a pile of robes. As soon as the Sun got to the doorway, he
stopped, and said, "I smell a person."

"Yes, father," said Morning Star; "a good young man has come
to see you. I know he is good, for he found some of my things on
the trail and did not touch them."

[1] Early Riser, *i. e.* The Morning Star.
[2] Night red light, the Moon.

Then Scarface came out from under the robes, and the Sun entered and sat down. "I am glad you have come to our lodge," he said. "Stay with us as long as you think best. My son is lonesome sometimes; be his friend."

The next day the Moon called Scarface out of the lodge and said to him: "Go with Morning Star where you please, but never hunt near that big water; do not let him go there. It is the home of great birds which have long sharp bills; they kill people. I have had many sons, but these birds have killed them all. Morning Star is the only one left."

So Scarface stayed there a long time and hunted with Morning Star. One day they came near the water and saw the big birds.

"Come," said Morning Star; "let us go and kill those birds."

"No, no!" replied Scarface; "we must not go there. Those are very terrible birds; they will kill us."

Morning Star would not listen. He ran toward the water and Scarface followed. He knew that he must kill the birds and save the boy. If not, the Sun would be angry and might kill him. He ran ahead and met the birds which were coming toward him to fight, and killed every one of them with his spear: not one was left. Then the young men cut off their heads and carried them home. Morning Star's mother was glad when they told her what they had done, and showed her the birds' heads. She cried, and called Scarface "my son." When the Sun came home at night, she told him about it, and he too was glad. "My son," he said to Scarface, "I will not forget what you have this day done for me. Tell me now, what can I do for you?"

"Haî-yu," replied Scarface. "Haî-yu, pity me. I am here to ask you for that girl. I want to marry her. I asked her and she was glad; but she says you own her, that you told her not to marry."

"What you say is true," said the Sun. "I have watched the days, so I know it. Now, then, I give her to you; she is yours. I am glad she has been wise. I know she has never done wrong. The Sun pities good women. They shall live a long time. So shall their husbands and children. Now you will soon go home. Let me tell you something. Be wise and listen: I am the only chief. Everything is mine. I made the earth, the mountains, prairies, rivers, and forests. I made the people and all the animals. This is why I say I alone am the chief. I can never die. True, the winter makes me old and weak, but every summer I grow young again."

Then said the Sun: "What one of all animals is smartest? The raven is, for he always finds food. He is never hungry. Which one of all the animals is most *Nat-ó-ye*[1]? The buffalo is. Of all animals, I like him best. He is for the people. He is your food and your shelter. What part of his body is sacred? The tongue is. That is mine. What else is sacred? Berries are. They are mine too. Come with me and see the world." He took Scarface to the edge of the sky, and they looked down and saw it. It is round and flat, and all around the edge is the jumping-off place [or walls straight down]. Then said the Sun: "When any man is sick or in danger, his wife may promise to build me a lodge if he recovers. If the woman is pure and true, then I will be pleased and help the man. But if she is bad, if she lies, then I will be angry. You shall build the lodge like the world, round, with walls, but first you must build a sweat house of a hundred sticks. It shall be like the sky [a hemisphere], and half of it shall be painted red. That is me. The other half you will paint black. That is the night."

Further said the Sun: "Which is the best, the heart or the brain? The brain is. The heart often lies, the brain never." Then he told Scarface everything about making the Medicine Lodge, and when he had finished, he rubbed a powerful medicine on his face and the scar disappeared. Then he gave him two raven feathers, saying: "These are the sign for the girl, that I give her to you. They must always be worn by the husband of the woman who builds a Medicine Lodge."

The young man was now ready to return home. Morning Star and the Sun gave him many beautiful presents. The Moon cried and kissed him, and called him "my son." Then the Sun showed him the short trail. It was the Wolf Road (Milky Way). He followed it, and soon reached the ground.

---

[1] This word may be translated as "of the Sun," "having Sun power," or more properly, something sacred.

IV

It was a very hot day. All the lodge skins were raised, and the people sat in the shade. There was a chief, a very generous man, and all day long people kept coming to his lodge to feast and smoke with him. Early in the morning this chief saw a person sitting out on a butte near by, close wrapped in his robe. The chief's friends came and went, the sun reached the middle, and passed on, down toward the mountains. Still this person did not move. When it was almost night, the chief said: "Why does that person sit there so long? The heat has been strong, but he has never eaten nor drunk. He may be a stranger; go and ask him in."

So some young men went up to him, and said "Why do you sit here in the great heat all day? Come to the shade of the lodges. The chief asks you to feast with him."

Then the person arose and threw off his robe, and they were surprised. He wore beautiful clothes. His bow, shield, and other weapons were of strange make. But they knew his face, although the scar was gone, and they ran ahead shouting, "The scarface poor young man has come. He is poor no longer. The scar on his face is gone."

All the people rushed out to see him. "Where have you been?" they asked. "Where did you get all these pretty things?" He did not answer. There in the crowd stood that young woman; and taking the two raven feathers from his head, he gave them to her, and said: "The trail was very long, and I nearly died, but by those Helpers, I found his lodge. He is glad. He sends these feathers to you. They are the sign."

Great was her gladness then. They were married, and made the first Medicine Lodge as the Sun had said. The Sun was glad. He gave them great age. They were never sick. When they were very old, one morning, their children said: "Awake! Rise and eat." They did not move. In the night, in sleep, without pain, their shadows had departed for the Sand Hills.

Old Legends

THE PROUD KING

By HORACE E. SCUDDER

Illustration by A. J. Walker

THERE was once a king who ruled over many lands; he went to war, and added one country after another to his kingdom. At last he came to be emperor, and that is as much as any man can be. One night, after he was crowned emperor, he lay awake and thought about himself. "Surely," he said, "no one can be greater than I am, on earth or in heaven."

The proud king fell asleep with these thoughts. When he awoke, the day was fair, and he looked out on the pleasant world. "Come," he said to the men about him; "today we will go a-hunting."

The horses were brought, the dogs came leaping, the horns sounded, and the proud king with his courtiers rode off to the sport. They had hunted all the morning, and were now in a deep wood. In the fields the sun had beat upon their heads, and they were glad of the shade of the trees; but the proud king wished for something more. He saw a lake not far off, and he said to his men:

"Bide ye here, while I bathe in the lake and cool myself."

Then he rode apart till he came to the shore of the lake. There he got down from his horse, laid aside his clothes, and plunged into the cool water. He swam about, and sometimes dived beneath the surface, and so was once more cool and fresh.

Now while the proud king was swimming away from the shore and diving to the bottom, there came one who had the same face and form as the king. He drew near the shore, dressed himself in the king's clothes, mounted the king's horse and rode away. So when the proud king was once more cool and fresh, and came to the place where he had left his clothes and his horse, there were no clothes to be seen and no horse.

The proud king looked about, but saw no man. He called, but no one heard him. The air was mild, but the wood was dark and no sunshine came through to warm him after his cool bath. He walked by the shore of the lake and cast about in his mind what he should do.

A. G. Walker

With these thoughts the proud king fell asleep.

"I have it," he cried at last. "Not far from here lives a knight. It was but a few days ago that I made him a knight and gave him a castle. I will go to him, and he will be glad enough to clothe his king."

The proud king wove some reeds into a mat and bound the mat

about him, and then he walked to the castle of the knight. He beat loudly at the gate of the castle and called for the porter. The porter came and stood behind the gate. He did not draw the bolt at once, but asked:

"Who is there?"

"Open the gate," said the proud king, "and you will see who I am."

The porter opened the gate, and was amazed at what he saw.

"Who are you?" he asked.

"Wretch!" said the proud king; "I am the emperor. Go to your master. Bid him come to me with clothes. I have lost both clothes and horse."

"A pretty emperor!" the porter laughed. "The great emperor was here not an hour ago. He came with his court from a hunt. My master was with him and sat at meat with him. But stay you here. I will call my master. Oh, yes! I will show him the emperor!" And the porter wagged his beard and laughed again, and went within.

He came forth again with the knight and pointed at the proud king.

"There is the emperor!" he said. "Look at him! Look at the great emperor!"

"Draw near," said the proud king to the knight, "and kneel to me. I gave thee this castle. I made thee knight. I give thee now a greater gift. I give thee the chance to clothe thy emperor with clothes of thine own."

"You dog!" cried the knight. "You fool! I have just ridden with the emperor, and have come back to my castle. Here!" he shouted to his servants, "beat this fellow and drive him away from the gate."

The porter looked on and laughed.

"Lay on well," he said to the other servants. "It is not every day that you can flog an emperor."

Then they beat the proud king, and drove him from the gate of the castle.

"Base knight!" said the proud king. "I gave him all he has, and this is how he repays me. I will punish him when I sit on my throne again. I will go to the duke who lives not far away. Him I have known all my days. He will know me. He will know his emperor."

So he came to the gate of the duke's great hall, and knocked three times. At the third knock the porter opened the gate, and saw before him a man clad only in a mat of reeds and stained and bleeding.

"Go, I pray you, to the duke," said the proud king, "and bid him come to me. Say to him that the emperor stands at the gate. He has been robbed of his clothes and of his horse. Go quickly to your master."

The porter closed the gate between them, and went within to the duke.

"Your Grace," said he, "there is a madman at the gate. He is unclad and wild. He bade me come to you and tell you that he was the emperor."

"Here is a strange thing indeed," said the duke; "I will see it for myself."

So he went to the gate followed by his servants, and when the porter opened it there stood the proud king. The proud king knew the duke, but the duke saw only a bruised and beaten madman.

"Do you not know me?" cried the proud king. "I am your emperor. Only this morning you were on the hunt with me. I left you that I might bathe in the lake. While I was in the water, some wretch took both my clothes and my horse, and I—I have been beaten by a base knight."

"Put him in chains," said the duke to his servants. "It is not safe to have such a man free. Give him some straw to lie on, and some bread and water."

The duke turned away and went back to his hall, where his friends sat at table.

"That was a strange thing," he said. "There was a madman at the gate. He must have been in the wood this morning, for he told me that I was on the hunt with the emperor, and so I was; and he told me that the emperor went apart to bathe in the lake, and so he did. But he said that someone stole the clothes and the horse of the emperor, yet the emperor rode back to us cool and fresh, and clothed and on his horse. And he said"— And the duke looked around on his guests.

"What did he say?"

"He said that he was the emperor."

Then the guests fell to talking and laughing, and soon forgot the strange thing. But the proud king lay in a dark prison, far even from the servants of the duke. He lay on straw, and chains bound his feet.

"What is this that has come upon me?" he said. "Am I brought so low? Am I so changed that even the duke does not know me? At least there is one who will know me, let me wear what I may."

Then, by much labor, he loosed the chains that bound him, and fled in the night from the duke's prison. When the morning came, he stood at the door of his own palace. He stood there awhile; perhaps someone would open the door and let him in. But no one came, and the proud king lifted his hand and knocked; he knocked at the door of his own palace. The porter came at last and looked at him.

"Who are you?" he asked. "And what do you want?"

"Do you not know me?" cried the proud king. "I am your master. I am the king. I am the emperor. Let me pass"; and he would have thrust him aside. But the porter was a strong man; he stood in the doorway, and would not let the proud king enter.

"You my master! You the emperor! Poor fool, look here!" and he held the proud king by the arm while he pointed to a hall beyond. There sat the emperor on his throne, and by his side was the queen.

"Let me go to her! She will know me." cried the proud king, and he tried to break away from the porter. The noise without was heard in the hall. The nobles came out, and last of all came the emperor and the queen. When the proud king saw these two, he could not speak. He was choked with rage and fear, and he knew not what.

"You know me!" at last he cried. "I am your lord and husband." The queen shrank back.

"Friends," said the man who stood beside her, "what shall be done to this wretch?"

"Kill him," said one.

"Put out his eyes," said another.

"Beat him," said a third.

Then they all hustled the proud king out of the palace court. Each one gave him a blow, and so he was thrust out, and the door was shut behind him.

The proud king fled, he knew not whither. He wished he were dead. By and by he came to the lake where he had bathed. He sat down on the shore. It was like a dream, but he knew he was awake, for he was cold and hungry and faint. Then he knelt on the ground and beat his breast, and said:

"I am no emperor. I am no king. I am a poor, sinful man. Once I thought there was no one greater than I, on earth or in heaven. Now I know that I am nothing, and there is no one so poor and so mean. God forgive me for my pride."

As he said this, tears stood in his eyes. He wiped them away and rose to his feet. Close by him he saw his clothes which he had once laid aside. Near at hand was his horse, eating the soft grass. The king put on his clothes; he mounted his horse and rode to his palace. As he drew near, the door opened and servants came forth. One held his horse; another helped him dismount. The porter bowed low.

"I marvel I did not see thee pass out, my lord," he said.

The king entered, and again saw the nobles in the great hall. There stood the queen also, and by her side was the man who called himself emperor. But the queen and the nobles did not look at him; they looked at the king, and came forward to meet him.

This man also came forward, but he was clad in shining white, and not in the robes of the emperor. The king bowed his head before him.

"I am thy angel," said the man. "Thou wert proud, and made thyself to be set on high. Therefore thou hast been brought low. I have watched over thy kingdom. Now I give it back to thee, for thou art once again humble, and the humble only are fit to rule."

Then the angel disappeared. No one else heard his voice, and the nobles thought the king had bowed to them. So the king once more sat on the throne, and ruled wisely and humbly ever after.

SAINT GEORGE AND THE DRAGON

By HORACE E. SCUDDER

Illustration by Warren Chappell

IN THE country of Libya in Asia Minor there was a town called Silene, and near the town was a pond, and this pond was the roving place of a monster dragon. Many times had great armies been sent to slay him, but never had they been able to overcome him. Instead, he had driven them back to the walls of the city.

Whenever this dragon drew near the city walls, his breath was so full of poison that it caused the death of all who were within reach of it; and so, to save the city, it was the custom to throw each day two sheep to feed the dragon and satisfy his hunger. So it went on, until not a sheep was left and not one could be found in the neighborhood.

Then the people took counsel, and they drew lots, and each day a man or a woman and one of their cattle were given to the dragon. And their lot spared no one. Rich or poor, high or low, someone must each day be sacrificed to the dreadful dragon.

Now it came to pass one day that the princess herself was drawn by lot. The king was filled with horror. He offered in exchange his gold, his silver, and half his realm if she might but be spared. All he could obtain was a respite of eight days, in which to mourn the fate of the girl. At the end of that time, the people came to the palace and said: "Why do you spare your daughter, and kill your subjects? Every day we are slain by the breath of the monster."

So the king knew he must part with his daughter. He dressed her in her richest apparel, and kissed her, and said:

"Ah, my dearest daughter, what an end is this! I had thought to die and leave you happy. I hoped to have invited princes to your wedding, and to have had music and dancing. I hoped to see your children, and now I must send you to the dragon."

The princess wept and clung to her father, and begged him to bless her. So he did, weeping bitterly, and she left him, and went like those before her to the lake where the dragon dwelt.

Now these people of Libya were heathen, but in Cappadocia, not far away, was a Christian named George, and this George was a young man of noble bearing. He heard in a vision that he was to go to Libya, and so he rode his horse toward the city, and he was hard by the lake when he saw the princess standing alone, weeping bitterly. He asked her why she wept, and she only said:

"Good youth, mount your horse again quickly and fly, lest you perish with me."

But George said to her:

"Do not fear. Tell me what you await, and why the vast crowd yonder are watching you."

Again she begged him to fly.

"You have a kind and noble heart, sir, I perceive," said she, "yet fly, and at once."

"Not so," said George; "I will first hear your tale."

Then she told him all.

"Be of good courage," said he. "It was for this I was sent. In the name of Jesus Christ I will defend you."

"I do not know that name, brave knight," said she. "Do not seek to die with me. It is enough that I should perish. You can neither save me nor yourself from this terrible dragon." At that moment, the dragon rose with a great bellowing from the lake. "Fly! fly!" said the trembling princess, "Fly, sir knight!"

But George, nothing daunted, made the sign of the cross, and went forward boldly to meet the dragon, commending himself to God. He raised his spear and flung it with all his force at the neck of the monster. So surely did the spear fly that it pierced the neck and pinned the dragon to the ground.

Then he bade the princess take her girdle and pass it round the spear, and fear nothing. She did so, and the dragon rose and followed her like a docile hound. George led his horse and walked beside her, and thus they entered the city. The people began to flee when they saw the dread beast, but George stayed them.

"Fear not," said he, "This monster can no longer harm you. The

Lord sent me to deliver you"; and so the multitude followed, and they came before the palace where the king sat sorrowing. And when the king heard the mighty rejoicing, he came forth and saw his beloved daughter, safe, with the dragon at her heels.

Then George took his sword and smote off the dragon's head, and all the people hailed him as their deliverer. But George bade them give glory to the Lord; and he remained and taught them the new faith, so that the king and the princess and all the people were baptized. And when George died he was called Saint George, and it fell out finally that he became the patron saint of merry England.

THE BELL OF JUSTICE

By HORACE E. SCUDDER

A ROMAN emperor had the ill fortune to lose his sight. He wished that his people might not be the worse for this loss; so he hung a bell in his palace, and a law was made that anyone who had a wrong to be righted must pull the rope with his own hands and thus ring the bell. When the bell rang a judge went down to hear the complaint and right the wrong.

It chanced that a serpent had its home under the end of the bell rope. Here it brought forth its young, and one day, when the little serpents could leave the place, it led them out for fresh air. While they were gone, a toad came and took a fancy to the place. Nor would he go away when the serpent came back.

The serpent could not drive the toad out, so it coiled its tail about the bell rope, and rang the bell of justice. Down came the judge, but saw nobody, and went back. Again the serpent rang the bell.

This time the judge looked about with care and espied the serpent and the toad. He went back to the emperor and told him what he had seen.

"It is very clear," said the emperor, "that the toad is in the wrong. Go down, drive out the toad, kill it, and let the serpent have its place again."

All this was done. Now, not many days after, as the emperor lay in his bed, the serpent came into the room, and toward the emperor's bed. The servants were about to drive the serpent away, but the emperor forbade them.

"It will do me no harm," said he; "I have been just to it. Let us see what it will do."

At that the serpent glided up to the bed, and laid a precious stone which it carried in its mouth upon the emperor's eyes. Then it slipped out of the room and no one saw it again. But no sooner had the stone lain on the eyes of the emperor than his sight was restored and he could see as well as other men.

WILLIAM TELL

By HORACE E. SCUDDER

SWITZERLAND is a republic, like the United States, and the men who live among its mountains are a brave, free people. But long ago the Emperor of Austria claimed the land as a part of his empire, and sent a man named Gessler to rule the people in his stead.

Gessler was a tyrant. He wished to stand well with his master, the emperor, and he ruled the bold Swiss with a rod of iron. He had soldiers at his command and he seemed able to do whatever he wished, but there was one thing he could not do: he could not make the proud people bow down to him when he came among them.

He was angry enough at this, and he cast about for some new way in which to make them feel his power. In those days, as now, every town had a public square called a market place. Here the people flocked to buy and sell of each other. The men and women came down from the mountains with game and cheese and butter; they sold these things in the market, and bought goods which they could not make or grow in their mountain homes.

In the market place of Altorf, a Swiss town, Gessler set up a tall pole, like a liberty pole. But on the top of this pole he placed his hat, and, just as in the city a gilt crown on some high point was the sign of the emperor's power, so this hat was to be the sign of Gessler's power. He bade that every Swiss man, woman, or child who passed by the pole should bow to the hat, to show their respect for him.

From one of the mountain homes near Altorf there came into the market place one day a tall, strong man named William Tell. He was a famous archer, for it was in the days before the mountaineers carried guns, and he was wont to shoot bears and wild goats and wolves with his bow and arrows.

He had with him his little son, and they walked across the market place. But when they passed the pole, Tell never bent his head; he stood as straight as a mountain pine.

There were servants and spies of Gessler in the market place, and they at once told the tyrant how Tell had defied him. Gessler commanded the Swiss to be brought before him, and he came, leading by the hand his little son.

"They tell me you shoot well," said the tyrant. "You shall not be punished. Instead you shall give me a sign of your skill. Your boy is no doubt made of the same stuff you are. Let him stand yonder a hundred paces off. Place an apple on his head, and do you stand here and pierce the apple with an arrow from your quiver."

All the people about turned pale wtih fear, but Tell looked Gessler full in the face and drew two arrows from his quiver.

"Go yonder," he said to the lad, and he saw him led away by two servants of Gessler, who paced a hundred steps and then placed an apple on the boy's head. They had some pity for Tell in their hearts, and so they made the boy stand with his back to his father.

"Face this way," rang out Tell's clear voice, and the boy, quick to obey, turned and stood facing his father. He stood erect, his arms hanging straight by his side, his head held up, and the apple poised on it. He saw Tell string his bow, bend it to try if it were true, fit the notch of the arrow into the taut cord, bring the bow slowly into place. He could see no more. He shut his eyes.

The next moment a great shout rose from the crowd. The arrow had split the apple in two and had sped beyond. The people were overjoyed, but Gessler said in a surly tone to Tell:

"You were not so very sure of your first shot. I saw you place a second arrow in your belt."

"That was for thee, tyrant, had I missed my first shot," said Tell.

"Seize him!" cried the enraged tyrant, and his soldiers rushed forward, but the people also threw themselves upon his soldiers, and Tell, now drawing his bow again, shot the tyrant through the heart, and in the confusion that followed, taking his boy by the hand, fled quickly to the lake near by, and, loosing a boat, rowed to the other shore, and so escaped to the mountain fastness.

THE IMAGE AND THE TREASURE

By HORACE E. SCUDDER

IN THE city of Rome was a graven image of a man. It stood upright and held out its right hand. On the middle finger of the hand were the words STRIKE HERE. No one knew what this meant, but all thought the image held some hid treasure. Thus the image was marred by blows where one person and another had struck to find the opening.

At last a learned man looked hard at the image to see if he could find out the secret. The sun was shining brightly. It was noon, and the shadow of the image lay upon the ground. The hand of the shadow was stretched out, and the learned man saw the shadow finger.

He marked the spot where the tip of the finger rested, and at night, when all was still, he came again. He had brought a spade with him, and he dug down at the spot he had marked. Soon he came to a trap door. He raised the door and saw some steps leading down. Then he closed the door above him and went down the steps.

He found himself in a great hall, and in the middle of the hall was a table. The table was set with dishes of gold and silver, with golden knives and cups of gold. At one end sat a king and a queen. He knew they were a king and a queen by their rich robes and by the crowns on their heads. Fine nobles, too, sat at the table, and all about were men standing.

The wonder was, there was not a sound and not a single person moved. The king sat still; the queen sat still; the nobles did not stir; the men were fixed. It was as if they were all of stone, and so they were; for when this learned man touched them, he found that they were stone.

He went into a room beyond. There he saw many women dressed in purple. They, too, were of stone. He went into a stable: there stood horses in the stalls, and dogs; but they had all been turned to stone. So he went about the palace, for palace it plainly was, and everywhere it was as still as death. Not a living thing was to be seen; but there were riches more than he ever dreamt of.

At last he came back to the great hall. He saw that the light which lighted the hall came from a precious stone in one corner. The light, as he gazed, fell upon a stone archer who stood with his bow drawn and the arrow pointed at the precious stone. On the archer's brow were the words.

"I am what I am. My shaft is sure; least of all can the precious stone escape me."

Now the learned man thought to carry away some of the treasure. He went to the table and chose some of the golden cups. They surely would be the easiest to carry. But no sooner had he hid them in his cloak than, whish! the arrow sped from the bow and struck the precious stone. In an instant the stone was shivered to bits and there was total darkness.

The learned man groped for the stairs. He could not find them. He went back and forth, but he never found the stairs. He, too, became a stone statue in the secret hall.

THE FLYING DUTCHMAN

By HORACE E. SCUDDER

ONCE upon a time a Dutch ship set sail from the East Indies to return to Holland. The Dutch had rich lands in the East Indies, and many a poor lad went out from Holland before the mast and landed at Java, it may be, and there settled and grew rich.

Such an one was a certain Diedrich, who had no father or mother living and was left to shift for himself. And when he came to Java he was bound out to a rich planter; but he worked so hard and was so faithful that it was not long before he was free and his own master. Little by little he saved his money, and as he was very careful it was not many years before he was very rich indeed.

Now all these years Diedrich had never forgotten what a hard time he had had when he was a boy; and at last, when he was a man grown and had his large fortune, he resolved to carry out a plan which he had made. He sold his lands and houses, which he owned in Java, and all his goods, and took the money he received in bags aboard a ship which was to return to Holland.

He was the only passenger on board, but he was a friendly man and soon he was on good terms with the captain and all the crew. One day, as the ship drew near the Cape of Good Hope, Diedrich was sitting by the captain and they each fell to talking about their early life.

"And what," said Diedrich to the captain, "do you mean to do when you make a few more voyages and have saved up money enough not to need to go to sea any more?"

"I know well," said the captain, as he pulled away at his pipe. "There is a little house I know by a canal just outside of Amsterdam. I mean to buy that house; and I will have a summerhouse in the garden, and there I will sit all day long smoking my pipe, while my wife sits by my side and knits and the children play in the garden."

"Then you have children?"

"That I have," said the captain, and he went on to name them, and to tell how old each one was, and how bright they all were. It was good to hear him, for he was a simple man and cared for nothing so much as his wife and little ones.

"And what," at last the captain said to Diedrich—"what shall you do?"

"Ah, I have no wife or children, and there is no one in all Holland who will be glad to see me come home." Then he told of what a hard time he had when he was a youngster, and at last, as the darkness grew deeper, and he sat there alone with the captain, he suddenly told him his great plan.

"I have made a great deal of money," said he, "which you know I am carrying home with me. I will tell you what I am going to do with it. There are a great many poor children in Amsterdam who have no home. I am going to build a great house and live in it, and I am going to have the biggest family of anyone in Amsterdam. I shall take the poorest and the most miserable children in Amsterdam, and they shall be my sons and daughters."

"And you shall bring them out to my house," said the captain, "and your children and mine shall play together." So they talked and talked, until at last it was very late and they went to their cabins for the night.

Now, while they were talking, the man at the wheel listened; and, as he heard of the bags of gold that Diedrich was carrying home, his evil heart began to covet the gold. As he steered the ship, and after his turn was over, he thought and thought how he could get that gold. He knew it would be impossible for him alone to seize it, and so he whispered about it to one and another of the sailors.

The crew had been got together hastily. There was not one Dutchman among them, and there was not one of the crew who had not committed some crime. They were wicked men, and, when the sailor told them of the gold that was on board, they were ready for anything.

The ship drew nearer the Cape of Good Hope, and the captain walked the deck with Diedrich and they both talked of the Holland to which they were going, when suddenly they were seized from behind and tightly bound. At the same instant the officers of the ship, the mate and the second mate, were seized, and now the ship was in the hands of the mutinous crew.

These wicked men made short work. They threw the captain and Diedrich and the two mates, each bound hand and foot, into the sea. "Dead men tell no tales," said the man at the wheel. Then they sailed for the nearest port. But as they sailed a horrible plague broke out on board. It was a plague which made the men crave water for their burning throats, and, as they fought to get at the water casks, they spilled all the water they had.

There they were, in the midst of the salt sea, which only to look at made them wild with thirst. Though they feared what might befall them if they made for the land, they could not stand the raging thirst and they steered for the nearest port.

But when they came into the port, the people saw they had the plague and they refused to let them land.

"We have great store of gold," the crew cried with their parched mouths. "Only give us water!" But the people drove them away. It was the same when they went to the next port, and the next. They turned back, away from their homeward voyage, to the ports of the East.

Then a great storm arose and they were driven far out to sea, and when the gale died down they steered again for the land. And when they drew once more, another gale sprung up and they were driven hither and thither. And once more they were swept far away from the shore.

That was years and years ago. But when ships make the Cape of Good Hope, and are rounding it, through the fog and mist and darkness of the night they see a ghostly ship sailing, sailing, never reaching land, always beating up against the wind. Its sails are torn, the masts are bleached, and there are pale figures moving about on deck. Then the sailors whisper to each other:

"Look! there is the Flying Dutchman!"

ARTHUR IN THE CAVE

By W. JENKYN THOMAS

ONCE upon a time a Welshman was walking on London Bridge, staring at the traffic and wondering why there were so many kites hovering about. He had come to London, after many adventures with thieves and highwaymen which need not be related here, in charge of a herd of black Welsh cattle. He had sold them with much profit, and with jingling gold in his pocket he was going about to see the sights of the city.

He was carrying a hazel staff in his hand, for you must know that a good staff is as necessary to a drover as teeth are to his dogs. He stood still to gaze at some wares in a shop (for at that time London Bridge was shops from beginning to end), when he noticed that a man was looking at his stick with a long fixed look. The man after a while came to him and asked him where he came from.

"I come from my own country," said the Welshman, rather surlily, for he could not see what business the man had to ask such a question.

"Do not take it amiss," said the stranger; "if you will only answer my questions, and take my advice, it will be of greater benefit to you than you imagine. Do you remember where you cut that stick?"

The Welshman was still suspicious, and said: "What does it matter where I cut it?"

"It matters," said the questioner, "because there is a treasure hidden near the spot where you cut that stick. If you can remember the place and conduct me to it, I will put you in possession of great riches."

The Welshman now understood he had to deal with a sorcerer, and he was greatly perplexed as to what to do. On the one hand, he was tempted by the prospect of wealth; on the other hand, he knew that the sorcerer must have derived his knowledge from devils, and he feared to have anything to do with the powers of darkness. The cunning man strove hard to persuade him, and at length made him promise to show the place where he cut his hazel staff.

The Welshman and the magician journeyed together to Wales. They went to Craig y Dinas, the Rock of the Fortress, at the head of the Neath valley, near Pont Nedd Fechan, and the Welshman, pointing to the stock or root of an old hazel, said: "This is where I cut my stick."

"Let us dig," said the sorcerer. They digged until they came to a broad, flat stone. Prying this up, they found some steps leading downward. They went down the steps and along a narrow passage until they came to a door. "Are you brave?" asked the sorcerer; "Will you come in with me?"

"I will," said the Welshman, his curiosity getting the better of his fear.

They opened the door, and a great cave opened out before them. There was a faint red light in the cave and they could see everything. The first thing they came to was a bell.

"Do not touch that bell," said the sorcerer, "or it will be all over with us both."

As they went farther in, the Welshman saw that the place was not empty. There were soldiers lying down asleep, thousands of them, as far as ever the eye could see. Each one was clad in bright armor, the steel helmet of each was on his head, the shining shield of each was on his arm, the sword of each was near his hand, each had his spear stuck in the ground near him, and each and all were asleep.

In the midst of the cave was a great round table, at which sat warriors whose noble features and richly-dight armor proclaimed that they were not as the roll of common men.

Each of these, too, had his head bent down in sleep. On a golden throne on the farther side of the round table was a king of gigantic stature and august presence. In his hand, held below the hilt, was a mighty sword with scabbard and haft of gold studded with gleaming gems; on his head was a crown set with precious stones which flashed and glinted like so many points of fire. Sleep had set its seal on his eyelids also.

"Are they asleep?" asked the Welshman, hardly believing his own eyes.

"Yes, each and all of them," answered the sorcerer. "But, if you touch yonder bell, they will all awake."

"How long have they been asleep?"

"For over a thousand years."

"Who are they?"

"Arthur's Warriors, waiting for the time to come when they shall destroy all the enemy of the Cymry and repossess the strand of Britain, establishing their own king once more at Caer Lleon."

"Who are these sitting at the round table?"

"These are Arthur's knights—Owain, the son of Urien; Cai, the son of Cynyr; Gwalchmai, the son of Gwyar; Peredur, the son of Efrawc; Geraint, the son of Erbin; Trystan, the son of March; Bedwyr, the son of Bedrawd; Cilhwch, the son of Celyddon; Edryn, the son of Nudd; Cynon, the son of Clydno."

"And on the golden throne?" broke in the Welshman.

"Is Arthur himself, with his sword Excalibur in his hand," replied the sorcerer.

Impatient by this time at the Welshman's questions, the sorcerer hastened to a great heap of yellow gold on the floor of the cave. He took up as much as he could carry, and bade his companion do the same. "It is time for us to go," he then said, and he led the way toward the door by which they had entered.

But the Welshman was fascinated by the sight of the countless soldiers in their glittering arms—all asleep.

"How I should like to see them all awaking!" he said to himself. "I will touch the bell—I *must* see them all arising from their sleep."

When they came to the bell, he struck it until it rang through the whole place. As soon as it rang, lo! the thousands of warriors leapt to their feet and the ground beneath them shook with the sound of the steel arms. And a great voice came from their midst: "Who rang the bell? Has the day come?"

The sorcerer was so much frightened that he shook like an aspen leaf. He shouted in answer: "No, the day has not come. Sleep on."

The mighty host was all in motion, and the Welshman's eyes

were dazzled as he looked at the bright steel arms which illumined
the cave as with the light of myriad flames of fire.

"Arthur," said the voice again, "awake; the bell has rung, the
day is breaking. Awake, Arthur the Great."

"No," shouted the sorcerer, "it is still night. Sleep on, Arthur the
Great."

A sound came from the throne. Arthur was standing, and the
jewels in his crown shone like bright stars above the countless
throng. His voice was strong and sweet like the sound of many
waters, and he said:

"My warriors, the day has not come when the Black Eagle and
the Golden Eagle shall go to war. It is only a seeker after gold who
has rung the bell. Sleep on, my warriors; the morn of Wales has
not yet dawned."

A peaceful sound like the distant sigh of the sea came over the
cave, and in a trice the soldiers were all asleep again. The sorcerer
hurried the Welshman out of the cave, moved the stone back to its
place and vanished.

Many a time did the Welshman try to find his way into the cave
again, but though he dug over every inch of the hill, he has never
again found the entrance to Arthur's Cave.

THE EMPEROR'S VISION

By SELMA LAGERLOF

I T happened at the time when Augustus was Emperor in Rome and Herod was King in Jerusalem.

It was then that a very great and holy night sank down over the earth. It was the darkest night that anyone had ever seen. One could have believed that the whole earth had fallen into a cellar vault. It was impossible to distinguish water from land, and one could not find one's way on the most familiar road. And it couldn't be otherwise, for not a ray of light came from heaven. All the stars stayed at home in their own houses, and the fair moon held her face averted.

The silence and the stillness were as profound as the darkness. The rivers stood still in their courses, the wind did not stir, and even the aspen leaves had ceased to quiver. Had anyone walked along the seashore, he would have found that the waves no longer dashed upon the sands; and had one wandered in the desert, the sand would not have crunched under one's feet. Everything was as motionless as if turned to stone, so as not to disturb the holy night. The grass was afraid to grow, the dew could not fall, and the flowers dared not exale their perfume.

On this night the wild beasts did not seek their prey, the serpents did not sting, and the dogs did not bark. And what was even more glorious, inanimate things would have been unwilling to disturb the night's sanctity by lending themselves to an evil deed. No false key could have picked a lock, and no knife could possibly have drawn a drop of blood.

In Rome, during this very night, a small company of people came from the Emperor's palace at the Palatine and took the path across the Forum which led to the Capitol. During the day just ended the Senators had asked the Emperor if he had any objections to their erecting a temple to him on Rome's sacred hill. But Augustus had not immediately given his consent. He did not know if it would be agreeable to the gods that he should own a temple next to theirs, and he replied that first he wished to ascertain their will in the matter by offering a nocturnal sacrifice to his genius. It was he who, accompanied by a few trusted friends, was on his way to perform this sacrifice.

Augustus let them carry him in his litter, for he was old, and it was an effort for him to climb the long stairs leading to the Capitol. He himself held the cage with the doves for the sacrifice. No priests or soldiers or senators accompanied him, only his nearest friends. Torchbearers walked in front of him in order to light the way in the night darkness, and behind him followed the slaves who carried the tripod, the knives, the charcoal, the sacred fire, and all the other things needed for the sacrifice.

On the way the Emperor chatted gaily with his faithful followers, and therefore none of them noticed the infinite silence and stillness of the night. Only when they had reached the highest point of the Capitol Hill and the vacant spot upon which they contemplated erecting the temple, did it dawn upon them that something unusual was taking place.

It could not be a night like all others, for up on the very edge of the cliff they saw the most remarkable being! At first they thought it was an old, distorted olive trunk; later they imagined that an ancient stone figure from the temple of Jupiter had wandered out on the cliff. Finally it was apparent to them that it could be only the old sibyl.

Anything so aged, so weather-beaten, and so giantlike in stature they had never seen. This old woman was awe-inspiring! If the Emperor had not been present, they would all have fled to their homes.

"It is she," they whispered to each other, "who has lived as many years as there are sand grains on her native shores. Why has she come out from her cave just tonight? What does she foretell for the Emperor and the Empire—she, who writes her prophecies on the leaves of the trees and knows that the wind will carry the words of the oracle to the person for whom they are intended?"

They were so terrified that they would have dropped on their knees with their foreheads pressed against the earth, had the sibyl stirred. But she sat as still as though she were lifeless. Crouching upon the outermost edge of the cliff, and shading her eyes with her hand, she peered out into the night. She sat there as if she had gone up on the hill that she might see more clearly something that was happening far away. *She* could see things on a night like this!

At that moment the Emperor and all his retinue marked how profound the darkness was. None of them could see a hand's breadth in front of him. And what stillness! What silence! Not even the Tiber's hollow murmur could they hear. The air seemed to suffocate them, cold sweat broke out on their foreheads, and their hands were numb and powerless. They feared that some dreadful disaster was impending.

But no one cared to show that he was afraid, and everyone told the Emperor that this was a good omen. All nature held its breath to greet a new god.

They counseled Augustus to hurry with the sacrifice, and said that the old sibyl had evidently come out of her cave to greet his genius.

But the truth was that the old sibyl was so absorbed in a vision that she did not even know that Augustus had come up to the Capitol. She was transported in spirit to a far-distant land, where she imagined that she was wandering over a great plain. In the darkness she stubbed her foot continually against something, which she believed to be grass tufts. She stooped down and felt with her hand. No, it was not grass, but sheep. She was walking between great sleeping flocks of sheep.

Then she noticed the shepherds' fire. It burned in the middle of the field, and she groped her way to it. The shepherds lay asleep by the fire, and beside them were the long, spiked staves with which they defended their flocks from wild beasts. But the little animals with the glittering eyes and the bushy tails that stole up to the fire, were they not jackals? And yet the shepherds did not fling their staves at them, the dogs continued to sleep, the sheep did not flee, and the wild animals lay down to rest beside the human beings.

This the sibyl saw, but she knew nothing of what was being en-
acted on the hill back of her. She did not know that there they
were raising an altar, lighting charcoal and strewing incense, and
that the Emperor took one of the doves from the cage to sacrifice it.
But his hands were so benumbed that he could not hold the bird.
With one stroke of the wing, it freed itself and disappeared in the
night darkness.

When this happened, the courtiers glanced suspiciously at the old
sibyl. They believed that it was she who caused the misfortune.

Could they know that all the while the sibyl thought herself
standing beside the shepherds' fire, and that she listened to a faint
sound which came trembling through the dead-still night? She
heard it long before she marked that it did not come from the
earth, but from the sky. At last she raised her head; then she saw
light, shimmering forms glide forward in the darkness. They were
little flocks of angels, who, singing joyously, and apparently searching, flew back and forth above the wide plain.

While the sibyl was listening to the angel-song, the Emperor was
making preparations for a new sacrifice. He washed his hands,
cleansed the altar, and took up the other dove. And, although he
exerted his full strength to hold it fast, the dove's slippery body
slid from his hand and the bird swung itself up into the impenetrable night.

The Emperor was appalled! He fell upon his knees and prayed
to his genius. He implored him for strength to avert the disasters
which this night seemed to foreshadow.

Nor did the sibyl hear any of this either. She was listening with
her whole soul to the angel-song, which grew louder and louder. At
last it became so powerful that it wakened the shepherds. They
raised themselves on their elbows and saw shining hosts of silver-
white angels move in the darkness in long, swaying lines, like mi-
gratory birds. Some held lutes and cymbals in their hands; others
held zithers and harps, and their song rang out as merry as child-
laughter, and as carefree as the lark's trill. When the shepherds
heard this, they rose up to go to the mountain city where they lived
to tell of the miracle.

They groped their way forward on a narrow, winding path, and the sibyl followed them. Suddenly it grew light up there on the mountain: a big, clear star kindled right over it, and the city on the mountain summit glittered like silver in the starlight. All the fluttering angel throngs hastened hither, shouting for joy, and the shepherds hurried so that they almost ran. When they reached the city, they found that the angels had assembled over a low stable near the city gate. It was a wretched structure, with a roof of straw and the naked cliff for a back wall. Over it hung the Star, and hither flocked more and more angels. Some seated themselves on the straw roof or alighted upon the steep mountain-wall back of the house; others, again, held themselves in the air on outspread wings, and hovered over it. High, high up, the air was illuminated by the shining wings.

The instant the Star kindled over the mountain city, all nature awoke, and the men who stood upon Capitol Hill could not help seeing it. They felt fresh but caressing winds which traveled through space; delicious perfumes streamed up about them; trees swayed; the Tiber began to murmur; the stars twinkled, and suddenly the moon stood out in the sky and lit up the world. And out of the clouds the two doves came circling down and lighted upon the Emperor's shoulders.

When this miracle happened, Augustus rose, proud and happy, but his friends and his slaves fell on their knees.

"Hail, Cæsar!" they cried. "Thy genius hath answered thee. Thou art the god who shall be worshiped on Capitol Hill!"

And this cry of homage, which the men in their transport gave as a tribute to the Emperor, was so loud that the old sibyl heard it. It waked her from her visions. She rose from her place on the edge of the cliff, and came down among the people. It was as if a dark cloud had arisen from the abyss and rushed down the mountain height. She was terrifying in her extreme age! Coarse hair hung in matted tangles around her head, her joints were enlarged, and the dark skin, hard as the bark of a tree, covered her body with furrow upon furrow.

Potent and awe-inspiring, she advanced toward the Emperor.

With one hand she clutched his wrist, with the other she pointed toward the distant East.

"Look!" she commanded, and the Emperor raised his eyes and saw. The vaulted heavens opened before his eyes, and his glance traveled to the distant Orient. He saw a lowly stable behind a steep rock wall, and in the open doorway a few shepherds kneeling. Within the stable he saw a young mother on her knees before a little child, who lay upon a bundle of straw on the floor.

And the sibyl's big, knotty fingers pointed toward the poor babe. "Hail, Cæsar!" cried the sibyl, in a burst of scornful laughter. "There is the god who shall be worshiped on Capitol Hill!"

Then Augustus shrank back from her, as from a maniac. But upon the sibyl fell the mighty spirit of prophecy. Her dim eyes began to burn, her hands were stretched toward heaven, her voice was so changed that it seemed not to be her own, but rang out with such resonance and power that it could have been heard over the whole world. And she uttered words which she appeared to be reading among the stars:

"Upon Capitol Hill shall the Redeemer of the world be worshiped—*Christ*—but not frail mortals."

When she had said this, she strode past the terror-stricken men, walked slowly down the mountain, and disappeared.

But on the following day Augustus strictly forbade the people to raise any temple to him on Capitol Hill. In place of it he built a sanctuary to the newborn God-Child, and called it HEAVEN'S ALTAR —*Ara Cœli.*

THE LEGEND OF ST. CHRISTOPHER

From THE GOLDEN LEGEND

CHRISTOPHER was of the lineage of the Canaaneans, and he was of a right great stature and had a terrible and fearful cheer and countenance. And he was twelve cubits of length. And, as it is read in some histories, when he served and dwelled with the king of Canaaneans it came in his mind that he would seek the greatest prince that was in the world and him he would serve and obey.

And so far he went that he came to a right great king, of whom the renown generally was that he was the greatest of the world. And when the king saw him he received him into his service and made him to dwell in his court.

Upon a time a minstrel sung before him a song in which he named oft the devil. And the king which was a Christian man, when he heard him name the devil, made anon the sign of the cross in his visage. And when Christopher saw that, he had great marvel what sign it was and wherefore the king made it. And he demanded it of him. And because the king would not say, he said, "If thou tell me not, I shall no longer dwell with thee." And then the king told to him saying, "Always when I hear the devil named, I fear that he should have power over me, and I garnish me with this sign that he grieve not nor annoy me."

Then Christopher said to him, "Thou doubtest the devil that he hurt thee not? Then is the devil more mighty and greater than thou art. I am then deceived of my hope and purpose; for I supposed that I had found the most mighty and the most greatest lord of the world. But I commend thee to God, for I will go seek him to be my lord and I his servant."

And then he departed from this king and hasted him to seek the devil. And as he went by a great desert he saw a great company of knights. Of which a knight cruel and horrible came to him and demanded whither he went. And Christopher answered to him and said, "I go to seek the devil for to be my master." And he said, "I am he that thou seekest." And then Christopher was glad, and bound himself to be his servant perpetual and took him for his master and lord.

And as they went together by a common way, they found there a cross erect and standing. And anon as the devil saw the cross, he was afeared and fled, and left the right way and brought Christopher about by a sharp desert, and after, when they were past the cross, he brought him to the highway that they had left. And when Christopher saw that, he marveled and demanded whereof he doubted that he had left high and fair way and had gone so far about by so hard desert. And the devil would not tell to him in no wise.

Then Christopher said to him, "If thou wilt not tell me I shall anon depart from thee and shall serve thee no more." Therefore the devil was constrained to tell him, and said, "There was a man called Christ which was hanged on the cross, and when I see His sign, I am sore afeard and flee from it wheresomever I find it." To whom Christopher said, "Then He is greater and more mightier than thou, when thou art afraid of His sign. And I see well that I have labored in vain since I have not founden the greatest lord of all the earth. And I will serve thee no longer. Go thy way then: for I will go seek Jesus Christ."

And when he had long sought and demanded where he should find Christ, at the last he came into a great desert to an hermit that dwelled there. And this hermit preached to him of Jesus Christ and informed him in the faith diligently. And he said to him, "This king whom thou desirest to serve requireth this service that thou must oft fast." And Christopher said to him, "Require of me some other thing and I shall do it. For that which thou requirest I may not do." And the hermit said, "Thou must then wake and make many prayers." And Christopher said to him, "I wot not what it is. I may do no such thing." And then the hermit said unto him, "Knowest thou such a river in which many be perished and lost?" To whom Christopher said, "I know it well." Then said the hermit, "Because thou art noble and high of stature and strong in thy members, thou shalt be resident by that river and shalt bear over all them that shall pass there. Which shall be a thing right convenable to Our Lord Jesus Christ, whom thou desirest to serve, and I hope He shall shew Himself to thee." Then said Christopher, "Certes, this service may I well do, and I promise to Him for to do it."

Then went Christopher to this river, and made there his habitation for him. And he bare a great pole in his hand instead of a staff, by which he sustained him in the water; and bare over all manner of people without ceasing. And there he abode, thus doing, many days.

And on a time, as he slept in his lodge, he heard the voice of a child which called him and said, "Christopher, come out and bear me over." Then he awoke and went out; but he found no man. And when he was again in his house, he heard the same voice, and he ran out and found nobody. The third time he was called, and came thither and found a child beside the rivage of the river: which prayed him goodly to bear him over the water. And then Christopher lifted up the child on his shoulders and took his staff and entered in to the river for to pass. And the water of the river arose and swelled more and more. And the child was heavy as lead.

And always as he went farther the water increased and grew more, and the child more and more waxed heavy: in so much that Christopher had great anguish and feared to be drowned. And when he was escaped with great pain and passed the water, and set the child aground, he said to the child, "Child, thou hast put me in great peril. Thou weighest almost as I had all the world upon me. I might bear no greater burden." And the child answered, "Christopher, marvel thou no thing. For thou hast not only borne all the world upon thee; but thou hast borne Him that created and made all the world upon thy shoulders. I am Jesus Christ, the king to whom thou servest in this work. And that thou mayest know that I say to thee truth, set thy staff in the earth by the house, and thou shalt see tomorrow that it shall bear flowers and fruit." And anon he vanished from his eyes.

And then Christopher set his staff in the earth and when he arose on the morrow, he found his staff like a palm tree, bearing flowers, leaves and dates.

LEGENDS OF BEASTS AND SAINTS

By HELEN WADDELL

THE ABBOT GERASIMUS AND THE LION

ABOUT a mile distant from the Jordan is a monastery called after the Abbot Gerasimus. On our coming to the monastery the old men who dwelt there told us of the Abbot Gerasimus, how one day walking on the banks of the Jordan he met a lion making a mighty roaring, and one paw dangling: and sticking in the paw was the sharp point of a reed, so the paw was swollen and full of matter. When the lion saw the old man, it showed him the paw with the thorn fixed in it, weeping after its fashion and beseeching him to have some care of it. And the old man seeing him in such sore straits, sat down and took the paw, opened it and drew out the thorn with a great deal of pus, cleansed the wound carefully, bound it up with a rag, and sent him away. But the lion finding himself cured would not leave the old man, but followed after him wherever he went, as a dear disciple his master, so that the old man marveled at the gratitude of a wild beast. And thenceforward the old man would feed him, setting bread before him and soaked herbs.

Now the monastery had a donkey to draw water from the Jordan for the brethren's needs. And the old man made it a rule that the lion should take charge of the donkey. And so he would go off with him along the banks of the Jordan, and watch him grazing. But one day while the donkey was browsing, the lion had gone some little distance away; and lo! a camel driver from Arabia came upon the donkey and took him and led him away. The lion, his donkey lost, returned sorely dejected to the monastery, and came with drooping head and neck before his abbot. Now the Abbot Gerasimus thought that he had devoured the donkey, and said, "Where is the donkey?" He stood silent and downcast, like any man. Then said the old man, "Thou hast eaten him: blessed be

God. Whatsoever the ass did, from this time forward thou shalt do." After which, at the old man's bidding, the lion wore panniers that held four jars, and carried the water for the monastery.

Now one day a certain soldier came to the old man for his blessing, and when he saw the lion carrying his burden, and learned the reason, he was sorry for him and offered three pieces of money to the old man to buy a donkey for this business of water-carrying, and release the lion from that necessity.

A little while had gone by after his deliverance from this task, when the camel driver who had stolen the donkey was coming with barley to sell it in the Holy City, and the donkey with him. He had crossed the Jordan where he came upon the lion: and at sight of him he left his camels and fled. The lion, recognizing the donkey, ran up to him, and holding the halter in his mouth as he was wont, drew him along with the three camels, and jubilant and roaring at finding his lost donkey, came to the old man. The old man who had originally thought that the lion had eaten the donkey now perceived that he had been taken unawares. And he called the lion Jordanes. And for more than five years the lion went about among the brethren in the monastery, never quitting the old man.

But when the Abbot Gerasimus passed over to the Lord, and was buried by the fathers, it befell, by the dispensation of God, that the lion was not to be found. After a little while he comes in, and begins looking for his old master. The Abbot Sabbatius Cilix, who had been disciple to the Abbot Gerasimus, saw him and said, "Jordanes, our old master has left us orphans, and has passed over to the Lord: yet take and eat." But the lion would not eat, but went ceaselessly here and there, turning about and looking round to see his old master, and signifying by a mighty roaring that he could not bear him to be absent. The Abbot Sabbatius and the other old men would ruffle his head and say to him, "The old master has gone to God and left us." But nothing they said could appease his roaring and lamenting: for the more they tried to caress and console him the more he grieved and the louder he roared, adding lament upon lament, and showing in voice and visage and eye the grief that he was in at not seeing the old man.

Then the Abbot Sabbatius said to him, "Come with me, since you will not believe us, and I will show you where our old master is laid." And he took him and led him to where they had buried him. It was about five paces from the church. And the Abbot Sabbatius, standing by the grave of the Abbot Gerasimus, said to the lion, "Look: our old master is buried here." And the Abbot Sabbatius bowed his knees beside the old man's grave. And when the lion heard it and saw the Abbot Sabbatius prone upon the grave weeping, he laid himself down, beating his head upon the earth and roaring: and he died there, on the old man's grave.

ST. WERBURGA OF CHESTER
AND THE WILD GEESE

IT was in the city of Chester that the girl Werburga, daughter of Wulfhere, King of Mercia, and Ermenhild . . . took her vows, and her goodness shone for many years. The story of one miracle done by her I now shall tell, which made a great stir and was long told about the countryside. She had a farm outside the walls, where the wild geese would come and destroy the standing corn in the fields. The steward in charge of the farm took all shifts to drive them off, but with small success. And so, when he came to wait upon his lady, he added his complaint of them to the other tales he would tell her of the day. "Go," said she, "and shut them all into a house." The countryman, dumfounded at the oddness of the command, thought that his lady was jesting: but finding her serious and insistent, went back to the field where he had first spied the miscreants, and bade them, speaking loud and clear, to do their lady's bidding and come after him. Whereupon with one accord they gathered themselves into a flock, and walking with down-bent necks after their enemy, were shut up under a roof. On one of them, however, the rustic, with no thought of any to accuse him, made bold to dine.

At dawn came the maid, and after scolding the birds for pillaging other people's property, bade them take their flight. But the winged creatures knew that one of their company was missing: nor did they lack wit to go circling round their lady's feet, refusing to budge further, and complaining as best they could to excite her compassion. She, through God's revealing, and convinced that all this clamor was not without cause, turned her gaze upon the steward and divined the theft. She bade him gather up the bones and bring them to her. And straightway, at a healing sign from the girl's hand, skin and flesh began to come upon the bones and feathers to fledge upon the skin, till the living bird, at first with eager hop and soon upon the wing, launched itself into the air. Nor were the others slow to follow it, their numbers now complete, though first they made obeisance to their lady and deliverer. And so the merits of this maid are told at Chester, and her miracles extolled. Yet though she be generous and swift to answer all men's prayers, yet most gracious is her footfall among the women and boys, who pray as it might be to a neighbor and a woman of their own countryside.

ST. GODRIC AND THE HUNTED STAG

IN the time of Rainulf, Bishop of Durham, certain of his household had come out for a day's hunting with their hounds, and were following a stag which they had singled out for its beauty. The creature, hard pressed by the clamor and the baying, made for Godric's hermitage, and seemed by its plaintive cries to beseech his help. The old man came out, saw the stag shivering and exhausted at his gate, and moved with pity bade it hush its moans, and opening the door of his hut, let it go in. The creature dropped at the good father's feet but he, feeling that the hunt was coming near, came out, shut the door behind him and sat down in the open: while the dogs, vexed at the loss of their quarry, turned back with a mighty baying upon their masters. They, none the less, following on the track of the stag, circled round about the place, plunging through the well-nigh impenetrable brushwood of thorns and briars; and hacking a path with their blades, came upon the man of God in his poor rags. They questioned him about the stag: but he would not be the betrayer of his guest, and he made prudent answer,

"God knows where he may be." They looked at the angelic beauty of his countenance, and in reverence for his holiness they fell before him and asked his pardon for their bold intrusion. Many a time afterwards they would tell what had befallen them there and marvel at it, and, by their oft telling of it, the thing was kept in memory by those that came after. But the stag kept house with Godric until the evening: and then he let it go free. But for years thereafter it would turn from its way to visit him, and lie at his feet to show what gratitude it could for its deliverance.

ST. CUTHBERT'S BIRDS AND BARTHOLOMEW,
THE HERMIT OF FARNE

FROM ancient time long past, this island has been inhabited by certain birds whose name and race miraculously persists. At the time of year for building nests, they gather here. And such gracious gentleness have they learned from the holiness of the place, or rather from those who made the place holy by their way of living there, that they have no shrinking from the handling or the gaze of men. They love quiet, and yet no clamor disturbs them. Their nests are built everywhere. Some brood above their eggs beside the altar. No man presumes to molest them or touch the eggs without leave. . . . And they in turn do harm to no man's store for food. They seek it with their mates upon the waves of the sea. The ducklings, once they are reared, follow behind their mothers who lead the way, and once they have entered their native waters, come no more back to the nest. The mothers too, their mild and gentle way of life forgotten, receive their ancient state and instinct with the sea. This is the high prerogative of the island, which, had it come to the knowledge of the scholars of old time, would have had its fair fame blazoned through the earth.

But at one time it befell, whilst a mother was leading her brood, herself going on before, that one of the youngsters fell down a cleft of a creviced rock. The mother stood by in distress, and let no one doubt but that she was then endowed with human reason. For she forthwith turned about, left her youngsters behind, came to Bar-

tholomew, and began tugging at the hem of his cloak with her beak
as if to say plainly: "Get up and follow me and give me back my
son." He rose at once for her, thinking that he must be sitting on
her nest. But as she kept on tugging more and more, he perceived
at last that she was asking something from him that she could not
come at by voice. And indeed her action was eloquent, if not her
discourse. On she went, she first and he after, till coming to the
cliff she pointed to the place with her bill, and gazing at Bartholomew, intimated with what signs she could that he was to peer inside.
Coming closer, he saw the duckling with its small wings clinging
to the rock, and climbing down he brought it back to its mother,
who in high delight seemed by her joyous look to give him thanks.
Whereupon she took to the water with her sons, and Bartholomew,
dumb with astonishment, went back to his oratory.

ST. MOLING AND THE FOX

THE blessed bishop Moling used to keep animals both wild
and tame about him, in honor of their Maker, and they
would eat out of his hand. And among these was a fox. Now one
day the fox stole a hen that belonged to the brethren and ate it.
The brethren brought their complaint, and the man of God scolded
the fox and accused him of being perfidious above other animals.
The fox, however, seeing his master wroth with him, gazed upon
him with solicitude, and made off to a convent of nuns that were
under St. Moling's care, captured a hen by guile, and bringing her
to his lord, presented her safe and sound. And the Saint, smiling,
said to him: "Thou hast offered rapine to atone for theft. Take back
this hen to her ladies, and deliver her to them unharmed: and hereafter do thou live without stealing, like the rest of the animals."
Hearing this, the fox took the hen between his teeth and deposited
her unharmed in her ladies' cloister. And those who saw so great
a marvel wrought in either place, made merry over it and blessed
God.

Another time another fox stole a book from the brethren and

carried it off to hide it in one of his earths, intending to come back shortly and gnaw it there. But on his return to the monastery he was found stealing and eating a honeycomb. Whereupon the brethren laid hold on him and brought him to St. Moling, and accused him of stealing the book. And the holy old man bade the brethren to let him go free. And when he was released, the Saint said to him, "O wise and crafty one, be off, and bring me back that book unharmed, and quickly." At that, off went the fox, and hasted to bring the book from his cave and set it down dry and unharmed before the holy bishop. And then he lay upon the ground before the man of God, as if seeking forgiveness. And the Saint said, "Get up, you wretch, and fear naught: but never touch a book again." And the fox got up rejoicing, and fulfilled in marvelous wise the Saint's behest: for not only did he never touch books again, but if anyone would show him a book in jest, he took to flight.

ST. COLMAN AND THE COCK, THE MOUSE, AND THE FLY

NOW, among the other virtues with which the Holy Ghost had endowed him, St. Colman was a great lover and keeper of evangelic poverty, and so marvelous a despiser of transitory things, that he would have no earthly possessions, nor gifts, nor kept any property of his own at all unless you could call property three small creatures that Ketinus saith he had in friendliness about him, a cock, a mouse, and a fly. The way that he used the cock was that its crowing wakened him at night to Lauds, as a bell might. But the offices rendered by the mouse and the fly were the stranger and more remarkable, in that these whom nature has designed to the fret and annoyance of mankind, the amazing kindness of God directed, against the weight of nature, to tendance upon His servants. For this was the service of the mouse to the man of God, that it would not allow him to sleep or lie at peace beyond the fixed hour that he had laid down for himself in his holy vows: but when his body and his tired limbs, worn out with vigil and prayer and his other austerities, would have craved sleep and rest beyond the stern limits of his vow, the mouse, sometimes by gnawing at his clothes, sometimes by nibbling at his ear, would drag him from all quiet. Dear was this office to the man of God, for by it he saw not only his vows fulfilled, but himself provoked by a dumb creature to the service of God.

Yet scarcely less remarkable was the office of the fly. For when the man of God had leisure to read his holy books, the fly would trot up and down his codex: and should some one call him, or he had to go about other business, he would instruct the fly to sit down upon the line at which he had halted, and keep his place until he should return to continue his interrupted reading: which the fly infallibly would do.

ST. KEVIN AND THE BLACKBIRD

AT one Lenten season, St. Kevin, as was his way, fled from the company of men to a certain solitude, and in a little hut that did but keep out the sun and the rain, gave himself earnestly to reading and to prayer, and his leisure to contemplation alone. And as he knelt in his accustomed fashion, with his hand outstretched through the window and lifted up to heaven, a blackbird settled on it, and busying herself as in her nest, laid in it an egg. And so moved was the Saint, that in all patience and gentleness he remained, neither closing nor withdrawing his hand: but until the young ones were fully hatched he held it out unwearied, shaping it for the purpose. And for a sign of perpetual remembrance of this thing, all the images of St. Kevin in Ireland show a blackbird in his outstretched hand.

SAINT MARTIN AND THE HONEST MAN

By PADRAIC COLUM

Illustration by Boris Artzybasheff

YOU must know that there is a certain day in the year on which the saints may leave the courts of heaven and come down upon earth for the space between daylight and dark. That day we call All Saints' Day. Then Saint Peter opens the gate, and the saints who would have their day upon earth come down.

Only a few ever come. These few are the best and the greatest of the saints. And of the few who come amongst us again I can tell you of only one—Saint Martin. I am told that never once has Saint Martin missed coming down to earth on All Saints' Day.

And what does Saint Martin do between daylight and dark when he comes down on All Saints' Day? I will tell you. He goes up and down the country that he went up and down when he was on the earth. He goes up and down upon it seeking for an honest man.

In the shape of a great white horse with wings he goes up and down the country he knew when he was on earth before. For you must know that the saints when they come down upon earth on All Saints' Day do not have the forms they had when they were on earth before. Oh, no! Each comes down in the form of the bird or beast that they were with most when they were upon the earth as men. And Saint Martin, because he was a high officer and rode a horse, takes the shape of a horse upon All Saints' Day—a white horse with great wings.

So up and down the land, in the shape of a white horse with wings, Saint Martin goes between daylight and dark upon All Saints' Day. And when he comes upon an honest man, he gallops around and around him, persuading him to mount upon his back. And when the man mounts upon his back, Saint Martin carries him off

347

to the place where honest men, honestly enjoying themselves, are doing the work that their hearts are set upon doing.

There was once a goatherd who lived near the place that Saint Martin had lived in. He was once given a very good riding boot that the King himself had worn. He hadn't been given the other boot. The King had ordered the riding boots to be given him one day when he had stopped at the goatherd's hut. But then he remembered that there was good leather in the sides of the left boot, and he ordered that it be sent to the cordwainer's, so that when his slippers needed repair there would be good leather to repair them with. So the left boot was taken to the cordwainer's and the goatherd was given the right boot only. It was a good boot and only slightly worn, and it would have lasted the goatherd many years—that is, if he had had the left boot to go with it.

He took it into his hut and he left it on a shelf above where he lay at night. It was a welcome sight to him in the mornings when he wakened up, that boot standing there so fine and so stately, as if it were waiting for him to put it on. And the goatherd lived hoping that some time he might come by another boot that would go with it. Then he would have a pair of boots for his feet, and then he would be able to go about in as much style and comfort as any man in the King's dominions.

One day, passing by the cordwainer's and looking sharply out as he always did when he went that way, he found the King's left riding boot. He picked it up out of the nettles, and, a happy man, he went into his hut and put the left boot beside the right boot upon the shelf. There was a real pair of boots for him to look at when he wakened up in the morning.

This left boot had a very good sole, but the sides of it had been taken out to put patches upon the King's slippers. He would get enough leather some day, the goatherd hoped, to make sides for this boot. Then he would put the King's two riding boots upon his feet, and he would go in as much style and comfort as any man in the King's dominions.

All that summer he used to sit near the shoemaker's bench while the goats were in the fenced field, and watch him while he cut out the leather and stitched the sides into the boots. He came to know how to do this job just as well as the shoemaker. He had a knife for cutting the leather, an awl for making the holes, a needle and waxed thread for stitching; he had even a cobbler's ball for rubbing on the leather when it was stitched in. But, the poor goatherd!—he could never get a piece of leather that would make sides for the King's riding boot.

He knew that he would come by so much leather some day, and he lived on in hope, while he had the comfort of seeing the two high boots on the shelf every morning when he wakened up. These two boots he knew would one day go upon his feet that never had had boots upon them before; then, with the King's boots upon his feet, he would go about in as much style and comfort as any man in the King's dominions.

Summer passed, and the days before All Saints' Day began. Now the goatherd had two very good pieces of leather. They were given him by a man whose goats he had saved from the flooding river. He was ready now to put sides into the boot that wanted sides. But, the poor goatherd!—he couldn't get any work for himself done now, night or day.

For it was about this time that the King, by the help of a good law that he himself made, had the Ancient Tribe shifted from the place they always had had by the edge of the forest. "It will be a good place for my goats to graze," said the King, and thereupon he had orders sent to the goatherd to take his two hundred goats to the edge of the forest. The goatherd used to take them there every day. He used to bring the leather, and the knife, and the awl, and the needle and the waxed thread, and the King's boot with him, always hoping that he would have an hour or two to cut out and put in the leather; but so it was not to be. The goats were always striving to get off that grazing ground and into places where they should not go, and the goatherd spent all his time keeping them where they should be. And when he would get back to his own hut at night, the light would be gone, and he had no way of making a light to cut or to stitch by.

Now I must tell you about the King. His family was known as "The Dynasty of the Honest Crown," for there was no one in that family, it was thought, but was an honest man. A long time before, one of the King's forefathers had been carried off by Saint Martin, and ever since that theirs was spoken of as "The Honest Crown." And on All Saints' Day every year the King would go walking the roads of his kingdom expecting that he would meet and be carried off by the white horse that was Saint Martin.

All Saints' Day came round again. The King went walking the roads of his kingdom in the expectation that Saint Martin would meet him and carry him off on his back. And as soon as the light came into the sky the goatherd rose up, and took his breakfast of whey and curds, got together the two hundred goats, and started off for the edge of the forest. He didn't forget to take with him the leather and the awl, the needle and the waxed thread, and even the cobbler's ball. And the King's boot was where it always was when he went out in the morning—hanging from around his neck. As he went out of his door he took his cap off to the rising sun and he said, "Glory and thanks to the day, and to God who has given me this day and the sense to use it." And then he shouted to the goats and drove them off.

He drove the goats in amongst the rocks and he kept them there till the King went by. The King, as always upon that day, was walking by himself, and the goatherd gave him the salutation that was always given him upon that day, "Good morrow, honest man." The King saluted him and went by, and then the goatherd took the road again, driving the two hundred goats before him.

He heard the sound of galloping behind him, and before he had time to look round him a white horse came up with him. It galloped around and around him. It had wings upon its back. The horse drove the goats on, and put them into a cave, and then it came back and galloped around the goatherd.

"Go on, go on, your reverence," said the goatherd. "Go on. The King is on the road before you."

But the great white horse with the wings would not go on. It kept galloping around and around the goatherd, persuading him to

Boris Artzybasheff

"Go on, go on," said the goatherd. "The King is on the road before you."

[See page 350]

mount upon its back. And at last the goatherd said, "If I get up on your back, maybe then you will go on to where the King is walking."

So up on the horse's back the goatherd got, and as soon as he was up, the horse spread out its wings and went up and up. High in the air went the goatherd upon the winged horse. Up and up they went, above the cave where the goats were, above the road where the King walked, above the forest along the edge of which the goats used to graze. Up and up they went, the goatherd upon the winged horse. Many's the story told of a man in the air, but there's none of them as strange as that of the goatherd upon the winged horse.

They went above where the King was walking, but although he was to be seen upon the road, the winged horse did not go down to take him up on its back. It took the goatherd at last to the place where the honest men were honestly enjoying themselves, each man doing the work that his heart was set upon doing. And there, with the rest of the honest men, the goatherd sat and ate what there was there to be eaten, and drank what there was there to be drunk, and set to and did what the rest of them were doing—the work that his heart was set upon.

He took the leather and cut it and shaped it; he took the awl and made holes for the needle to go through; he took the needle and the waxed thread and stitched the sides into the boot. He pared away the leather and he rubbed it with the cobbler's ball, making it all fine. And when the work was done the winged horse came before him again, and took him down to the cave where the two hundred goats were. Then the white horse galloped away. The goatherd drove the goats to the edge of the forest, and there was still time for them to graze to their hearts' content.

And in the morning when he wakened up, the goatherd looked to the shelf, and there before his eyes were the two high boots that were his very own. They were the finest sight the goatherd had ever looked on. He rose up and he put them on his two feet, and every minute in the day he looked down on them, saying to himself, "I have as much style and comfort now as any man in the King's dominions! Praise to God and Saint Martin for it!"

HOW THE SON OF THE GOBHAUN SAOR SOLD THE SHEEPSKIN

By ELLA YOUNG

THE Gobhaun Saor was a great person in the old days, and he looked to his son to be a credit to him. He had only one son, and thought the world and all of him, but that was nothing to what the son thought of himself. He was growing up every day, and the more he grew up the more he thought of himself, till at last the Gobhaun Saor's house was too small to hold him, and the Gobhaun said it was time for him to go out and seek his fortune. He gave him a sheepskin and his blessing, and said:

"Take this sheepskin and go into the fair and let me see what cleverness you have in selling it." "I'll do that," said the son, "and bring you the best price to be got in the fair."

"That's little," said the Gobhaun Saor; "but if you were to bring me the skin and the price of it, I'd say you had cleverness."

"Then that's what I'll bring you!" said the son, and he set off on his travels.

"What do you want for that sheepskin you have?" said the first man he met in the fair. He named his price.

"'Tis a good price," said the man, "but the skin is good, and I have no time for bargaining; here is the money; give me the skin."

"I can't agree to that," said the son of the Gobhaun Saor. "I must have the skin and the price of it too."

"I hope you may get it!" said the man, and he went away laughing. That was the way with all the men that tried to buy the skin; and at last the son of the Gobhaun Saor was tired of trying to sell it, and when he saw a crowd of people standing around a beggar man he went and stood with the rest. The beggar man was doing tricks and everyone was watching him. After a while he called out:

"Lend me that sheepskin of yours and I'll show you a trick with it!"

"You needn't ask for the loan of that skin," said one of the men standing by, "for the owner of it wants to keep it and sell it at the same time, there's so much cleverness in him!"

The son of the Gobhaun Saor was angry when that was said, and he flung down the skin to the juggler man.

"Do a trick with it if you can," said he.

The beggar man spread out the skin and blew between the wool of it, and a great wood sprang up—miles and miles of a dark wood —and there were trees in it with golden apples. The people were frightened when they saw it, but the beggar man walked into the wood till the trees hid him. There was sorrow on the son of the Gobhaun Saor at that.

"Now I'll never give my father either the skin or the price of it," he said to himself, "but the least I may do is to take him an apple off the trees." He put out his hand to an apple, and when he touched it he had only a bit of wool in his hand. The sheepskin was before him. He took it up and went out of the fair.

He was walking along the roads then and it was growing dark and he was feeling sorry for himself, when he saw the light of a house. He went toward it, and when he came to it the door was open, and in the little room inside he saw the beggar man of the fair and another man stirring a big pot.

"Come in," said the beggar man; "this is the house of the Dagda Mor, the World Builder. It isn't much, as you see, but you may rest here and welcome, and maybe the Dagda will give us supper."

"Son Angus," said the Dagda to the beggar man, "you talk as if I had the Caldron of Plenty, and you know well that it is gone from me. The Formorians have it now and I have only this pot. Hard enough it is to fill it, and when it is filled I never get a good meal out of it, for a great, hulking, splay-footed churl of a Fomorian comes in when he smells the meat and takes all the best of it from me, and I have only what remains when he has gorged himself; so I am always hungry, son Angus."

"Your case is hard," said Angus, "but I know how you can help yourself."

"Tell me how," said the Dagda.

"Well," said Angus, "get a piece of gold and put it into the best part of the meat, and when the Fomorian has eaten it up tell him he has swallowed the gold; his heart will burst when he hears that, and you'll be rid of him."

"Your plan is good," said the Dagda, "but where am I to get the gold? The Fomorians keep me building all day for them, but they give me nothing."

"I wish I had a piece of gold to give you myself," said Angus. " 'Tis a bad thing to be a beggar man! The next time I disguise myself I'll be a prince." He laughed at that, but the Dagda stirred the pot and looked gloomy. The son of the Gobhaun Saor felt sorry for him and remembered that he had a gold ring his father had given him. He pulled it off his finger and gave it to the Dagda.

"Here," said he, "is a piece of gold and you can be rid of the Fomorian."

The Dagda thanked him and gave him his blessing and they spent the night in peace and happiness till morning reddened the sky.

When the son of the Gobhaun Saor started to go, Angus set him a bit on the way.

"You are free-handed," he said to him, "and a credit to your father, and now I'll give you a bit of advice—Say 'Good morrow kindly' to the first woman you can meet on the road, and good luck be with you."

It wasn't long till the son of the Gobhaun Saor saw a woman at a little stream washing clothes. "Good luck to the work," he said, "and good morrow kindly."

"Good morrow to yourself," said she, "and may your load be light."

"It would need to be light," said he, "for I'll have far enough to carry it."

"Why so?" said she.

"I must carry it till I meet someone to give me the price of it and the skin as well."

"You need travel no farther for that," said she; "give me the sheepskin."

"With a heart and a half," said he, and he gave her the skin. She paid the price, and she plucked the wool from the skin and threw him the skin.

"Now you can go home to your father," she said.

He wasn't long going, and he was proud when he gave the Gobhaun the skin and the price of it.

"What man showed you the wise way out of it?" said the Gobhaun Saor.

"No man at all," said the son, "but a woman."

"And you met a woman like that, and hadn't the wit to bring her with you!" said the Gobhaun Saor. "Away with you now, and don't let the wind that is behind you come up with you till you ask her to marry you!"

The son didn't need the second word, and the wind didn't overtake him till he asked the woman to marry him. They came back together, and the Gobhaun made a wedding feast for them that was remembered year in and year out for a hundred years.

HOW THE SON OF THE GOBHAUN SAOR SHORTENED THE ROAD

By ELLA YOUNG

ONE day the son of the Gobhaun Saor was sitting outside in the sunshine, cutting a little reed into a pipe to make music with. He was so busy that he never saw three stranger-men coming till they were close to him. He looked up then and saw three thrawn-faced churls wrapped in long cloaks. "Good morrow to you," said the son of the Gobhaun Saor. "Good morrow," said they. "We have come to say a word to the son of the Gobhaun Saor." "He is before you," said the son. "We have come," said the most thrawn-faced of the three, "from the King of the Land Under Wave to ask you to help him; he has a piece of work that none of his own people can do, and you have the cleverness of the Three Worlds in your fingers." " 'Tis my father has that," said the son of the Gobhaun Saor. "Well," said the other, "bring your father with you to the Land Under Wave and your fortune's made."

The son of the Gobhaun Saor set off at that to find his father. "I have the news of the world for you and your share of fortune out of it," he said. "What news?" said the Gobhaun. "The King of the Land Under Wave has sent for me; if you come with me your fortune is made." "Did he send you a token?" "No token at all, but do you think I would not know his messengers?" "O, 'tis you has the cleverness!" said the Gobhaun Saor.

They set out next morning, and as they were going along, the Gobhaun Saor said: "Son, shorten the way for me." "How could I do that," said the son, "if your own two feet can't shorten it?" "Now, do you think," said the father, "that you'll make my fortune and your own too when you can't do a little thing like that!" and he went back to the house.

The son sat down on a stone with his head on his hands to think how he could shorten the road, but the more he thought of it the

356

harder it seemed, and after a while he gave up thinking and began to look round him. He saw a wide stretch of green grass and an old man spreading out locks of wool on it. The old man was frail and bent, and he moved slowly spreading out the wool. The son of the Gobhaun Saor thought it hard to see the old man working, and went to help him, but when he came nearer a little wind caught the wool and it lifted and drifted, and he saw it wasn't wool at all but white foam of the sea. The old man straightened himself, and the son of the Gobhaun Saor knew it was Mananaun the Sea God, and he stood with his eyes on the sea foam, and had nothing to say. "You came to help me," said Mananaun. "I did," said the son of the Gobhaun Saor, "but you need no help from me." "The outstretched hand," said Mananaun, "is the hand that is filled the fullest; stoop now and take a lock of my wool, it will help you when you need help." The son of the Gobhaun Saor stooped to the sea foam; the wind was blowing it, and under the foam he saw the blue of the sea clear as crystal, and under that a field of red flowers bending with the wind. He took a handful of foam. It became a lock of wool, and when he raised himself Mananaun was gone and there was nothing before him but the greenness of grass and the sun shining on it.

He went home then and showed the lock of wool to his wife and told her the sorrow he was in because he couldn't shorten the road for his father.

"Don't be in sorrow for that," said she, "sure everyone knows that story-telling is the way to shorten a road."

"May wisdom grow with you like the tree that has the nuts of knowledge!" said he. "I'll take your advice, and maybe tomorrow my father won't turn back on the road."

They set out next day and the Gobhaun Saor said—"Son, be shortening the road." At that the son began the story of Angus Oge and how he won a house for himself from the Dagda Mor: it was a long story, and he made it last till they came to the White Strand.

When they got there they saw a clumsy ill-made boat waiting for them, with ugly dark-looking men to row it.

"Since when," said the Gobhaun Saor, "did the King of the Land Under Wave get Fomorians to be his rowers, and when did he borrow a boat from them?" The son had no word to answer him, but the ugliest of the ill-made lot came up to them with two cloaks in his hand that shone like the sea when the Sun strikes lights out of it. "These cloaks," said he, "are from the Land Under Wave; put one about your head, Gobhaun Saor, and you won't think the boat ugly or the journey long." "What did I tell you?" said the son when he saw the cloaks. "You have your own asking of a token, and if you turn back now in spite of the way I shortened the road for you, I'll go myself and I'll have luck with me." "I'll go with you," said the Gobhaun Saor; and he took the cloaks and they stepped into the boat. He put one round his head the way he wouldn't see the ugly oarsmen, and the son took the other.

As they were coming near land the Gobhaun Saor looked out from the cloak, and when he saw the place he pulled the cloak from his son's head and said: "Look at the land we are coming to." It was a dark, dreary, death-looking country, without grass or trees or sun in the sky. "I'm thinking it won't take long to spend the fortune you'll make here," said the Gobhaun Saor, "for this is not the Land Under Wave but the country of Balor of the Evil Eye, the King of the Fomorians." He stood up then and called to the chief of the oarsmen: "You trapped us with lies, and with cloaks stolen from the Land Under Wave, but you'll trap no one else with the cloaks," and he flung them into the sea. They sank at once as if hands pulled them down. "Let them go back to their owners," said the Gobhaun Saor.

The Fomorians ground their teeth and cursed with rage, but they were afraid to touch the Gobhaun or his son because Balor wanted them; so they guarded them carefully and brought them to the King. He was a big misshapen giant with a terrible eye that blasted everything, and he lived in a great dun made of glass as smooth and cold as ice. "You are a firesmith and a wondersmith, and your son is a wise man," he said to the Gobhaun. "I have brought the two of you here to put fire under a pot for me." "That is no hard task," said the Gobhaun. "Show me the pot." "I will," said Balor, and he brought them to a walled-in place that was guarded all round by warriors. Inside was the largest pot the Gobhaun Saor had ever laid eyes on;

it was made of red bronze riveted together, and it shone like the Sun. "I want you to light a fire under that pot," said Balor; "none of my own people can light a fire under it, and every fire over which it is hung goes out. Your choice of good fortune to you if you put fire under the pot, and clouds of misfortune to you if you fail, for then neither yourself nor your son will leave the place alive."

"Let everyone go out of the enclosure but my son and myself," said the Gobhaun Saor, "until we see what power we have." They went out, and when the Gobhaun Saor got the place to himself he said to the son: "Go round the pot from East to West, and I will go round from West to East, and see what wisdom comes to us." They went round nine times, and then the Gobhaun Saor said: "Son, what wisdom came to you?" "I think," said the son, "this pot belongs to the Dagda Mor." "There is truth on your tongue," said the Gobhaun, "for it is the Caldron of Plenty that used to feed all the men of Ireland at one time, when the Dagda had it, and everyone got out of it the food he liked best. It was by stealth and treachery the Fomorians got it, and that is why they cannot put fire under it." With that he let a shout to the Fomorians: "Come in now, for I have wisdom on me." "Are you going to light the fire," said the son, "for the robbers that have destroyed Ireland?" "Whist," said the Gobhaun Saor; "who said I was going to light the fire?" "Tell Balor," he said to the Fomorians that came running in, "that I must have nine kinds of wood freshly gathered to put under the pot and two stones to strike fire from. Get me boughs of the oak, boughs of the ash, boughs of the pine tree, boughs of the quicken, boughs of the blackthorn, boughs of the hazel, boughs of the yew, boughs of the whitethorn, and a branch of bog myrtle; and bring me a white stone from the doorstep of a Brugh-fer, and a black stone from the doorstep of a poet that has the nine golden songs, and I will put fire under the pot."

They ran to Balor with the news, and he grew black with rage when he heard it. "Where am I to get boughs of the oak, boughs of the ash, boughs of the pine tree, boughs of the quicken, boughs of the blackthorn, boughs of the hazel, boughs of the yew, boughs of the whitehorn and a branch of bog myrtle in a country as barren as the grave?" said he. "What poet of mine knows any songs that are not satires or maledictions, and what Brugh-fer have I who never gave a meal's meat to a stranger all my life? Let him tell us," said Balor, "how the things are to be got?" They went back to the Gobhaun Saor then and asked how the things were to be got. "It is hard," said the Gobhaun, "to do anything in a country like this, but since you have none of the things, you must go to the Land of the De Danaans for them. Let Balor's son and his Sister's son go to my house in Ireland and ask the woman of the house for the things."

Balor's son set out and the son of Balor's Sister with him. Balor's Druids sent a wind behind them that swept them into the country of the De Danaans like a blast of winter. They came to the house of the Gobhaun Saor, and the wife of the son came out to them. "O Woman of the House," said they, "we have a message from the Gobhaun Saor. He is to light a fire for Balor, and he sent us to ask you for boughs of the oak, boughs of the ash, boughs of the pine tree, boughs of the quicken, boughs of the blackthorn, boughs of the hazel, boughs of the yew, boughs of the whitethorn and a branch of bog myrtle. You are to give us, he said, a white stone from the doorstep of a Brugh-fer, and a black stone from the doorstep of a poet that has the nine golden songs."

"A good asking," said the woman, "and welcome before you!" "Let the son of Balor come into the secret chamber of the house." He came in, and she said: "Show me the token my man gave you." Now, Balor's son had no token, but he wouldn't own to that, so he brought out a ring and said: "Here is the token." The woman took it in her hand, and when she touched it she knew that it belonged to Balor's son, and she went out of the room from him and locked the door on him with seven locks that no one could open but herself.

She went to the other Fomorian then and said: "Go to Balor and tell him I have his son, and he will not get him back till I get back the two that went from me, and if he wants the things you ask for he must send a token from my own people before I give them."

Balor was neither to hold nor to bind when he got this news. "Man for man," he said; "she kept one and she'll get back one, but I'll have my will of the other. The Gobhaun Saor will pay dear for sending my son on a fool's errand." He called to his warriors and said: "Shut the Gobhaun Saor and his son in my strongest dun and guard it well through the night. Tomorrow I'll send the son to Ireland and get back my own son, and tomorrow I'll have the blood of the Gobhaun Saor."

The Gobhaun Saor and his son were left in the dun without light, without food, and without companions. Outside they could hear the heavy-footed Fomorians, and the night seemed long to them. "My sorrow," said the son, "that ever I brought you here to seek a fortune! But put a good thought on me now, father, for we have come to the end of it all." "I needn't blame your wit," said the father, "that had as little myself. Why did I send only two messengers? Why didn't I send a lucky number like three? Then she could have kept two and sent one back. Troth, from this out every fool will know there's luck in odd numbers!"

"If we had light itself," said the son, "it wouldn't be so hard, or if I had a little pipe to play a tune on." He thought of the little reed pipe he was making the day the three Fomorians came to him, and he began to search in the folds of his belt for it. His hand came on the lock of wool he got from Mananaun, and he drew it out, "Oh, the fool that I was," he said, "not to think of this sooner!" "What have you there?" said the Gobhaun. "I have a lock of wool from the Sea God, and it will help me now when I need help." He drew it through his fingers and said: "Give me light!" and all the dun was full of light. He divided the wool into two parts and said: "Be cloaks of darkness and invisibility!" and he had two cloaks in his hand colored like the sea where the shadow is deepest.

"Put one about you," he said to the Gobhaun, and he drew the other round himself. They went to the door; it flew open before them; a sleep of enchantment came on the guards and they went out free. "Now," said the son of the Gobhaun Saor, "let a small light go before us"; and a small light went before them on the road, for there were no stars in Balor's sky. When they came to the Dark Strand the son struck the waters with his cloak and a boat came to him. It had neither oars nor sails; it was pure crystal, and it was shining like the big white star that is in the sky before sunrise. "It is the Ocean-Sweeper," said the Gobhaun. "Mananaun has sent us his own boat!" "My thousand welcomes before it," said the Son, "and good fortune and honor to Mananaun while there is one wave to run after another in the sea!"

They stepped into the boat, and no sooner had they stepped into it than they were at the White Strand, for the Ocean-Sweeper goes as fast as a thought goes and takes the people she carries at once to the place they have their hearts on. "It is a good sight our own land is!" said the Gobhaun when his feet touched Ireland. "It is," said the son, "and may we live long to see it!" There was no stopping after that till they reached the house of the Gobhaun, and right glad was the Woman of the House to see them. They told her all their story, and she told them how she had seven locks on Balor's son. "Let him out now," said the Gobhaun, "and ask the men of Ireland to a feast and let the Fomorian take back a good account of the treatment he got."

Well, there was the feast of the world that night. The biggest pot in the Gobhaun's house was hung up, and the Gobhaun himself put fire under it. He took boughs of the oak, boughs of the ash, boughs of the pine tree, boughs of the quicken, boughs of the black-thorn, boughs of the hazel, boughs of the yew, boughs of the white-thorn, and a branch of bog myrtle. He got a white stone from the doorstep of a Brugh-fer, and a black stone from the doorstep of a poet that had nine golden songs. He struck fire from the stones, and the flames leaped up under the pot, red blue and scarlet and every color of the rainbow.

It is not dark or silent Gobhaun's house was that night, and if all the champions on the golden-crested ridge of the world had come into it with the hunger of seven years on them they could have lost it without trouble at Gobhaun's feast.

SOURCES OF STORIES IN VOLUME III

Phaeton, from The Age of Fable, by Thomas Bulfinch. David McKay Company.

Prometheus the Firebringer, from Orpheus with his Lute, by W. M. L. Hutchinson. Longmans, Green & Company.

Perseus: The Argonauts, from The Heroes, by Charles Kingsley. The Macmillan Company.

The Hunting of the Calydonian Boar: The Winning of Atalanta: The Divine Musician, from Children of the Dawn, by Elsie Finnimore Buckley. Frederick A. Stokes Company.

The Golden Touch: The Chimaera: The Miraculous Pitcher, from The Wonder Book for Boys and Girls, by Nathaniel Hawthorne. Houghton Mifflin Company.

How All Things Began: How All-Father Odin Became Wise: The Apples of Youth: How the Fenris Wolf Was Chained: How the Pride of Thor Was Brought Low: How Thor's Hammer Was Lost and Found: The Story of Balder the Beautiful: How Hermod Made a Journey to the Under world: How Loki Was Punished at Last, from Stories of Norse Heroes, by E. M. Wilmot-Buxton. The Thomas Y. Crowell Company.

The Spirit That Lived in a Tree: The Hare That Ran Away: The Monkey That Saved the Herd: The Elephant That was Honored in Old Age: The Faithful Friend: The Banyan Deer, from Eastern Stories and Legends, by Marie L. Shedlock. E. P. Dutton & Company, Inc.

The Coyote and the Fox: Pah-tay and the Wind Witch, from Taytay's Tales, by Elizabeth Willis DeHuff. Harcourt, Brace & Company, Ltd.

The Porcupine's Quills: How Rock-Dweller the Chipmunk Gained His Stripes, from Skunny Wundy, by Arthur C. Parker. Doubleday, Doran & Company, Inc.

How the Coyote Danced with the Blackbirds: The Serpent of the Sea, from Zuni Folk Tales, by Frank Hamilton Cushing. Alfred A. Knopf, Inc.

Scarface, from Blackfoot Lodge Tales, by George Bird Grinnell. Charles Scribner's Sons.

The Proud King: Saint George and the Dragon: The Bell of Justice: William Tell: The Image and the Treasure: The Flying Dutchman, from The Book of Legends, by Horace E. Scudder. Houghton Mifflin Company.

Arthur in the Cave, from The Welsh Fairy Book, by W. Jenkyn Thomas. Frederick A. Stokes Company.

The Emperor's Vision, from Christ Legends, by Selma Lagerlöf. Henry Holt & Company, Inc.

The Legend of St. Christopher, from The Golden Legend. E. P. Dutton & Company, Inc.

Legends of Beasts and Saints, from Beasts and Saints, by Helen Waddell. Henry Holt & Company, Inc.

Saint Martin and the Honest Man, from The Forge in the Forest, by Padraic Colum. The Macmillan Company.

How the Son of the Gobhaun Saor Sold the Sheepskin: How the Son of the Gobhaun Saor Shortened the Road, from Celtic Wonder Tales, by Ella Young. T. Fisher Unwin, Ltd.